# JAUNT

ISBN: 978-0-9833317-3-5

Cover illustration, book design
and layout by
Erik J. Kreffel.

# JAUNT

*The First JauntWorld Thriller*

# ERIK J. KREFFEL

*To SMV,*
*I love you.*

*In the midst of the 22nd Century, humanity struggles to overcome 70 years of a dim age, where a series of global economic meltdowns have precipitated the collapse of the People's Republic of China, the Russian Federation, the Dominion of Canada and other BRIC states. Billions starve and die in environmental and political distress. Technological progress grinds to a halt. The dreams of prosperity languish in a medieval nightmare.*

*Nationalistic factions seize the spoils of formerly great powers and carve fiefdoms throughout the globe. Regional warfare convulses the bastions of freedom. By deliberate action, the last free powers lock down many conflicts, creating a second Cold War. Uneasy tensions build. The United States and Canada merge into a single entity—the United States of North America. Russian generals and oligarchs fuse a new Eastern European empire in the form of the Confederation of Independent States. China consolidates a wide western bulwark, a second Bamboo Curtain—the Central Asia Conglomerates.*

*A near century-long ban on nuclear weapons causes the few nationalistic powers, enflamed by megalomania and schemes of conquest, to experiment with far deadlier technologies in the years to come....*

# CHAPTER ONE

"Give me one good reason why I shouldn't put a bullet through your skull, Yastanni!" Special Agent James Gilmour spat, leveling his E4.10c "Bull" sidearm against the temple of Doctor Nouhri Yastanni, who cowered on the bedroom floor of his four-star Parisian hotel.

His head held taut by Gilmour's partner, Special Agent Greg Mason, Yastanni answered in his thick Iranian accent, "What're you doing in my room? I'm here for the trade show! My government will be very displeas—"

"We don't care about your leisure activities while you're in town!" Drawing his face closer to the stunned man, Mason produced a palm-size black canister. "Look familiar? Where and how did you receive these neutronic particles? Why do you have this canister, which was reported missing from the Sudbury Quantum Laboratory last month!"

Shivering under the grasp of both Gilmour and Mason, Yastanni's mouth contorted, his words weak. "I've...I've been producing them for the past sixteen months...since I've...received seed particles and schematics for a neutronic device from a mole code named HADRON in North America...."

Gilmour nuzzled the barrel of his E4.10c into Yastanni's sallow skin. "And...?"

"The neutronic particles are being funneled to the Confederation government in Russia...they've paid me one hundred million euros for every batch of particles I can produce that will yield a neutronic warhead—"

"Who is HADRON's handler? What is HADRON's location!"

"I—I don't know...contact was arranged by someone in the

Confederation—"

Gritting his teeth, Gilmour fought against every fiber of his being not to strike Yastanni in the gut. "You'd better hope you have a good advocate, Doctor...you're gonna need one now. Have you got all that, Mason?"

"Every second," Mason said, removing a circular device adjacent to his left eye; it was a webeye, which had recorded in its blue iris the proceedings of Yastanni's capture for his prosecution. "He's going down."

The agents pulled Yastanni to his feet and smoothed out the wrinkles in his suit jacket and trousers, making him presentable again. Yastanni started to straighten his tie, but Gilmour slapped his hands away.

"I think that's good enough."

"Ready for your day in the World Court?" Mason taunted. "You'd better clear your schedule for the next few years...."

"Hey, Chief! We've got Nouhri! Web A.D. Leeds!" Gilmour shouted, craning his head back.

"Already on it," acknowledged Section Manager "Chief" Grant Louris, the pair's immediate supervisor. He left his observing post at the room's threshold and walked into the corridor brandishing a holobook—a multi-purpose holographic ledger—in his left hand.

Keeping Yastanni in line with his E4.10c between the doctor's shoulder blades, Gilmour wore a triumphant smile. "Thanks, Doctor... you just made our sweat all worthwhile." He glanced to Mason. "I think he's sorry, don't you?"

Mason clapped Yastanni's arm and pulled him forward. "Sorry he got busted!"

Racing out the hotel, Gilmour, Mason, Chief and a squad of Parisian gendarmes headed towards an idling paddy wagon, scurrying before the webmedia converged with skydrones to witness the catch.

"Keep your head down!" Gilmour barked. A sack had been placed over Yastanni's head, but he was still lit by the sodium lights from the hotel front despite the team's best efforts.

The trio hoisted Yastanni aboard the paddy wagon, but instead of a waiting celebration, another agent, Tommy Bell, pulled the trio aside at the wagon's rear doors. "Agents! A.D. Leeds is recalling you immediately! He's scrambling a jumpjet to take you back to D.C. this evening."

"What?" Gilmour flashed an indignant look to Louris, but Chief merely shrugged.

Mason not so subtly dismissed the greenhorn's message. "Agent, we're going to Brussels to arraign Yastanni. Those're the laurels, got it?"

"I'm sorry, sir. A.D. Leeds has invoked Clause 452."

452...that was an immediate recall back to the Intelligence and Investigation Agency's HQ, with grounds for permanent dismissal from the Agency if disregarded. Whatever the hell was happening, Gilmour thought, Leeds wasn't fooling around. Only an international incident on par with Congress declaring warrated so high in the IIA's protocols.

Gilmour shook his head and sighed. "Talk about a whimper."

"I'm sure there will be others that'll be a bang," Louris said, the weariness in his voice betraying his decades of service to the IIA. "Agent Bell, web A.D. Leeds our acknowledgement. Boys, looks like we're going home."

Fighting off the flight lag back to Washington, Gilmour and Mason put on their best professional countenances and swiftly made their way through the IIA's stuffy basement corridors—a relic of the defunct Federal Bureau of Investigation—and towards the Level Three Conference Room, where they expected Leeds to be awaiting them. Instead, Agent Bell diverted the pair to the office of Leeds' secretary.

Harold Leeds and his secretary were inside, as was a slight, taller figure, dressed in a stereotypically Ivy-League professorial manner. Tension oozed from the place, making Gilmour pause.

"Agent, why are we going here?"

"A.D. Leeds' orders, sir." Bell gestured the pair inside, then locked the door.

Gilmour and Mason noticed that Leeds didn't appear particularly pleased by this older man in his battered tweed coat and tie; he had all the hallmarks of someone who normally disdained the work of the intelligence community, let alone be seen wandering the Agency's recesses.

"Doctor," Leeds said, "these are my top agents in the Global Intelligence Directorate of the Washington Bureau, James Gilmour and Gregory Mason."

The visitor, his once-red hair flecked with silvery strands, extended his hand. "Pleased to meet you. I'm Doctor Richard de Lis, of the theoretical studies laboratory in Ottawa. I have been sent here specifically on orders from Solicitor General Rauchambau and Secretary of Defense McKennitt to secure both of you."

Gilmour shook de Lis' hand. "Why us?"

"There is a situation in Ottawa demanding the critical attention of the IIA—"

"Just a moment," Mason interrupted. "I don't think you realize the severity of the situation my partner and I are currently embroiled in. We've invested years in uncovering the ties the Confederation has with illicit neutronic technology trafficking—"

"I understand, but this operation has been declared a Presidential Priority, superceding all else," de Lis declared. "Your presence has been requested from the highest echelons, agents. As of now, all other assignments you have are on hold. Without you at my disposal, the balance of power in the world could be lost to the Confederation or the Central Asian Conglomerates. And I don't mean temporarily."

Beneath the doctor's near-stoic demeanor was a twinge of fear. "I mean forever."

# CHAPTER TWO

"Your sidearms and badges!" the Marine sergeant at the check-in gate barked to Gilmour and Mason as the agents and de Lis appeared. Behind the sergeant were two other Marines brandishing conspicuous M-119 semi-automatic rifles, each weapon twice the thickness of a man's forearm.

Gilmour opened his jacket, eliciting a stern "Slowly!" from the sergeant. He complied and handed over his E4.10c, then displayed his badge prominently enough that the spit-polished and starched MP couldn't possibly mistake it for anything but government-issue.

After accepting Mason's two items, the sergeant gestured towards the gate, handed the two agents small RFID chips, then announced, "Cleared. Upon your exit from this facility, reclaim your sidearms from the armory with those chips."

Gilmour looked to de Lis with contempt, waved a less-than-conciliatory hand to the MP, then walked past the gate, which, he was sure, was now thoroughly scanning his body for other illicit devices or materials.

"Nice welcome mat you lay out here," Mason said to de Lis once the trio were out of earshot.

"Gentlemen, we're at Threat Level Red...so expect nothing but the utmost of inconvenience while in the U Complex facility."

"And what kind of facility is this, Doctor?" Gilmour asked, knowing only the basics he and Mason had discerned on the flight, taking note of the U—Underground—Complex and its mundane, above ground, twin hangar decks. Being all that were visible to untrained eyes, the jumpjet and skycraft landing pads masked the extensive basement levels dug deeply into the Ottawa soil.

"North America's most premier and revered quantum, particle and experimental extra-forces research facility, Agent Gilmour. We also deal with phenomena the government otherwise has no category for."

"You split particles?" Mason asked, ignoring the latter part.

"Well, they're usually already smashed before we get our hands on them, but yes, in a manner of speaking."

Gilmour flashed a pleasant look to Mason, as if he'd just placed the next-to-last piece in a log-jammed puzzle. "Doctor, do you deal with anyone who plays with neutronic particles?"

"Quite a few." De Lis lifted a finger. "You pair are quick...I think I have chosen correctly. I was a little concerned at your apprehension, but you'll do nicely."

Gilmour put his hand on de Lis' arm. "We'll do nicely?"

"Follow me...it'll speak for itself. I am loath to explain in these... corridors."

Gilmour furrowed his brow as de Lis sped ahead. The corridors de Lis mentioned were cramped, and positively ancient, not exactly what one would have expected for the government's "premier quantum research facility." Fluorescent light bounced off the tile floor, reminding Gilmour of the Washington Bureau; some things were the same no matter where.

De Lis led them through the corridor for several minutes, passing dozens of doorways. Only after they appeared to come to a dead end did de Lis cross over to a particular door. Producing a set of pass keys from his pocket, he selected one and slid the card through a slot on the panel, which beeped, accepting it.

Gilmour noted the room's denomination as they were led in: U5-29. Instinct told him this would be the first of many treks here.

Mason took a few seconds to study the sparse room. The cream walls contained their only other companions—an oval, chrome-inlaid conference table with a dozen chairs. No holobooks had been set out, only a few pens. Green-shaded secretary lamps extended from the table's edges at each chair's location, providing a traditional look to the otherwise hodgepodge office.

"Make yourselves comfortable at the table, gentlemen," de Lis said, gesturing. "The remainder of our contingent will be along at any moment."

The pair sat down and subsequently noticed a smaller oval concavity at the table's center, which appeared to be merely for decoration. Gilmour's hand brushed against the smooth gold polish, which was cold to the touch. Tapping it with a finger, it sounded solid. "Quite a piece you got here."

"No wonder the rest of the place is falling apart," Mason quipped.

"This is just a small example of a larger facility—the gallery," de Lis explained. "You'll find out that appearances aren't everything."

The door beeped behind him, admitting a man and a woman, both of whom were dressed informally in denim trousers, short-sleeved shirts and bruised trainers. The two newcomers nodded to de Lis, then hastily sat themselves, placing a stack of holobooks on the table, paying almost no heed to the visitors.

De Lis seated himself between the newcomers. Picking up a holobook, he scrolled through the device's virtual interface for a moment before saying, "Sorry...I just needed to update myself on the latest intel. The situation here changes almost second by second."

His eyes glanced to the two mystery people, then back to the agents. "Allow me to introduce two of my colleagues: Doctor Stacia Waters, out of the DoD's Defense Advanced Research Projects Agency, and Doctor Javier Valagua, an old friend on loan from the IIA's historical department, specializing in twentieth century research."

Waters and Valagua nodded, voicing light pleasantries.

An historian and a theoretical scientist; Gilmour sensed this wasn't going to be the usually sanctioned IIA case. Whatever this Presidential Priority was, it was definitely out of their typical domain. But yet, here they were.

"Let's get down to business," de Lis started. "Secretary McKennitt notified this facility at oh-three-twenty GMT yesterday of the detection of a crater in the Himalayan Mountain Range, twenty-nine degrees north by eighty-three degrees east. The Global Security Network's topographical and spectral analyses have determined that this crater could not have been created by any known, natural object, nor has NORAD reported any man-made, orbital objects as lost."

Valagua tapped a button on his holobook, bringing the table's concavity to life; within the gold ring a topographical holograph of the Himalayas materialized, an image obtained by the Global Security Network within the past few days, Gilmour surmised. The level of detail was extraordinary, even as Valagua commanded the magnification below sub-meter scale.

Peaks lining the range flew past the holograph's circular border and out of view while the image scaled down to a crater situated in the center. With the magnification paused, the holograph added a red outline that hovered over the crater, bringing the arguably hard-to-discern impact to light.

Mason grabbed a holobook to review the statistical analysis of the crater. "Doctor, the Confederation routinely performs flyover maneuvers of the Central Asian Conglomerates. Could they have lost an atomic bomber?"

De Lis nodded to Waters. The DARPA doctor explained, "At first, the DoD believed it was indeed a lost bomber, due to the configuration of the crater and its blast patterns. But, the residual nuclei decay just don't match predicted levels for that kind of accident, especially for an atomic reactor. The physical, however, is a different story—the crater is two hundred years old."

Gilmour's and Mason's jaws dropped. Both agents looked straight into the crater.

"How could it have escaped detection so long?" Gilmour asked, his eyes plainly discerning the crater's definition without the embellishing outline.

"The technology simply wasn't sophisticated enough until now. And to be honest," she added, almost as an afterthought, "no one bothered to look. The CAC hasn't exactly been on anyone's watch list for some time."

Gilmour looked to de Lis. "Do you believe it to be a threat?"

"Causing as much damage as it did, and by virtue of its perceived age, yes. Right now, with affairs being as they are, we need to find out exactly what it is, how it happened, and most importantly," de Lis added, "keep it out of Confederation hands."

"And that leads to us," Gilmour said.

"Exactly. Our mission is to travel to the crash site in Chinese-occupied Nepal and ascertain its contents, integrity and origin, if at all possible."

"At all costs," Mason presumed.

"At all costs," de Lis confirmed. "Everyone here is expendable if the greater mission requires it. I believe you know that, Agents?"

Regrettably, Gilmour and Mason did indeed.

# CHAPTER THREE

The spine of the world silhouetted the Milky Way, the dark majesty of the Himalayas ahead of them capturing the collective gazes of Gilmour and Mason as they rode the C-255 Grasshopper "jumpjet" through a pack of cirrus clouds. The hybrid delta-wing/helicopter's engines soon switched off, leaving the vertical takeoff and landing craft to glide for several moments as glistening, snow-peaked summits rotated below.

"Prepare for descent," the pilot's muffled voice said. "Engage seat restraints."

Gilmour secured himself, taking a second to sneak a glance out the circular starboard window. "Prettier all the way up here. Sometimes wish I could stay in flight forever."

"Eh, you'd get bored before too long," Mason commented. "I know how you are...the adventure sounds great now, but you'd miss saving the world with me."

"These days I'm not so sure about it. Can't the world stop for a little while, maybe just long enough to enjoy what's out there, sample a little of what life's like?"

"Do people really know what life's like, outside of their internal universe?" Mason asked, laughing. "Most of the modern world doesn't have the luxury of globetrotting like us. Too bad it doesn't pay better, or get women easier." Mason reclined and folded his hands behind his head. "Oh, well, my philosophy's always been to live it up while you can, 'cause tomorrow, it could all be taken away. Keep it in mind."

The overhead and running lights in the jumpjet's corridor darkened as the mainland appeared below from a curtain of altocumulus clouds. In a matter of about fifteen minutes, the jumpjet had descended a height of eleven kilometers. Seconds passed until the jumpjet trembled, its rear engines roaring to life again. The agents' bones rattled as the twin ramjets' horsepower coursed through the craft, pitching them towards the Earth once more.

A riverbed snaked a groove into the mountains, soon splitting the rocky shield into a narrow valley. The jumpjet's VTOL engines rolled them gently into the mountain pass, following the winding valley like a weary bird migrating home, welcomed by the patches of scrub grass sprinkled amongst the riverbed's upper reaches.

Within the hour, the jumpjet had arrived at the landing zone, its vertical descent dropping them amidst an open scrub plain. Gilmour and Mason waited for the "All clear" from the pilot, then unstrapped themselves and headed to the craft's cockpit.

De Lis propped open the jumpjet's forward starboard hatch, which extended a short stepladder down to a dry riverbed. Valagua, packed with several briefcases and a rucksack, stepped out next, followed by Waters, who stowed only a minor arrangement of baggage. Gilmour and Mason brought up the rear, toting their own hastily assembled rucksacks from Washington.

The jumpjet had been parked a good distance away, presumably to preserve the site's integrity for the next day's expedition. De Lis retrieved a holobook, which had been equipped with a crude map of the location, and gestured to the team to follow him. They came upon a bend in the riverbed, where their eyes were soon flooded with light; ten meters away, several tents equipped with portable lights and generators stood, awaiting their arrival.

To his left, Mason's eye caught a glint on the rock floor. Walking past, he dismissed the glint before rethinking and reversing his steps. His curiosity piqued, Mason scooped up the object and dropped it in his jacket pocket before rejoining the group.

Two small men emerged from the first tent and approached de Lis, who shook the hand of one dressed in a seemingly uncomfortable three-piece suit. "Secretary Buhranda, good to finally meet you."

Buhranda, the local representative of the Central Asian Conglomerates' Chinese contingent, cracked a toothy, smarmy smile. He ran his hands through his tousled, jet-black hair. "Your flight was good, Doctor?" he asked in clipped English.

"A little bumpy. But we're glad to finally be here."

Buhranda sized up the other Americans. "I...suppose you are exhausted. Please, come inside. You can refresh before we have business tomorrow."

De Lis nodded again. "Thank you." He turned to the group and stepped back, allowing all four to proceed ahead of him.

Buhranda's apparent major-domo, fitted with climate-appropriate woolen jacket, khakis and boots, took the lead, showing them to the temporary domiciles. Waters and Valagua were first inside, having been assigned the left end of this particular tent.

The major-domo then turned to Gilmour and Mason, and gesturing with the flick of an index finger, assigned them the right section. Handing Gilmour a small lamp, the major-domo grunted, proclaiming this small pocket Gilmour's and Mason's area. He then exited, stalking past the two doctors.

Gilmour lit the lamp and set it into a corner. Placing his rucksack next to it, he said, "Charming."

Mason glared at Waters and Valagua across the way. Throughout the flight, neither Waters nor Valagua had so much as uttered a syllable to the two agents. They continued that trend by huddling close on the opposite side of the tent, speaking their scientific jargon while emptying scientific equipment out of their bags.

"So, are we on a separate mission, or are they just very quiet?" Mason whispered.

Gilmour stood mute, not knowing what to think. Their chilly reception threw him quite off guard; he half-expected de Lis to change his mind and send them back home. They would appear to be just as useful there as here.

"Well, how about a little science experiment of our own?"

Gilmour furrowed his brow. "What?"

Grinning, Mason produced the glinting object from inside his jacket pocket. "Found something to play with."

Gilmour drew closer, picking the stone out of his partner's hand, which he held to the warm lamp light. "This from the LZ?"

Mason nodded. "It's much different than the floor here. Take a look at the scoring. Maybe subjected to intense, incredible heat and pressure."

The stone was encrusted with pitted and cracked silicates, but a discerning eye turned up another, clearer material at its core, which was amazingly lightweight.

"This isn't at all like the meteorites I've ever seen," Gilmour said. "All the ones you see are always grainy, rough, or metallic. This looks like there's a gem inside."

"That was my first thought as well. I'm not a geologist, but a good detective doesn't have to be. This is definitely in the realm of the exotic."

Mason's mind went wild, imagining all sorts of strange and otherworldly explanations; but none seemed to be explanation enough to him.

Gilmour balled the stone in his hand, making a fist, then smiled. "I can't get over how light it is."

Mason caught his partner's convivial mood. "What?"

"I just felt like a kid again, almost like I was reliving a memory... to when my old man and I would go rock hunting." Gilmour placed the stone back in Mason's open palm. "Hadn't thought about that in a long time."

Morning came with a sudden pull of the wool tent divider. De Lis crouched beneath the tent's short canopy and informed the two agents their mission was set to begin. After a quick sponge wash to their faces, the two agents changed into hiking gear and exited the domicile.

Waters and Valagua had not been roused much earlier, and were equally drowsy. Mason felt a sense of victory, since they, too, must have stayed awake a good portion of last evening discussing the mission.

Now in the new daylight, Gilmour and Mason could fully comprehend the extent of the valley. It stretched on for kilometers to the northwest, before finally disappearing from view behind another wall of pale mountains. Their camp was set off to the foot of a smaller mountain face, just a bit taller than an ordinary hill. Surrounding them like a crown, however, was the more massive mountain chain, standing firm one to two kilometers in height, by far the most impressive summits they had seen.

De Lis returned from a brief meeting with Buhranda, toting his holobook. The secretary then entered his private tent and quickly expelled what Gilmour and Mason determined was a Sherpa guide. The guide slowly made his way behind de Lis, catching up to him only as de Lis paused to brief the group.

"According to the data given to me by the Chinese occupational government, the main crash site is located—" he pointed his index finger to the northeast, "approximately four hundred and forty-three meters from here. Shajda, our guide, will lead the way. Stacia, is your equipment ready?"

"Yeah. We prepared everything on the flight."

"Excellent. Agents, how are your hiking legs?"

Gilmour traced the peaks with his eyes. "We're in pretty good shape even though we don't have those," he pointed to the mountains, "in Washington."

The doctor chuckled. "I'll make sure we check up on you every so often." De Lis tightened his rucksack over his shoulders. "Let's go. Shajda...."

Shajda nodded methodically, giving all appearances that this was just another ordinary day. He gathered his pack over his shoulders to begin the long journey.

The sun climbed its ladder in the sky, burning off the vapor in the valley. As the group walked in single file, Mason brought up the rear, allowing him ample opportunity to closely study the gravel floor. From his limited experience, the valley appeared to have flooded several times within the last two centuries, obscuring any overt traces of the crash. His strange rock must have been a complete fluke, because no other stones glinted in the sun the way that one did.

Shajda blazed a trail, stopping only long enough for the team to do cursory research at de Lis' urging. Gilmour noticed Shajda's misgivings, but the Sherpa said nothing; he was doing what he was compensated to do.

Mason stood next to Gilmour, both men taking great interest in Waters' and de Lis' quick study. Waters unpacked a selection of clear sample bags large enough to hold several kilograms of specimens. Both then collected various stones and other candidate debris from over nine square meters of area before de Lis halted their progress to resume the journey. Gilmour detected a surprising hint of exasperation from Waters, which evaporated when she saw the two agents watching her. Shajda wasted no time in directing the team to a mountain face ahead of them, tempting the Westerners to believe that the trail had come to an end. Drawing the team closer, Shajda's trek revealed a fissure deep within the mountain, creating another, narrower trail.

De Lis consulted his holobook, not recalling this particular trail. "Shajda, halt. Where are we? This isn't here," he said, pointing to the cartograph.

Shajda confidently shook his head, agreeing with the doctor. "More."

"More? No, take us to the site."

Shajda gave a toothless smile. "More...follow."

*There wasn't time for this.* De Lis called again, "Shajda, halt."

Shajda paused, turning his head around.

"Good. Now, take us to the site."

"Site, yes. Follow, now." With that, he started again.

De Lis mused on abandoning the Sherpa, but knew the guide was too important to the mission, let alone to the group. Without him, it was doubtful they'd ever find the crash site or their way back again, at least within the short time they had available. Resigned to that fact, he followed the Sherpa down to the fissure.

A path through the fissure was damp, dark and stale. Repeatedly, the forward members of the team pulled the trailing members through, resulting in scratches and scrapes. Once daylight reigned again, de Lis and Waters played medic to Valagua, Gilmour, Mason and themselves. Only Shajda remained unscathed; apparently, he had done this many times in the past.

After de Lis was satisfied that the team had been thoroughly patched up, he turned his attention to the Sherpa. Thanks to him, the team was not only deviating from their time-constrained mission, but cut up.

"Where are we?"

"A lone path," Shajda said, before viewing the trail ahead of them. Now outside the crown of peaks, the team had ventured to a region completely foreign to de Lis' cartograph. De Lis was certain that this was not a short cut. If anything, it was a reason to fire this guide and hire another. The group walked on hesitantly, evidenced by de Lis' repeated attempts to find this location on his holobook. In his frustration, he handed the device to Valagua, telling him to "stow it."

They wound through another dry riverbed, which soon descended a sharp twenty-five degrees. At the foot of the incline, Shajda took a simple, carved path, whose traffic pattern couldn't have been more than perhaps one person per month, but used consistently over the centuries. A rock face loomed ahead, beckoning them to its solid wall. Shajda walked further, giving pause to de Lis and the others, all of whom rightfully pondered where he was going; the path seemingly ended there. Sensing the group's pause, he gestured them forward without a single turn of his head.

De Lis again acquiesced. Shajda waited for them to catch up, then started his trek once more. The path brushed against the foot of the mountain, curving round it as the trail started another ascent.

Tall pines and other indigenous trees formed a dark curtain around the path ahead, bringing to Gilmour a strange sense of awe. He had not noticed any of these trees in their long journey here, none especially within the confines of the mountainous crown mapped for them. Warm tingles pricked his nerves once the path had become one with the treeline. It was indeed a mysterious, if not intriguing, sensation to have. Their very perception of time slowed as they traversed the spiral pathway up the mountain, so much so that not even de Lis felt compelled to complain about the tremendous waste of usable sunlight this journey was.

None of that was a concern now. A calm breeze overtook the five, washing away their desperation, pacifying the mission. Gilmour's eyes met Mason's, both realizing the effect the woods had on their mindset. Neither could remember quite why they had been rushed to this land. All was so...quiet.

The path opened into a clearing, spotted with small, decorative scrub grass. Beyond that, to the group's astonishment, was a temple situated deep within the mountainside, shaded in darkness and ringed by strings of multicolored prayer flags. Shajda halted at the temple's gate, allowing the five to drink in the beautiful mountain garden that had suddenly appeared, its spectral blooms and sweet scents surprisingly complimenting the flapping flags above and the wafting incense below. Ornamental wood carvings and meter-tall monoliths of various religious and mythological motifs were patterned and grafted onto the temple itself and spread throughout the angled grounds, lending a divine aura to the already rarefied atmosphere.

With trepidation, the two agents stepped up to the main gate. This was holy ground, and both felt uneasy—as Westerners—to even be setting foot on its soil. Waters and Valagua appeared equally uncertain, while de Lis was deeply entranced studying a particular wooden beam near him. Shajda patiently waited for whomever was expecting him. At least Gilmour hoped he was expected; with the lack of civilization in this region, they were bound for a long wait if Shajda was not.

Moments passed before a Buddhist monk, his head clean shaven and his body draped by the traditionally simple, but bright, robes of the monastery, crossed over to the group from a narrower path behind the temple. Shajda immediately spoke to the dark man in a mellifluous tongue. The monk nodded his head enthusiastically, heartening the two agents, and most likely de Lis, also.

Maybe this Sherpa wasn't such a bad guide after all. If these monks had any clues to the origins of the crash and its contents, including the bizarre stone Mason had discovered, then that was one advantage the group had over the Confederation. And seeing as how Shajda was on such good terms with the monastery....

Shajda beckoned the group forward with his good, toothless grin, raising de Lis' grey eyebrows. He quickly took up the guide's offer—also realizing the monks' potential value—and followed the two men into the interior of the monastery. Waters, Valagua, Mason and Gilmour hustled to catch up with the invigorated doctor's high steps.

The monk rested his arms on the temple's large wooden doors, and with a small push, introduced the foreigners into his sanctum. They were received by a brisk, dark corridor lined with prodigious candles billowing a hypnotic wave in the new breeze. Each member of the group stared incredulously at the spartan quarters that these monks inhabited, marveling at their modest, yet majestic, domicile.

Gilmour noted silently how awed the three scientists he accompanied had become. Yes, they could appreciate a culture as serene and orderly as this one; science was a curious and intuitive study. However, he was discovering that their fascination with the temple was not purely about knowledge...but faith.

The monk picked up a lit candle and made his way to a closed door at the side of the corridor, stopping at its threshold. Speaking his strange tongue again to Shajda, he cracked the door, giving them his permission to enter. His business finished, he gave a nod to each team member as they approached, before finally taking his leave.

Shajda's hand peeked through the crack, admitting himself and the other five. Inside sat an elderly abbot hunched over a wooden desk, meticulously inscribing script into a small, antique paper book and immersed in a haze of candle and incense smoke. Decades of India ink splashes had stained his fingers black, but he didn't appear to mind as he skillfully manipulated a stylus between them. Surrounded by hundreds of relics, books and a small Buddha behind him, the abbot seemed small in comparison, but Gilmour felt a vibrancy from him that he could only describe as larger than most lives.

Seeing that he had guests, the abbot rose from his seat, placed two fingers to his mouth to stifle a yawn, and greeted Shajda. The Sherpa returned the welcome with his palms together, bowing in deference. The abbot nodded to the team, also welcoming them to his quarters.
Shajda spoke to him, gesturing excitedly with his hands. Their dialogue continued for several moments, as it appeared that Shajda was informing the abbot of the team's entire journey here. Mason wondered if Shajda had mentioned de Lis' impatience with their Sherpa guide, but thought better of it. Besides, Mason figured the guide was probably oblivious to these odd Westerners' habits and eccentricities, anyway, so why bring it up?

The abbot nodded and crossed over to a cabinet set to the side of his quarters. He gingerly removed a wooden chest and placed it on his desktop. Unlocking it, the abbot produced a folded, dark mahogany cloth, embroidered in yellow thread and encrusted with dozens of stones or jewels that gleamed warmly in the candlelight. Mason and Gilmour instantly recognized the ornamentation: Mason's stone.

Swallowing their surprise, the agents watched the abbot hand the cloth to de Lis, who shared it with Waters. The pair spoke in enthusiastic whispers, careful to not only handle the cloth with a delicate touch, but their voices as well.

Shajda nodded and pointed to the cloth's ornamentation. "He wait for you."

De Lis furrowed his eyebrow. "What?"

The Sherpa smiled. "He knew you come...some day."

Behind the guide, the abbot also grinned, as if knowing the punch line to a joke in a foreign language the Westerners couldn't comprehend.

"A gift...for you," Shajda said, his eyes finding the jewels on the cloth.

Waters turned to de Lis. "I think he means, the monk has been expecting us."

"Expecting?" de Lis asked. "But we just discovered...." The journey here, the monastery, Shajda's deviation from the crater...was it all planned? But Buhranda said nothing about...unless he didn't know. None of it made any sense.

"But perhaps they've known all along," Valagua said. "This is a heavily guarded region, Doctor. Not many foreigners travel here. We are the first to look exclusively for this crash site, and the monks realized that too."

De Lis, holding the cloth up so that jewels sparkled in the pale candlelight, returned his attention to Shajda. "What is this?"

"A gift...." His eyes rolled towards the ceiling of the quarters. "The eternal candles."

# CHAPTER FOUR

Valagua gingerly handled the cloth as he received it from de Lis. "I'm not an expert on Nepalese religious culture, Richard, but I'd say it's similar to twentieth century contemporary robes." He unfolded it, recovering more of the mahogany weave. "Not much changes here over the centuries."

"Just who rules them," Mason said from behind.

Valagua agreed. He refolded the robe and tried to hand back to the abbot, but the old man refused, simply pushing it back into Valagua's hands.

"It's a gift, Javier," Waters said.

"Stacia, can your field equipment run a test on it?" de Lis asked, oblivious to Valagua's attempted return.

Her eyes scanned its exotic adornment. "I could, but I'd prefer the mobile lab. I don't recognize these jewels encrusting it to be native to this region. I could be wrong...I'd have to double-check our geology files for a definitive answer."

De Lis nodded. "All right. We'll do that after we return. For now, stow it for the trip to the crater." His eyes turned sharply to Shajda. "Which, I presume, we are headed to now?" he said, more of a command than a question.

Shajda nodded his head happily. "No...more!" The Sherpa faced the abbot.

De Lis' eyes widened. Another gift?

The abbot obliged, closing the chest. He returned it to the cabinet and retrieved a metallic lock box, setting it also on the desktop. The lid opened with a clack as he reached his hand deeply into the box and shuffled it among the unseen contents. His hand returned seconds later with a yellowed document, which he then gave to de Lis.

De Lis sneezed from the dust showered about the room. After wiping his nose, he unfolded a large, green and blue sheet of paper, revealing a series of graph lines littered with abbreviated graphite handwriting.

Valagua took immediate interest in the relic, nearly ripping it from the doctor's hands. "It's a military topo map...of Nepal." His eyes and fingers darted around the map's periphery. An index finger ran a straight line over a piece of small text. "United States..." he recited, "War Department. It's from the Second World War."

"Where did they get this?" de Lis asked Shajda.

The abbot spoke quietly, nearly imperceptibly, in his native speech. Shajda bobbed his head while listening to the abbot give his testimony. The Sherpa turned away from the old man, translating the passage in his head before saying, "Long...uhm...many centuries past. Military men...Westerners bring it here."

The abbot gestured excitedly with his hands, flaring them about his head.

"Military men...very scared—yes!" Shajda reiterated.

"No, that's not possible," Waters said. "This site, this crash, wasn't discovered until three days ago. Nobody knew it was here! Certainly not the military."

The abbot grinned coyly once more. Another set of papers, this time a small spiral notebook, was thrust into de Lis' hand.

De Lis nearly tore the tattered remains apart as his fingers turned it about.

"Careful!" Valagua cautioned, reaching for the notebook.

De Lis lightened his hold of it, relieving Valagua. He then flipped through the ancient journal, reading its quick scrawls. "What happened to these men?"

Shajda turned to the abbot, who jutted his lips in a doubt.

De Lis frowned. It was bad enough they were belatedly informed of eyewitnesses, but it was worse that no trace of their whereabouts were to be remembered at all. The best clues to the crash's origins would lie with them. But, perhaps without meaning to, the abbot had provided them with a better record of the crash than a two-century-old tale. They would need to pore over this notebook, however, and any other treasures the old abbot could dig out of that lock box of his.

"Shajda," de Lis asked, pointing his hand to the lock box, "ask him if he will give us the other papers in there."

Shajda started to translate, but the abbot handed de Lis the rest of the stash.

De Lis quickly bowed, showing his appreciation. "Thank—thank you. You have been too kind."

The abbot bowed as well, his fingers steepled.

Valagua gently guided the ancient papers into a sample bag.

"Shajda...the site?" de Lis asked once more.

The Sherpa nodded; his work was now nearly complete.

With the group shown the monastery's door a short while later, de Lis wasted no time following Shajda down the path; their diversion had already cost them two hours of precious sunlight. Just past the garden, however, Waters took several digigraphs with a holo-imager and lidar readings using laser pulses to document the monastery's precise topographical coordinates; besides, no one back at the lab would believe them if she didn't employ every means to authenticate the monastery.

Some time later Shajda led the team back to the mountain fissure. Before allowing his team to pass back through the narrow way, de Lis had the team cover their exposed flesh. De Lis then consolidated the rucksacks and gave them to Shajda to carry, which allowed them the optimal amount of crawl space, lessening any chance for new injuries. They all crossed through the passage with less difficulty, emerging in two-thirds the time. Each member reclaimed their gear from the waiting Shajda, then rested a moment to focus on the upcoming trail.

De Lis pushed the team forward again, paying particular attention to his creeping chronometer, which was not the team's friend. Meticulously tracing their journey with his holobook, he marked their every step, correlating Waters' lidar data into a holographic cartograph, which produced an extended view of the region. If indeed they did have to return to the monastery for any reason, he'd make sure that Shajda was not along for the trip.

Shajda soon led them to the familiar section of the path. He continued onwards, beyond a series of outcroppings that formed a natural barrier to the unaided and unfamiliar eye. Mason noted again the absence of crash strata, lending more credence to his private hypothesis of river flooding, which conveniently hid any immediate connection to a crash site.

A bowl in the structure of the mountains soon opened up, and they realized they had ventured into the bottom of a thousand-meter crater. De Lis and Waters crouched, scrounging around the exterior of the bowl with sample bags, ready to collect the first specimens. De Lis was curiously quiet, Gilmour thought. The agent at least expected the doctor to give some profound announcement, perhaps justifying their presence there. But true to the scientist he was, the doctor silently gathered his samples.

Grappling for a useful purpose, Gilmour and Mason walked around the bowl's perimeter, studying the layout of the land. Mason even briefly conferred with Valagua, but the historian could only serve to validate Mason's flooding theory as the explanation for no visible signs of a meteor or other "normal" crash debris. Whatever had crashed here, neither the landscape nor the scientists were forthcoming.

At least yet.

Shajda suddenly tugged at de Lis' and Waters' arms, gesturing down to the bowl's nadir. At first trying to ignore the guide's incessant commotion, de Lis finally acquiesced and rose to his feet. Sighing, he and Waters followed Shajda's descent. The Sherpa raced ahead some five meters into the crater, almost as if he knew what was down there.

"Slow down!" de Lis said, fanning the dust from his face. "You're kicking up potential evidence."

Shajda pointed to the bare ground repeatedly, drawing de Lis and Waters to the spot. The two trailed behind him with trepidation, regarding the soil cautiously.

At the lip of the crater above, Gilmour and Mason watched the trio's exchange with interest, if not outright amusement. Venturing that this was the best—if only—use of their time, they inched down the tracks left by the trio, taking note of the crater and its desolate contents, mainly its lack of eye-catching stones.

"Stacia, get some more samples from the bottom, just for measure." De Lis looked back to their guide, exasperated. "I don't see anything out of the ordinary here. Why do you keep telling me that?"

Waters retrieved several kilos of material and placed them in her bag while Shajda shoved a pile of loose rubble into de Lis' hands.

"This is the same material Doctor Waters is getting. Why do you keep giving it to me?"

Shajda smiled and pretended to shovel with his hands. "Dig."

De Lis paused; if Shajda was anything like that old abbot, then he knew this place's secrets as much as he knew its trails. The doctor peered over to Waters, ready to give the Sherpa another chance. "Stacia, break out your pickaxe!"

Gilmour, Mason and Valagua walked up behind de Lis, puzzled at his swift call to action.

"Everyone, your pickaxes!" de Lis yelled. "Start digging!"

The five lowered their backpacks and removed their collapsible pickaxes, unfolding each to their full length. De Lis gathered the group at the very center, pointing out Shajda's hand-scooped holes, then began his assault on the crater.

Cracks from all five pickaxes broke the hardpan open, revealing soil unseen for decades, centuries even. Ten hands peeled away the broken earth and tossed it aside, exposing the dark, rich underlayer.

Waters clawed a palmful and inspected the cake of burnt and unaffected desert humus closely. Flicking out a piece of burnt soil with her index finger, she compared it to a holograph of similar soil from her holobook. "This is definitely debris strata, Richard...maybe two hundred years old."

"Keep digging," de Lis instructed. "Let's try to find the impactor by sundown."

After several hours of excavation through two meters of ground, Valagua, Gilmour and Mason had uncovered a twisted chunk of metallic debris from its earthen cage, which, just moments earlier, Valagua had unknowingly whacked into with his pickaxe. Facing the darkness, de Lis and Waters rushed over to the trio and helped scoop out the reclaimed debris, eager to catch their first glimpse of the impactor before night reclaimed it. Taking shifts with their pickaxes and shovels, they managed to gain enough leverage to forcibly extract the metallic debris after several moments, lifting it out of the pit ever so slightly.

With the team breaking for a moment, Waters scanned the meter-long debris with her holobook, allowing the device to estimate the material's density and mass by its composition. Seeing the results, her eyes bugged out; the metal was denser than all but the most advanced industrial steel alloys humankind had yet conceived, little wonder it was able to survive a collision and remain in a good state. If this relatively small piece made it through, she had to wonder where the rest lay....

Calling their break over, de Lis produced a line of osmium-nanotubular cord and tied it to one end of the debris, securing it with a winch that Gilmour and Mason had earlier drilled into the lip of the bowl. On command, the two agents and Waters pulled on the cord, while de Lis and Valagua pushed the debris up and out of the excavated hole, then clearing the lip of the bowl, where they left it lay. Hunched over and grabbing their knees, the team paused for a few breaths.

Looking up from his work, de Lis caught sight of a lone planet twinkling high in the ultramarine atmosphere. Clapping his hands once, he said, "All right, we've just lost the sun! We need to get this back to the camp."

Waters retrieved the winch while Valagua wrapped up the cord and placed it over his shoulders. With Shajda donning the group's ruck-sacks and leading the team back to the camp, de Lis, Valagua, Gilmour and Mason hoisted the debris up between the four of them and arduously began the trek back with their cargo.

What are we doing here?

The two agents headed away from the jumpjet after leaving the impactor in the mobile lab. De Lis had dismissed the group afterwards, instructing them to get a good night's rest. But the same question kept repeating in Gilmour's mind, forcing him to rethink their true purpose here.

"Why did de Lis select us? Our specialty is intel and investigation, not archaeology," Gilmour said, his irritation getting the better of him. "De Lis said we'd do nicely, but at what? So far, we're just his grunts."

After entering and sealing off their end of the tent, Mason removed his rucksack and his hiking clothes, replacing them with his warmer slumber garb. "This is the government's baby...there's a reason they sent us. The Russians don't know we're here. If we can keep this quiet, then we've won." He rubbed his eyes and sighed. "Maybe that's why. We're discreet."

Gilmour slung his rucksack to the floor. "Get me behind the lines...but don't have me digging up two-hundred-year-old garbage. That's not my game, nor the IIA's." Privately, he wondered just who de Lis was really serving; himself, or someone above them all.

## CHAPTER FIVE

The morning alarm roused Gilmour and Mason from their respective cots. A blinding dawn sun steadily infiltrated the tent canopy's thin fabric, inciting them to dress once again into their hiking gear.

Exiting the tent after a sponge wash and a quick course of field rations, Gilmour's and Mason's ears picked up the jogging footfalls of Javier Valagua rounding the corner from the jumpjet. The historian stopped before the two and removed his sunglasses, his feet blowing dust into the morning air.

"Agent Mason, Agent Gilmour. We're about ready to open up the wreckage."

Gilmour's attitude hadn't shifted much since the night before. "And we're needed for this...?"

Oblivious to the agent's facetious words, Valagua said, "This is the big moment, why we're here." He checked his wrist chrono. "We've got two minutes, agents."

Trained to obey their orders despite any personal misgivings, Gilmour and Mason joined Valagua on the return path to the jumpjet, shelving their thoughts for now.

Once inside, the trio bypassed the cramped seating to enter the mobile laboratory, situated at the rear of the craft. The lab itself was not much larger than three square meters, and came equipped with a island centered exam table, which was now inhabited with the debris recovered from the crater. Each wall was sloped down from the ceiling to the floor, brimming with cabinets, racks and shelves of diagnostic tools and other scientific equipment unknown to the two agents.

De Lis welcomed the trio back to the lab, where he and Waters had donned goggles. Waters crossed in front of the trio to a box-shaped console bolted to the lab wall, where she drew a half-meter long laser torch. After typing in a short sequence of buttons on the console, Waters stepped back to the exam table and the wreckage.

De Lis tossed goggles to Valagua, Gilmour and Mason. "You'll need those."

Whipping the torch's hose around her, Waters soon fired up the device, eliciting a blue spark from its curved head. She minutely adjusted its intensity with a twist of its nozzle, then subjected the debris to the torch without hesitation.

Gilmour and Mason watched the invisible laser pierce through the debris' outer layer, a twisted bar of dark metallic material. The scream of the wreckage bounced between the tight walls of the lab, making Mason think that de Lis should have provided earplugs, too.

De Lis, now outfitted with thermal gloves, assisted with the procedure, lifting the first bar away after Waters had removed it from the carcass. She then cut her way around the perimeter of the debris over the next few minutes, working to expose what appeared to be a compacted sheet lying flat against the interior of the wreckage. Once the sheet had been cut, de Lis peeled back the charred metal canvas, allowing it to rest open halfway.

Inside, more twisted metal lay compressed together, perhaps due to the centuries it had spent locked in earth. De Lis picked at the various layers of material with pliers, eager to learn what lay beneath. He gestured Waters to gently cut down the center of the metal, enough to unlock more of the layers.

Waters skillfully maneuvered her way into the wreckage like a surgeon. Adjusting the laser accordingly, she started to uncover the central layers, which proved to be difficult; the metal whined under her torch, resisting her efforts to pry it open.

She looked at de Lis for a course of action; he gestured for her to up the power. Again, Waters adjusted the torch, strengthening the photon frequency. Refocusing on her task, she took the torch to the metal while de Lis worked at it with his pliers, attempting to wrench the compact material loose.

A loud hiss and a pop from inside the wreckage startled the assembled group, leaving de Lis shouting, "Stop!" In his pliers were clamped the last metal layer, smoking fiercely.

Waters extinguished the torch and removed her goggles. Setting the torch down, she inspected the specimen in the doctor's pliers. Valagua, Gilmour and Mason followed her study with their own.

De Lis placed the metal into a sample dish, saving it for future analysis.

With a lamp, Waters spotlit the hole in the wreckage, examining the crumpled layers for any other hidden layers of composition. She threw her gloved hands inside and rummaged around, feeling the tough metallic material on all four sides. Her fingers detected nothing different until they brushed against a smooth, bulbous object lodged between several layers of twisted debris.

"Richard, there's another object in there...it's not part of this metal."

"Can we get a better look?"

"I think we can." Waters crossed to the other side of the lab and opened a cabinet, removing a long, slender wand. At one end was a centimeter-wide sphere, which she grabbed with her right hand, extending the wand out to a full meter.

Waters made her way back to the table. Above it was situated an holographic monitor, planted on a descending deck, which she pulled down to view. With the flip of a button, Waters activated the monitor, giving them access to the three-dimensional view produced by the spherical holo-cam at the end of the wand.

She fed the wand into the mouth of the debris, producing alternating infrared, ultraviolet and optical views of the shaft on the monitor. The group watched as the holo-cam wound its way through the hole, finally coming to a halt at the end. Waters rotated the sphere until it caught a glimpse of her quarry: a black, globular object that separated itself from the other, similarly colored metal by its unusual UV spectrum. De Lis placed an index finger near the monitor. "There—Stacia, get a closer view."

She magnified the holocam's image threefold.

Intrigued, de Lis tapped a button on the monitor deck, which performed a cursory analysis of the object's EM spectrum. Below the image, a series of peaks and troughs were displayed. "You're right, Stacia. That's not metal. Spectrum is organic, heavy in calcium and oxygenated minerals." He exchanged a look with Waters. "Let's get it out of there."

Twenty minutes later, Waters and de Lis had carved up the remaining wreckage, temporarily placing the disjointed pieces around the lab's walls. Waters, with a pair of pliers in her hands, reached over to the metal layers containing the organic object. De Lis held the metal while Waters extracted the object from its centuries-old entrapment.

The object popped out sooner than Waters anticipated, dropping out of the pliers. Only good reflexes by her left hand kept the object from hitting, and most likely smashing, on the lab's reinforced metal floor. Throwing the pliers down, she grasped the object in both hands, allowing all in the lab to glimpse the unusual artifact under the glare of real lighting. A shade of mottled brown stained the artifact, as if bruised.

The five said in immediate synchronicity, "A skull."

Waters soon found a strange glint lodged inside a crack at the base. "Hold on...."

"What is it?" de Lis asked.

Waters picked up the pliers again, and working it into the crack, grasped an object in its teeth. Pulling gently but firmly, she plucked a glittering jewel from inside the wound, exposing it to the overhead light.

"Are you shitting me?" Mason said.

# CHAPTER SIX

"It's not Homo sapiens," de Lis announced, clamping the skull in a spectrometer.

Gilmour took a close look at the relic, noting the two large eye sockets, cheek bones and upper mandible. "Some sort of simian, a native species here?"

"It doesn't fit any profile of the hominids, past or present," Waters explained. "I'd bet my money against the missing link, too."

De Lis closed the hood over the skull and tapped a button below the spectrometer's scanning plate, activating the device's spectrum sensor. A small monitor attached to the spectrometer read out the object's atomic spectrum: a dozen peaks and valleys, rapidly drawn from a single red line.

A spike near the middle of the spectrum caught de Lis' attention. "Look at that!"

Waters closed in. "That...that can't be right."

De Lis keyed in a series of buttons on the spectrometer. "Readings are good. Everything's online." He pointed a finger to an unassuming spike. "Hmm...interesting."

"What is it?" Gilmour asked.

"The signature of yttrium. An isotope, actually...one I've only seen in laboratories."

Gilmour recalled the chemistry classes from his youth. "Isn't that a rare element? How could it be in this skull?"

"Yttrium itself isn't that rare," Waters explained. "In fact, it's more common than silver. Its isotopes, particularly the Y-90 here, are different than the Y-89 found in Earth's crust, and are found in asteroid and meteorite crater strata. As rare as those isotopes are compared to ter-restrial Y-89, they're only a fraction compared to the seven parts per million that are in this skull. The Y-90 here is a major constituent of the skull's minerals, although I can't see how a radioactive isotope with its short half-life got to Earth without decaying as soon as it made contact with our atmosphere."

"Well, if it's not a hominid," Gilmour said, "what is it?"
De Lis looked at Waters. "Uh, we don't know."

All five were drawn again to the thirteen-centimeter-long skull, resting anonymously on the spectrometer. It seemed so peaceful.

"The only way to find out will be to catalogue its DNA," Waters said after a moment's pause.

"That can wait for now," de Lis said. "I think, in light of our dwin-dling time, our next course of action should be to split our resources. Agent Gilmour, Javier, we've got to see if we can find any other pieces of that impactor out there. Stacia, start work on those jewels...I want to know what's so special about them, why that abbot had them, and what one is doing inside that skull."

Waters nodded. "Good luck."

Pausing at the hatch's threshold, de Lis continued, "If we don't get anything else out of that crater, this will be all we have to show for ourselves."

Waters didn't have to have de Lis spell it out for her; whatever they potentially left behind was fair game to not only the Chinese, but the Confederation, if they decided to start sniffing around their back-yard. And whatever they had here was just strange enough to get the Confederation ample reason to dig around for more.

"Then I'll try to exhaust every avenue at our disposal," Waters answered.

De Lis nodded, then departed with Gilmour and Valagua, leaving Mason as her sole assistant.

"Ready for some action?" Waters asked the agent.

"What can I do, Doctor?"

"First of all," she smiled, "stop calling me doctor. It's Stacia, all right?"

"Gotcha."

Mason retrieved a sterile container from across the lab and brought it over to Waters. She removed the lid, exposing the opalescent jewel and its many facets to the light again. Waters' gloved hand envel-oped the jewel, cradling it as she gently placed it inside the spectrom-eter's hood, then dialed a set of commands into the keypad.

The scanning plate hummed while the pair waited patiently for several moments, more than long enough, Waters thought, to receive a good spectrum from the relic.

Scanning the spectrometer's monitor for activity, Waters let out a deep, confused groan when the readout remained static, merely droning its usual mechanized voice, as if no object had been placed on the plate at all. She turned to Mason.

His right eyebrow arched on his face. "Maybe it's just shy."

"I've never seen a spectrometer do this before...I don't understand...." Waters tapped the scanning plate with her hand, causing the device to whine. Undaunted, she gave it a smack to its side for good measure.

"Can we try scanning it again?" Mason asked. "If it's malfunctioning, maybe there's another analysis you can perform."

She sighed. "None as sensitive as this." Waters tapped another button. "I'm programming it to run a simultaneous self-diagnosis while it scans the object. If it is a malfunction, we'll be able to pinpoint it."

With the "START" button toggled, the spectrometer began its second attempt at solving the mystery of the jewel's identity, and perhaps origin.

Everything seemed normal, Mason thought, since the spectrometer hummed like before. He also didn't see any black smoke streaming from the device, so they had that in their favor. His eyes drifted back to the spectrum readout. Once more, a dull red flatline was displayed, giving them no hint or clue as to the jewel's composition.

After the scan cycle had been completed, Waters looked at the machine with disguised disgust, the same visage she had tried to hide from Doctor de Lis a day ago, Mason noted. She linked her holobook in with the spectrometer's computer and accessed the device's self-diagnosis.

Mason drew closer to glimpse the holobook's results. "Well?"

"There's nothing wrong with the spectrometer," she said, switching her holobook off. "It's this jewel. Somehow it's obscuring the sensor."

Incredulity crept into Mason's eyes.

"Don't ask me how," she intoned, before Mason could even find the words. "I've never heard of any substance ever having been theorized to possess no spectrum."

They soon succumbed to the power of their collective awe, each wondering precisely what it was they had discovered in this remote corner of the world.

Mason soon broke the silence. "What about a good old

microscope?"

"Hmm?"

"Is there a microscope on board to get a visual picture of the jewel's quantum structure?"

"Yes...we have one." Even as Waters crossed over to an equipment cabinet, she still seemed to be lost in a daze, perhaps even lost to herself. When faced with an object that appeared to be contrary to all that she had learned and observed with her education, the young doctor became a shadow of her professional self, perhaps unfairly humbling herself into self-doubt.

Waters set the half-meter-barreled gamma particle microscope on a mobile tray cart. She then removed the jewel from the spectrometer, placed it on the microscope's probe plate, and secured it under the radiation hood. She toggled several buttons located on the 'scope's barrel before activating the quantum battery inside.

Above them, the monitor displayed a snowy pattern after Waters had linked them to the microscope's data transmission. Looking into the microscope's binocular eyepiece, Waters adjusted the outgoing image, which displayed a twofold exterior of the jewel on the assembled monitors.

Over the next several moments, Waters peeled away the layers of the bizarre object, but not the mystery itself. Midway through her tunneling, she paused; instead of the atomic folds and plains she had expected to see, all that greeted her was a barrier of impenetrable matter, so impassable that even high velocity gamma rays were turned away, an impossible feat save for the most densely packed material known to exist—the cores of pulsars.

Mason turned away from the monitor to Waters. "Why'd you stop?"

"I haven't...the microscope won't penetrate the object. I—I don't know why."

The agent crossed over to the microscope and lowered his eyes into it to examine the binocular eyepiece for himself.

Waters rubbed her forehead, trying to formulate a solution to this new quandary, but nothing became apparent. However impossible, and theoretically unlikely, this object refused to subject itself to their probes.

Mason backed away from the scope and its disappointing view. "Are there any other tests, anything even remotely feasible?"

"A Casimir," she said, then pondered the consequences. "But that may be unwise."

"What's a 'kaz-ee-meer'?"

Waters rested her back against the edge of the island table. "Two sheets of metal designed to test the presence of negative energy in space."

He cocked his head. "Pardon?"

"An experiment. We can view the negative curvature of spacetime with it, as well as the dimensional topology of this object." She sighed. "In other words, find out what exactly this thing is, and its effect, or distortion, of the curvature of spacetime."

"Is this a bad thing?"

"Well, nobody has exactly used it for what we're talking about."

"Why not?"

"Allow me to explain it this way: no one likes fooling with Mother Nature."

Mason nodded his head; a justifiable response. Unfortunately in his line of work, he knew little about the theoretical bending of nature. Most of the cases he dealt with involved global terrorism, or genocide for political means. And if that was his version of fooling with Mother Nature, he wanted no part of theirs. "Is there any guarantee of its safe use?"

A smile formed over Stacia's face. "There are rarely guarantees in science, Mr Mason."

Regardless of his suspicions, he knew he had no real authority to stop her from performing this negative energy experiment. And if doing the experiment would help them get a leg up on the Russians, then he had no reason, nor room, to dissent.

"All right. What do we do?"

A cascade of brilliant white grains bombarded the monitors above, presenting Mason with a show unlike any other in nature. His brain, much as it did when he was a child, imagined a scene of tremendous forces at work. Despite a love of nature as a youngster, Gregory Mason never had the aptitude for studying it, so he pursued other areas to fuel his creativity, leaving science behind. Watching the fireworks on the screen, a part of him wished he had tried a little harder to grasp the concepts he was too fidgety all those years ago to appreciate.

He didn't attempt to hide the grin on his face. "What is it! It's so beautiful!"

"The annihilation of virtual particles. Spacetime is a stew of these matter and antimatter reactions," Waters explained. "They're just too small for us to see with conventional instruments."

"And we're creating this inside the Casimir plates?"

"To a degree," she said, marveling at the quantum explosions as well. For a professional dedicated to a stereotypically cut and dry career, she freely expressed her wonderment.

"Most of the annihilation occurs naturally. We're just going to influence them a bit more."

Waters manipulated the holo-cam's position on the device formally known as the Casimir Symmetrical Virtual Particle Reaction Cavity. The machine was nothing but a pair of parallel metal plates inside a vacuum chamber, which, upon its invention, had the peculiar habit of confirming a cornerstone of quantum theory: the curvature of spacetime. The device was rarely practical until a method of "seeing" this curvature could be discerned by the same theory. Now, with the holo-cam firmly in place, the trio could witness for perhaps the first time the definitive spacetime topology of this bizarre and inconspicuous little jewel, and determine what exactly it was.

Satisfied with the holo-cam's image of the cavity's interior, Waters set to work on their final test. She started the Casimir's aspirator, evacuating the atmosphere from the cavity. After confirming that the cavity was indeed cleared of gasses, Waters next switched on the gear for the twin metal plates. The two plates would then converge, creating a space devoid of ninety-seven percent of the virtual particles and antiparticles naturally found in the spacetime continuum.

Jury-rigged to the top of the chamber housing was a clear dropchute, wide enough to fit the jewel. Acting as an airlock, the dropchute maintained the integrity of the vacuum without a "leak."

Waters consulted the particle annihilation image on the monitor, confirming that the Casimir was in proper working order. She popped the dropchute's top hatch open, gingerly situated the jewel inside, then closed the hatch again. The doctor pulled the bottom hatch open and watched as the vacuum cavity sucked the jewel into its hungry maw.

Mason witnessed an immediate shift in the image of the particle explosions. Instead of the random activity he had allowed his eyes to gaze upon, a pattern emerged in the timing of the various particle annihilations. Not only was this evident, but also a shape, although none Mason could place a name to. A void, he thought again, to be more precise. This amorphous darkness, devoid of explosions, dominated the center of the monitor image to the agent's growing curiosity.

To his left flank, Waters pointed to the image, placing her fingers near the monitor and tracing an outline of the mysterious, dark pattern. Wearing a smile so large that Mason couldn't believe it was Stacia Waters, she said, "Do you see it! Do you see it!"

Mason nodded his head, although hardly matching her

enthusiasm. "What is it?"

"The jewel!" she answered. *Could Mason really be so dense?* "I—I can't believe it worked!" Waters' eyes teared. She could no longer hold back a yelp, a half-laugh, half-cry. All of her dreams, all of her career goals were breaking through. She was breaking through. If only everyone back at Ottawa could see this....

Mason's finger traced the oscillating dark patch. He squinted, trying to fathom what bizarre object this jewel was, what history it had seen, who had first held its smooth facets. Above all else, he pondered what it all meant.

"What is this shape?" he asked.

"I...I can't be sure. It's large, much larger than what I calculated it to be. There are absolutely no particle annihilations inside the boundary. It must have an immense effect on the spacetime fabric."

"But gravity should also do the same, and this weighs no more than several grams."

"True," Waters allowed. "But there are more effects than just gravity." She stared back at the image. "Whatever that object is, it's no jewel. And this is no ordinary spacetime curvature, either."

De Lis, Valagua and Gilmour returned to the jumpjet later, after a fruitless scavenge through the crater site. Despite the abundant presence of more metal shards buried deeper within the bowl, the absence of other artifacts similar to the skull dissuaded de Lis from staying longer than three hours.

Gilmour noticed throughout the second dig how distracted de Lis seemed; his thoughts were back in the lab. With de Lis' career resting upon this mission, Gilmour wondered if it was a boon to him, or an albatross. Nobel prize aspirations aside, de Lis had been ordered here by the Defense Secretary, so he couldn't focus solely on his dreams—the world's safety was on all their shoulders. Doubtless, that made good science pretty difficult.

"Richard, drop everything!" Waters exhorted. "Get back here!"

The mobile lab quickly grew quiet as Waters displayed the incredible image on the monitor deck, enthralling all eyes to its eerie otherworldliness and seemingly playing with their perceptions.

De Lis' eyes sparkled. He angled his head in marvelous rapture. "This... this is phenomenal, Stacia! Absolutely...the curvature, the topology, much higher than I've ever seen, even in the lab simulations."

Waters crossed her arms, locking her eyes on the holographic object. "Doctor, I...I'm not certain I have the experience necessary to even begin an adequate analysis. Quantum theory is one thing, but cosmological topology—"

"Pshhh," de Lis scoffed. "You're precisely the person for this moment. Tell me what you think it is. Use your most outlandish idea... nothing spared."

Gilmour raised an eyebrow to Mason, who were both completely foreign to this schoolyard scientific method. The pair looked on while Waters massaged her jaw, employing her years of education to lend a hand in deciphering this most complex of puzzles.

"Logically," she said, "it conflicts with gravity. The object itself has a mass of only a few grams, but has no quantum structure, as yet we can determine. It leads me to only one belief, and that is it's as dense as matter can possibly be, even more so than a typical pulsar core. But that would be in defiance of all natural laws." She took a breath. "In fact, quite absurd."

"Good," de Lis said, clapping his hands once. "Good. I like it. It makes no sense, but I like it!" He smiled back at her, lifting the tremendous weight from her mind. "Now, let's see if we can tweak this a bit."

De Lis manipulated the plate gears, bringing them closer. Inside, sheltered from the macroscopic world by the twin plates, an infinite number of virtual particles and antiparticles continued the eternal cycle of creation and annihilation, in the process distorting the curvature of the very fabric of space and time—the universe. Twisted and contorted beyond the stresses allowed by Mother Nature herself, this crude manipulation by mere men could lead to only one conclusion.

The monitor displayed the spectacular results. All eyes were drawn to the amorphous shape, which quickly grew from occupying one quarter of the monitor to eating up the available viewing area, leaving almost no room to visualize the remaining virtual particle explosions. The three scientists gasped, clearly awed by the increasingly dynamic structure of this object.

"Look at that!" de Lis exclaimed.

Below them, almost lost amongst the excitement of the shifting image above, the Casimir hummed louder, but not perceptibly, underneath the scientists' thrill. A miniature earthquake rumbled throughout the solid vacuum device, rattling it a millimeter from its former position on the island table. Only when the holo-cam's image itself become distorted did the odd behavior draw attention.

"Doctor," Gilmour said, pointing out the Casimir device shaking its way across the table.

Waters and de Lis grabbed the device to halt its migration, but the violent shaking persisted, nearly shoving off the pair's hands. De Lis reached for the button to deactivate the parallel plates' gear mechanisms, but failed to reach it before the Casimir's quaking reached a dangerous level.

Snow was the only image on the monitor now while the group fought to contain the animated machine. They wrestled delicately with the expensive device, hoping to salvage its cargo without having to take a sledgehammer to it.

With the hands of de Lis, Valagua, Gilmour and Mason on the casing of the machine, Waters devised a newer strategy. "The dropchute! Open it!"

The four wrestled the unwieldy device onto its side long enough for Waters to land her left hand onto the dropchute. She retrieved a wrench from the top of the table, and using the leverage of her left arm to steady herself, placed the tool's twin teeth over the clear housing of the dropchute. The rigged airlock hissed as she pulled it open, admitting the atmosphere to invade the pristine vacuum chamber below.

Despite this, the Casimir continued to quake. Whining horribly, the machine's casing fractured, launching the dropchute into the lab's ceiling. Gilmour and Mason pried de Lis and Valagua away from the mechanical volcano just before it cracked in two. The remains of the plates and gear mechanisms spilled out as the shell halves were blown past the exam table and onto the floor.

But that incredible explosion paled compared to the sight now before their eyes. Hovering in the remains of the Casimir—for a mere second—was a bizarre optical hole, an electromagnetic siphon curving light waves around its tight, spherical core. The jewel itself orbited the core, swiftly spiraling into the heart of the phenomenon before the assembled group could reach for their instruments to study it. The team gasped as the siphon instantly collapsed upon itself with a dreadful sucking echo, ending the anomaly and the mystery of the jewel all too soon.

"Jesus," Valagua muttered.

"Break camp! We're going back now!" de Lis shouted in the jumpjet.

Without hesitation, Gilmour and Mason, followed by Waters and Valagua, ran to the camp, hastily gathering and evacuating their gear from the temporary domiciles while de Lis secured the mobile lab for flight lockdown status.

Liftoff had been scheduled for 2047 hours, local time, under the descending layer of night, but the incident in the mobile lab virtually guaranteed their return to Ottawa should be as swift as possible. If the Confederation had indeed been aware of their presence here, there wasn't much this tiny group could do to evade the Russians' satellite platforms. The best they could hope for was to effect a quick exit, arousing as little notice as possible.

De Lis took a few minutes to devise a satisfactory explanation for their abrupt departure, mentioning nothing of the jewel, to Secretary Buhranda; the jumpjet's pilots, meanwhile readied the jumpjet for emergency takeoff, fueling the craft with just enough hydrogen pellets to get back to USNA airspace, but no farther. It was truly a last-minute operation.

After performing final inventory checks of their equipment, Gilmour, Mason, Waters and Valagua boarded the jumpjet, leaving Nepal and the mysterious crater behind them. De Lis stepped aboard a few moments later via the starboard hatch, then signaled the pilots to depart. Wiping his jaw, de Lis took a seat and a deep breath. Deep down, he knew the easy part was done; the hard part was just beginning.

# CHAPTER SEVEN

USNA airspace once again greeted them, lending a palpable ease to the craft. From what they could tell, the Confederation had not detected the team's access to the Central Asian Conglomerates, a small comfort with the potentially hazardous cargo the team had retrieved from the earth.

The jumpjet made a smooth descent back at Hangar Building B, gliding under the opened doors which led to a cavernous subterranean chamber. Once the craft had set down, a grounds crew, loaded down with equipment cases, poured out an adjacent compartment. They hurried over to the jumpjet and flooded its interior, scanning the deck with an array of instruments. Gilmour and Mason watched the men with keen interest, remarking that they were probably searching for bugs, but not of the arthropod variety.

After a pair of MPs arrived to lead the agents to a chemical de-radiation and de-biological washroom, Gilmour and Mason were issued appropriate attire to wear, then handed decorum guidelines to be employed throughout the Ottawa facility. Their previous visit here was too brief to be a proper introduction, so the agents were isolated inside another meeting room for an hour before they were released.

Dressed like blue-suited twins, the agents were accompanied by another pair of MPs downstairs to one of U5's dark corridors, the jarheads saying nothing, per their reputation. The lead Marine soon found his pass key and slid it through the door panel to U5-29. The agents proceeded inside, this time met by de Lis, Waters, Valagua and several other personnel unknown to them, all seated at the conference table.

"Agents Gilmour and Mason," de Lis said, gesturing, "have a seat."

"Thank you, Doctor."

Gilmour and Mason rounded the table and sat down across from de Lis. To Gilmour's right was Waters, and over one was a new staff member, a dark woman with slim features who appeared to be a staff scientist. A mustached Native American man in USNA officer's uniform was next to her, and across from this man was a taller, bespectacled gentleman. A Latina woman with greying temples sat adjacent to de Lis, who surveyed the agents with a discerning stare.

De Lis leaned forward, placing his hands on the table. "Let me introduce you to the rest of our senior staff. To Doctor Waters' right is our chief anthropologist and sociologist, Doctor Carol Marlane. Next to her is our lead liaison with the North American Army, Lieutenant Colonel Benjamin Dark Horse. Next to you, Agent Mason, is our quantum mechanics lead theorist, Doctor Lionel Roget."

Roget smiled and shook hands with Mason, lending the agent his first sign of cordiality since they arrived here.

De Lis continued, "And last, our facility's State Department liaison, foreign policy scholar and analyst, Professor Inez Quintanilla. All of my esteemed colleagues and I, as well as you, Agents Gilmour and Mason, will work closely to decode the mystery of the crash site, and the various artifacts we have found therein."

Once the briefing had adjourned for the day and the agents had read up on the latest mission reports, de Lis and his staff introduced Gilmour and Mason to U5's theoretical studies laboratory, a set of contiguous offices spanning most of the floor space, located in its central square and bounded by an outer perimeter corridor. Upon entry, the first room that met them was also the largest: U5-1, the main diagnostic and experimental laboratory, a hexagon-shaped room. Six smaller units branched off from it, creating a space reminiscent of a beehive. Around them, a dozen junior scientists outfitted with goggles, clear antiseptic exam suits and holobooks scurried about, relaying information to one another from an array of computer terminals situated throughout the lab. Gilmour imagined that each was performing a separate test on the jewels found in Nepal, quantifying and cataloguing the specifications of each object.

Sterility permeated the lab, granting a scrubbed feel and smell to it, owing to the enormous quantity of North America's finest quantum computers and diagnostic equipment spread amongst the complex and narrow rows of office tables and chairs. An ever present hum vibrated in the air, coupled with an electric crispness, like ozone from a spring thunderstorm.

The lighting here was particularly bright, more than making up for the dim corridors. Each agent took note of the five-centimeter-thick fullerene glass separating the adjacent offices, a clear, ceiling-to-floor material, sufficient to observe any and all the smaller labs at once, and capable of containing any accidents with Level-3 bio- and chem-safety protocols. Fullerene glass also had the ability—due to its remarkable carbon-60 structure—to become opaque on command for private briefings and provide, if need be, instant security behind its bullet-resistant surface.

Ordinary walls here were nonexistent, save for U5-6, a room sequestered to their far left, which de Lis identified only as the aforementioned gallery, a multibillion-dollar mini-facility for large-scale holographic presentations. The agents could only wonder what the good doctor had in store for them in there.

De Lis soon ushered them over to his own office, U5-3, inhabiting the north wall of the theoretical studies lab, to their right. Sliding his pass key into the round, fullerene-suspended panel, de Lis led them inside. He walked behind his small desk and quickly read from a holobook, then set it back down, looking both agents in the eyes. "This is your home from now on. This is what we do to keep the world out of harm's grasp. All of this," he gestured with his outstretched hands, "is our first line of defense."

De Lis stepped over to the two men, leading them to the fullerene wall overlooking the area. All three observed the busy scientists on the other side, each doing his or her duty to decipher the secrets of the microscopic universe.

"I just hope our defense isn't too late."

Despite the vast pressure exerted by the government to decode the mystery of the jewels, the next several days passed by fleetingly. Various tests on the remaining jewels extracted from the robe revealed no more than before, and de Lis was hesitant to employ another Casimir experiment until all other avenues had been exhausted.

While work on the bizarre, unforgiving objects proceeded with fits and starts, Valagua and Marlane made many examinations of the cryptid skull, as well as the topographical map handed to them by the abbot. A complex, three-dimensional holograph of the skull by the two scientists reconstructed areas on the original specimen that had long ago been crushed or fractured, allowing them a better chance of perhaps defining a genus and species for the cryptid, and just maybe figure out who or what brought these jewels to Earth, and for what purpose.

Marlane had begun work on cataloguing the cryptid's DNA and

ribosomal RNA protein sequences, concluding—until better evidence could be uncovered—that the skull was of "no known terrestrial origin," and, due to the presence of Y-90 isotopes, "most likely extraterrestrial," eliciting the highest echelons of the USNA government to seek access to it. That, however, was on hold indefinitely, until all other avenues of cross-checking could rule out laboratory errors.

Valagua, on his own time, had analyzed the US government map and written a computer program that displayed a holographic representation of the topology of the Nepalese region. Consulting known records from the time, he was able to extrapolate the terrain of the former country during the mid-twentieth century with a margin of error of positive or negative one-three-thousandth of a percent. This holograph would also take into account the shifting sub-Indian continental plate, the changing course of mountain rivers, flooding and cumulative rainfall over the centuries, and the regular shifting of Earth's climate and magnetic field strength.

With these factors plotted, Valagua set to work discerning the angle of approach the extraterrestrial body responsible for the crash may have taken. In this way, he could perhaps correlate these data with past or future satellite observations to determine any additional crash sites, if they existed. Thanks to nearly two hundred years' worth of orbital astronomical observations, Valagua knew that often enough, if not always, more than one extraterrestrial object could be involved in any impact on Earth. Armed with all the Global Security Network data he could ask for and the knowledge of hundreds of government astronomers, Valagua set out to decipher the mystery.

Amid the scientific pursuits of de Lis' staff, Gilmour and Mason were treated to a DoD and State Department update on the ongoing St. Petersburg summit involving the President and the Premier of the Confederation. Lieutenant Colonel Dark Horse, practical as he was for a career Army officer, proved to be an easy man to hold dialogue with, even providing the agents insight on how to approach de Lis, whom he had known for the better part of a decade.

Professor Quintanilla, in contrast, was aloof, perhaps due to her years of dealing with foreign diplomats, and the games of chance government negotiators often played. She possessed a no-nonsense air about her, keeping to herself even when Dark Horse actively included her in his discussions on the summit proceedings.

The colonel had arranged a daily briefing for the agents to read, a summary similar to what Defense Secretary McKennitt would be given with his breakfast. Quintanilla would also make herself available to discuss current foreign affairs, by appointment, only, of course. In the agents' eyes, she was perhaps here strictly by order of de Lis, or the State Department itself.

Despite Quintanilla, the agents readily anticipated the reports. If nothing else, to do their duties more efficiently and keep the DoD off their backs, as well as Quintanilla.

After three days—two since the MPs had allowed the agents to travel from their quarters to the lab unaccompanied—the scientists were still fruitless in their various examinations of the jewels. They had been no more successful gleaning additional data from the remaining samples than at the mobile lab. Valagua, on the other hand, had succeeded in recreating the circumstances and geography of the former Nepal.

Honing the holographs in his office alone, often late into the evening, Valagua had meticulously generated the exact conditions for the date of the crash. The Allied armed forces kept remarkable records for that particular theater; the topographical map itself had several pen-ciled-in references to the day, as well as weather and other, shorthanded, communications reports. Employing these field notes, and coupling them with official records from the National Archives and the spectral dating taken from the crash strata by Waters, Valagua was able to calcu-late a rough date for the event, a reckoning of sixth October, AD 1940.

Valagua had duly warned de Lis that his research might drag on for several weeks, perhaps not even accomplishing all of his goals. But in his usually understated way, Valagua had somehow managed to outdo himself once again, not only squeezing every exabyte of data out of his computer, but substantially beating his own estimated timeline.

Now, with his holographic presentation ready to be unveiled, Valagua had downloaded the research for transport to the U5-6 gallery, where the three-dimensional work would best be viewed in its entirety, giving the assembled scientists a startling look at the day the world was changed.

# CHAPTER EIGHT

Gilmour and Mason dressed hastily in their response to the summons from Doctor de Lis to report directly to the U5-6 gallery. As if to reinforce the urgency of this briefing, an MP rapped on each quarters' door with the subtlety of a jackhammer until the two agents made prompt exits.

The MP led them to the theoretical studies laboratory, saying nothing while the two wondered privately what de Lis had up his sleeve. He had failed to give the agents details, only that the promised gallery visit was at hand.

Gilmour and Mason lined up behind several of the junior scientists at the gallery's entrance, their anticipation of visiting the mysterious mini-facility nearly overpowering their curiosity about the hasty briefing. Walking inside, an oval, two-meter-diameter monitor affixed to a large wall greeted them; this small area was the observation anteroom, where guests were allowed unparalleled access to the holographic chamber's many activities, as if one were indeed a participant in the gallery itself. A computer terminal below the monitor provided constant streams of data to observers in the event of a failure or error in the gallery's systems.

Moving past the monitor, a narrow door appeared to the right, bearing a tiny, obliquely inscribed word: GALLERY. With their heads craned upwards, then cranked around, they absorbed as much of the atmosphere as possible while filing through the threshold. Measuring at least thirty square meters, the facility was devoid of any and all equipment. Illumination was provided by a circle of lights directly above the assembled staff that cast a smattering of shadows across the walls, giving the gallery a rather spartan appearance belying its reputed price tag.

On the west wall was an affixed panel twenty centimeters in height, wafer-thin and smooth, which Gilmour realized was the control panel for the holographic simulation. Standing near it was de Lis, gesturing broadly with Roget, appearing to be having quite the animated discussion. The junior scientists stood with the senior staff, forming a semi-circle in the center. Checking faces, Gilmour accounted for everyone but Valagua.

The assembled staff had but a few moments to mingle before Valagua showed up, brandishing an equipment case slightly larger than a holobook. He parted the crowd and headed straight to the control panel on the wall. Presenting the MP with a pass key, the Marine ran it through a groove at the head of the panel, allowing Valagua's codes to activate the controls underneath. Valagua slid the security panel up, revealing a touchscreen. He attached his equipment case squarely onto the control panel's surface, which accessed the gallery's software.

As Valagua finished, de Lis cleared his throat, grabbing the crowd's attention. "Thank you all for coming at such short notice. As you are aware, Javier has been putting in some long nights here at the office. You're about to discover what his hard work has accomplished."

De Lis then backed away, letting Valagua have his presentation.

Valagua tapped an icon on the control panel, dimming the overhead lights. Only two beacons remained, permitting Valagua to see his panel. He followed with a series of buttons, each emitting a tiny chime during the machine's warm-up period.

After a moment, light barraged the group from all directions, like an interrogation. Once Gilmour and Mason had regained their wits, they saw that the blinding brilliance was the gallery's walls turning translucent, letting through a stream of photons from an array of pyramids sandwiched between the gallery's opaque exterior and now-revealed fullerene interior.

Photons spilled forth into the seven colors of the spectrum, flowing and pooling into a flat, amorphous holograph hovering a meter-and-a-half above the floor. The project scientists backed away from the image, watching it maneuver. A squared plane condensed from the amorphous photons, which was soon sculpted into a series of blue troughs and red peaks, with a smooth green sheet as a median of the two.

Valagua's simulation evolved further for several more minutes, rendering a virtual terrain, complete with snow caps, rivers, flora, and various soil strata. Even a scaled sun rose to the zenith and descended in the west, appropriately situated for his reckoning of the date. A final touch brought dusk and the appearance of the constellations above the heads of the scientists.

Valagua stepped to the edge of the image and began, "Allow me to present Nepal, sixth October, Nineteen hundred and forty. Our research indicates a small team of Allied reconnaissance officers were traveling along this route..." a single gesture from his index finger illuminated a blue beam, which traced a path over a low mountainside, "...and witnessed what I—and the senior staff—believe to be the crash of an extraterrestrial object."

Out of the simulated night sky an interloper crashed the length of the terrain at an angle. A red circle flashed where the earth was impacted, corresponding to the crater.

"This occurred midway in the evening...the soldiers present noted that a particular smudge was seen to advance against the constellation Cygnus. The crash you saw was an interpolation of the notes retrieved from the Allied topographical maps. A transcript I have created from the written report of the event notes two more related objects crashing somewhere beyond the horizon."

His blue beam continued on through the mountainside, descending slowly, while overhead, the stars drifted, edging closer to dawn.

"The officers traveled through the night, following the observed crash. The distance from the sighting and the crater was twenty-seven hundred meters."

The blue beam met the valley floor and snaked around a dry river bend before hitting the red circle of the crash site.

"Dawn," Valagua said, before the sun peaked over the eastern edge of the simulated terrain. "The officers arrive at the crash site, finding...?"

De Lis' form broke through the holograph. "That's what we're here to discover. We have all the right pieces, and Javier has provided us with a dramatic reconstruction of the crater's first hours. But we still have inaccessible avenues. The DoD is researching their military and civilian archives, attempting to dredge up any records of the officers involved in this reconnaissance. The Global Security Network is currently scanning the region for the two other supposed crashes. Javier will also continue to modify his simulation as new data arrive to supplement it."

De Lis glanced at Valagua, then back to the group. "Dismissed."

"Take a look at this," Waters said, plopping a clear rod into Roget's hands. "I scraped the carbonized material off this morning. The rest is metallic hydrogen."

Roget lowered his glasses before bringing the rod closer to his eyes. He brushed his fingers along the odd material, which felt—and looked—like normal glass. "Metallic hydrogen? This?"

Waters nodded. "Pure, one hundred percent, no bonding atoms at all. Tensile strength equal to thirteen times that of fullerene glass. It was locked inside that twisted debris we recovered."

"Beautiful." Roget tapped the rod with his index finger, sounding a tiny clink. "DoD received a sample?"

Waters scrolled down her holobook. "Dropshipped at noon. Lionel...I think we should...keep this one for ourselves and Richard. Perhaps even the other samples."

He raised an eyebrow; Waters rarely considered confidentiality among the Ottawa group. He wondered why she bothered to now, after all of the trouble de Lis had gone in assembling the best and brightest Canada had to offer.

"Why?" Roget said, pacing in front of her desk. He carefully looked out the fullerene glass before continuing, checking for eavesdroppers. "There are no factions here. We don't keep our research privy to a specific department. This is—"

"I...I was wanting to keep our security in check. You know the rumors."

"Not the men and women here. No." Roget watched the working scientists, like ants in a nest. "I'm not keeping this all to myself. If we're to fulfill our respective assignments, we can't hide research."

Pursing her lips, she rose from her chair. "It'll be Richard's call."

As Waters passed him to open the door, he said, "You're making a mistake."

She ignored him as she left, leaving him alone in her office. How confidential was this? He could pour through her personal files, if he wished to.

Roget stole a peek at the holobook on her desktop, sighed, then followed her out.

De Lis rotated the holographic skull around 180 degrees. His index finger traced the virtual surface suspended before him, his eyes comparing the reconstruction to the genuine object he had first caught sight of several days ago, halfway round the globe.

Marlane typed a series of buttons on her keyboard, which then displayed a crude image of an anthropoid skeleton on her monitor. "Without a specimen from the rest of the body, I can't do much better than this."

His eyes shifted from the exquisite rendering of the complete skull to the highly speculative framework. "This is an approximate head/body proportion? The skull's rather large in comparison to the whole."

"I agree. Human children exhibit this, as well as those of other hominids, as you are aware, but not to this degree." Marlane glanced back to the reconstruction. "I'm convinced. What about you?"

De Lis nodded. His eyes roamed the holograph's cranial roof, noting the absence of unfused cranial plates. Human children are born with highly malleable bones, which knit themselves together, particularly in the cranium, as they mature. If this was indeed a hominid, it was not a child. Its size could potentially mislead a less educated person, but its unusual characteristics would not fool an anthropologist, or anyone with a basic understanding of human anatomy.

Despite this, the skull remained unknown. Although she had been encouraged to investigate its potential genus or species, Marlane hesitated to create a new label for the specimen, especially if it was extraterrestrial, which would have to be peer debated by all the world's primatologists before she'd even get a paper released. She had been witness to—and nearly part of—many groups that had employed a new find to try to gain prestige by creating exotic, but ultimately worthless, nomenclatures.

"Right now," she said, "we're performing cell analysis. Hopefully, we will also find some fossilized protein chains in the remnants of ligaments, or perhaps some other biomolecular systems, to do a full genome and proteome, or at least partial ones."

De Lis clapped her shoulder. "Good work, Carol. Take a break every so often, would you?" He smiled at her, hoping his conviviality would boost her confidence.

Marlane managed a grin, but it was all that her exhausted muscles could achieve. Her reputation was her stamina—which was nearly boundless—but this case was one of only a few that had brought her to her knees. The usual fuel of choice was coffee, but even that had failed her. For reasons unknown, it seemed like time itself was slowly sapping her strength.

Dark Horse coughed in his hand before releasing the latest reports to Gilmour and Mason. The two agents, who had days ago fully mastered the content and form of the less-than-smooth reading of the DoD's reports, eagerly digested the data while Colonel Dark Horse relayed updates from Washington.

Contrary to the media clips praising the St. Petersburg summit as a first step to a thawing of relations between East and West—the usual hyperbole—the DoD thought less highly of the President's trip. So less that half the North Pacific Fleet's submarine units had been dispatched to secure various positions in the Pacific Ocean in anticipation of renewed Confederation maneuvers, thanks to the confidence gained in part by their Premier's webcasted flag waving.

Dark Horse replayed the President delivering his rhetoric concerning arsenal downsizing, promises to deter future weapons development, pledges to the peoples of the Confederation of full North American support (whatever that meant, allowing any commentator to fill in the blanks), and North America's willingness to cooperate with the civilized Eastern nations in rebuilding the shattered global economy.

The lieutenant colonel was brutally honest: the President may as well have stayed home. Showing newly processed images obtained from the subterranean Sudbury Quantum Laboratory, Dark Horse ably demonstrated that the Russians had accelerated their neutronic particle production. A dozen green points on the holobook represented key sites across the Confederation frontier where neutronic particle decay had been emitted, leaving deadly fingerprints. Stockpiling enough particles to detonate a bomb would take only a matter of months.

The summit, at second glance, had dissolved down to nothing more than empty promises and breast beating. Unfortunately for de Lis' team, they were in the middle of this mess. Retrieving the specimens from Nepal had been highly dangerous, and had the Confederation known that the North American government had brokered a hush-hush deal with the CAC, war would become even more imminent. The freedom of the world seemed to be increasingly in their unsteady, and untested, palms.

# CHAPTER NINE

Week one at U5 was over. Gilmour and Mason rushed through the dark corridor, putting their jackets and ties on for the hastily adjourned briefing called by de Lis. The doctor had promised never to call on such short notice—only ten minutes—but he had insisted that this situation was of the utmost importance. So, the two agents scrambled from their quarters at oh-five-forty-five, their morning breakfast still an hour in the future.

Once let inside to the theoretical studies lab, Gilmour and Mason headed for the junior staff gathering at the closed door to de Lis' office. The senior staff were confering with de Lis inside, nodding their heads as he spoke.

Crossing over to his door, de Lis opened it and said, "Thank you all for coming swiftly. Colonel Dark Horse a major break to announce, a find that might shift the course of our investigation. Colonel."

Dark Horse stepped out from behind de Lis, holding a holobook. "NorthPacCom has informed the DoD of a significant find, discovered at oh-thirty-one hours this morning. According to the Global Security Network, two craters have been discovered in the Northern Hemisphere, each matching the characteristics of the crater discovered some eleven days ago in Nepal."

"Here we go again," Mason whispered into Gilmour's ear.

"After pinpointing the exact coordinates," Dark Horse continued, "NorthPacCom has verified the first crater to be lying off the coast of Russia, in the Okhotsk Sea." The lieutenant colonel scrolled down further. "The second crater, or third, total, if you will, is believed to be in Northeast Russia. Precise coordinates will be forthcoming."

Two more craters, Gilmour thought, each again buried deeply inside Russia's backyard. The recovery of similar specimens at the sites by the Russian government, if they did indeed harbor the same objects, would seal the world's fate. Armed with both the awesome power of the neutronic bomb, and the seemingly infinite possibilities of the bizarre jewels, the Russians could conceivably conquer the planet in a matter of months, or weeks.

Damn, wasn't this ever going to get easier?

De Lis spoke again, "As you can see, the developments today will force us to change our priorities. Agents Gilmour and Mason," he said, looking to the back of the crowd of scientists, "this is your area. I want your expertise in developing our strategy."

"I assume we're going to go after the craters, Doctor?" Gilmour asked.

"We have no choice. The Confederation's already beaten us just by virtue of having the craters in their neck of the woods."

"I thought we'd agree." He nodded, glancing at Mason before returning his eyes to those of the senior staff. "Let's get to work."

Gilmour and Mason seated themselves at the table of U5-29, armed with holobooks while de Lis, Valagua, Waters, Dark Horse, Marlane, Roget, and Quintanilla sat next to them. Finally in the environment of their training and vocation, Gilmour and Mason truly felt like members of the Ottawa team, and they intended to take full advantage of this unforeseen opportunity to pull off the mission their way.

"If we may, Doctor," Gilmour started, "Agent Mason and myself have various contacts throughout the IIA capable of dealing with covert missions such as this. Missions that are not...kosher, if you read me."

De Lis understood perfectly. "Get Colonel Dark Horse a list. He'll take care of the rest."

"All right. Colonel, I'm sure the DoD will be requesting a mission profile from me and Agent Mason. Give us an hour, and we can have one to you, also."

"Understood."

Mason scrolled through the data on his holobook. "The first objective will most likely be to attempt a retrieval of specimens from the Russian landfall sight. Of all the craters sites discovered so far, this one will be the most hazardous, if only because the Confederation can access it rather easily and give us all kinds of trouble. Doctor, Colonel, I recommend that this briefing be allocated the highest security clearance. This won't be legal by anyone's means."

De Lis glanced at Colonel Dark Horse. "The colonel has arranged for that. We can speak freely."

"Good." Mason leaned forward, clasping his hands together on the conference table. "This is where the fun part begins."

Mason scrolled up the page again, reading this paragraph for the third time in the last five minutes. Staying up to finish a DoD report was never as much fun as catching the cineweb, but business always took first prize for his attention.

He heard a commotion that reawakened his senses, driving him to the door of his quarters. Several stern voices echoed loudly in the corridor, each talking over the other. Unlocking his door, he spied a group of MPs racing past his quarters, sidearms drawn.

Mason threw a semi-appropriate button-down shirt over his head and ran into the corridor. Gilmour, who also appeared to have just been roused, met him in the hall outside of his quarters.

"What's happening?"

Mason started down the corridor. "Something big!"

The two agents could hear the MPs gathering at the entrance to U5-1, just around the turn of the corridor. Behind them, appearing less urgent, were Valagua, Marlane and Waters. Coming around, Gilmour and Mason saw that de Lis and Dark Horse had already beaten them to the main offices. A sergeant at the entrance quietly relayed information to the chief scientist and the DoD representative, while five Marine MPs swarmed inside.

On the other side of the corridor, Quintanilla and Roget were just now meeting up with de Lis. The two agents and the three senior scientists were halted with an outstretched palm by the lead MP.

Waters walked between Mason and Gilmour. "Richard, what's going on?"

De Lis shook his head. "Can't talk now."

"Richard!" Waters protested before the lead Marine cleared her out of the way.

All heads turned to the side to see five new MPs escorting a medevac team down the hall towards them. Marching in rhythm, the new wave of MPs had brought with them holo-imagers, presumably to catalog whatever had transpired inside the lab. The MPs entered the main offices in single file, summarily relieving the first squad. Without warning, these MPs cordoned off the entrance, forming a shield with their armor and weapons, which prevented the project scientists from even seeing their own workplace.

Upon finishing with the MPs, the Marine sergeant took hold of de Lis' arm and whispered into the doctor's ear, away from the inquisitive assemblage. The conversation was one-sided, and de Lis nodded several times, as if receiving instructions.

Before this incident, de Lis had appeared haggard to begin with; the agents wondered if he had caught any rest at all the last few weeks. Remarkably, though, he must have had an iron will. During their duty hours, de Lis was quite alert and spritely, always exuding his enthusiasm for the research. Hell, he nearly out-hiked them all in Nepal.

But this development couldn't be weighing easily on his soul. Tensions were already prevalent due to the political situation, and de Lis' department had been tearing apart in the wake of the recent troubles. Now, this had occurred, leaving the project in jeopardy if the DoD had decided the risk was too great to carry on in the traditional fashion.

A final nod from de Lis sent the lead MP on his way, allowing the doctor to rejoin his staff. The doctor eyed the scouring Marines inside the lab offices as he passed, and motioned for the scientists and agents to step a few paces out of earshot.

The group encircled their leader. De Lis glanced back to the MPs before saying, "There's been an incident in the lab...." he jerked his thumb back to the entrance, "All we can ascertain is that U5-5 has been left unsecured."

"The Lockbox?" Waters blurted, incredulously.

De Lis wiped his forehead before inhaling deeply. "Again, we don't know. Trust me, all I want to do is get in there and see what's been contained, but I'm not allowed access until the preliminary investigation has been completed."

"When will that be, Richard?" Roget asked.

"Whenever they decide. Until then, we should try to keep our nerves calmed."

De Lis' advice was met with a chorus of sighs and groans, most notably from Waters.

"Look, we're going to have to deal with this." De Lis' skin wore a dark pallor, much like a man held prisoner. "Everyone take a few hours of rest, and meet..." he paused to check his wristwatch, "in U5-29 at oh-eight-hundred. All right?"

Grumbles and the nearest approximations of acknowledgements came from the group as they split up, less than certain that the security of the world was anything they were capable of controlling.

Sleep will revive, food will save, Gilmour believed. The nonstop race towards deciphering the secrets of their finds had sapped his strength, and only a slight indulgence in his two passions could restore his soul. Despite the alarming incident during the early hours of the morning, Gilmour was refreshed and ready for de Lis' briefing in U5-29.

Everyone seated themselves in their customary chairs, all arriving with holobooks. The scientists looked clear-eyed, but Gilmour and Mason detected hints of dreariness in their spirits, save for Dark Horse, true to the military man he was. This lingering uncertainty in the mission projected itself strongly into the spirits of the Ottawa scientists; they all needed de Lis' encouragement and support to reinforce their confidence and pride.

De Lis stood at the head of the table, behind his usual seat. His normally reserve, calm manner was replaced by uneasiness, no doubt influenced by the gravity of his forthcoming report.

He rested his hands against the back of the chair. "Let's get this over with. I've just finished a long web conversation with Secretary McKennitt and Solicitor General Rauchambau. Suffice it to say, they're not pleased with this morning's incident."

The staff grumbled among themselves.

He raised his hands in defense. "I know—I know what you think. They're politicians. But they're also the ones who cut the checks, and without them, our research wouldn't be possible. They have called for tighter security measures, which I believe are necessary. I know we all agree on that issue."

The assembled group nodded and voiced their positive opinions.

De Lis sat down, finally relieving himself of his most pressing task. "Excellent. Now that we've covered that, the DoD has authorized us to inform you of the event this morning. Colonel, your report."

Dark Horse held up his holobook, manually scrolling down its screen. "This is the official report from the Department of Defense. Please refer to page one, paragraph seven."

Tapping a button on their respective holobooks, the group scrolled through the report and found the appropriate text.

"Preliminary scans of the laboratory sub-room U5-5 indicated that at approximately one hundred nineteen hours, tampering with the Secured Sample Lockbox resulted in the absence of specimen X-two-six-alpha-two-one-five-six-four. The person or persons involved does not preclude anyone in this room or complex."

"Oh, Christ," Waters muttered, before burying her face in her hands.

Other sighs of disbelief and panic trembled throughout the room as several of the scientists chose to console themselves instead of hearing any more of the devastating news.

Mason flashed a look to Gilmour; one of the jewels was missing. How the hell could this have happened? After all the hard work, and all the precautions....

"Now wait a minute!" Marlane said, her holobook clattering to the table top. "Colonel, what motive would any of us here have for theft?"

"I am not suggesting any motive, Doctor Marlane," Dark Horse answered. "I am reporting simply what the DoD has said. Tests will be administered to clear everyone in this complex of any wrongdoing. Allow me to reiterate," Dark Horse continued, shifting into damage control mode, "no one here is above suspicion, including myself. My superiors have questioned me thoroughly, and will continue to do so as required by military law."

"Military law," Marlane spat. "Colonel, I should hope that the military is interested in enforcing their own Civilian Employee Protection Act. Or will we be subjected to the same level of questioning as you?"

"I assure you all," de Lis answered for him, "the government is interested in protecting the rights of all of its employees here. Please, let's not reach premature conclusions."

Roget looked to Marlane. "The military have their reasons, whether you believe them to be legitimate or not, Carol."

"Than what are they, Doctor?" Marlane's hands flew wildly about as she looked to her dejected colleagues. "The Lockbox has been broken into! Nothing here is safe! Any of us could be blamed for this! It will be impossible to carry out the—"

*Enough.* He had heard the concerns, and despite his status as a foreigner here in this enclave, Gilmour knew his piece must be voiced. "Doctor Marlane, if I may." The IIA agent pointedly eyed each scientist, making sure he was understood. "The lieutenant colonel has made us all aware of this breach, which cannot be undone, no matter the amount of soul-searching by anybody at this table. It is important that we not lose our resolve, that we maintain our commitment to this project, and our duty. Despite the tragedy this morning, we must move on, and redouble our efforts to determine the nature of the finds from the field."

Were they listening? He double-checked their eyes, their mouths. Not one of the eminent doctors here, despite the probable and deserved attitude towards this decided non-scientist, looked askance. Gilmour had their ears, and most importantly, their attention.

Pointing to the corridor outside, Gilmour finished, "As an agent of the IIA, my duty is to go out into the field and face danger everyday.

Because our hand has most likely been tipped to the Confederation now, we have new dangers, new challenges to face. Does this mean we fold? Hell no. Complete this mission, finish what Doctor de Lis and Colonel Dark Horse have tasked us. I'm not a scientist, but I'll do my duty to the utmost. It's the least we can do."

De Lis found his seat, stunned by the man's fluent and earthy appeal. He felt envious in a certain way; Gilmour had communicated better to de Lis' own staff than he sometimes could. Nonetheless, he was pleased; Gilmour had earned their full respect.

"Thank you, Agent Gilmour...I think...that sums up everything." De Lis turned to Dark Horse. "Colonel, I think that's good enough for now. Thank you."

Dark Horse parted his lips, but thinking better, closed them; his years of experience with the military allowed him to understand the doctor's need to rally his staff. The lieutenant colonel silently offered his best wishes for the difficult task ahead.

"I trust my staff can return to the lab?" de Lis said to Dark Horse.

"Yes...yes. Our investigation will be concluded off-site."

"When will we be questioned, Colonel?" Valagua asked, moving the subject on.

"The timetable is confidential. Doctor de Lis and I will call each and every one of you when in turn." He looked to the staff, eliciting their acknowledgement.

"Sounds fair," Waters said. She had been with the theoretical studies laboratory for the shortest time of all those gathered here, save for the two IIA agents, but possessed a sense of how the military operated during her formal education with DARPA; Marlane, conversely, was actually one of the few scientists recruited straight from the civilian fields. And, despite Marlane's vocal protestation, Waters could understand her concerns. All too often in North American history, the military had suspended the rights of the lesser informed and the ignorant in times of crisis, destroying careers and ruining lives in the operation of that juggernaut.

"If there are no more questions..." de Lis paused, and hearing nothing further, continued, "dismissed."

U5-29 emptied out quicker than usual. Marlane and Waters exited the room together, followed by Valagua, Roget and de Lis. Only Quintanilla remained, and she paired off with the lieutenant colonel away from the other scientists. Gilmour and Mason rose from their seats and approached Dark Horse, holobooks in hand.

The lieutenant colonel paused his conversation with Quintanilla.

"Agents...."

Gilmour handed his holobook to the lieutenant colonel. "Colonel Dark Horse, my list of candidates."

Mason watched the curiously calm Quintanilla exit the conference room without so much as a word spoken, nor a look back to the three.

"Oh yes." The lieutenant colonel scrolled through the text, inspecting the government bioinfomatics, his head bobbing almost imperceptibly. He tucked the holobook under his arm. "Interesting. I'll examine them further as soon as possible."

Gilmour allowed his mouth a simper. "Just don't lose my holobook, sir. It's my favorite."

"Ah, yes. I understand." He patted the device's exposed top with his right hand, as if it were a pet, then exited the conference room, making sure not to lose Quintanilla's trail.

Gilmour raised an eyebrow. "What do you make of Quintanilla?"

"She's cool under all this boiling tension, that's for sure." Mason shook his head. "I don't know. She's secretive, even more so than when we met her."

"Is that good or bad in this group?"

"Nothing is at it seems here, James."

"We're one short on specimens, Richard," Waters said, spinning in her seat to face de Lis, who stood at the threshold to her office. "I can't afford to misstep and risk destroying the remaining artifacts."

"I realize that. Time is of the essence, though. If our worst fears are reality, we may not be able to afford to be careful. We need to be ruthless in our examinations."

She sighed, hating having her hands tied. "Do you really think there are more jewels to be gathered at these new sites?"

De Lis stepped over to Waters, his arms crossed. "There's a good probability. Dark Horse is busy preparing a retrieval mission to Russia."

Her eyes were tired and unfocused; objects in her office blended, melding together as she contemplated this most dangerous of circumstances. God, if the Confederation discovered us.... "I should go, Richard. I'll be needed."

He shook his head. "No, Stacia, I need you here. If Gilmour and Mason don't re—" he caught himself, "aren't successful, we'll be lost without our research here. There's no more to it than that."

Waters' eyes met de Lis'. "Are you going?"

He doctor remained mute for a moment, finally saying, "I haven't discussed this matter with Dark Horse in any depth. As it stands, I'm still here to carry on this research."

"As am I." Waters stood and walked out from her desk. "Which means I need to get back to the lab."

De Lis remained in her office as Waters headed back to U5-1. He removed his glasses to wipe his eyes clear, the memory of his last web correspondence ripping his mind apart. De Lis had been kind when describing the conversation, hoping to ease the tensions already present in his staff. McKennitt and Rauchambau had not only been displeased, they had given him a royal reaming.

He breathed deeply. If results were not immediately produced, it was let known by the two offices that he would be swiftly retired from active duty in Ottawa. If that did indeed occur, he'd never be able to live with the knowledge that he had let his staff down. They had to succeed. Not for his own sake, but for theirs, and the world's.

A succinct round of knocks outside Gilmour's quarters startled him. He set down an auxiliary holobook and scrambled to the door. Once open, his favorite holobook met his stomach with a thump before Dark Horse made himself welcome.

Gilmour inspected the device for scratches, but finding none, greeted the officer.

Dark Horse clasped his hands behind his back and walked a few healthy paces into the abode. "You have good contacts, Agent Gilmour. I'm pleased with their credentials."

Smiling to himself, Gilmour knew his candidates had been quickly secured and shanghaied to Ottawa. "When are they due to arrive?"

"Within the hour." Dark Horse swiveled on his heels. "That speech you gave this morning at the debriefing...I've been waiting for that leadership of yours to exert itself."

Gilmour picked up a mug and filled it with his own blend of coffee from a thermal container. "I thought it prudent. Doctor de Lis didn't seem to be breaking through to the staff. The whole matter with the Lockbox isn't good for morale, especially these days."

Dark Horse eyed the coffee container like a predator; Gilmour figured the man had been going for nearly thirty-six hours.

"May I?" the colonel asked.

"Certainly, sir."

"Morale," he said, before pouring and sipping his own share of the beverage. "We need that from you and Mason, Agent Gilmour. Now more than ever. Times are not good for us. This mission to Russia...the

Secretary is not certain it will succeed."

"I believe otherwise. Agent Mason and I have penetrated most of the deadliest principalities the globe has to offer. With adequate training and reconnaissance, we'll be able to do whatever is required of us."

Dark Horse pursed his lips, the first time Gilmour had ever seen a military man do so. Deep down, the agent sensed Dark Horse was truly troubled. "There will be no training, nor reconnaissance, besides what sensor data the Global Security Network can provide us. We have no time to do this the way Uncle Sam taught us."

"Improvise." Gilmour took a swig. "If that's what's needed. For our own sake, my men will be capable...more than so, if you ask me."

"That's what I wanted to hear." Dark Horse set his mug back to the table, having only sipped it once. "Thank you."

Gilmour furrowed his brow. "Something wrong? Too much roast?"

"No," he said, walking to the door. "It's damn good."

# CHAPTER TEN

"Here they come now, sir," the Marine Flight Control Officer reported, breaking her attention away from the monitor to peek out the vestibule's open-air window.

Gilmour and Mason stepped away from the security checkpoint, pausing five meters from the subterranean entrance of Hangar Building B, a stiff backwash roaring through their hair and clothes. Four grounds crew scurried over to the approaching jumpjet once it had cleared the threshold, waiting with instruments to scan the craft's hull. The jumpjet landed on the yellow neon tarmac markers and exhausted its thruster gasses, briefly fogging up the hangar.

A moment later, the starboard hatch opened, admitting the grounds crew with their bulky equipment. Exiting after them were three well-dressed gentlemen—Special Agents William Constantine and Neil McKean, along with Chief Grant Louris—each hoisting rucksacks of their own.

"William! Neil! Chief!" Mason shouted, running over to the hatch.

The newly arrived agents dropped their rucksacks and exchanged vigorous handshakes and warm smiles with Gilmour and Mason.

"I see you've all made it in one piece," Mason remarked.

Louris couldn't hold the smirk cracking over his face. "Those security goons you sent sure made us nice and cozy on the flight here."

"We've got our reasons, Chief." Gilmour gestured towards the security checkpoint. "I'm afraid that's as cozy as it'll get."

The five agents crossed the tarmac, signed in, then were expeditiously shown their way into the bowels of the U Complex.

"Normally, you'd receive the standard decontamination shower once you'd entered the complex," Gilmour said, glancing back to his colleagues, "but Doctor de Lis managed to have that protocol overridden in light of the circumstances."

"Tell him to reconsider next time, Gilmour," McKean said. "I wouldn't mind getting a good delousing from Washington."

Security in the U Complex tightened hour by hour as more Marines were rotated in to serve throughout the six levels. Before, MPs were only guarding various doors and acting as escorts; now, squads were paired off and actively patrolling the corridors. The new IIA agents were impressed by the show of force, perhaps more so by the open brandishing of M-119s.

Louris eyed the rifles a pair of MPs held as the five traversed the corridors of U5. He brought his head forward to Mason and whispered, "Nice accouterments. Had some trouble?"

"You noticed...we had a breach yesterday morning."

"Thought so. Quite a number of Marines to be pulled from outside, even for this facility."

"That's one of the reasons why you're all here on such a short schedule," Gilmour said. "The U Complex is under Threat Level Red-plus."

U5-29 loomed ahead, denoted by the twin MPs orbiting the door. Gilmour paused at the entrance, long enough for the lead MP to hand a secured holobook. The Marine then slid one of his pass keys through the panel, allowing the group of agents inside.

"Gilmour turned back to Louris, Constantine and McKean before entering. "All right, gentlemen, that was the easy part. What you'll hear inside is where the real shit begins." With that warning, he led them inside to de Lis' briefing, where the enormous responsibilities they would soon face slowly encompassed not only their minds and bodies, but their souls.

"Congratulations, gentlemen," Dark Horse announced some time later, "you passed."

Mason blew a breath from his lips, relieved. Gilmour's hands remained steepled; he had been stationary, awaiting their formal exoneration since he and Mason had been called into de Lis' office.

"Was there ever any doubt?" Gilmour finally asked.

"No, not in my mind. We have had rumors spreading throughout the U Complex of a mole in our midst. Rumors we haven't been able to corroborate."

Gilmour sat straight up...a mole? De Lis had said he was loath to discuss their reassignment to the theoretical studies laboratory; was he referring to HADRON? If HADRON was here, that would understandably make de Lis nervous about discussing the neutronic situation with Mason and him. Was that truly why de Lis had handpicked them? To root out HADRON?

"I'm glad to have that over with," Mason said, exchanging a knowing glance to Gilmour. "What are you to do now, colonel?"

"Doctor de Lis and I still have to administer questions to the other staff. I received permission from my superiors to clear you two first, so that we could proceed to the retrieval mission ASAP." Dark Horse stepped out from de Lis' desk and crossed over to the two agents. "There was a time, not too long ago, when I would have been commanding a mission similar to the one you two are embarking upon."

Dark Horse paused to stroke his fine, salt-and-pepper mustache. Did Gilmour detect a hint of contrition in the officer?

"Remember this time. This is when you are truly alive." A fire lit in his eyes, unleashing a flood of memories in his mind. "I've made mistakes in my career, many I have never told anyone about, not even my closest of family. But despite that, above everything else, just come home alive."

The pair listened, wondering what had happened to Benjamin Dark Horse; the lieutenant colonel was quiet, his eyes focused not on some distant object within the laboratory, but on another time, another place, so confidential that Gilmour and Mason would never have heard or seen of it.

He cleared his throat before turning back to the pair. "That will be all, gentlemen. At a thousand hours, your colleagues are to be awaiting you in Hangar Building B, complete with instructions and a holographic briefing from Doctor de Lis and myself. The jumpjet has been fully stocked and equipped to meet all of your mission objectives."

Dark Horse's hand was outstretched to shake the agents' hands. "Good luck, Agent Gilmour."

"Thank you, sir."

"Good luck, Agent Mason."

"Thank you."

The agents exited, speaking no words between themselves. Somehow, it didn't seem right.

Gilmour's last shower for the foreseeable future was hot and neat, but much too fleeting. Running his hands through his damp hair after stepping out, he buttoned up his most practical field uniform—a layered, long shirt and coat coupled with black khaki trousers—plucked his rucksack and equipment case into his hands and dashed out his quarters' door, meeting the similarly well-disciplined Mason right behind him.

Heading into the down lift, one of a pair of MPs wished him good luck. The courtesy seemed so odd, if only that none of the MPs had ever spoken to the pair without first greeting them. Odd, indeed.

Moments later, the security checkpoint became a haven for frenzied activity; not just from the five waiting special agents, but also with the flight and ground crews bounding in and out of Hangar Building B, busily preparing the patient jumpjet for launch. The agents gained admittance from the Flight Control Officer and rounded the tarmac, weaving between the two crews.

Once on board, a co-pilot took the agents to their seats, which were located aft of the cockpit bulkhead. Politely informing the agents that they would be departing soon, the co-pilot produced a thick metal tube from his equipment case and unrolled it, revealing a square, ten-by-ten-centimeter plane with tiny, one-centimeter-tall pyramids featured on its top side. The co-pilot plugged the bottom end vertically into a matching ten-by-ten-centimeter socket in the bulkhead, then tapped an icon on a touchscreen above the socket. The device shimmered and hummed as the pyramids glowed brightly, emitting a shaft of light into the faces of the agents.

A photon field soon coalesced into a flat, two-dimensional, ten-centimeter-tall version of Doctor de Lis, eliciting the agents' laughter at the strange dwarfish figure. "Welcome, gentlemen," de Lis' simulacrum greeted them.

Constantine leaned over to Gilmour, giggling. "Is he going to sprout wings?"

"If you will please refer to your holobooks," the holograph prompted.

The five agents sorted through their rucksacks, and once in hand, booted the devices up while the holograph began its briefing.

"Your mission parameters provided by the Department of Defense have been downloaded to each of you for your instruction. Our objective is to penetrate the Sakha Republic, or as the Russians refer to it, Yakutia, a large province of the Russian Far East."

On the holobooks, a large red outline appeared on the respective cartographs of the Confederation of Independent States, centering on the particular area of Siberia where the Sakha Republic lay, a vaguely heart-shaped region bordering the Laptev and East Siberian Seas, south of the Novosiberskiy Islands. Pages of text materialized, providing facts and statistics about the republic. Scrolling through the text while de Lis narrated, they discovered that the crash site was particularly inhospitable, lying just within the Arctic Circle, and accessible by river only. Permafrost sealed the ground, adding nothing but hard labor to their mission.

"...In order to facilitate our guidelines," the holograph went on, "it will be necessary to burrow under the Confederation's lidar. To accomplish this, your jumpjet will take you as far as Ellesmere Island, where a waiting Icebreaker-class submarine will deliver you under the physical North Pole to the East Siberian Sea. The two-hundred-kilometer journey along the Indigirka River and its branch, the Kolymskaja, will take you approximately three weeks, camping under camouflage during the short day hours. You will then proceed across the Ulahan-Sis Mountains to reach the crater site, which is marked on your cartographs."

A red semicircle, located nowhere near any viable travel path, flashed deep within the over seven-hundred-meter tall Ulahan-Sis Mountains. The range was quite hostile, especially on foot, and infamous for its extreme temperatures, anywhere from forty degrees Celsius in the summers to minus fifty in the winters. They would not have the benefit of a jumpjet to fly them in, nor the guide of any natives to lead them to one of the remotest regions on Earth. Traveling to the crater site was technically feasible, given their training; if they could only survive the frozen river passage without being discovered by the Russians or the natives, or succumbing to the weather, then that was half the battle....

White blindness. The polar ice sheet—large as a continent—loomed under the approaching jumpjet, the arctic at its most welcoming. Ellesmere Island, a jutting landmass less than eight hundred kilometers from the roof of the world, rose from the wastes of this icy sea. Bucking to the force of the angry polar gales, the jumpjet descended from the space-scraping cirrus clouds towards the lands of northernmost Canada. They circled a remote coastal port at the tip of the island, gradually shedding their altitude and momentum. Fresh snow kicked up in the craft's wash, swirling around the cobbled concrete runway and creating new drifts half-a-meter high.

Once on the ground, the jumpjet was boarded by a USNA Navy chief petty officer, garbed in a heavy white parka. After a brief introduction, the five agents departed, braving the harsh polar desert. Behind them, a Navy crew unloaded and began to haul the IIA equipment and gear to the waiting submarine's stores, where the cargo would be held for the voyage to the Russian coast.

Under their boots, the powered snow cracked, echoing through-out the pristine wilderness. The wind howled in Gilmour's hood, inflict-ing its sad song into him. Nothing could have adequately introduced them to the frozen north more than the seizing, crushing cold.

In the distance, a slate blue conning tower peaked over the low snow bluffs, standing tall against a powdery wind. Five NCOs milled about the runway's small shelterhouse, smoking and conferring with the two jumpjet pilots. Paying no heed to his crewmates, the chief petty officer led the agents off the last vestiges of civilization and into the snowcapped trail beyond.

A temporary platform bridged the massive conning tower to Ellesmere's solid shelf. Meters below the narrow walkway a mighty gash had been ripped through the ice by the quadruple-hulled bullet curves of the Icebreaker-class submarine. Their boots clanging harshly as they walked along the graded walkway, each agent took the opportunity to glance down at the particles of snow careening into the deeply plowed shelf; soon they'd be descending into those same depths.

Two more officers—without parkas and visibly shivering—met the group at the open mouth of the submarine, all too ready to shut their mobile city's hatch. The agents were shuttled inside the mechanical behemoth and summarily sent down a vertical crawl space. A moment later they were in a narrow corridor, lined by horizontal metal pipes over the low ceiling. Stenciled on every conceivable piece of equipment in sight were yellow warnings, indicating either high pressure liquids or merely sensitive, for-eyes-only data. Suspended caution lights and dis-tant monitors provided the only illumination, casting a sickly pall to their faces.

Gilmour's ears were inundated by the whine of gears near and far, as well as the regular shouts of the crew down the low, tight corridors. Walking single file behind Louris throughout this dark artery, Gilmour was reminded of the U Complex and its dim illumination. Perhaps he could get used to this vessel; after all, it wasn't much different than what he had been quartered in for two weeks.

Louris looked at the ceiling, just centimeters over his scalp. "We're breaking through the ice. They're moving out."

"How do you know that?" Constantine asked. "I can't feel a thing."

Louris gave a cryptic grin. "Experience."

He said no more. It was widely rumored in IIA circles—but never discussed openly—that Louris had spent many years with the Agency in mysterious circumstances. This lead to many interesting, if not totally believable, theories about his prior career. It never paid to ask him directly; one rookie dared to prod him about it, and his reward was to be reassigned an entire week's worth of work from an experienced field agent. At least Mason had benefited from the overeager lad's mistake, managing to snag a few day's leave in the process.

They spent the next few minutes loosening their garb and rubbing life back into their extremities as they moved through the sub, which wasn't much warmer than outside, giving them plenty of incentive to keep the pace quick.

A man soon approached from the opposite direction, dressed in a starched white shirt, blue tie, slacks and epaulets. "Gentlemen, welcome aboard the *Hesperus*," he greeted, shaking each of their hands stiffly. "I'm Commander Roger C. D'Avid, at your service. If you'll follow me."

Commander D'Avid led them further into the subterranean corridors, passing various stations and monitors. Crewmember after crewmember courteously pushed through the cramped artery, like ants bent on a single purpose. Just another day on the *Hesperus*, Gilmour imagined.

Their escort finally brought them to a small wardroom, considerably smaller than U5-29 or the D.C. bureau conference room. Unlocking the cabin with a set of pass keys, D'Avid admitted the agents into the darkened room. "Watch your step," he warned.

The five looked down to clear their feet over the high bulkhead. Bypassing that obstacle, they walked into the relatively spacious room, stretching their arms and backs. D'Avid hit the lights, throwing low, but warm, illumination throughout the cabin. Five cots lay in a row on the floor, with folded, woolen blankets set upon each.

D'Avid locked the door behind them, securing the nearly illegal cargo and himself together. "This will be your home for the next week. Get used to it."

Gilmour glanced at both Mason and Louris; their executive officer was blunt.

"Their will be no fraternization with the crew," he continued, "nor will you discuss this mission outside of this cabin. The only two people who know the precise nature of this voyage are myself, and my commanding officer. Please report to the duty officer before lights out."

D'Avid looked to each man. "Any further questions?"

Silence from the agents answered him.

"Good. Dismissed."

Over the course of the next two days, Louris massaged out of the crew that the *Hesperus* was approximately one thousand kilometers from the East Siberian Sea, still a good day away. Twenty hours ago, they had diverted a kilometer to the south aft experiencing a close call from sinking ice sheets. And finally, intercepted communiques indicated that the majority of the Confederation Navy was in the North Atlantic and Mid-Pacific Oceans, partially allaying their fears of detection.

For now, the agents were reduced to preparing for their extended mission, memorizing geographical sites, brushing up on their Russian, writing contingency plans, and above all else, practicing severe climate survival training.

The USNA Navy wasn't any more accommodating than they legally had to be. Perhaps it was the secrecy of the mission that prevented them, or the orders from the captain, a man named Conway. Either way, the agents perceived a hands-off attitude from the senior officers. Once the IIA agents and their equipment had been off-loaded, the *Hesperus* would be efficiently, and conveniently, out of range. If the mission went to hell before reaching the first night's objective, then the agents were SOL.

Gilmour had to admit, despite the chilled atmosphere above and below decks, the ride so far had proved fairly smooth, in contrast to the angry flight the jumpjet had given the group. Small miracles, he thought. He then cautioned himself of the sores, aches and blisters he'd be lucky to have when the agents were hiking their way to the Sakha Republic. That is, if they weren't hunted down before then.

He quieted his anxious mind and focused on the objective ahead; no use dreading over possibilities. Anxiety would not keep him alive, nor would fear.

Just his abilities, his training, and a determination to save the future.

# CHAPTER ELEVEN

"You do realize we could lose another sample by pushing forward."

De Lis stroked his chin. "I've made my decision, Stacia. Is the Casimir ready?"

Waters peered through the fullerene glass to Roget's exam table. "Looks like Lionel is just about finished."

The pair left de Lis' office and headed over to the main examination table, where Roget and two junior scientists, Cory Crowe and Alik Ivan, were completing work on a larger, sturdier version of the Casimir device. The grey vacuum chamber was twice the size of the jumpjet's now defunct machine, and capable of supporting several samples. Crowe slipped a holo-cam snake into the device's open dropchute while Roget read off the final checklist for the modifications.

"Richard," Roget said, "we're nearly completed. Another moment or two, and the holo-cam will also be set to broadcast."

De Lis nodded, satisfied.

A circular bank of four monitors to the group's left sprouted from the center of the floor, administered by Ivan. He hurriedly connected various optical bundle wires into the rear of the holographic receptors, which then wound underneath the shelf to the Casimir device.

Marlane entered from another room carrying a heavy, reinforced equipment case in her hands. With a loud thump, she set the case down adjacent to the Casimir device. De Lis and Waters crossed over to the sturdy examination table.

"Thank you, Carol," de Lis said, his fingers keying in a code sequence on the lid of the case, which unlocked the mechanism. Inside were a dozen jewels laid bare on dark molded velvet, their iridescence refracting into the beguiled eyes of the assembled scientists.

De Lis slipped a pair of radiation gloves over his hands in case the objects were toxic. Gingerly lifting a single jewel from its hold, he cupped it in his hands like a sacred offering. He paused for a moment and held it at eye level, looking deeply into its dozens of facets, which held perhaps hundreds of secrets, all of them calling his name, coaxing his curiosity. Shaking his head, de Lis broke out of his reverie and placed the jewel on an adjacent glass plate while Roget, Crowe and Ivan finished the modifications on the Casimir.

A moment later, Crowe set a tool down, proclaiming, "Finished."

Roget nodded and for the last time, checked the restraints on the Casimir. He had personally welded it to the lab floor, hoping to prevent this more robust device from meeting the same fate as the last one. In the event of a catastrophe, however, not much could indeed be done to stop it from exploding and ruining their chances of ever penetrating the enigmatic jewels.

Roget rubbed his hands together after testing the vanadium-welded rods, then turned back to de Lis. "Ready?"

De Lis retrieved the extraterrestrial object from the glass plate, while Waters closed and sequestered the equipment case several meters away, just to be sure.

Ivan signaled to Roget that the monitor signals were good. Roget then activated the Casimir Symmetrical Virtual Particle Reaction Cavity, which oscillated on the exam table as the interior quantum battery began charging the device. A green diode on a side panel informed Roget that the Casimir was at full power and in optimal working condition.

Ivan unlatched the dropchute, permitting de Lis to place the jewel inside, then sealed it again. Roget punched the aspirator control button, evacuating the ambient atmosphere from the vacuum cavity before dropping the jewel into the metal Casimir plates at the chamber's heart.

Waters and Marlane monitored the laboratory's holobooks, using the devices to record the progress of the jewels as they were subjected to the virtual particle/antiparticle annihilation. Throughout the experiment, the pair would be scanning for a method to control the reaction, and perhaps utilize the nano-explosions to their own benefit, whatever those may be.

"Releasing dropchute," Roget announced, resting his hand on the holding switch. Flipping it, the jewel fell into the chamber, where the holo-cam glimpsed the fuzzy object pause between the Casimir plates.

The assembled group, many of whom had never witnessed such an event, scrunched shoulder to shoulder before the monitors, transfixed by the incoming telemetry. A holograph of the jewel suspended in the chamber appeared on the twin holobooks, coupled with a continually updated data stream. The eyes of Waters and Marlane never strayed from the miniature screens while the devices displayed the condition of the object in the Casimir.

White grains exploded onto the monitors, bringing cries of joy and wonder to the scientists. Deep at the center of the nano-explosions, a void took shape, shifting and twisting a non-descript black mass onto the screens of the curious group. Numerous fingers tapped the amorphous shape's image, anxiously tracing an outline while furious discussions began about the meaning and circumstances of this new discovery. "Chronometers at peak," Marlane said, checking the sequencing numerals on her holobook's holographic face, as well as the control face.

Inside the vacuum chamber, Roget's customized quantum timepiece measured the chronometric spin rate of protons, which were synchronized to run parallel with the control timepiece—Chronometer A— located in the laboratory. These were necessary to discern what effects the object would create upon the normal fabric of spacetime.

Waters' holobook recorded the relative strength of the vacuum chamber's zero point virtual particles, represented by repeatedly overlapping red and green spheres, a holographic interpretation of old-time field isobars. "Highest field strength at negative three millielectronvolts, lowest at negative one point nine millielectronvolts." She shook her head. "No change, Richard."

Roget toggled a dial on the chamber's exterior. "Decreasing plate distance by...nine micrometers." He looked back to her, ready for any sign, any flicker that they were making progress.

The holographic jewel held steady on Waters' holobook. "No change."

"Wait...." Marlane's eye double-checked the parallel timepieces. The control scrolled by at the perceptibly normal rate, but the customized chronometer's numerals slowed, and actually stopped. "Chronometer B...it's paused."

"Paused?" Roget stepped over to Marlane and glanced at her holobook. There, in bright green, the numerals to Chronometer B lay frozen at 09:49:31:09571.

"Stacia, the field strength," de Lis asked, almost giddily.

"Negative eight millielectronvolts, ninety-two percent uniform." Her holographic isobars ran smoothly together, save for the center of the field, which represented the small space between the Casimir plates.

"Doctors," Ivan yelled. Pointing a finger to the monitors, he brought attention to the larger void mass flowing out from the center of the screen, exterminating the nano-explosions all around.

From beside the gathered group, Waters consulted the incredulous data on her holobook. "Chronometer B...is going backwards. It's reversing! Field strength at negative eleven millielectronvolts...fifteen... nineteen!" The holographic jewel distorted horribly, as if her holobook's sensors could no longer register the object's presence. "Richard, we're losing the jewel."

"My god...look at it."

No eyes could break away from the jewel on the monitors. Despite the incessant static clouding the image, de Lis, Roget and the other staff watched the mass invade the entire vacuum chamber, obscuring even the twin plates.

"The plates, they're fading...what's going on in there?"

Waters and Marlane shook their heads; they had no better explanation.

De Lis peeked at Waters' data readings, to see if he could decipher the images they were all witnessing. "Spacetime curvature must be awesome in there...it's at negative thirty-two millielectronvolts and rising! Lionel, what topology can you—"

Roget lunged for the Casimir twin plates control dial. "Richard, it's going to destroy the vacuum chamber."

"Lionel...no, let it go, for just a little long—"

The two men fought for the dial, one hand grasping another like two schoolyard adversaries.

"Richard, we have to preserve the equipm—"

De Lis forced Roget's hand back and twisted it around, away from the Casimir device. "Stand down, Lionel. If we can just get a few more readings...."

"But the—" he protested, his eyes still burning with the image of the void mass' invasion of the vacuum chamber. All his hard work....

Waters ignored the internecine squabble before her, instead focusing on the rapidly depleting data at her eyes. Now, the jewel's holograph had disappeared completely from her holobook screen. "Richard, all sensor data have been cutoff! I'm receiving no telemetry."

"Nor am I," Marlane said. "Nothing but flatlines."

Static on the monitors drowned out any useful images from the holo-cam, but contrarily, the Casimir device still hummed, its own interior sensors declaring it at optimal power. Somewhere mysteriously between the two, rationality and logic had been distorted, twisting reality.

An inkling popped into de Lis' mind. Freeing Roget's hand, de Lis mulled over the conflicting reports for a moment. "Carol, status on Chronometer B."

Marlane glanced at her holobook. "Last contact was at reading eight-sixteen-fifty-seven point seven-four-three-six-two. Telemetry ceased at that point."

"It lost an hour and forty minutes." He lifted his spectacles to rub his eyes, then gazed at the reticent Casimir device. "You...what are you hiding?"

To de Lis' surprise, the instant after his question, the vacuum chamber's exterior diode went red, indicating a loss in power or operating efficiency. Roget stepped up to it, eyeing the Casimir for any indication or cause for the energy drop.

"I don't understand," Roget said, inspecting the power ports on the chamber's rear. "Everything's functioning normally, just how I designed."

De Lis steadied Roget's fidgety hands. "Lionel, it's not the device's set-up that's the cause. If I'm right, there's nothing inside for it to function."

Roget crinkled his face. "What?"

"Give me a hand."

Following de Lis' instructions, Ivan cut power to the device, while de Lis and Roget forced open the lid of the vacuum chamber, using a crowbar and hammer. The pair wrenched off the top, revealing the burnt shell of the Casimir's vacuum chamber. Roget's face registered his horror; where once there had been parallel metal plates, the mechanisms for them, various internal sensors and a holo-cam, there was merely a hollow chamber, devoid of circuitry and machinery.

Roget looked to de Lis, awestruck, then scraped the edge of the chamber's wall, removing flakes of ashen metal with his fingernail. "It did this? Incinerated it?"

"No, not incineration," de Lis explained. "What we saw in Nepal was different. The jewel...ripped open some type of spacetime vortex. I think this one did as well, taking some presents with it."

"Spacetime rips...vortices...the Casimir doesn't have the power to do that, Richard. If I could have created one, I would have done it with a Casimir years ago."

Waters smirked. "We all would have, Lionel."

Roget furrowed his brow, sublimating his irritation. "If this could be done, where would it all have gone?" He checked his wrist chronometer. "I don't see any difference in our local environment, no evidence of change. Surely it would have affected something."

"Perhaps. The jewel, and everything inside, broke with our present timeframe. They all went back to the past." De Lis grew somber, feeling rather foolish once more. "Spacetime was briefly fractured, and nature abhors a vacuum. Somehow, these extraterrestrial objects have the capability to do just that, apparently rather easily, with our current technological level. We've now sent two of these objects to the past, practically handing them over to anyone with the will and the means to employ them for whatever gains. Nobody in recorded history has ever been able to substantiate the manipulation of spacetime. Now, we can do it with ease. Too much ease."

He stepped away from the troublesome Casimir. "From here on out, now that we all have firsthand knowledge of what these jewels are capable of, we must prepare ourselves, in the event that someone from the past has acquired the objects we unwittingly sent to them. Let's just hope that our friends are successful in their mission. If not, we could all be in trouble."

# CHAPTER TWELVE

Strapping on their arctic camouflage, Louris, Gilmour, Mason, Constantine and McKean were led to the conning tower's docking tunnel, where the *Hesperus* personnel would shove off their gear to the pack ice above. The submarine had surfaced through the frozen shelf just moments prior, after an extended lidar survey of the East Siberian Sea, coupled with data from the Global Security Network, eliminated the chances of any potential witnesses.

Clambering up the stepladder after their gear had been unloaded, the five agents were wished a reserved farewell by Captain Conway. Once Constantine was grounded on the thick ice, the docking door was hastily shut, severing the agents' links to the world, leaving them to their own wits in the arctic twilight.

They wasted no time hoisting their gear onto their backs. With hand gestures to another, signaling their readiness, the five men began their trek inward, crossing the iced-over Indigirka River delta. The *Hesperus* had deposited them one-and-a-half kilometers from the Russian coast, but the vast sea ice had created its own LZ, visible to the horizon. Walking the distance of the delta would not prove too difficult for the agents; keeping their arctic gear—goggles, thermal gloves and face guards—secured to protect against frostbite would be the paramount concern.

Mason turned to see the conning tower disappear into the breeze-blown snow. Behind that white shield, nothing could be discerned, not even the stars from the evening sky. The sea ice creaked under their boots as they left tread impressions in the powder, which were promptly consumed by the breeze, erasing any note of their presence.

It really was a shame this was enemy territory, Gilmour thought. Beautiful in its own manner, the overcast sky gave the ice a sheen he could only imagine existed as a child. The Indigirka had a serene spirit, perhaps inherent in its remoteness from the rest of "civilization." Gilmour hoped that if time could heal old wounds, then he could return here some day, not as a soldier, but as a friend, with the blessing of the land, and its people.

Thirty-five minutes after disembarking, McKean pointed the way to the true coast, where lichen-rich rock protruded from the ice. All five joined hands to assist one another up the coastal land, surprisingly bare of snow. Today's fine powder had difficulty adhering to the taiga of the coast, all the better to help conceal their presence.

Now that landfall had been achieved, the group's first priority would be to scout along the river edge for a suitable encampment for the night. They all wore lowlight goggles, enhancing the ambient illumination without having to blatantly blast torchlight across the terrain and flag their wanderings to anyone who cared to look. Despite having at least five more hours' worth of walking time left, there was never a bad time to be on the watch for a good shelter, even if they had to retire earlier than necessary. In this climate, that made the difference between meeting your eventual goal, and dying the first night.

This far north, the river country was flat and night came early, giving the men little assistance in fostering shelter. They pressed forward, becoming increasingly aware of the limited time they had to set camp for the optimal rest required in this harsh land. Following the river south, by an hour's passing they had traversed nearly three kilometers, a good start, but only a skip compared to the nearly two hundred kilometers needed to reach the crater site.

Throughout their journey, McKean would be taking continuous lidar surveys of the country, in anticipation for their return, tentatively scheduled four weeks from now. Dark Horse had arranged for a Navy vessel to retrieve the five agents upon achieving their goal, or act on their distress signal after a mission abort. If the agents did abort, a prolonged stay would be most likely, so familiarity with the coastal taiga and its terrain would be a paramount concern. Louris and his men hoped it wouldn't come to that, but illegally entering foreign soil almost never went according to schedule.

Ninety minutes later, McKean detected a ravine that carved out a nice angle from the Indigirka, sloping at twenty-three degrees towards the frozen banks. Crossing the ground to the ravine, the agents broke out their hammers and constructed their tents, then placed thermal camouflage over the site to obscure their presence from eyes in the sky.

Commanded by Louris to get a good dose of rest, the agents settled in with their rifles as bedmates, content to know that this would probably be the most secure slumber they would have for their entire stay.

With each successive day, the sun lowered its grip on the arctic lands, bequeathing its domain minute by minute to the moon and stars until finally, the great burning sphere remained hidden, hibernating for the duration of winter. Darkness gave the agents more flexibility in their route, and the less daylight there was for any natives to be wandering the taiga, the better for the team to slip in, and then flee.

To Louris' discontent, most of their travel schedule the first night had been consumed by the *Hesperus'* and Global Security Network's sweep of the East Siberian Sea's coastline, necessitating a belated shove off, but not this night. Louris had rousted his agents just prior to dusk, allowing them time to prepare for the next leg. The day's MREs were consumed by all, and their waste was collected and recycled into emergency rations in the event of an extended mission. Despite having enough supplies for a month-and-a-half in the wilderness, experience had taught the agents that missions could go for much longer than planned, sometimes necessitating the consumption of "prior matter," or as Mason quipped, "shit on a stick."

Before exiting their sheltered ravine, Mason took readings from his meteorological lidar, indicating a cold front would be moving in over the region within the next few hours, bringing potentially severe winds and temperatures. The group tied a line between themselves, enacting a hazard precaution in the event the weather threatened to separate them. Setting off, the five hastily covered ten kilometers in the few hours prior to the inclement weather blowing in. Although this heightened leg would prove quite exhausting, it was worth the extra effort to traverse now, rather than double timing it during a snowstorm or minus fifty degree winds.

A howling gale soon roared above the river valley, slamming down upon the agents from the distant, dominating Cherskiy Mountains and, further southwest, weather twisting Verkhoyansk range. Shelter was constructed on the quiet side of a ravine, and the agents waited out the storm with a few hours of rest.

Journeying to the iced branch of the Indigirka, the Kolymskaja, proved monotonous, with only the occasional, curious fox or two to break the endless landscape of taiga. Now a full week into the mission, the agents were on the second, longer leg of the mission, about five days from penetrating the large land plate, Kondakovskaja Vozvysennost', forming the north end of the Ulahan-Sis.

Time had actually passed faster than anticipated, due to the exceedingly flat terrain of the Kolymskaja bed, allowing them to nearly double their usual hiking rate for the ninth and tenth days. Another branch of the Indigirka, the ascending Keremesit, revealed to the group the full breadth of the East Siberian Sea from behind them, and the opportunity to scout the upcoming terrain from a distance.

Climbing to the zenith of a hill, Gilmour utilized a forward tele-scoping eyepiece, capable of discerning landmarks tens of kilometers away in a two-centimeter-diameter focal lens from his goggles. Flashes of light to the west, along the artery of the Indigirka, revealed four tiny villages, flickering like fireflies in the turbulent mountain air, which the group doubtless would have met up had they continued along the river-bank. Despite the range of tools and modern technology the men had been outfitted with, Gilmour could've done for some alcohol to proffer the natives in exchange for some local hospitality. Perhaps another day, when he didn't have to surreptitiously travel the quiescent river bends to dig holes in the ground.

After they had concluded their surveys for the night, the agents retired to a copse of abundant spruce and birch trees, which provided a good shelter for their camp. That night, and for three successive, the agents received the most restive hours of sleep, despite the high eleva-tion lowering the temperature several degrees further.

Seven days since beginning the rise to the Kondakovskaja Vozvysennost', the agents soon glimpsed the the seven-hundred-meter-tall Ulahan-Sis Mountains—their final destination—lingering in the sky at twice their current elevation through a slash in the flank of the Keremesit valley.

Gathering themselves for the final push, the agents headed through the forested taiga, locking eyes on the mountain peaks that concealed secrets perhaps no man should possess, certainly not the Confederation and its *siloviki*. Survival now hinged on what the five would find; hopefully, an undisturbed range gathering snow like any other, silent for almost twenty decades.

The twenty-third morning seemed the longest of all, and a heavy air crawled over Gilmour's and Mason's skins, a feeling of relief, but anx-iousness. Constantine had mapped out a route to the coordinates de Lis and the DoD had furnished them, and all they had left to do was reach a basin carved into the northside spine of the range. Satellite analysis determined the crater basin spread over an area of roughly five square kilometers, a rather large region in which to achieve their stated mission goal of securing every object resembling the Nepal jewels.

They didn't hesitate, knowing the sooner they reconnoitered the area and determined what status it was in, the quicker they could retrieve any samples and head home. Louris had repeatedly drilled this into their heads, but only Gilmour and Mason truly understood how difficult this would be. Keeping this to themselves, they hustled through the thickly brushed route, calculating and recording every meter of the way. Gilmour's eyepiece found the foot of the basin, a depression seemingly kicked out of the face of a mountain. Plotting these datapoints into Constantine's holobook, the agents created a cartograph of the area to match up with the Global Security Network-based one.

Once inside the basin, the five men noted the way nature had reasserted itself after such a cataclysm; black spruces dominated the slopes, coupled with birch and willow trees, the higher ones curiously lying parallel to the ground, even up the side of mountains. Without foreknowledge of the crater, the agents would have had difficulty believing this basin had been created by a spectacular crash.

Unpacking their magnetic and gravimetric resonance detectors, the agents fanned out, allowing several meters between them. The devices fired electromagnetic pulses, enabling them to map the basin's subsurface for the extraterrestrial specimens they knew were here. The work was tedious, but perfect for five agents groomed to perform hours of long, fastidious labor. Years of underground missions proved to be ideal training for the patient men, who dutifully combed the virgin taiga ground, gradually encircling the perimeter of the basin.

Their schedule for the first day was to thoroughly scan the ground, disregarding any other scientific work. Most of that day shift had elapsed before each man had even completed their assigned segment of the basin. As night fell, the agents convened in the center of the crater, at Louris' predetermined quarters. Louris collated the respective data from each holobook into one large, multifaceted cartograph, following de Lis' instructions. Meanwhile, they sampled various floral and soil specimens to return to the Ottawa lab for contamination analysis. De Lis was adamant about this part, strictly emphasizing the importance these samples would have on their knowledge of the area, mostly the effects on the quantum structures of the samples by the jewels.

Louris ended the shift unceremoniously, ordering his agents to break out their equipment and prepare for rest. The next day would be the most strenuous of all, as the group would begin excavating the already promising site, scrabbling around like the moles de Lis had sent them out there to be.

The chiming alarm threw Gilmour's eyes wide; he rose from the taiga, weary and tender. In the area beside him, he could hear Constantine and Mason already moaning about the six hours of restlessness. Three weeks of roughing it had reduced them to bedsores, strained muscles and fruitless rest. Each man, save for Louris, of course, had mentioned the lack of worthwhile sleep, but all dutifully, but not so rightfully, dismissed it as contemporary laziness, brought about by the conveniences of modern life. Despite his allegiances to his agency, there were days Gilmour grew tired of quoting the Agency line for the sake of mission morale.

Presentable for work once more, Gilmour and the others stretched their muscles and yawned, ready to resume their duty shift. Louris retrieved their optically connected holobooks from his tent, updating himself on the status of the data collation.

"Congratulations, gentlemen, looks like we have a good relief cartograph here. Take a peek." Louris held out his holobook, which displayed an image of the basin's subsurface. Horizontal striations combined in the taiga strata with red, unnatural clumps to paint a picture of the unseen world beneath their feet.

Gilmour looked up from the holograph. "What's our first order of business?"

"Locating those red splotches. De Lis gave me a simulated image of the strata, with instructions on what to dig for first. According to him, the clumps are more of the metal specimens you and Mason encountered in Nepal."

"The ground is cluttered with them, Chief," Mason noted. "There's much more here than we ever found in Nepal. How are we going to transport them all back?"

"We're not. A few samples of the metal for good measure, but our prime mission is to find those jewel objects. The doctor believes by digging up the metal, it'll lead directly to them. That's why we're here. Any other questions?"

Silence provided his answer.

"All right then. Get out your pickaxes and shovels so we can go home."

Sectioning the basin off into quarters, the agents gridded the alpha segment and began the rigorous process of uprooting its first set of specimens, a target just meters away, under the rocky terrain. Because the cartograph was so precise, the agents ably predicted how far they needed to dig before striking the crater's riches.

Diamond-tipped industrial pickaxes broke open the taiga perma-frost, allowing their shovels to take the team to depths of one to three meters, more than enough to reach the metallic debris waiting patiently for them. In the event standard tools weren't hardy enough to crack the earth, Louris had packed a rather heavy instrument they referred to as "The Liquidator," but more prosaically called the Solidified Strata Fluidation Device, capable of temporarily liquefying soil by sound waves in order to more easily dig for specimens. Its use was limited, but could come in handy in the event the taiga below ground was rock solid.

Gilmour and Mason positively identified the first specimen as belonging to the extraterrestrial debris. The five men then released the twisted metal from its encapsulated home and hauled it out for the first round of spectral analysis. The mass was about twenty kilograms—remarkable for its dimensions—but this fact had allowed it to be easily buried quickly after its plunge to Earth. Gilmour's holobook scanned the interior of the debris, piercing the entire mass except for a scattered group of small, unidentifiable materials suspended inside.

He glanced at Louris. "Chief, we've got some. Let's open her up."

The five agents, armed with a variety of cutting and grasping tools, invaded the tangled scraps of metal. Working feverishly, they revealed the pitted remains of the mass, guided along by continual scans of its interior by their holobooks. After an hour of peeling away the lay-ered debris, Louris shuddered to think how long it would have taken the agents to search for the jewel objects had they not had the advantage of spectral analysis available to them.

With a gentle unwrapping of the thin metal, Mason revealed a deposit of two jewels, which Constantine, wearing radiation gloves, removed. The group marveled at the quivering objects now in their possession, taking the time to appreciate their quarry before sequester-ing the twin jewels into a portable lockbox. Pursuant to de Lis' orders, the agents lifted the emptied metallic debris and placed it back into the earthen tomb, careful to snip off a small specimen before reburying it.

The group headed for the next target, sixteen meters up the side of a collapsed mountainside, where debris was embedded inside an ava-lanche of rock and earth once comprising a near-plateau thirty meters or more tall. After defining the exact coordinates of the site, they removed their hiking gear, putting on the appropriate climbing footwear and gloves. Once pitons had been hammered into the rock-studded earth at the foot, they ran a reinforced cord through to begin the ascent. Louris took the lead, gingerly sliding his feet into the best available slits in the rock slab. Mason, McKean and Constantine scurried up the rock behind him, leaving Gilmour to stand watch on the ground, a sentry over the newly acquired specimens.

Climbing the fifty-degree slope took no more than forty minutes; the four agents moved at such a clip, Louris privately predicted they'd be on the floor again in just under two hours. He scanned the face with his holobook, and upon reaching the correct height, secured the cord inside the final piton. Louris then lightly hammered out two lateral bootsteps to allow himself room as Mason ascended. Mason caught up next, using his gloved hands to clear out the sparse flora that wound up the side of the slope, making their retrieval and analysis of the remains much simpler. McKean and Constantine remained a few steps below to facilitate the quick removal of material from the site.

Pickaxes in hand, Louris and Mason lightly tapped into the slab, careful not to disturb too much of the surrounding rock, or damage the important material just centimeters under the surface. Piece by piece, the subsurface was exposed, revealing rock not seen by the elements in two hundred years.

Mason scraped away orange and yellow lichen from his side, evidence that at one time this rock had been exposed to the elements. So far, so good. Their scans of the area, while nearly guaranteed, were only as good as the programmers and users, so it was a relief to know that the team was doing something correctly.

Louris' gloved hand uncovered a deep sublayer of rock, a piece large enough to rest in his open palm. Beneath it, a glint caught the ambient light of the atmosphere. Consulting his holobook, he tapped out a larger piece of rock, soon revealing a shiny vein that appeared to run nearly horizontally. Using his fingers, he tugged at the vein, which stubbornly clung to the rocky sublayer. Deciding to dispense with gentleness, Louris wedged the tip of his pickaxe just under the vein, and applying elbow grease, pushed down on the axe's handle, coaxing the material from the rock. To his vast surprise, the horizontal material readily separated, cracking the rock around it. He continued to wedge his pickaxe at intervals along the vein, diligently removing the eight-centimeter-wide metal.

Meanwhile, Mason had caught on and worked his way to Louris, the two meeting at some point in the middle. Determining that the vein's breadth was for the most part exposed, the pair produced their industrial pliers and began wrenching the vein away from its rock cage. As they did so, the rock slab directly underneath the vein—but many centimeters thicker—cracked under the stress of the pair's tugging. A terrible creak paused them both in mid-pull.

Louris inspected the fissure he had created. "Mason, you too?"

"Yeah. I've got a crack about the size of my leg running under my initial separation point. Looks like its going for my footholes."

Louris nodded. The footholes the pair had tapped out were weakening the slab, which now threatened to crash to the ground in pieces, with them in tow. Unfortunately, the holograph of the mountainside showed that this site's two red splotches were approximately eleven centimeters inside the metallic debris; the first, just straight ahead of Louris, and the second, about one meter below Mason's position. They might be able to pry out the first object, but with the stress they created excavating it, the second jewel would be next to impossible to reach.

Louris frowned. "Mason, abandon your target. We're going to devote as much manpower as possible to get this one," he pointed at the rock in front of him, "out of here."

Mason needn't say anything. Yes, their primary concern was to excavate any and all possible jewels, but they were also burdened with the caveat of concealing their activities at all times. Louris could probably use The Liquidator on the rock slab to get to the concealed jewel, but they ran the risk of showing up on a seismograph. Clearly, tiptoeing around while performing industrial excavation were almost beyond possibility. Mason had no doubts that this was indeed a government operation.

Mason vacated his target and moved back to the dangling cord, where he and Louris would then employ their collective power to wrest the debris from its two-hundred-year-old tomb. Anxiously watched from below by McKean, Constantine and Gilmour, the pair gradually pulled the debris out a piece at a time, not fighting to keep it wholly together, if only because they would be hanging from the rock for the next few weeks. Ever so smoothly the flattened metal was released from the slab, creating only minor cracks in the mountainside throughout the delicate surgery. Using his holobook as a guide, Louris secured the largest chunk of the debris, the section that happened to house the jewel, and handed it to Mason. The section wasn't particularly heavy, but cumbersome, measuring by Mason's standards a good seventy-five centimeters. Descending three leg-lengths, Mason entrusted the specimen to Constantine and McKean, who then delegated it to the waiting Gilmour. Mason quickly returned to Louris, who had already prepped the slab to be restored to its pre-excavation condition. Despite their efforts to the contrary, the mountainface would bear the scars of their climb for decades to come, until flora re-grew and erosion wiped away the traces of the dig. Louris descended soon after Mason, his final efforts being the removal of the pitons and—to the best of his ability—covering their footholes.

Once that had been accomplished, Louris met up with his agents, and all then changed out of their climbing gear and into their arctic garb. A bitter chill was blowing into the mountains, and the men were more than willing to bundle up to face the oncoming front.

"Number three secured," Gilmour announced, placing the newest jewel into the lockbox, next to the other two.

"How bad does that front look, Mason?" Louris asked while buttoning up his overcoat. The air temperature had dropped by several degrees, and the chill was palpable, despite the perspiration from the heat of the climb.

Mason oriented his holobook towards the sky, discerning the air mass' exact size and coordinates. "Doesn't appear to be cause for much concern. Temperatures will be ten below zero, but shouldn't be any precipitation."

"All right, the third site we should be able to excavate before nightfall," Louris said, referring to his holobook, which displayed the third site. Thankfully, he thought, it was another ground dig.

The five stowed their climbing gear back at the camp before heading out. Above them, the feeble sun began numbering the minutes of light on its return to the horizon, propelling the group to make use of the quality time remaining. The day would finish soon, rewarding them well. When the stars would twinkle again, the agents could take comfort in the fact that their mission had proceeded nearly to schedule, and they could only hope the accomplishment of their goal went as well.

# CHAPTER THIRTEEN

Gilmour scrubbed his face, removing the last pebbles and particles of earth from his burgeoning beard. Stroking his wooly countenance, he forgot how many days the team amassed in the basin. Guessing by his beard's length, he double-checked the mental count on his wrist chrono. The tiny device reported today as 18.10. Forty-one days! Gilmour moaned...somehow his memory erased a good week. Thinking back, he could recall why; the team had methodically surveyed ninety-four percent of the entire basin, bringing them to this morning, Louris' projected final day. The exhausted agents were hours away from packing up for good, and they couldn't have been more ready, judging by the bruises, scrapes and tendinitis each of them attained.

Over the weeks of the dig, the team accumulated enough samples to necessitate storing portions inside each agent's tent. The situation was cramped enough with the marginal elbow room they were initially provided, but adding the spoils of their better-than-expected success only hastened their irritability and eagerness to finish the job on schedule or before. To its credit, the weather was playing a critical part in the team's ability to secure nearly every jewel they set out to find. Mason forecasted one more good day of average autumn temperatures to accommodate the group's efforts, and Gilmour made a pact with himself to do all that was humanly possible to ensure this day was the last.

Pulling his triple-layered parka over his head, Gilmour finished his morning routine. It was time to go home.

Louris and the four agents traipsed through the steep brushland of the Ulahan-Sis basin before reaching the delta quarter, the final section of ground excavated by the men. Five previous targets had already been extracted from this quarter, leaving the sixth, and most delicate, for today's ultimate dig.

Arriving at the target—which Constantine had previously scanned and mapped—the agents produced their pickaxes and shovels. Louris saved this target for last, as it was buried two to three meters under the basin soil, requiring the efforts of all five men over the course of the day to reveal. All previous excavations required only a few hours at the most; this one, a full man's height in depth, would be the most arduous. There was the temptation to use The Liquidator to disturb the earth, thanks to their crying muscles and bones, but de Lis' explicit instructions to remain as inconspicuous as possible overruled that, if only slightly.

Mason swung his pickaxe first, cracking open the frozen topsoil. Successive efforts loosened and created a half-meter crater; McKean and Gilmour shoveled out the spoil, while the others chipped open the adjacent soil. Their survey of the basin eighteen days ago had revealed this target's treasures lay scattered through the various strata, rather than heaped together. The first scraps of debris couldn't be too deep, as successive rainfall and tectonic activity over the centuries had migrated the particulates of earth and shards of metal upwards from the original blast location.

Pausing his work, Louris set his pickaxe down and consulted his holobook. Two hours had gone by and there was still no sign of the debris. Looking at the holograph, the team should be just centimeters from the metal clumps.

"Chief."

Louris' eyes left the device and met Constantine, who pointed out a spectral glint in the black soil. Taking radiation gloves out of his pockets, Louris slipped them on and scooped the shard from the permafrost. The metal-encrusted jewel soon made its way from Louris to the portable lockbox, which Mason had strapped around his waist for the duration of the dig. Behind his partner, Gilmour sampled the surrounding soil, placing the humus into small bags for later analysis.

More perspiration yielded another metal shard, larger this time, from the permafrost. Deeper down, the rock-saturated soil proved quite immune to pickaxes, so Constantine jumped into the meter-deep hole with shovel in hand, ramming the floor like a posthole digger. Despite his renewed vigor, Constantine managed to dig no better than the men had before.

He sighed, then glanced up to Louris. "Damn if this permafrost ain't moving. Anybody else?"

Louris frowned. He alone had decided to leave this target, one of the few sites almost never to see the weakened sun, until the very end. Here they stood, exhausted to the breaking point, sweating while throwing their backs out to retrieve the final half-dozen or so objects from this damned basin, and the ground rejected each try past one meter. Louris signaled for Constantine to come out of the hole.

"Is it time?" Constantine asked, soothing his left tricep.

Louris nodded. He stepped away from the group, towards his backpack. Opening it, his hand sifted through various unseen objects before pulling out a dull grey tube, complete with hinged handlebars at the top and a bulky, cone-shaped device at its bottom.

He carried The Liquidator back to the site, cradling it over his forearms like a cumbersome bouquet. Louris paused at the hole's edge, eyed the floor, then proceeded to the bottom. With Louris unfolding the tube's appendages, the device blossomed to its full width of twenty centimeters, handlebars and a pair of stabilizing legs at the end included.

Louris first placed his goggles on, then rested The Liquidator's cone flat against the stubborn permafrost, aligning the device like a fulcrum into the soil to achieve the optimal angle. Tweaking a series of switches along the tube's top collar, he charged the quantum battery. After determining he had properly prepared and attuned The Liquidator, Louris said, "Gilmour, you've got monitoring duties."

Gilmour routed his holobook to scan The Liquidator's progress and vital statistics, making absolutely certain Louris didn't overdo the sonic assault on the permafrost and running the possibility of attracting Confederation seismological surveys.

A green light between the handlebars flashed on The Liquidator's top collar; the device was synchronized to go. Louris flexed his right hand on the handle's palm trigger, activating the first pulse. A muffled thump sounded in the permafrost, reverberating throughout the ground, even under the feet of the four agents. Another thump, and two more followed, before Gilmour signaled with an upright thumb that all was functioning below threshold.

On Gilmour's display, a holograph of the permafrost layers, overlayed by the agents' scans of metallic debris, showed blue isobars spacing out in sequential waves. Beside that graphic was a tally of the site's sonic threshold, which peaked every few seconds as another blue isobar appeared.

Gilmour scrolled down on the holobook, revealing a second holograph, this time of the soil's density. Each isobar increased the distance between the earthen particulates, slowly transforming the ground from nigh steel to manageable topsoil consistency.

One by one, the metallic debris sifted out of the earthen cocoon, rising to the floor of the hole. After Gilmour's signal, Louris deactivated the device and hoisted it up to McKean, who returned it to Louris' baggage. Constantine joined him below, and the two shoveled the loose soil, taking only minutes to retrieve the first few objects.

Mason's portable lockbox now brimmed with additional extraterrestrial samples, more than enough to justify the expense of The Liquidator on this last target. Holobook in hand, Gilmour confirmed the exhaustion of material at two-point-eight meters, at which his fellow agents exhaled thankfully.

Their cleanup of the final site took an hour, in which time the five men had redeposited the spoil back into the hole, and for good measure, topped with small boulders found nearby to help conceal their activities for a long, long while.

With camp broken, the agents scurried to collect their gear and ration out the specimens piecemeal; each man would carry a share of the load, in the event one or two became lost, or victims of a greater catastrophe. Final thermal garb was slipped on and food rations ingested as the sun drew close to the horizon, throwing a curtain on the sky. Once again, the group would be traveling at night, as they had done entering the country. Fully loaded, the men descended the Ulahan-Sis, reaching a lower altitude and a blanket of warmer air, although at night temperature was all relative. The land of forested spruce and willow would soon give way to distant peaks, leaving them in open country until they could reenter the core of the Keremesit valley, the southern end of the Kondakovskaja Vozvysennost', about three nights hence. There, the naturally mountainous terrain, while not as looming as the Ulahan-Sis, would conceal their exit route from any powerful surveillance in the Indigirka River villages. Eight days into the return journey, the five men set foot on the frozen Keremesit's final curve around the northeastern quarter of the Kondakovskaja Vozvysennost', a shallow cradle of hills allowing excellent viewing of three out of four of the largest Indigirka villages. Gilmour's steady capturing of the activities from the forty- to eighty-kilometer-distant hamlets prepared the agents for any municipal surprises, such as mass fishing expeditions or clandestine mining of the diamond hills. So far, no reason for deviating from the planned leg to the coast had been warranted.

Gilmour, aching step by step, returned from the hill summit. "Negative," he whispered to the waiting men.

Louris took the point once more, leading the group towards the frozen river bank ahead. Moving past the highlands, murmuring insects fluttered in and out of dank crevices, becoming constant companions along the winding river branch until dawn flexed its rays over the horizon.

Another night stirred the agents, impelling them to begin anew. Gilmour broke from the group, finding the highest point in the region. The task was not easy, given the depth they had descended to, but he continued on until a suitable clearing allowed him to spy just two of the villages. Again, he saw no one, and no traces of any equipment. On one hand, he felt relieved that their trek could continue unabated, although an unease soon gnawed within him. If a people subsisted in the wilderness for centuries, in one of the remotest and most unforgiving regions of the world, wouldn't they make routine and periodic expeditions out of the community for hunting and trading purposes? His observations didn't lie, but they couldn't answer the subtlest questions his mind thought they should.

Pausing a second longer to unequivocally rule out activity, he doubled back, the gnawing only beginning to deepen. Gilmour relayed his report to Louris, who then moved the men forward. Once on the icy banks, Gilmour gestured to Mason, bringing his partner within earshot. "I can't keep these observations out of my mind," he uttered.

Mason looked on, beckoning him to elaborate.

"Instinct...doesn't seem natural that no one's home."

"We all know what happened to this country; the government didn't hesitate to drive them out."

Gilmour nodded. He granted Mason his point, but that still didn't assuage his gut.

Mason's gaze drifted ahead. "Come on, we're falling behind."

The pair accelerated, putting themselves a few paces behind the other three. Mason hadn't lent too much thought to the inactivity of the distant villages, crediting it to the coming season. Now that Gilmour had brought his worries to his partner only, however, he committed them for consideration. Gilmour wasn't one to voice minor troubles; if anything, the fact that he went to Mason and not Louris should have distressed Mason even more than it did.

Mason checked Gilmour's body language the next few hours, attempting to gauge his partner's thoughts. He remained agitated, his hands flexing and balling into fists while his eyes scoured the taiga; the entire display, despite its extended period, was palpable.

Gilmour then halted, his right hand brushing Mason's forearm.

He squinted, scanning the frozen Keremesit. "Insects...."

"What?"

"There aren't any insects...no fauna to run into, either."

By now, Gilmour had aroused the other three, who turned back.

Mason scanned the hills also, wondering if his partner had finally cracked, before realizing, "He's right." He looked at the others. "It's been quiet the entire three hours we've been out here."

"Wait a moment," McKean said. "Gilmour, you said the villages were nearly deserted. The bugs out here wouldn't be quiet unless they're weren't any animals to prey on."

Mason eyes locked with Gilmour's. "Then where are they? We sure as hell haven't scared them off before."

"Something has." Gilmour swallowed. "We're not alone."

# CHAPTER FOURTEEN

Soft thumps approached from beyond the nearest crest of hills, scattering the agents among the low brush. Gilmour and Mason hit the permafrost chest first, rolling onto their sides to retrieve the sidearms hidden inside their parkas. Mason was the first to produce his holobook, using its meteorological lidar to scan for the location and nature of the gaining intruder.

Mason held up the holobook's screen at half-arm's length, allowing Gilmour a look. "Goddamn it."

Gilmour's finger traced the object's trajectory; it was making quick time—fifty meters per second—straight to them. "*Akilina*-class."
"Troop carrier...perfect."

Six meters away, Louris signaled his parallel assessment with a rough gesture of his hand, mocking a zooming aircraft.

The thumps grew quiet again, before mechanized rips tore through the air five minutes later, echoing into the night. Peeling tires cut into the taiga, followed by the roar of hyped up engines.

Crouching low, Mason and Gilmour watched the lidar representations of the vehicles bound over the river bank, before raising their heads to see the real machines, silhouetted across the near horizon. Five in all, the squat vehicles—too small and fast to be armored fighting vehicles—slowed to unleash beams of infrared energy into the valley, scanning for the illegal party.

Each of the five agents, outfitted in their IR-desensitized thermal garb, froze in place while the vehicles meandered over the rocky valley. Exchanging glances, Gilmour and Mason readied their respective E4.10c sidearms. Once the vehicles—now clearly ATVs—drew within optimal range, the pistols were gradually raised, tracking their quarry until the vehicles gained speed, spitting stones out from underneath in pursuit.

Gilmour and Mason hardened their stances, commanding their vox activated sidearms to project blue laser sights onto the marauders. Finding worthy targets on the lead vehicle, the E4.10cs fired, connecting with the vehicles' riders before the agents themselves could be marked. Swift return fire from one of the backup vehicles lit the valley. Mason grunted as a round nicked his abdomen; a quick swipe of his fingers revealed that the gash didn't penetrate his skin. Motioning that he was fine, the pair and the three agents at their right flank separated, opening up their spacing to misdirect the oncoming fire.

Gilmour ran to the left, then landed hard on the ice, his winter head gear protecting him from a fractured skull. After sliding a meter on the permafrost bank, he gathered his wits and timing, recovering the location of the circling band of submachine-gun-armed ATVs. He squatted and fired his E4.10c once more, but unable to attain knowledge of a positive hit, kept plugging at the closest marauder, five meters at his eleven o'clock flank. A sickening squeal followed by the crunching of metal on metal silenced the customized engine, beckoning Gilmour to investigate.

Rising to his feet, he approached the collapsed mass within seconds, both hands clutching his pistol while he roamed for survivors. A groan, coupled with shuffling boots, answered his question.

"Hello," Gilmour said, less than warmly, in his best Russian. "Identify yourselves."

Two lean soldiers, one hampered by a limp, went to their feet. The maimed one, no doubt attempting his best poker face, rubbed at his thigh and replied, "You are under...under arrest, by the authority of the Confederation of Indepen—" His hand felt up the wound again. "Independent States," he blurted, as if scripted.

The agent drew nearer, his eyes giving a cursory glance to the leg. "How badly are you hurt? It looks broken."

A hand belonging to the other man flashed towards Gilmour's left flank, which the agent promptly pulled to his chest. Wresting the leverage away from the young Russian, Gilmour pinned the soldier's arm behind his back, so that the boy faced his injured companion.

"I wouldn't do that, son," Gilmour spat in the boy's ear.

"Go to hell!"

If I could do that, do you think I'd be in this mosquito-infested swamp right now?" Gilmour cranked the boy's arm up further, eliciting a whimper. "All I came here to do was save us." He looked to the man across from him, his three sergeant's chevrons glowing in the gunfire. "That goes for you, too."

Additional gunfire illuminated Gilmour's face as he heard the rampaging engines circling about his comrades.

"Your friends will die if they resist," the sergeant said, his breath visible in the chilled air.

Gilmour snapped open the young soldier's holster and withdrew his sidearm, placing it inside his own parka. The agent then scanned for the sergeant's holster, but saw it had already been emptied. He pushed his E4.10c into the man's face. "Your weapon. Give me your sidearm."

"I can't...I lost it when we crashed...it's over there." His head swung back, nodding to the opposite edge of the heap.

Gilmour pursed his lips. Reaching within a side pocket of his trouserleg, he produced a length of cord. Relinquishing his grip on the young soldier's left arm, Gilmour tied one end of the cord around the boy's wrist, then joined it with another tie around the other wrist, effectively immobilizing him.

Fidgeting and cursing at the agent now that he had been bound, the young Russian was shoved to the taiga by a high kick to his back from Gilmour, letting the boy fall on his chest.

"Those are very adult words you're using," Gilmour warned. He ripped off the boy soldier's glove, scrunched it into a ball, and fed it to the cesspool of a mouth.

Despite the violence taken against one of his men, the sergeant continued to nurse his wound, a black stain leaking from a horrendous tear. "What about me?" he asked, his brow heavy with perspiration, even in the cold.

Gilmour discerned an island of exposed bone in the blood. "You probably have a compound fracture. I'm surprised you haven't fainted yet. But I'm not going to do anything."

With a mighty groan, the sergeant's knees imploded, surrendering him to the ground. Clutching the shred of flesh and bone, the sergeant's eyes followed Gilmour as the agent walked behind the wounded vehicle and found the missing pistol. Before long, the sergeant and his subordinate had been abandoned to the freezing Keremesit bank, while their singular, and now former, prey rejoined his comrades under continued fire.

Permafrost soil vaporized behind Mason as he stayed a pace ahead of the gunfire tracking him. Diving into a growth of low, nearly bare spruces, he caught his breath, and then his bearings before more shots pecked at the flora above him. His holobook provided the position of the chase vehicle and its riders, allowing him an opportunity to know their exact distance to return fire. Stowing the black device, Mason sat on his haunches, careful not to lose his head.

The ATV's engine clicked off, and a momentary lapse in gunfire afforded him time for his E4.10c's barrel to clear a small tunnel through the spruces' taut branches. Blue laser light streamed from the barrel's circumscribed sight, finding a pair of dark, amorphous shapes advancing to Mason's two o'clock. With two quick bursts from within the spruce, the men were felled, never seeing the scattered blue dots on their helmets.

Leaping over the spruces, Mason ran to the parked vehicle and commandeered it. Fumbling through the Cyrillic stamped on the vehicle's rusted controls, he managed to get the engine started, although it coughed and grumbled. Choking out exhaust, the vehicle lumbered past the fallen soldiers and headed for the remaining Russian team.

Pumping the throttle, he raced forward, jumping over cracked boulders and other deposited debris from the Keremesit's past. Ahead, he could see two other ATVs circling around Louris' last known location. Craning his head back, Mason looked for the other two vehicles, but found none, at least none with lamps shining into the night.

Mason heard the chink of gunfire from the attacking vehicles, but just minutely over the rumble of his ATV's engine. Twisting the steering column to the right, he rounded an accumulation of prostrate birch trees to gain a straight avenue to the pair of machines. Mason fed the engine more fuel, increasing his speed despite fighting the steering column to maintain his dominance of the vehicle, which threatened to buck him. The two enemy vehicles, tightening their circle around Louris, were now just meters away. Clamping his left arm onto the steering bar, Mason's other hand retrieved his E4.10c and sighted the first approaching ATV. He fired three times before his hand was forced back to the steering bar, which had caused his vehicle to drift leftward sans a steadying pair of hands.

The rear chase vehicle, rounding the circle, narrowly missed Mason head-on as he struggled to retain command. Clouds of dirt rose in his eyes when his ATV's front tires carved into the loosened silt and rock soil, fishtailing hard. The motor gagged hard, then died, sputtering Mason forward with inertia until the tires locked up. His left hand fingered the starter several times while he pumped the throttle repeatedly, but without success.

Mason cursed at the hobbled vehicle before jumping out of the fractured vinyl seat. Potshots meant for him whined through the air, puncturing the ATV's front tires and what remained of a quarter panel. The agent ducked and fell to his haunches, allowing the stationary vehicle to block the gunfire, for now. A hiss, followed by a soft whoosh, sounded in his ears as the left front tire lost pressure, eliminating the ATV as a means of escape.

Looking ahead, he estimated Louris, Constantine and McKean were at least ten meters away, a solid ten-second run to their positions. Of course, he wasn't going anywhere while those Ruskies were aerating his shield. His holobook projected an image of the other three—minus Gilmour, whom he had lost a while back—spread along a semi-circle over a distance of fifteen meters. Constantine was the nearest, followed by McKean and Louris. Their vital signs looked good, not tremendous, but alive. Small blue isobars at the end of their arms signaled that the agents were returning gunfire, meaning they hadn't been incapacitated.

Mason peered over the curved body of the vehicle during a slight pause in weapons fire, just long enough to glimpse the enemy machines heading away from him and back to the three holed-up agents. Spotting his chance, Mason's E4.10c sight located the spine of the armed, rear soldier in the backup ATV. A dark splatter erupted from his overcoat, sending the soldier cascading from the edge of the vehicle.

Mason launched himself, timing the distance in his head. At three seconds to go, the front ATV bisected the region harboring Constantine and McKean from Louris, turning back around to the running Mason. One second from the frozen river bank, Mason prompted himself to dive, throwing his arms towards the ground, leaving his feet to propel him. He heard the gunfire buzz pass him as the pain of peculiarly sharpened stones in his left flank broke his fall. His legs and arms flopped about while he rolled over himself fourfold, stirring up a heap of pebbles and soil.

Spitting out a glob of saliva and dust, Mason clutched his E4.10c, slowly realizing the ache of the fall was not ebbing. He groaned; it was increasing.

"Sonuvabitch!"

A gnawing burning deafening screaming shock then bit his torso, crawling and acidizing his organs, the angriest and most terrorizing sensation his nerves had ever given him.

"Get up, fucking yankee!"

Swirling greens and reds mingled with the pitch in Mason's eyes, the excruciating tendrils choking his mind into dumbness. Another boot to his abdomen later, and he was too deep into his anguish to hear the round silence his tormentor.

"Oh, Jesus...Greg! Greg, can you hear me?"

Gilmour crouched down to the balled-up Mason, by now face first in the soil, spattered blood caked into his nostrils and beard. Gingerly, Gilmour rolled his partner belly up, his hands roaming Mason's body for possible wounds. His fingers caught on two sticky, black holes in Mason's flank. Entrance holes, leading straight to Mason's cardiac system, possibly perforating his heart.

"Greg, it's me, James. Can you understand me?!"

His twisted countenance, streaming with porphyric tears, froze as his body succumbed to shock. The poor man's skin already looked cadaverous.

Gilmour found Mason's holobook and programmed it to run a medical scan of his partner's body. The holograph revealed a pair of clean piercings in Mason's pericardial tissue, with no remnants of the rounds to be discovered. Gilmour deepened the scan, and located two exit wounds in Mason's left shoulder; the rounds had burned straight through his body. He probably didn't even know he had been hit.

Mason's heartrate became arrhythmic, the damaged muscle flailing all over its chamber, pouring its vital fluid into his lungs, unaware of the damage it had sustained. His lungs had filled with blood fast—drowning him in his own chest—a wound exacerbated by the impacts done to him by the formerly living soldier behind them.

Gilmour's hands scooped up the clotting blood bubbling out of Mason's throat and mouth, fruitlessly trying to clear an air passage to his foundering alveoli. Periodic gurgling gave Gilmour a fading sense of hope that he could save his fallen friend, despite the fanatic beeping of the holobook's cardiac sensor.

"Oh, Greg...I'm sorry God I'm sorry I...."

Next to him, the cardiac failure alarm sounded, contrasting the degenerating cardiac sensor. A second later, his heartrate monitor flattened, leaving nothing but a monotone from the holobook's audio alarm.

His stained hands pulled away from Mason's gaping jaws, allowing his partner's limp cranium to rest easy against the wet soil. With the back of his left parka sleeve, Gilmour wiped the remains of perspiration from his forehead and collapsed onto his haunches, small breaths only escaping his mouth.

"Gilmour, we've got to get the hell out of here! Gilmour! Do you hear me!"

Constantine grabbed two handfuls of Gilmour's backpack and pulled him off the permafrost. Yanking the agent's face to his, Constantine looked deeply into Gilmour's eyes. "Goddammit, Gilmour, we've got to get rolling! The Russians are sure to find a mess of things in the morning. Do you have Mason's equipment?"

Gilmour's dreamy gaze found his partner's corpus before he nodded. He looked down at the lockbox in his hands. Equipment; Mason's pack, check. Mason's dead body, left for the mosquitoes and foxes. Fuck.

"I'm sorry, man. You did the best you could. We couldn't save Chief anymore than you could save Mason." Constantine put his arm around Gilmour's shoulder and hurried him away. Ahead, McKean readied the two ATVs captured by the agents; one by Constantine and McKean, and the other by Louris, with which he was leaving behind his body and soul as payment.

Driving out of the Keremesit valley and into the Indigirka's many frozen basins, the three agents made the last leg of their journey in the span of three days, more than quadrupling their leg speed. Stopping only to rest and refuel themselves in the limited daylight, the three men damned de Lis' mandate of inconspicuousness.

Beyond the mist and fog of the waste sea, a dark tower rose from the horizon, solidifying as the twin ATVs tracked across the snowpack, roaring away from the haunted taiga. The conning tower shone a blue laser light towards them, signaling to the trio of agents that the *Hesperus* had arrived to take them home.

Once the agents crossed over the shallowest section of the shelf, they cut a two-meter hole in the ice, then scuttled the pair of ATVs into the depths of the East Siberian Sea. Walking into the relative comforts of the submarine's vertical shaft, the men held tight to the retrieved cargo, completing their assigned duty. Burying their dead comrades, however, and committing them forever to the ultimate tomb of memory was the one duty they could not yet do.

# CHAPTER FIFTEEN

"Two Americans are dead, sir, the rest fled. We are presuming a ship, perhaps a subma—"

"Presumptions are not what we require," Lieutenant Vasily Nicolenko snapped. "Facts, get me facts. If there was an American vessel in our sovereign waters, I need to know the specifics: deuterium decay, infrared detection, hell, even visual confirmation from one of the local fishermen."

"Yes, sir." The sergeant trotted off to meet up with his men, who had busied themselves with the scanning of the permafrost soil.

In the grey morning hours, he could see the numerous tread tracks and half-formed footprints where the valiant effort to neutralize the invading Americans had taken place. Walking up an incline onto the banks of the Keremesit River, the pair of black bags containing the American corpses fluttered in the bitter wind to his left, disappointing him greatly. The orders from down high had been to shoot to kill if necessary, but capture the interlopers alive, more importantly. Judging by the wounds Nicolenko had seen on these bodies upon arrival this morning, the two Americans had been needlessly silenced, leaving him the unenviable task of reporting the failure to St. Petersburg.

Of a lesser concern were the three dead of the detachment of Muscovite regimental soldiers, who had been assigned the task of interceding here. For all Nicolenko cared, they deserved what they got; his orders were to clean up the mess left by the botched assignment. Fortunately for their wretched hides, his captain had ordered the Muscovites back home, before Nicolenko could have them gunned down and thrown into the Keremesit.

Walking away from the mess, he lit a cigarette and damned the cold. The sergeant's men were several hours from gleaning any forensic evidence from the site; if the Americans were clever, they would have removed any clues from the taiga. Nicolenko still couldn't imagine what drove their military here; didn't they have their own diamond and oil fields to exploit? Surely the Premier had sent the Muscovites here for something far more essential to the security of the Confederation than black gold?

He shook his head, dismissing his curious thoughts. It wasn't his concern to know why, just do. Too many years had passed since he had been the eager young man, ignorant of proper decorum. Now the fresh young men he commanded must learn the lessons he had been taught, or end up fodder, like the Muscovites.

"Lieutenant!"

The clamor outside the *Akilina* carrier broke Nicolenko away from his scheduled webcast with the captain. Rising out of his tight seat in the rear of the craft, the lieutenant produced fur gloves from his pockets and slipped them on before rejoining the men outside.

A light snow had coated the taiga, covering all but the recent tracks made by the sergeant and two corporals behind him as they crossed over to the aircraft.

"Sir, come quickly!"

He doubled his pace, keeping up with the fleeing sergeant. Steam crept from his nostrils and ruby lips, inevitable given the front that had pushed through this morning.

A circle of soldiers divided the sergeant, his two men and Nicolenko from a segment of heavily surveyed permafrost. Cutting through the gaping soldiers, the sergeant led Nicolenko to the secured ground, which still underwent scans from a soldier brandishing a portable EM spectrometer.

The sergeant shoved the obstructing soldier out of the way, allowing Nicolenko to view a shiny patch of material littering the soil, deceptively diamond-like to the eye, but possessing far more...presence.

Crouching down, the lieutenant's gloved hand fingered the first of the pair of objects, noting its peculiar gleam in the snowy air, seemingly reflecting and refracting far more than the simple Yakutian light pouring through the lattice. Despite the jewel's intrinsic beauty, Nicolenko did not pretend to be a gemologist.

He craned his head back to the soldier. "Diamonds?"

"No, sir," the boy said, a native Yakut. His own bare hands, nearly frostbitten, pointed to the object's natural facets; in all probability, its exquisite structure and complexity were of such remarkable design work that duplication would be nigh impossible, even in specialist laboratories. "They are unique to anything I have ever seen before."

Nicolenko nodded; perhaps there was a way to salvage this mess before he had to report to his superiors. "Very well, Corporal. Collect these gems and secure them inside the carrier." He checked his wrist chronometer, then rose to tower over the assembled men. "You have one hour to clean up! We leave at dusk!"

"Yes, yes, bring him in."

A creak admitted Nicolenko into the spartan office. Removing his cap, he deferred to the old man, who stood, not noticing the gesture, at the room's sole window, staring away, as if into infinity. The old man's worn hand placed a tiny phone into his pocket. Turning to the officer, he finally welcomed him. "Ah."

"Lieutenant Vasily Nicolenko reporting as ordered, sir."

"You have returned from Yakutia, correct?"

Nicolenko nodded. "I bring a field report on our maneuver." Unbuttoning his overcoat, he produced a small holobook from an inner pocket, then tapped a series of buttons.

The old man held up a hand, halting the upcoming recitation of events. "What of your men? How did they fare during this expedition to the cold north? Are they resilient? Do they like it?"

Taken aback, Nicolenko masked his awe with deep thought. "They do not question their orders, if that is what you ask."

"Good, then they are not Muscovites, eh?" He laughed, then stepped closer to the officer. "That is reassuring."

"Sir," he began, pursing his lips, "perhaps I am dull from my long flight. I was under the belief that you required my report, per Capt—"

"In a moment. We here," his weary arms opened, signifying the whole of St. Petersburg, "are interested in you, Lieutenant. You have risen fast from the mire of your postings. This matter in Yakutia was a simple cleansing, yet you relished it with such fervor unheard of in other officers of your caliber. Above that, the expedition was a prologue to greater duties, if you are willing."

"Sir, I have always been at the mercy of my country's will and greater judgment. I do what must be done, no matter the circumstances."

A flame lit in the old man's eyes, a burning that was once believed to have been snuffed out. "Good, good." Uncharacteristically, a palm now rested on Nicolenko's shoulder. "There are several colleagues of mine, important men you would do well to become acquainted with."

"What of my report?"

The old man ushered Nicolenko towards the paint-flecked door. "Tell me on the way. It is a tedious walk, and I rarely have good drinking company."

A waft of tobacco smoke, cloyingly sweet, met Nicolenko's nostrils, and he wished he had received a box of homegrown, studiously rolled cigarettes from his sisters the past holiday instead of the bathtub vodka he hated. No matter, he could always dream of next season.

He was beckoned inside a larger office, sans windows, by the old man, where a motley assemblage of military officers—some he recognized, others not—and men in high-priced suits, were seated on leather couches and chairs. Each eyed Nicolenko intently, studying his stature, facial features, gait and military dress. They made obvious gestures to one another, some nodding while others murmuring behind a cloak of cigarette smoke. Curiously, he caught the gaze of a solitary gentleman off to one corner, his white, disheveled hair and dress distinguishing him from the other men, very much not belonging in the same room, let alone organization, as the other men.

"Have a seat, Lieutenant," one of the suited man said, gesturing to a wooden chair centered in the room.

Nicolenko eagerly nodded, noting all the trappings of a traditional interrogation. Sitting down, the men continued their silent conference, betraying no hint of the meeting's purpose.

The suited man stood before Nicolenko, his eyes locked with the old man in silent dialogue before returning to the seated lieutenant. "We are pleased to finally meet you, Lieutenant. Your mission to the Yakut Republic was a success?" The question was more rhetorical than query. "Details of our expedition will be found in my report." He produced his holobook and held it out to the man.

"Thank you." The suited man received the holobook and unceremoniously handed it to another man next to him, not even committing it a glance. "Reports are not our priority. Your country needs your expertise, dear lieutenant. My comrades have kept a very close eye upon you, and you have distinguished yourself well. I trust you have been informed of this already, hmm?"

Nicolenko looked to the old man, then to the suited man again. He nodded. "Yes, sir."

"There is a situation, a problem that needs to be resolved." He folded his arms over his chest. "The Americans have created a new weapon of mass destruction, capable of destroying all that we have labored so long to preserve. Several weeks ago, a specialized team invaded our sovereign soil to test the strength of this weapon on our innocent citizens of the Yakut Republic."

So, there was more to the mission, Nicolenko thought. And the dispatch of the expendable Muscovites to stop the Americans started to make more sense as well.

"Our people cry out for security from this threat," he continued. "You, Lieutenant, have been selected to be the vanguard of our sovereignty."

Nicolenko tightened his collar, then rose to his feet. "I will do my utmost, sir."

The suited man nodded, satisfied. Raising a hand, he gestured to the peculiar, solitary man, who came forth from the smoky shroud. "Lieutenant, your first duty as vanguard will be to train with Doctor Vasya Zaryov, our chief scientist with the Cosmoscience Institute. He has spent much time studying this new class of weapon."

Nicolenko clenched his jaw, stifling his imminent confusion; what business did that man have training a career officer?

The suited man detected Nicolenko's smugness. "Are there any problems, Lieutenant?"

"No, sir." Nicolenko's knees knocked together, reinforcing his confident stance.

The suited man smiled, revealing alcohol- and tobacco-stained teeth. "Excellent." Stepping away from Nicolenko, he allowed Zaryov, tufted shock of hair and rumpled overshirt in all, to look over his new pupil.

Nicolenko bowed in deference to the elder Zaryov.

Vasya Zaryov placed a hand on Nicolenko's shoulder, much the same way the old man did earlier, and led him out of the darkened room. The old system still thrived well, indeed.

"You are very quiet, Lieutenant," Zaryov observed. The pair sat together in a car of the old regime's private subterranean railway, a stingy, stubborn, and oftentimes insolent system built to expedite the Soviet and New Democratic Republic's leaders to safehouses in the event of nuclear confrontation. Now, the railway had been relegated to simply ferrying government men under St. Petersburg's various canals.

"I've known lots of men as yourself," Zaryov continued. "You are probably thinking, 'Why is this crazy man training me?'. Well, you would do well to think that, Lieutenant."

Nicolenko's eyes did not wander from the window view opposite him.

"You are a steely one. They have done well."

"I serve where commanded, sir. My duty is to my country, not my feelings or thoughts. They are good in bed only."

At that, Zaryov laughed heartily, leading to a coughing fit. Nicolenko looked at the scientist, wondering if the old man was going to keel over next to him. Zaryov wiped the tears from his eyes, finally gaining control of his spasmodic lungs.

"Good, good. You do have humor. It will come to good use where we are going."

Nicolenko turned to the disheveled man, asking, "Which is?"

"The fate of our Confederation is in our hands, now, Lieutenant. The Premier and all the *siloviki* who elected him cannot influence the events of the future, as you will soon do. It is not a light responsibility. The Institute—my home—will be the forefront of world diplomacy. And you'll be our ambassador, Lieutenant."

"What is out there? What is so important?"

"Power, my young sir. The power to shift world governments. To crumble them. To reset the world as one sees fit. It is a race against the very fabric of spacetime itself. It curves back upon itself, prevents us from ever exposing its secrets...until now."

"Why now? Why here?"

"A tremendous event, two centuries in the past. A craft...a vessel of unearthly origins. It holds the potential you see in these jewels. Our enemies possess a minute quantity of them. You saw firsthand what transpires when governments clash for supreme power. These are worth dying—killing—for. You will do the same, like they have."

"I am a soldier. That is my duty, sir. If I am to...retrieve these jewels, how shall I accomplish this?"

"Therein lies the secret, young lieutenant. Look deeply into the objects, perhaps you will see...."

# CHAPTER SIXTEEN

Outside U5-10, de Lis heard the door vibrate in unison with a melancholy strain of music, a piece he recognized but couldn't place. A swirling violin gave him a start before he composed himself and toggled the door's buzzer, confident that the occupant wouldn't hear his knock. After a moment, he raised his finger to toggle again until the door opened unexpectedly, revealing a man who had willingly severed himself from the world, waiting at the threshold.

"Agent Gilmour," de Lis uttered, the sight of the fully bearded and pallid man shocking him. He had to push his lips open to say, "May...I come in?"

Gilmour nodded reticently.

De Lis tread carefully behind the agent, as if walking onto hallowed ground. "I'm sorry I didn't come by sooner," the doctor apologized, closing the door behind him. De Lis' eyes roamed around Gilmour's quarters, noticing the room was as spare as the day the Ottawa Bureau had assigned it to him. Baggage, not emptied since his return, had clustered in one corner, joined by several days' worth of stacked meal trays. Like an afterthought, he remembered the still-playing piece: Beethoven's Seventh Symphony, one of the maestro's most moving, and particularly recently, in de Lis' opinion, dirge-like compositions. How better to drown one's sorrows then in a sorrowful elegy for lost ones?

Gilmour crossed over to his bureau and tapped a button on its metal surface, silencing the music. "Pardon my decor. I hadn't much cared to pick up after myself."

De Lis dismissed the carelessness and stepped over to the disheveled man. "I'm sorry for your loss. I wish I had had the opportunity to get to know Mason and Louris better."

"This is the nature of our profession, Doctor." He turned around to face de Lis, ready to drop the matter. "Why are you here, exactly? Didn't you receive my notice to be left alone?"

"Agent Gilmour, it's been three days since your return, just as you specified. Have you even kept track of the time?"

Gilmour laughed inside. The mission to Russia had destroyed time in his mind; how did one follow a nonstop routine of day sleeping and night hiking, then compartmentalize in one's brain the passage of time, when the stars were your only companions? Time was the invention of madmen.

De Lis checked the condition of Gilmour's clothing, and seeing the stains and rips, concluded he hadn't an inkling of the day. "You have a new mission, Agent. We have been provided with a new objective from the Department of Defense, stemming from your retrieval of the specimens from Sakha."

Gilmour stroked the curls on his jaw. "With all due respect to Colonel Dark Horse, I request a leave of absence."

"There are no requests to be granted, Agent Gilmour. Your assignment to Ottawa stipulates your willingness to perform all duties as ordered by the DoD. As you quoted me just now, it 'is the nature of our profession.'" De Lis' teeth ground together. "I'm not above pulling rank. I am truly sorry for the loss of your partner, but don't make me shatter your chances for directorship. We need you, Gilmour. The country, the world needs you."

The agent placed his palm to his chest, just to see if his heart had continued to beat, just to see if he hadn't actually died, too. Four days ago he wished he had.

Finally, Gilmour lifted his eyes to the doctor, and after the consideration and hindsight of nearly a week, nodded. "I'll need a physical, and pain medication."

De Lis' lips curled at their edges. "I wondered how long you'd forgo treatment since your refusal in the hangar. We'll get Doctor Anaba to look over you." He then studied the growth on Gilmour's jawline. "After that, lose the beard. I'm not sure the colonel or the DoD would approve, even though Doctor Anaba might. Unfortunately for her tastes, she doesn't see too many men here with facial hair."

Despite the various greetings and slaps on the back he had received from the Ottawa scientists, Gilmour didn't feel as though he had truly returned; a part of him still lay dead in Sakha, a part he didn't know if he'd ever get back. Walking stiffly into the U5-1 laboratory, a finger slid down his shaven jaw, reinforcing the changes of the past weeks. No, he wasn't comfortable here at all. In fact, he wasn't too much in the mood for the debriefing he was certain to receive from Dark Horse, which, to Gilmour's curiosity, was not in U5-29, but here, with de Lis' staff present. Unusual for the lieutenant colonel.

De Lis slid his pass key through the circular panel suspended in U5-3's fullerene glass wall, admitting the pair into the doctor's office. "Have a seat."

Gilmour eased his tender body into the chair, then noticed Dark Horse's absence. "Where's the colonel?"

"This is a laboratory status report, not a debriefing, Agent Gilmour," de Lis said, taking his own seat. "Colonel Dark Horse felt the need for one marginal at best. You know what's involved, we know what's involved. No reason to drag it out for our ears."

Gilmour nodded; a silent thank you.

De Lis slid a holobook across the desk to Gilmour. "This is our latest update. While you were gone, the staff and I added quite a few pieces to our puzzle, as well as digging up new ones, pardon the pun."

The agent scrolled down the report and examined the holographs accompanying it. This went on for a moment before pausing, then furrowing his brow. "Uh, what do you mean by losing an hour forty minutes?"

De Lis stroked his chin; this would be the hard part. "The specimens have a tendency—when exposed to a Casimir vacuum—of warping spacetime." He discerned Gilmour's well hidden disbelief, then continued, "That's why our first Nepalese specimen seemingly disappeared."

"Pardon?"

De Lis leaned forward, so Gilmour could fully comprehend. "Extradimensional travel, Agent Gilmour. We unknowingly sent it into the past. Twice."

"Oh, God." He collapsed into the chair. "You can't be serious...I hope you're not serious."

De Lis gave a curt nod.

"Then they have it too, don't they? Sweet Jesus, they have one too."

The doctor remained mute. HADRON, their little mole, the anonymous critter inside their own walls, perhaps inside U5-1's walls, had done it. If the Russians knew what was in their hands—Gilmour couldn't see why not—then it was all over. Memory could be erased like a fragged file, written over by someone with the will and the means to redo history in his own image.

"How long have you known this?"

De Lis sighed. "Three days after your team left."

Gilmour rubbed his eyes. Reality didn't seem so real anymore. "Well, then. What do we do about it?"

"Lionel is working on that. First, you need to finish the report. It doesn't get any better."

The succeeding pages had been composed by the DoD, complete with several holographs of the Asian continent. Dozens of green points—a multiplication of the sites from Dark Horse's report six weeks ago—popped up from the cartographs, followed by a smattering of reddened spikes. The green points coincided ominously with a smuggled list of factories and industries located inside the Confederation. The red spikes, while only a handful, were centered on remote regions of the continent, areas Gilmour knew to be hard to access, even with military transportation. His finger tapped a peripheral button, providing a DoD quantum analysis of each spike. They were explosions...neutronic test blasts.

The holobook clacked on the desktop.

"What exactly is my objective, Doctor?"

De Lis raised a finger to his lips before knocking on Stacia Waters' office door. Inside, Waters rose to her feet and opened the door, allowing the two into the room. Shutting the door behind her, she gestured to the chairs.

"Welcome back, Agent Gilmour. I trust Richard has updated you?"

Gilmour nodded. "Regrettably."

De Lis glanced to the device in Waters' palm. "Stacia."

Gilmour received the holobook thrust to him by Waters, then scrolled through the text. A holograph of a miniaturized Casimir chamber, small enough to be affixed to a man, appeared in the report.

"This is all well, Doctor, but what good does this do me?"

De Lis pointed to the holograph. "This is your new objective, Agent Gilmour. We need you to penetrate the Confederation and wipe out their potential extradimensional capabilities."

"Bomb them?"

"It's not quite that simple," de Lis corrected him. "For all we can discern, the samples themselves are infinitely dense, incapable of being reduced to a more fundamental—hence, safer—state. The Secretary of Defense is ordering you to eradicate the extradimensional potential at the source: returning to the moment of the specimens' landfall."

"You mean," he raised an eyebrow, "you want me to use one of those things to erase history?"

"No, not erase," Waters said. "We think we can construct a way for you and a team to retrieve the jewels before they are covered by the elements. But it would involve utilizing the jewels we have to do so."

Gilmour covered his nose and mouth. "I think I'm going to be sick."

De Lis put a hand to the agent's shoulder, steadying him. "At this moment, the DoD believes the Confederation is preparing to utilize a neutronic device to unearth the Pacific Ocean site. According to Javier, this site is potentially the largest one yet, capable of yielding several tonnes of the jewels. We've beaten them to the punch twice, but there's a mole here, and it knows what only a few of us have been privy to."

The doctor's eyes narrowed. "If we blink, sneeze, or hesitate long enough to even lick our wounds, the Confederation has won. I don't need to tell you what that means."

"Just how do you know this...harebrained idea will succeed? Do you have exact evidence that these jewels went back to the past?"

"We're pretty sure," Waters said, glancing at de Lis.

Gilmour looked to the doctor as well.

"Well, empirical evidence is scant, honestly."

The agent rolled his eyes and turned away.

"Gilmour, listen." De Lis touched the agent's sleeve, grabbing his attention. "Everything we do here is risky. We've never done this before. My staff and I have been working since your departure to determine the precise meV charge that will activate spacetime warping. A narrow margin has been discerned, and we're continuing to narrow it further until exact."

"All right."

"Gilmour," Waters stood, "we wouldn't have even presented this as a possibility to the secretary unless we knew there was a chance it would work. Richard and I need you to work with us during the lab experimentation. That means your input on design procedures and other practical considerations, since you'll be the one performing the mission...we're just the eggheads in the lab coming up with the stuff."

"Where do we start?"

"Lionel's office," de Lis answered, heading for the door. "He's been working on a way to construct a miniaturized Casimir vacuum chamber."

"Any luck?" Gilmour asked as the trio exited.

Waters looked to de Lis, who merely raised his eyebrows.

De Lis, Gilmour and Waters walked into Roget's office in time to smell the acrid air wafting to the ceiling. At their feet lay the remains of some mechanism, now blown to thousands of irretrievable shards. The trio stepped over the larger debris to find Roget shaking his head at his exam table, holding a shard in his hand. "That was Mark II. I guess it needs more work."

Gilmour picked up one of the curved shards and rolled it over, soon realizing that it was a fractured section of the Casimir. "And this is what's supposed to take me back?"

A petulant look crossed Roget's face as he tried to ignore Gilmour's not-so flippant comment. "Richard, I've got two more housings in the wings. We'll get it completed."

"Good. Three days, no more."

"Not much of a deadline for the work everybody's being asked to do," Gilmour said to de Lis.

De Lis returned a few pieces of the shattered Casimir to the table before leading the three out. "The secretary understands the difficulties involved, but we've had some successes. As we speak, several of my associates are finalizing a series of hazard suits to deploy for the missions, and—"

"Missions? How many missions?"

"At least one for yourself, Agent Constantine and Agent McKean. There are three sites to reconnoiter," de Lis explained, raising a finger. "Agent Gilmour, we're sending you to the Pacific Rim, per Colonel Dark Horse's recommendation. It is the most complex—and dangerous—of the missions, requiring your expertise as the lead agent in the Temporal Retrieve Project to execute. Agents Constantine and McKean will each be sent to a separate site deep within the Confederation: Irkutsk and Magadan, respectively, two industrialized cities suspected of being important neutronic facilities, where they will conduct reconnoitering on the Confederation's current neutronic capabilities."

"We've been directed to manufacture hazard suits flexible enough for multiple missions," Waters added. "If need be."

Gilmour gave a small sigh. "Then I'll be sure to do it right the first time. I'm not given to being kicked around time repeatedly."

"We can't afford to lose you, either," de Lis said. "If, for any reason, the other site retrievals go awry, we'll need the other agents to take up the failed mission. To counter this, Javier will brief your team extensively on the conditions of the century to which you will be traveling, even though you're slated to be the only agent going back to the twentieth century, Agent Gilmour. We can't lose. Period."

Forty-eight hours of almost non-stop preparation had the three agents' minds reeling from mass data input. Valagua made excellent time on de Lis' schedule to brief the trio of men, squeezing in copious references about the times, including customs, political affiliations, language, clothing styles, popular culture, and most importantly, the Second World War, which was just entering its second year by late 1940.

De Lis and Waters periodically spelled them from the intense research by involving the trio in the final construction of the hazard suits, supervised by Ivan, Crowe, Lux and Jaquess. U5-7, the theoretical studies lab's hardware bay, was the current home of the suits, each of which hung from the ceiling in the center of the office. A deck of monitors ringed the haz suits, displaying dozens of design graphics and schematics. Tools pertinent to the suits' maintenance—modern quantum tunneling microscopes and EM pulsers, time-tested mallets and screwdrivers—were arrayed on several shelves lining the four walls. Above them, a bay of lights exposed every square millimeter with pleasant, warm illumination.

Handed a batch of holobooks by Waters, the trio looked over the holographic designs, comparing theory to the actual results. The half-completed exolayers of the outfits were composed of a beige, quilted material—tough to the touch—underneath which was a layer of quanta-conducting fiber, enabling the myriad mechanisms and sensors to draw power from a secured quantum battery deep inside. Concentric metal rings formed the shoulder-to-neck harnesses, where helmets would be latched to the suits to maintain livable atmospheric pressure.

"So we need to run around in these things to prevent us from broiling alive?" Constantine asked. The thought of wearing twenty-kilogram spacesuits weighed heavily on his mind; just one more operational hoop to jump through.

"A precaution, Agent," de Lis explained. "I've seen firsthand what the last object did to Lionel's Casimir chamber. Quantum analysis of the charred remains revealed that the interior material had been stripped of ninety-five percent of its bosonic matter, reducing the chamber to the equivalent of atomic ash."

McKean playfully plucked a portion of one of the hazard suits with his finger. "Ouch. Sounds like a plan, Doctor. When do we have our measurements taken?"

De Lis checked his wrist chronometer. "We have twenty-one hours, Agents. Now would be a fine time."

Laser-light dimensions of each respective agent was recorded by the four junior scientists, and work commenced on the final phases of the hazard suits, while the flesh and blood embodiments of the trio assisted in the fabrication of bodysocks to be worn underneath the hazard suits. These sublayers would facilitate the easy removal of waste liquids from the agents, as well as provide an extra layer of comfort and cushion impacts.

Soon the men had been stripped down to nothing and ordered to wear the bodysocks, or "diapers," as Constantine referred to them. The khaki fabric stretched over their feet and hands, slipping up to their jawline. Restrictive at first, the agents soon adjusted to the uniquely reptilian feel of the 'socks clasping to their skin, and assured by de Lis that yes, the wicking action of the 'socks would indeed eradicate any unmentionable moisture.

Once the agents and de Lis were satisfied with the undergarments, the remaining hours of the day passed swiftly. Under the DoD's strict schedule, the agents concluded their assigned research of the prospective era a few hours early, allowing them time to revisit the just-minted hazard suits waiting for them.

De Lis and Waters conferred with Ivan, Crowe, Lux and Jaquess before bringing the trio of agents in to inspect the final versions of the garb. When all had been settled between the project head and his associates, the agents were reintroduced to the hazard suits, now fully installed with compact interior scanning equipment. Adorning the outfits from the exterior were life support systems units melded into the quilted exolayers, connected to the now-concealed quanta fiber layers. From the front, the suits had been personalized by the junior scientists, with each agent's surname stitched onto a chest patch.

Waters and de Lis, with holobooks in hand, guided the agents through a crash course in the operation of each suit, providing a holographic checklist of each system, its function, and its energy requirements. The only remaining component left to be completed from the list was the miniature Casimir devices, promised by Roget before the deadline. A flat, circular panel on the backs of the hazard suits indicated where the devices were intended to be placed, patiently waiting for the possibly too-experimental mechanisms. Until delivery of the devices, the three agents would have to postpone their first fitting of the hazard suits, tightening the DoD's already rigid schedule.

# CHAPTER SEVENTEEN

Roget wasted no time perfecting his prototype Casimir devices, despite exhausting all but three-and-a-half hours of their allotted timeframe. Even now, while the three agents in their bodysocks were being connected to the hazard suits via a series of narrow, translucent optical fibers, Roget and his four associates sweated away the final details of the intricate connections to the backs of the suits, dodging de Lis' and Waters' helpers as they did their own maneuvers.

De Lis instructed the three men to ease their feet into the bottom portion of the hazard suits, one at a time, as if climbing into a sturdy pair of trousers. While Ivan and Crowe held the torso locking mechanisms, the trio sat themselves onto nearby chairs, pulling the leggings taut. Despite the laser measurements taken of each agent's body, the suits were tighter than anticipated, if de Lis could take the complaints he received as the truth.

"I assure you, gentlemen, the suits conform to your exact measurements. Perhaps you've gained water weight?"

The agents groaned, giving de Lis the only answer he expected. Entrenched now in the beige leggings, the agents stood again, testing out the firmness of the boots and the flexibility of the knee joints. Constantine dropped to his haunches once and rose back to his feet, while Gilmour and McKean practiced moving laterally, hoping the quoted mobility of the suits held up in the heat of their respective missions.

"I think we're ready to go," Roget announced. With his associates, he carried over the first completed upper body unit, which was inscribed with "GILMOUR."

Once Roget, Ivan and Crowe were at his side, Gilmour held out his arms, ready to climb into the empty abdomen. As the agent wormed his hands through the suit and found the bulky sleeves, the scientists pitched the suit upwards and slid it down Gilmour's trunk, resting the metallic abdominal collars together. Swift fingers latched the two halves, locking Gilmour into his hazard suit. Gilmour's bare hands pulled and tugged at the suit's abdominal half like a nervous bridegroom; the entire suit felt like one big diaper, and was probably as a pretty as one, too. He flexed his sleeves and tested the extent to which they allowed his arms to maneuver.

"Looks well," de Lis said. "How does it feel?"

"Heavy, especially with this contraption strapped to my back," Gilmour answered, jutting his thumb back to the Casimir. "I'll manage, though."

"We took thirteen grams off the original design specifications," Roget said, rising to the device's defense.

"Good. That's thirteen less grams to explode into my shoulder blades."

"Agent Gilmour—" Roget protested.

De Lis held out a hand, quieting Roget. "Lionel, we need to suit up Agent Constantine and Agent McKean."

Roget sighed, deferring to his boss. Retrieving the next suit piece, the scientists finished Constantine within moments, and concluded with McKean. Waters wheeled into the room a portable tray, displaying three pairs of gauntlets, three fifteen-centimeter-long flat black objects, and the bubble-shaped helmets, complete with fullerene glass faceplates and a set of Heads-Up-Display sensors lining the interiors.

Roget toggled a button on the front panel of each hazard suit, activating all three quantum batteries. A soft hum sounded as power now coursed throughout the fibers lining the hazard suits, vibrating the rib cages of the men.

"You're all in full power mode," Roget confirmed, eyeing the green systems status diodes on the chest plates.

De Lis nodded. "Thank you, Lionel. You gentlemen should have sufficient power to run all critical systems in your suits for about a decade, specifications holding true, of course. If for some reason battery power begins to fluctuate or degrade, an immediate infusion of quarks will have to be performed."

The trio exchanged glances; they'd be damned if they spent more than a few days in those hazard suits.

"We'll try to make it back before than, Doctor," Gilmour said.

"Please see that you do."

"What wonderful toys do we have here?" McKean asked, picking up one of the black objects next to the gauntlets. Holding it up to his eyes, the object betrayed no outward use, looking like nothing more than trim from a military stealth project.

"These are the modes of visualizing your hazard suit's compliment of sensory devices, as well as system functions," Waters explained. "A simple voice authorization command activates the holographic interface, eliminating the need for a multitude of material buttons and dials. What's more, the holographs are visible through your Heads Up Display only, making your suit's systems that much more covert."

Gilmour handled a display in his own hands, feeling the smooth surface over his skin. "Will they work? You've only had a few days to get this up and running."

"I've got a few friends throughout Washington working on some pet military projects," she answered, cracking a smile. "They'll work."

Gilmour nodded. He hoped Stacia was right, and the short R-and-D period wouldn't leave them high and dry during the mission.

Waters took the holograph projector from Gilmour and placed the device on his hazard suit's left forearm, locking it into an empty slot. She locked the two remaining devices onto Constantine's and McKean's respective suits, then programmed all three with the wielder's personal authorization code.

"Refer to the helpware if for any reason you should need assistance in utilizing this," de Lis said, citing the holograph projectors again. "Stacia and I personally programmed a virtual guide in the case of an emergency. In that unlikely instance, our voices will lead you to troubleshoot any problems. Right then?"

The trio nodded their heads before familiarizing themselves with the holograph projectors' angle on their sleeves along with the proper methods of utilizing the invaluable hardware.

Waters handed the agents their gauntlets and pointed to an insignificant tab at the base of Constantine's right gauntlet palm.

"This is the talon manipulator Richard and I diagrammed to you earlier." She took back the gauntlet and tugged the tab, revealing a pair of two centimeter-long metal styli, one each from the tips of the index and middle fingers. "Just in case you have to manually manipulate your equipment."

Constantine opened his mouth to make a crude joke, but McKean's quick hands covered Constantine's lips, stifling it in time.

Waters, ignoring Constantine's attempt at sophomoric humor, pushed the tab in and returned the styli to rest, then handed the gauntlet back to him. The three agents then holstered the gauntlets like sidearms, where electromagnets below their suits' abdominal rings would hold the gauntlets until needed.

"And lastly...." De Lis proffered the surplus military helmets to the men—customized to form fit each agent's respective cranial shape, eye equidistance, and vision—then glanced at his wrist chronometer. "We'd better hurry. Javier is expecting us for a final briefing before you depart."

Unexpectedly to the three agents, U5-1's ambient buzz had been superseded by a louder smattering of voices, which reached a crescendo as de Lis opened the door out of U5-7 to the main lab.

A circle of the theoretical studies laboratory staff, everyone from Valagua, Marlane and Dark Horse down to the lowest echelon of junior scientists, had gathered in the center of the pristine room, awaiting the "chrononauts." Rounds of echoing applause greeted the crew, startling the agents into smiles, a gesture they had not expected after the previous weeks' experiences.

The circle tightened around the three men; generous shoulder clapping and "Good luck", "Godspeed," and even "Thank you" filled the air, raising the goodwill to deafening levels, drowning out the doubt that had washed over them.

De Lis raised his hands, momentarily lowering the circle's intensity, and gestured to Javier Valagua.

The historian produced a holobook and read, "On behalf of the Secretary of Defense of the United States of North America, we wish to thank you courageous men for daring to undertake such a hazardous, but necessary, action. We wish you godspeed, and may you return in success. Thank you."

With equal efficiency, and grateful that the DoD's message was curt, Valagua replaced the holobook into his jacket pocket and addressed the agents. "It has been a pleasure and privilege to work with a group of such fine agents of this nation. Sharing my knowledge of the circumstances of your mission to you all has been a delight, and I couldn't have asked for better students. Thank you all."

Valagua bowed to the trio, bringing a sense of pride and accomplishment to Gilmour, Constantine and McKean, three men who, despite losing two close friends, one a mentor, pressed on with the perhaps foolish operation because it was not only their sworn duty and obligation, but a private vow between them and their lost comrades.

De Lis turned to his senior staff. "Are we ready for final procedures?"

Waters, Valagua, Marlane and Roget consulted their respective holobooks, running down the checklists and searching for any omitted or outstanding entries. Finding none, the four nodded, agreeing that all was ready to go.

"Colonel Dark Horse, web the secretary that Project: Temporal Retrieve is commencing. Stacia, Lionel, distribute the specimens and begin monitoring the Casimir chambers. All right, ladies and gentlemen, let's get this over with."

While Valagua, Marlane, Dark Horse, Quintanilla and the junior scientists backed off from the featured agents, Waters and Roget opened the Lockbox and extracted several jewels. Crossing over to the suited and waiting agents, Waters portioned out a pair of jewels for each man, handing them over to Roget, who then unsealed a tiny, circular drop-chute on the chestplate of each agent's hazard suit. Once the first jewel was placed inside the fabric-laden dropchute, a tube located below the exterior layers inhaled it and settled the object inside the miniature Casimir chamber on the backs of each agent. The second jewel was given as a replacement, in the event the inexact science of the Casimir vacuum chamber happened to send the primary specimen hurtling through spacetime, which had occurred more often than any of the scientists wished to admit.

"Suit 'em up."

At de Lis' command, Lux and Jaquess stepped forward and gloved the three agents, then topped off the hazard suits with each man's helmet, latching them into place with a click. The two associates clapped the agents' arms and gave a thumbs up, signaling all had been completed. Hearing the okay given from the junior scientists, de Lis gave his own thumbs up to the men. "Good luck."

Gilmour turned to his two colleagues, and gesturing to his holographic interface, tapped the black device. A flat blue circle, a half-meter in diameter, exploded onto his HUD, astounding him with its brightness, boldness and clarity. Gilmour adjusted his vision to the new technology, reciting the holographic layout he had memorized the day before during their hasty training. Next to him, Constantine and McKean did the same, readying the hazard suits' systems for the phenomena they were about to experience.

Marlane monitored the three HUDs on a screen along the circular bank of monitors. "Holographic interfaces functioning normally. All systems go."

"Specimens active," Waters reported. "Good for start-up."

"Excellent," de Lis said, before nodding to the trio a final time, giving them his approval.

Toggling a holographic green sphere on the interface, Gilmour activated his Casimir vacuum. He began counting along with the virtual chronometer, all the while holding his breath and praying that he wouldn't be blown to subatomic nuclei.

Waters' and Roget's monitors displayed the three pairs of Casimir plates and the jewels suspended between them, as well as the proton spin rate of the individual chronometers manufactured into each Casimir device, which would allow—in theory—the agents to select the particular era for any mission objective.

Gilmour tapped his Casimir plate controls, closing the gap between the plates to within several micrometers, consequently decreasing the zero-point particle field strength to negative ten millielectronvolts.

A black mass now consumed each monitor, raising the heartbeats and voices of Marlane and the assembled scientists.

"Negative twelve millielectronvolts," Waters read out, her gaze alternating between the monitor bank and watching the final seconds of the agents' presence.

"Systems nominal," Marlane confirmed again.

Dark Horse turned to de Lis, a smile barely carved out of the lieutenant colonel's stern face.

"Come on, do it," de Lis repeated over and over to himself. His face was flush, with his collar and tie abysmally tight once more, but too transfixed in the drama to relieve the stranglehold.

"Negative fifteen millielectronvolts."

A tiny bead of perspiration, too small to roll down his nose without force, tickled Gilmour's skin, causing him to shake his head. Refocusing his eyes, the last image retained by his retinas read "-32 meV." His ears heard a muffled buzz before—

De Lis stepped back from the trio; their chests were now emblazoned with widening spheres of pure energy, electromagnetic siphons curving light—and this time, matter—around their respective cores. Within a microsecond the four limbs of each man were pulled inside the optical holes, leaving nothing save the dreadfully familiar sucking echo of air to fill the vacated space.

"Contact...lost."

## CHAPTER EIGHTEEN

All that was...all that could be done...all that is....

Quanta flowed, a river in the spacetime ocean, beckoning at the omnipresence of gravity, the evacuation of quintessence, the unknown of the mind, the depths of the soul...a particle, a drop in the splash that was the membrane of the universe, a vibrating fabric woven with infinite strings stretched taut over incalculable eras, spaces and memories, times that had been imagined, dreams that had been lived.

Together, they were one, innumerable, unfathomable, indistinguishable, borne apart, a stew of species of scintilla, God's DNA, the genome of the multiple universes, oneness.

The city had changed much before his day; the people...their numbers astounded him, forcing him to remember that at one time, his city of birth was a thriving second capital, not a sparsely populated, commuter's destination. But much had shifted since then, many had fled, many had perished. He couldn't begin to ask why it had happened....

Lighting a rolled cigarette, he hoisted his gear onto his shoulders and boarded the train, melding with the mass, becoming a mere drop in the sea. Odors of poverty, despair, even prosperity in some, yes, reminded him of home, telling him through the ages that not much really changed here, just the shadows in charge. Despite this, he was vigilant not to reveal himself, not to betray his differences. Times change, languages permutate, he thought. Even the threads he had buttoned up this very morning had to capture the flavor of the old country; nothing could be allowed to expose him for what he truly was. Because on this day, in this era, all the loyalties to his home country could not save him if he mis-stepped before the wrong person.

Deep sea water broke over the stem of the *Marinochka* as the trawler headed into the North Pacific under the stars of the October midnight. Darkness gave the ship and its trailing sister vessel, the *Amiliji*, security from roving Japanese cruisers, intent on protecting the sovereignty of their expanded empire of the sea. The journey to the edge of the continental shelf had taken seven days, several more than usual, in order to pass cleanly around the declared Japanese territorial limits, avoiding any conflicts between the uneasy goodwill of the mightiest two nations of Asia, won only by a brutal war thirty years before.

Nicolenko found the *Marinochka's* corridors cramped, forcing himself to remember the circumstances of this time. Materials were scarce for the war effort; modern techniques for manufacturing steel composites and lighter weight, non-corrosive materials had yet to be formulated, necessitating the need for rationing. His eyes studied the rust stains smearing the cabin's walls, and he wondered how his people ever emerged victorious in this war.

Despite this, he knew this vessel was perfect for recovering what was sitting on the ocean bed, waiting for him to claim it. Alone in his quarters, Nicolenko pored over the hard copy prepared for him of the craft's remains, its exact dimensions, and what to look for once the *Marinochka* had arrived over the site. All he had left to do was lie in wait until the vessel had reached the prearranged coordinates.

By the next morning, the *Amiliji* had caught up with the *Marinochka*, allowing the two sisters to proceed on to the undersea trench together. Nicolenko had risen early, as his custom, and walked the upper deck of the ship, breathing in the Pacific air, hoping the atmosphere lent him some sense of what it held many meters below. *Marinochka's* captain, Krasnowsky, ordered the vessel to lower anchor, parking the ship near the mysterious trench and its secret inhabitant.

Nicolenko crossed over to the bridge in anticipation of the lowering of the cargo nets overboard. Inside, officers and crewmen hustled to their respective stations, barking out commands while they set to work. Krasnowsky turned to one of his officers before acknowledging Nicolenko's presence. "These depths are more than this ship is accustomed to, but we won't have problems bringing up your loads."

"See to it that you don't. The Navy has invested much into this retrieval process. The Japanese aren't easy to dissuade from our borders."

"Yes, sir." The captain gestured to his men, and a verbal response signaled that the lowering of the nets had proceeded.

Throughout the bridge the strains of the motor lowering the nets could be heard. Nicolenko counted the seconds, then minutes, away, while the weighted nets sank to the bottom of the ocean shelf. His heart drummed against his ribcage; maintaining his composure during this perilous leg of the operation proved quite difficult, even for his seasoned mind.

A buzzer on a station board sounded, reporting that the nets had descended to their fullest depth, ending Nicolenko's growing anxiety.

"Retrieve anchor," Krasnowsky commanded, "ahead two knots."

Unmoored, *Marinochka* trotted ahead, allowing the unfurled nets to scour the ocean floor as thoroughly as possible and dredge up the remnants of the newly grounded craft on the edge of the teetering slope.

Nicolenko left the serenity of the bridge to observe the ocean water pouring through the lowered booms, hoping to see any remnants of the crash return to the surface, but better yet, willing the remains into the nets. He paced from portside of the vessel to starboard, running contingencies through his mind and hoping the calculated mass of the debris was the correct figure, and not orders below or above. Everything had to be right; he had to be efficient and not arouse suspicions. Above all else, he couldn't fail. There was nothing else.

Periodic reports throughout the afternoon and night by the crew allowed Nicolenko to map the *Marinochka*'s route onto his hard copy, giving him an exact catalog of their search so far, and what was found where. Krasnowsky, relying on the best judgment of his boom operators, estimated that over six old-style tons of material had been recovered in the nets, with more dredged every hour. Behind the dredging ship was the *Amiliji*, tracking the *Marinochka*'s progress, and keeping an eye open for unwanted visitors. Paying for both trawlers had been expensive, but ultimately, Nicolenko hoped, having two would double his chances of returning home successful.

By morning, in conjunction with Nicolenko's rise, *Marinochka*'s first transit of the site had been completed. On the deck, the booms were hoisted into position, and with Krasnowsky's commands voiced, the operators began raising the nets. Orders were barked on the outer deck and the bridge, all ignored by Nicolenko, who steadfastly watched the nets appear from the water's surface, carrying in their taut mesh the hopes of his once and future country.

Creaks and groans were the first sensations Nicolenko heard and felt during the nets' rise, followed by the out rushing of seawater back to the murk. Straining his eyes, Nicolenko discerned metallic debris heaped into piles, caged together like such refuse. The booms were directed over the *Marinochka*'s holding bay and methodically lowered down, where the nets would soon be emptied of their cargo.

Nicolenko exited the outer deck and descended to the holding bay, where the stench from years of use and disregard for cleansing slammed into his lungs, eliciting a dry cough before he covered his nostrils and mouth. Metal debris coupled with seawater fell to the bay's floor, creating a tremendous scattering of sound, deafening Nicolenko with successive pressure waves. Gritting his teeth, he crossed over to the mounting pile, careful to maintain a safe distance from the nets, which still expelled their mysterious cargo on the floor.

Crouching down and extending his arm, he picked up a fallen bar. Thin glints of light from the holding bay's open doors rained down from above, allowing Nicolenko to study the artifact closely. Scoring on the debris limited the level of naked-eye examination, but Nicolenko's other senses provided enough information to satisfy his innate curiosity, regardless of his own lack of scientific training. He wielded the piece with ease, not at all expecting its lightness; the alloy must have been of some supercarbonic composition, perhaps a variation of the modern day industrial fullerene composites, capable of binding with standard steel metals in a sort of jacket. Again, his ignorance lent him no further clues, but he understood this to not be of earthly origins; it just didn't feel right. Long ago he had trained himself to rely on instinct in the field; this was one of those times.

The nets soon retreated to the upper deck of the ship, leaving him alone but for a few moments, until the crewmen were sure to arrive for inspection. Clambering into the stack of soaking debris, Nicolenko began a cursory search for his primary objective, his hands rifling among the metallic shards.

"You got here fast."

Nicolenko rose to his feet and stepped back to the foot of the ladder, where the shadowed form of Krasnowsky now descended.

"This is just the first wave? When do we get more?" Nicolenko asked, deflecting the captain's attention away from his scrabbling.

"We're starting the cross salvage now."

"Excellent."

Krasnowsky surveyed the debris pile. "Need any help down here? My men are really good at salv—"

"No," Nicolenko said, waving his arm. "Classified material. My administrators would be most unpleasant if I enlisted the aid of your crew beyond the dredging operations."

"All right. Wars and crises aren't good times for making the Party mad, right?" The captain let out a faint, exhausted laugh.

Nicolenko nodded. "If you will excuse me."

Krasnowsky laid his hands on the rusted ladderbars. Pulling his tired body back to the upper deck, he struggled to accept his position in the greater scheme of the war efforts, and of the motherland. Matters changed so fast anymore, leaving the skipper to abide by archaic regulations, altered shipping lanes, and most indignantly, allowing Moscow to run his way of life, nearly eliminating his family's sole means of support. He just prayed this latest trawl—so near Japanese territory—wouldn't be his last.

Once the captain had finished his ascent, Nicolenko locked the cargo doors from the inside, ensuring his security. He produced a well-hidden holobook from his uniform and a folded specimen bag. Opening the bag, he set it down at his feet and booted up the holobook, beginning the covert search for the objects—those strange, enigmatic jewels he'd first seen in Yakutia.

It would be a long night.

# CHAPTER NINETEEN

"Do you know how difficult it'll be for me to take you all the way out into the North Pacific?" Captain Stanley Clayton asked before flicking a spent cigarette onto the concrete floor, then stubbing it out with the sole of his shoe. The trawler skipper, many sizes larger than the man next to him, produced a small, battered book from his back pocket.

"This says I can't go nowhere near the Nips. Who do you think I'm gonna listen to, the government—which has told me that they'll revoke my license if I disregard these regulations, or you, saying you'll pay me on delivery?"

"I realize the extent of my request, but allow me to assure you that I am good for any price...just name it," Gilmour asserted.

Clayton tugged at his jaw stubble. "One thousand, in US gold certificates. Our Canadian is more worthless than theirs." He lit another cigarette. "And no less."

"No less," Gilmour agreed, nodding. "And payment before embarking." After risking his life to jaunt this far forward, he wasn't about to let this portly fisherman end his mission before leaving the Canadian coast.

This time, Clayton nodded. He then left Gilmour to attend to his gear, which he had set down at the front door of the Skippsen Marina's office. Back in his possession, Gilmour took out a stack of bills and counted out the required deposit. The sequence of bills were molecular copies of original documents Valagua had recreated for this mission, eliminating the need to counterfeit contemporary currency during the mission.

Hoisting his bag over his shoulder once more, Gilmour headed for the marina itself, where the skipper's trawler awaited him. He located the small vessel, its name, *Bradana*, painted along its hull. Stepping onto its quarterdeck, he found himself not the least bit intimidated, unlike his previous stint aboard the *Hesperus*, which now seemed a lifetime ago.

Several men came up from below decks hauling equipment to the top level, presumably readying the ship for another voyage. The men—really boys, under closer inspection—ignored the stranger, except for one, wearing a brown beard and black, navy cap.

"You Gilmour?"

"I am."

The man threw a thumb behind his back. "Clayton wants you below deck. Bring your pay, and don't bother renegotiating once you're down there. We've all got families, we need that money."

Without uttering another word, the bearded man walked past Gilmour, giving him the distinct impression that his money was welcome, but Gilmour was not. Whatever the case, Gilmour needed this crew, despite their individual or collective misgivings towards him, and they needed him. They were embarking for the North Pacific; his payment to Clayton dictated no less from the men, and was more than generous enough, if he remembered the twentieth century's Depression-era economy correctly.

Vancouver Island bid the *Bradana* farewell that next morning, with unusual winds blowing back west to push the vessel into Johnstone Strait, then to Queen Charlotte Sound. Soon they would be sailing on to the Gulf of Alaska, where, closely following the Fiftieth Parallel, Clayton would over the course of several weeks navigate the *Bradana* to the Kuril-Kamchatka Trench. This deep gouge in the sea bordered the International Date Line, the scene of a tense, and private, little war the Soviets were waging with the expanding Japanese Empire; Clayton had heard enough stories that he had bought firearms for himself and a couple of his other crewmen before leaving port.

To make matters worse, the coming winter posed a mounting threat to the expedition; as the season progressed, the ocean waters would quietly freeze around them, threatening to seal them inside an ice floe if they veered too far north. Biting polar winds could be deadly, too, known to kill men less protected against the forces of nature.

Several brushes with the Japanese Navy over the course of the journey's first half were to be expected, even in far western American waters, but Clayton's expertise in dealing with the curious scouts, and his crew's status as Canadian fishermen, helped to dispel the Japanese from lingering, or better yet, boarding, uninvited. Seemingly surprising no one but Gilmour, one particular Japanese captain was more than helpful in guiding the ship to good fishing grounds, as he had been there many times as a young man, before the Navy had come calling.

Perhaps more intriguing to the crew was the absolute absence of the Soviets, whose waters they entered soon after their casual encounter with the Japanese. Complaints weren't to be heard, however; the less trouble encountered, the better. Clayton kept surveillance of the horizon constant, hoping to bypass any possible ships in the area. Radio scanning of all normal frequencies revealed distant murmurings in various Russian dialects, which the bearded man, who Clayton had earlier called Ghoukajian, translated for the crew. Positions of Soviet and Japanese civilian and naval ships were plotted by the navigator, which Gilmour took into account while directing Clayton to the precise coordinates of the crash site.

Referring to his memorized coordinates, Gilmour pinpointed the crash site at about one hundred and fifty kilometers east of the Kuril Island chain, at the eastern edge of the Kuril-Kamchatka Trench, balanced on a precarious shelf. According to Pacific seismic records from the late twentieth century, that same trench shelf collapsed just months later, taking the crash remnants and whatever lay inside down to nearly five kilometers, much too deep for Gilmour to reach with 1940s diving and dredging technology. If he intended on retrieving this object's specimens, this year was the time to do it.

A furious rapping on Gilmour's quarters door roused him from his tiny bunk. Throwing on his shirt, the agent opened the door, revealing a silhouetted crewman.

"Mr Gilmour, you're needed on deck."

Gilmour detected a tremor running through the boy. He acknowledged the request, then followed the crewman into the corridor. Once the pair were on deck, Gilmour noticed the crew alive with activity, much more so than all the days and weeks beforehand. Around the radio were gathered Ghoukajian and Clayton, as well as the navigator, Andersson, and the radioman, Osipiak. Gilmour heard the distinctive Soviet radio traffic, but a particular voice piqued Ghoukajian's attention.

The agent crossed over to the hunched foursome, allowing his own admittedly rough translating skills to decode the Russian shorthand. His briefings in Russian were based on his own era's evolved dialect; despite this, he maintained a grasp on the syntax. From what he heard, it wasn't good.

Ghoukajian's dark eyes fixed upon Gilmour's; somehow, the

crewman knew Gilmour was following along with ease. For now, that overlooked fact didn't concern the man, just the translations he relayed to Clayton.

"Well, looks like your coordinates are garnering more attention than planned for," Clayton said. "Not only is the site occupied, two Soviet vessels are patrolling the trench area, Mr Gilmour."

Gilmour translated for himself just a moment before, giving him time to ponder just how the hell the Russians had discovered the crash site. Dark Horse and Valagua had assured them that the site would remain unknown well into their present century, two hundred years after the crash. What the hell was he going to do now? They couldn't just turn tail and run.

Clayton stood erect, his teeth grinding inside his stubbled jowls. A finger was quickly planted into Gilmour's breast. "What are we doing out here? You said nothing about the Soviets being involved."

Gilmour clenched his fists. "They weren't invited. Believe me, I don't want them here."

"Weren't not getting enough for this," Ghoukajian growled.

Gilmour pointed to the translator. "You're getting what your captain demanded. I didn't hear any complaints from you when we embarked...you all knew the danger."

"Keep your eyes on the horizon," Clayton ordered one of the crewmen at the forward window. He then turned to Andersson and asked, "How far are we from the trench?"

Andersson studied the large paper cartograph on the desk before him. Grabbing a pencil and compass, he recorded the measurement on the sheet. "Eleven miles, Captain."

Clayton folded his arms and peered out the forward window, his eyes scanning the blue horizon, as if he could actually see the Soviets from this distance. "Keep on course. These are still international waters, and we're not at war."

Gilmour nodded his satisfaction, but Ghoukajian turned his back on the men, fuming silently.

For now, the tiny ship continued sailing, its crew, save but one, unaware of the otherworldly treasure soon to be beneath their hull, if they made it there alive.

## CHAPTER TWENTY

"They're trawlers," Andersson announced, lowering the binoculars from his eyes. "Two fishing ships."

Osipiak looked at Clayton from the radio post. "Too much radio traffic to be normal trawlers. Something has aroused their curiosity."

The captain nodded. He turned to his secretive passenger, who continued to listen in on the radio conversation, as if he understood what the Soviets were saying; now just how was that possible? "What do you know, Gilmour? Did the Reds lose a ship? Is that why we're here?"

"I can't say for certain, sir. I have been commanded to bring cargo back as quietly as possible."

"Well," Clayton began, rising his bulk from his worn seat, "they're sure interested in your cargo. I doubt it's fish they're netting over there." He then shuffled over to Gilmour, employing his red face and stout body as a silent threat to the agent. A spent cigarette sputtered from his lips to the floor, and he exhaled the last puff of grey smoke into Gilmour's general direction. "Care to explain why I've endangered my crew to bring us here?"

Gilmour stood steadfast to the imposing man, not allowing Clayton's bullying posture to faze him. "I paid you your money, Clayton. That is the only explanation you require."

He grunted, realizing he wasn't going to get anything better from the icy man, then circled back to his chair.

Gilmour suppressed a burgeoning smile. "Besides, Clayton, you made sure to arm yourself. You're not worried those arms will fail, are you?"

At that, the three crewmen on the bridge locked eyes with their captain, now uncertain as to whether Clayton would actually endanger their lives with faulty weapons.

Clayton, in disbelief at the faces of the crewmen, pointed his finger at each of them and yelled, "Get back to work!" He stepped over to Gilmour again and whispered, "Don't ever question me in front of my crew. Ever."

"Don't question me either, Clayton," Gilmour replied sotto voce. "You'll live to regret it."

A rise in the volume level of the radio traffic brought the attentions of Clayton, Gilmour and Ghoukajian back to Osipiak's post. Excited Russian voices, now loud and rushed, filled the wooden walls of the *Bradana*'s bridge.

"Captain," Ghoukajian said, "the Soviets are visually inspecting the *Bradana*. They want to know what a Canadian trawler is doing all the way out here."

Clayton rubbed his chin, the prickly hairs poking at his fingertips, much as this voyage did to his soul. "Raise our friends the Russians...tell them we are here as fellow fisherman, led to this sea by the good grace of the Nipponese." And pray it succeeds, he thought.

"A Canadian trawler? Why wasn't I informed?"

The young crewman maneuvered his way to Nicolenko in the holding bay, hoping to avoid his death by slipping on the abundant debris and water. "The captain had to be certain, sir."

"Of all the damnable...." Nicolenko threw down the metal rod in his hand and picked up the sample bag at his feet, tossing it over his shoulder. "Tell Krasnowsky I wish to speak to him."

The stunned boy nodded but was cemented to the floor, still in awe of the mysterious man's cargo.

"Get out!" Nicolenko's index finger pierced the air, pointing to the ladder a few meters away.

After the boy had fled, Nicolenko took the concealed holobook from his pocket and placed it inside of his sample bag, which threatened to slide off his shoulder from the weight of the jewels. Redoubling his discipline, he plowed and grunted his way up the ladder, emerging from the darkness into the blue sky above.

Locking the sample bag into his quarters, Nicolenko headed for the bridge, whereupon reaching the top deck again, his eyes sighted the intruder vessel off starboard, less than a kilometer away. His jaws tightening, he flung open the bridge hatch and stepped inside.

"Have you responded?" Nicolenko asked Krasnowsky. Without

waiting for an answer, he hastily crossed over to the radioman.

Krasnowsky noticed the ire in Nicolenko's glare. "A standard hail—"

"Send the *Amiliji* to intercept it," the lieutenant commanded the radio operator, bucking Krasnowsky's authority.

"Belay that!" Krasnowsky jumped between Nicolenko and the radioman. "This is a civilian vessel...we have no authority here to block a foreign ship—"

Nicolenko jabbed his finger into the captain's chest. "Under the authority of the security forces, I am in command of this retrieval operation." He turned back to the operator. "Do as ordered."

"Yes, sir." The operator tuned the radio to a different channel, then spoke into the transmitter, ordering the *Amiliji* to change course and intercept the oncoming vessel.

The sister ship's radio operator acknowledged, and the bridge crew watched from the window as the smaller vessel steered to starboard and headed for the approaching trawler.

"The second trawler is doing an intercepting run," Andersson yelled, his back to Clayton. From his vantage, he could see the smaller of the pair circling around toward the *Bradana*.

Gilmour pushed his way past the crew. "Clayton, we can't allow them to block our access to the trench."

The captain froze, his head and heart unable to reach a decision.

"Clayton!" Gilmour grabbed the burly skipper's coat and jerked the man's attention back to him. "Clayton!"

Ghoukajian leapt up from the radio and headed for the vessel's controls. Behind him, Gilmour saw the bearded man commandeer the *Bradana*'s conn and attempt to reverse the trawler's course away from the coordinates. The agent ran over and tackled Ghoukajian, forcing the Armenian's head against the wooden instrument panel, splattering blood down his face and beard.

Ghoukajian elbowed Gilmour in the ribcage, causing the agent to release his grip. Collapsing on each other, the pair scuffled on the grimy floor before Gilmour landed a punch to Ghoukajian's jaw, stunning him. The agent managed to claw his way to his knees, then to his feet, his hands outstretched to the vessel's helm. Placing his fingers on the tiller, Gilmour's ears heard an unfamiliar click.

"Don't move, Mr Gilmour. Now, get away from my helm."

Gilmour shifted his head back a centimeter, just enough to feel a cold metal cylinder brush his ear. Releasing the helm, he walked backwards, seeing the revolver in Clayton's hand for the first time.

"Raise the approaching trawler," Clayton ordered Osipiak.

"Yes, sir." The boy sat down at the radio transmitter and tuned it to the corresponding channel. "Approaching vessel, this is the Canadian trawler *Bradana*."

"You're too late, Clayton," Gilmour said, spying the Soviet vessel circle around them outside.

Clayton's trembling hand reached for his forehead to wipe off the gathering perspiration. Clearing his throat, he ordered a second time, "Keep trying to raise them."

After a second attempt and subsequent silence, Osipiak shrugged. "I'm sorry, sir."

The *Bradana*'s hull then lurched to port, followed by a series of furious rappings against the quarterdeck. Footfalls and distinctly Russian voices soon echoed throughout the cabin, growing louder each second. "Congratulations, Clayton," Gilmour scoffed, "you've managed to get yourself boarded by the U of S-S-R."

The skipper waved his revolver hand in Gilmour's direction. "Close your mouth!"

Two meters aft of the bridge, the hatch burst open, easily admitting two men onto the floor. The first man, dressed in the simple attire of a fisherman, walked forward, bearing no threatening demeanor.

"Afternoon," he said in his best, approximate English. "Please...no resist."

Clayton, with his revolver still squarely at Gilmour, attempted a strained smile. "I am Captain Stanley Clayton, skipper of the *Bradana*. Do you understand?"

The Soviet pair exchanged glances, then the first man looked back to Clayton, nodding his head. "Nyet."

"We are passing through," Clayton explained, simplifying his speech as though talking to a child. "We are leaving now."

The two studied Clayton, their glances shifting from his blood-shot eyes to the revolver in his outstretched arm. Clayton, noticing this, tried to hide the weapon by resting his arm at his side.

Terse words were uttered by the second Soviet, who inexplicably left his friend alone and walked back up to the quarterdeck. Clayton and Gilmour heard a flurry of Russian spoken between the man and another on the boarding vessel, but spoken too quickly and distantly for Gilmour to translate in his head.

"Put that damn revolver away," Gilmour hissed, "or you're going to be the recipient of a cold Russian goodbye."

Clayton ignored Gilmour's advice, instead saying to the Soviet, "We are simple fishermen, here for the season."

The Soviet furrowed his brow, not comprehending Clayton's repeated pleas of innocence.

"Allow me," Gilmour interjected. Pausing to put his speaking skills in a Russian frame of mind, he asked, "Why are you here? We are trawling for fish. We were informed these are excellent grounds."

"Fishing?" he responded. "The man has a revolver to you, and there's a man passed out in front of you. What sort of game is this? Why are you in our seas?"

"We had a misunderstanding. An argument, that is all. Please, leave us be. We would very much like to trawl these waters—"

The Soviet waved his hand, stopping Gilmour in mid-thought. "My supervisor will make that decision. I am just here under his order."

"Is he a just man, your captain?"

He paused, rolling his eyes in thought, then continued, "My captain, yes. But I am not under his orders. The supervisor, however, is a private man. I have not known him for long. A week, in fact."

Odd, his supervisor and captain were two different men. What was going on? "Then perhaps I may persuade him."

The Soviet nodded his head. "Perhaps. He will be here before long."

Hearing a diesel engine powering up, Gilmour looked out the window to see the boarding vessel crawling back to the larger trawler. Within a few minutes, the second vessel had parked next to the larger ship and then circled back around to head for the *Bradana* again.

His brow perspiring as each moment passed, Gilmour recalled the exact location of his equipment in his cabin, the jaunt procedures, and most importantly, the E4.10c strapped snugly beneath his left trouserleg, with enough rounds to take out the crews of two trawlers, one per man.

Nicolenko walked out into the fading afternoon, adjusting his wool jacket to the decreasing temperatures on the deck of the *Amiliji*. His nose recognized the pungent odor of diesel exhaust, returning him to his days as a youth in the old city. Scanning the horizon, his eyes met the Canadian trawler growing closer, the brine wind forcing him to wipe moisture from his tear ducts. The mystery of the trawler's appearance at the exact time of his retrieval operation goaded him along, despite his inner reluctance to expand the length of time he spent in this era. But a good officer never questioned his training and experience, he just smoked sweet tobacco to forget his troubles. Too bad he had run out of that on the journey here. Nicolenko laughed silently; what did that say about him?

Slowing their orbit about the Canadian trawler, the *Amiliji* pulled to within five meters, allowing Nicolenko to study the ship's exterior, even to discern the interior of the bridge. Krasnowsky had ordered *Amiliji*'s engines cut and, per Nicolenko's command, sent two crewmen to board the Canadian trawler. An inflatable boat was unfolded and tossed into the water by the men, with two of them climbing down a rope ladder into it, followed by Nicolenko himself. The men paddled Nicolenko over to the trawler, and a moment later, all three were aboard the upper deck, heading for the bridge hatch.

Even before lowering himself onto the bridge, Nicolenko could detect the mildew and rust permeating this ship's hull, stenches he fought by taking small gulps of air through his mouth. Pausing as the men opened the hatch, he gritted his teeth, wanting nothing more but to get this mission over with.

Five men, one obscenely large, greeted Nicolenko's eyes. As the lone remaining fisherman relayed the trawler's status to the lieutenant, Nicolenko studied the central hull of the ship, the comatose man on the floor, and most importantly, the intriguing stranger standing over the comatose man, scouring Nicolenko with his own stare.

Nicolenko nodded once the man had finished his scattered report; his lack of efficiency definitely marked him a civilian...he wouldn't stand a minute under Nicolenko's interrogation. His ancestors weren't really this soft back then, were they?

Waving his men forward, Nicolenko gestured to the Canadians. "Clear them out."

As the men came forth for the Canadians, the lieutenant laid a hand on the lead Soviet fisherman and said, pointing to Gilmour, "All but that one. Let me speak with him. Alone."

"What the hell are you doing?" Clayton yelled. "What the hell are you doing!"

The two Soviet fishermen went over to Clayton, only to be stopped by the lead Soviet fisherman announcing that Clayton concealed a revolver in his right hand, behind his back. The two men backed off, stepping back behind Nicolenko.

Scowling at the stupid man's omission, Nicolenko drew his own pistol and aimed it at Clayton; he'd deal with the Soviet later. "Surrender your sidearm. Now."

Clayton's head bobbed back and forth from Nicolenko's pistol to

Gilmour. "What the hell is he saying? What the hell is he talking about!"

"He said to surrender your weapon, Clayton, just like I warned you. Do it, you fool!"

"But my ship! My money—"

"You'll be dead!"

A whimper sounded from deep within his jowls. The captain's hand crept around from his flank, and with a slight toss, the revolver tumbled to the floor below, centimeters from Nicolenko's feet. Taking their captain's lead, the other crewmen dropped their revolvers as well.

Nicolenko nodded, and the two men again made their way to Clayton, Andersson, Osipiak and the unconscious Ghoukajian, leading them out one by one, then carrying the bleeding Ghoukajian back to the *Amiliji*.

"You...you speak Russian well. Who are you?"

"Just a simple crewmen, sir." Gilmour had scrutinized the man's face, uniform and boots throughout the confrontation with Clayton; he was too neat, too pristine for previous field service of any length. A raw recruit, perhaps? No, his handling of the situation was a prime example of a man with considerable experience. Gilmour's gut felt a presence beyond the visual with this soldier.

Nicolenko beckoned him forward with a wave of his hand. "Come with me."

"Am I a prisoner of war?"

Nicolenko smiled. "I didn't realize we were at war with Canada."

Gilmour didn't return the smile. "This is a trawler. Why have you evacuated our crew from this ship? We are here on a long voyage—"

"Your grasping of my language is impressive. I am not convinced you are a fisherman, let alone a member of this crew."

"Then you are welcome to check our cargo holds. We have nothing to hide."

Nicolenko nodded. "We will. But first, we have a mission to complete. You are welcome to rejoin your crew on my ship, the *Amiliji*."

"I would prefer to stay on my own vessel."

He waved a dismissive finger. "I am sorry, but that is not possible, at least yet. Please, come with me." Nicolenko laid hands on the agent's chest and torso, patting and smoothing down his clothes, searching for concealed weapons. "We have much to offer while we conduct our research," he continued, his hands roaming down Gilmour's trouserlegs.

Gilmour's breathing quickened as the Russian crept closer to his E4.10c. He hiccuped suddenly, distracting Nicolenko enough to make eye contact.

Satisfied, Nicolenko stood eye-to-eye with the agent again. "You can have clean quarters," he paused to inhale more stale air, then continued, "and a fresher environment."

Knowing he was going to lose no matter what, specifically with the man's finger on his trigger, Gilmour complied and headed for the hatch. "Tell me, sir," he said, passing Nicolenko without looking or stopping, "are all of the NKVD as accommodating as you appear to be?"

Nicolenko halted to consider carefully what this mysterious man was up to, and what the lieutenant was up against. "One does what one must. Survival is a pivotal factor in today's world."

Gilmour turned and then peered deeply into the Russian's cobalt eyes. Who was he? "Right you are. How right indeed."

"I must ask you this: Why are you interested in this part of the ocean? Why two ships?"

Gilmour and Nicolenko walked side by side as they entered the interior of the *Amiliji*. The agent noted the remarkable difference in his previous vessel and this one, which, while not an ocean liner, was of a magnitude better in condition and upkeep.

"I have sworn an oath to remain silent. Suffice it, these are our waters, and we do as we please."

"I understand." Gilmour followed the lieutenant around a corner, which led the pair to a tight corridor, lined with thin doors on either side. Surmising that the mysterious Russian was going to lock him in one of these rooms, he spoke, "May I lend you a hand? I do have some experience with trawling." It was perhaps the only way to discover what they were truly searching for out here, though he already had an idea.

Nicolenko stopped in mid-stride and narrowed his eyes as he looked at Gilmour. "What do you have to offer me that I don't already possess in this crew?"

"A fresh perspective." For the first time, Gilmour cracked a smile. He had piqued the Russian's interest, perhaps offsetting his judgment as well. Now was the time to jump at his only chance. "Experience. Most importantly, the will to work. The men you have aren't interested in trawling...they just want to be home. I can provide you with some much needed manpower, perhaps even opportunities that hadn't crossed your mind."

Nicolenko thought in silence for several seconds before he said, "I...I will think about it some more. For now—"

Gilmour's hand found Nicolenko's jacket sleeve. "I would seriously suggest you take my offer. The weather is only going to become worse, and the men are going to want to return to the coast." He hardened his grip. "We need each other."

Nicolenko contemplated the strange Canadian's—if he was at all Canadian—cryptic statement. "I will think it over. Please, come with me. Your quarters are waiting for you. I trust you will find them most enjoyable."

The lieutenant produced a key from his jacket pocket and unlocked the cabin door to his left. Opening it, Nicolenko led Gilmour inside, where a narrow bunk and no additional amenities greeted the agent.

"If I may request my baggage," Gilmour said before Nicolenko managed to lock him up, "I have essential medical needs, important to my health," he finished, lying in his most practiced manner.

Nicolenko nodded. "I will see what I can do."

"No." Gilmour grabbed Nicolenko's sleeve again, pulling him close. "I need it now."

Nicolenko ripped his jacket from Gilmour's hand and rose his revolver up to the agent's chest. "You will make no demands of me. I offer you nothing, just the chance to redeem your mistakes. I have no qualms about killing men."

Gilmour backed up a few paces, holding his arms out with palms skyward.

"Excellent choice. You are not a stupid man, contrary to my colleagues' opinions of Westerners." Nicolenko lowered his revolver, putting his captive in a state of less than ease, but not alarm. "I will mull over your suggestion. But I ask you to think of your future as well. Here, I hold control over every life on these two vessels. I recommend you think about telling me everything you know about this part of the sea, starting with your expedition to 'fish.' You have until I return."

Gilmour stood mute as the Russian slammed the cabin door shut and locked it from the outside, leaving the agent in solitary confinement.

"Shit."

# CHAPTER TWENTY-ONE

Gilmour's mind raced. Constructing, then tearing down, contingency plans in his brain, he balled his fists, not realizing until his cuticles bled that he had injured himself during his brawl with Ghoukajian. Despite the pain, he knew that bastard Soviet was right then salivating to get his hands on Gilmour's gear, find whatever treasures lay inside—the hazard suit and its jewels—and no doubt attempt to activate his holobook, which thankfully would evade his curiosity with an encryption lock.

The secrets buried inside the holobook didn't concern Gilmour; it was the hazard suit that consumed his thoughts. If the goddamned NKVD found some way to activate it, despite their lack of knowledge of its technology, then he may as well throw the operation, and himself, to the North Pacific depths. He just hoped the bastard was distracted before he could retrieve it from the *Bradana* with the rest of his goons.

"What's the problem? Why have we stopped?" Nicolenko yelled, his boots clacking as he dashed to the *Amiliji*'s bridge.

The smaller vessel's radio operator listened while the transmitter played a second broadcast from the *Marinochka*. Over the radio, the larger ship's radioman informed the crew that they had ceased dredging the trench shelf.

Nicolenko's eyes bulged with fury. He stepped over to the radioman. "Tell them I am ordering them to continue with the dredging procedure. I do not care what they insist. They will finish their duty!"

"But, sir," the radio operator insisted, "we're intercepting storm warnings from Vladivostok. Potential late season typhoon in the ocean."

"All the more reason to continue!"

Furrowing his brow, the youth nodded his head slowly, more out of fear of what Nicolenko was capable of doing to him then authority.

The insolence of those men; Nicolenko would not hesitate to punish them once he returned to the *Marinochka*. Every fiber and nerve in him cried out to ravage the fools for disobeying his authority. How could they wantonly disregard the power of a representative of the NKV—

Nicolenko stepped away from the bridge; he had to get out, get to the corridor, breathe. His trembling hand reached for the taut skin of his forehead, where he wiped off droplets of perspiration his anger had invoked. He chided himself for his mental outburst...he was not NKVD, he was not the persona he had assumed to bring these men out to sea. He was so exhausted. Rest had eluded him, his duty had consumed him; now, deep inside his soul, he feared the spectre of this war of nations, this Great Patriotic War his ancestors had called it, was destroying him, tearing apart his mind, his body. What times these were...how he longed to finish this mission and leave forever...damn Zaryov, the siloviki and their ways.

Once this mission was over, once the Americans had been defeated, never again was he going to do their bidding...to hell with duty.

Krasnowsky peered at the horizon through his binoculars, scanning the darkening sky for signs of this weather system the coast had been warning every ship about for the last few minutes. This was a fine time for his two ships to be caught dredging up these damned heavy materials. The captain wondered what kind of fool he was to continue honoring Nicolenko and the NKVD, despite their ruthless agenda.

He inhaled heavily on his cigarette, not noticing or caring about their short supply, just that they took his mind off his worries, if for a few moments. Krasnowsky sighed; he turned to his crew. "Bring up the nets. We're not doing any more dredging tonight."

His crewmen seconded their skipper's orders, happy to oblige staying inside their cabins this evening.

"Keep me apprised of the weather reports. If things look worse, we're setting home."

"Yes, Captain," the radioman acknowledged, more than willing to listen for any inclement report, no matter how distant or sketchy, that could have them heading back to port.

Krasnowsky sat down in his seat; what was taking Nicolenko so long to get back? Surely the Canadian fishermen couldn't have been putting up too much resistance.

A clatter to the aft bridge heralded Nicolenko's return moments later. Unbuttoning his overcoat, the lieutenant walked past the crewmen to the forward window, uttering nothing. His eyes searched the blue horizon for several quiet minutes, oblivious or outright ignoring Krasnowsky's repeated questions.

Finally, the lieutenant broke his gaze from the glass. "The sea appears peaceful...I see no reason to stop now."

"Have you lost your mind? There's a storm warning. I can't risk losing my equipment because of your secret dredging operation. One gust and I'm—"

Nicolenko swiveled on his heels, putting his face within centimeters of Krasnowsky and his cigarette stub. "I am not concerned about your livelihood, Captain. I have one priority here: completing the dredging of the shelf."

Krasnowsky clinched his teeth. "You're a bastard."

The *Marinochka* crew dropped their jaws, pausing at their posts to stare at the two; they were all sure Krasnowsky's unflinching insult would provoke a swift reprimand.

"I have a mission to finish," Nicolenko continued, brushing off the captain's curse like water down a duck's back. "Give your men the evening off. After the storm breaks, I expect them all to return to the nets to finish their commission. And nothing less."

The captain inhaled one last drag from his cigarette before taking it from his lips. He grudgingly nodded and cranked his head back to the surrounding crewmen. "Do as he says. We'll rise early to wait out the storm."

Nicolenko left Krasnowsky and his crew to seethe in private. He was certain he had solidified his status as an enemy of the crew, but he reminded himself sacrifices were sometimes essential for missions to come to fruition. And if it meant getting home sooner, he'd make the entire world his nemesis.

"All right, Gilmour, let's find a way to get the hell out of here." The agent shelved his troubles for the time being and focused on the locked door in front of him. Taking stock of every potential tool available to him, he forged several ideas on how to break himself out of the cabin.

One, there was the possibility of bedsprings inside the shallow mattress on the bunk. Ripping those out, he could fashion a crude lockpick. Second, anything capable of becoming a blade could help him cut his way through the wood-paneled door, although, on the other hand, he could waste two of his rounds popping the lock out of the frame, if he wanted to go the less surreptitious route.

Having had the opportunity to count heads once he had been taken aboard the *Amiliji*, Gilmour knew there were at most seven crewmen on board, enough for him to take out, or if at all possible, hold hostage long enough for him to retrieve both his hazard suit and whatever amount of the jewels the Soviets had dredged from the shelf. Doing so would be difficult—hell, probably impossible—but he didn't have the luxury of backup from Constantine or McKean. Although, if he so phrased it, Clayton and his crew might be enticed to join him in his little rebellion. Granted, the captain would have qualms about accompanying Gilmour in a potential shootout, but the gains would far outweigh whatever squeamishness the man possessed.

Unbuttoning his trousers, Gilmour reached into the left leg and found his E4.10c. After rebuttoning them, he double-checked the magazine in the pistol's hilt, memorizing the number of rounds he had to expend; it would do.

Stepping back a few paces until he was against the far wall, Gilmour crouched, steadied his left knee to the floor, and then sized up the pistol's barrel to the door lock at a zero-degree angle.

Two quick shots later, the doorlock fell to the floor, splinters following. Rising quickly, he ran for the door, steeling himself for the attention that was to come. Sure enough, he could hear a commotion on the bridge, what sounded like crewmen cursing and scrambling to investigate the gunfire in the corridor.

Gilmour hid himself just next to the entrance, the damaged door closed, with his E4.10c drawn and ready. The agent estimated the crewmen's closing distance by the volume and pitch of their voices and footfalls, which echoed well through the tiny vessel's hull.

The voices paused just on the other side of the wall. Gilmour heard heavy respiration as a hand brushed against the door, its frame bolts squeaking open to reveal a crewman peering inside, a torchbeam piercing the dark cabin.

Gilmour kept his timing, waiting for the optimum moment when the crewman had begun to step inside. At once, Gilmour pounced, cracking the butt of his pistol against the man's head, felling him cleanly to the floor. Another crewman was still out there, but upon seeing Gilmour he fled back to the bridge, screaming madly in Russian about the maniac on board.

Gilmour retrieved the fallen man's torch and followed the second crewman to the bridge. At the entrance, Gilmour tried the closed door with his free hand, rattling it hard. Someone must have locked it just seconds before, sealing the only way in or out. The crew had cordoned Gilmour off from the vessel's controls, but most importantly, prevented themselves from meeting the same fate as the crewman a few seconds ago.

He thought about shooting the lock off, but realized a better tactic could open the metal door; Clayton and his men. Gilmour returned down the corridor and pounded his fist on each of the doors, listening for pleas of help, which weren't hard to find.

"Who's in there?" Gilmour said near the door. "Clayton? Where are you?"

A monstrous banging on the cabin to his right answered his question. Crossing over to it, he yelled, "Clayton?"

A muffled "Get us the hell out of here!" came from inside; Gilmour could recognize the man's unrestrained voice anywhere.

"Stand back! Everybody, stand away from the door!"

Bracing his E4.10c in his hands, Gilmour fired at the doorlock twice, rendering the wood to pulp. One swift kick of his foot released the skipper, Andersson and Osipiak from the cabin, all three of whom tumbled over themselves to get out.

Clayton looked over the agent's twenty-second-century piece. "Where the hell did you get that?"

Gilmour didn't answer, instead switching Clayton's focus to the locked bridge. "If you want to get off this ship and back to the *Bradana*, we'll need to get in there," he said, pointing to the door. "Problem is, it's locked, and they've got at least six men in there holed up."

Clayton folded his arms; a miraculous feat to Gilmour's eyes. "I see. So, you want my crew to help you raid their bridge, huh?"

"Why else free you?"

The skipper pursed his lips, not thinking of a quick enough comeback. "Get my other men out of their cages, and we'll get that bridge back."

Gilmour nodded once, then gestured for the three to step away. Once again, a pair of rounds took out the lock, and two more men, each supporting the comatose Ghoukajian, exited the cabin.

Clayton relayed Gilmour's plan to the newly freed men, one of whom would stay behind the raid to watch over the injured Armenian. Once the details had been sorted through, Gilmour and Clayton led the way to the bridge door, Gilmour sizing up the lock carefully before proceeding.

"This one will be a little bit trickier," he told Clayton, pointing out the metal panel that served as the door. Simple wood was by far easier to blow apart, but metal required a savvier hand. Then, the idea sprang to Gilmour. "Who here has experience as a lockpick?"

The men, all of whom had not served for long under Clayton, looked at each other, unsure who possessed what skills, or how superior they were. Finally, Clayton pointed to one of the youths.

"Samuels can do it."

Gilmour glanced to the boy—the same timid youth who had roused him out of his bunk his first night on the *Bradana*—almost asking him by his eyes alone.

Samuels nodded. "I can...I served some time. Got pretty good at it—"

Gilmour waved his hand; no explanation was necessary—everybody had a past. "All right. Pull out whatever amount of springs you need from the bunks. Make it fast!"

The boy nodded and was off down the corridor. A moment later, he returned with a length of wire he was already fashioning into a lockpick. Gilmour created room, and Samuels went to work on the lock.

A minute later, after some difficulty with his ersatz pick, Samuels unbolted the door. Pushing his way to the point, Gilmour monitored the still closed door, careful to keep their presence quiet. Raising three fingers, he counted down three seconds. On the last signal, the men rose up and burst through the door, Gilmour's E4.10c leading the way.

"Everybody stand down!" he yelled in Russian. "Drop your weapons!"

The six crewmen, startled by Gilmour's blitz, backed themselves against the bridge walls, uncertain what to do next.

"Drop your weapons! Get your arms in the air!"

Small pocket knives and a couple of hammers went clanging to the floor, bringing laughter to Gilmour and the *Bradana* crew. So much for sidearms, Gilmour told himself, but probably all for the better.

With his E4.10c, Gilmour directed the Soviet crewmen to one corner of the bridge. "Everyone over there! Samuels, keep an eye on them."

The youth nodded before rounding up the six crewmen, utilizing one of the surrendered knives to keep the men under control.

Gilmour and Clayton crossed to the helm, studying the Cyrillic marks on the controls.

"Can you read Russian?" Gilmour asked the skipper.

"No. But I can pilot a boat...navigation is really universal."

Gilmour clapped Clayton's shoulder. "Good." His eyes scoured the ocean for the *Bradana*, and upon finding her, pointed to Clayton. "Just get us back to your boat."

Gilmour braced himself against the *Amiliji*'s metal deck as one more high wave crashed onto the ship's hull. He looked out over the darkness of the sea, trying to fathom out what the disturbance was. "What's going on out there?"

"Judging by the chop, I'd say we're in for a storm...maybe a typhoon," Clayton guessed.

"Damn...." Gilmour saw the *Bradana* venture past the Soviet trawler's forward window. "How much longer?"

"About five minutes...maybe longer. It's difficult enough to steer in this mess when in port. Try at sea."

Gilmour clenched his teeth; it was about all he could do while waiting to get back to the *Bradana* and find out the fate of his hazard suit. If there was so much as a fingerprint on the suit's exterior, he'd hunt down that NKVD goon and—

"Shit!"

Looking over to Clayton, Gilmour witnessed the captain struggle with the tiller until it was wrenched from his control, spinning wildly. Both men's hands went for its grips to calm the ship's steering before a massive vibration rippled through the *Amiliji*'s hull, followed by a horrendous din of metal grinding against metal.

The *Amiliji* jolted and pitched to port, sending both crews screaming and toppling to the deck floor. Gilmour landed next to Clayton and one of the Soviet crewman, all three in a daze and unsure what the hell went wrong.

Once the ship had slowly evened itself out, the men climbed back to their feet and went to the windows. Roiling green water, illuminated by their deck lighting, was the only thing in sight.

"We must have collided with the *Bradana*," Clayton said, his voice cracking with fear.

"Are you sure?" Gilmour asked.

"Well something happened!" Andersson shouted.

Gilmour tucked his E4.10c away and lowered his hands, trying to ease already heightened tensions. "All right, everyone calm down. We need to find out what condition the *Bradana* is in...a couple of men to go on deck and try to spot her. I'm volunteering to go. Anyone else?"

"I'll go," Samuels spoke up.

"All right, okay." Gilmour turned to Clayton. "See what you can do about assessing damage to this ship. We should attempt a boarding pass regardless of the *Bradana*'s condition."

Clayton nodded, but with a caveat. "If either one of these boats are damaged enough to take on water, we don't have but less than an hour to sink."

"I'll keep that in mind." Gilmour looked to Samuels. "Come on."

The pair made it to the upper deck with little difficulty, thankful that no large waves came over the top to snatch them into the dark, frozen sea below. Continual spray quickly rendered both men's coats and trousers wet, giving them almost no defense from the bluster of the evening wind.

Gilmour flashed his torch across the wide expanse, catching no more than high crests and water droplets. Next to him, Samuels caught sight of a dark patch in the water, which the crewman directed to the agent's attention with an outstretched finger. Gilmour sent the torch-beam further starboard stern, soon picking up the glint of *Bradana*'s rusted hull. Tracing the beam down the vessel's flank, a series of cracks made themselves briefly visible before being reclaimed by the sea crash.

"We hit her pretty bad," Samuels proclaimed. "I'd say she won't make it until morning."

Gilmour took a breather from torch duty. "If the *Bradana* is that bad, what about us?"

"Hard to know. Seen bigger ships go down with hairline fractures you'd thing wouldn't drown a dinghy. Seen smaller trawlers haul back to port with entire flanks wiped clean. The sea's a fickle mistress."

Gilmour nodded, not so much from experience, but life in general. "Think we can cross the eight meters in one of the inflatables?"

"Only if you want to meet the creator sooner than most," Samuels said, remembering the questionable construction of the rafts with which the Soviets had evacuated him off the *Bradana*. "What's so important to you? Why risk your life to go back?"

Gilmour wiped his face of seaspray. "If I don't go back, there won't be a world left for either one of us to go home to."

Samuels squinted; what did that mean?

"Come on, help me find an inflatable." With that, Gilmour left the deck's railing and headed for the vessel's central platform.

The pair fought the storm all the way to the exterior closet where the four inflatable craft were hastily thrown in after the *Bradana*'s evacuation. Gilmour grabbed the top raft, a pair of paddles, and a pair of rope bundles, then ordered Samuels to grab a second inflatable in the event their primary sprung a leak midway through their excursion.

With Samuels' help, Gilmour found the *Amiliji*'s exterior descending ladder. He tied the first length of rope to one end of the inflatable, then tossed the raft into the sea, which quickly blossomed into its full length. Descending the ladder, Gilmour tied the opposite length of the rope to the bottom rung, using the rope to anchor the raft during Samuels' following descent. Once both men were safely aboard, Gilmour let the raft end of the rope loose, giving the ocean control of the slackened hemp.

Handing Samuels his paddle and the second rope bundle, Gilmour and the youth began the extraordinary challenge of rowing to the injured trawler, which now seemed five times as far. Samuels had taken the lead position at the fore of the raft, deeming himself the better of the pair to lead them with his superior skills and experience. Following every instruction to the letter that Samuels gave him, Gilmour poured his strength into the task, coordinating his rowing rhythm with his partner, which would, they hoped, get them to the *Bradana* safer and faster. Getting to the damaged and adrift vessel took all of Gilmour's strength; fighting the sea and its crosswinds forced his body to perspire much more than he thought healthy, and he realized his body wasn't replenishing the heat it was expended. If they didn't reach the ship before long, Gilmour was going to end up at the bottom of a vicious cycle, a mass of frozen and congealed tissues.

"Gilmour," Samuels said, "quit rowing. We've reached the *Bradana*."

Gilmour looked up to see the rusted hull of the trawler looming over the inflatable. He had been too concerned with preserving every ounce of energy to heed the approaching vessel.

After some quick instructions to Gilmour, the pair acquired the proper angle to board the ship. Once next to the vessel, Samuels produced the second length of rope and tied it around the raft and the lowest rung of the trawler's descending ladder. The pair ascended with haste, Gilmour particularly so, and headed for the interior cabins, minding the ship's swaying decks.

Finally inside, Gilmour rubbed his palms together and blew on them, trying to restore heat to his deprived body.

"What is it that you need? Where is it?" Samuels asked after securing the door against the rampaging winds.

Racing down the corridor, Gilmour blurted out a curt "Wait here."

"Gilmour," Samuels said again, straining to see down the darkened path.

The agent had already opened the cabin door to his former quarters once the sound of Samuels' voice echoed throughout the *Bradana*'s empty hull. Flicking on his torch, Gilmour shined the yellow beam over the deck floor, scouring the cabin for his abandoned gear. He dropped to his knees and crawled about, running his hands in wide, circular swaths. No doubt the repeated pitching of the *Bradana* in the storm had shifted the equipment several times since Gilmour left hours ago, forcing him to look about the entire cabin.

Another wave smashed against the *Bradana*'s hull, throwing Gilmour across the cabin and slamming him to a wall. His torch yanked from his hand during the toss, Gilmour rose to his feet without illumination. Taking a step, his foot tripped over a dark object, nearly felling him once more. Gilmour crouched down, his fingers clasping a leather strap; he had his quarry.

The agent burst out of the cabin. "Samuels! Let's get the hell out of here!"

# CHAPTER TWENTY-TWO

Gilmour and Samuels breathed heavily upon entering the *Amiliji*'s bridge, just minutes short of encountering several cresting, six-meter-tall waves. The battered trawlers now yawed, pitched and rolled amidst the angry ocean, cutting out power to the countermanded *Amiliji*.

Clayton turned away from the window to see the returning men. "Christ, I'd never thought I'd see you two again."

Gilmour passed the astounded captain and peered out the forward window, putting his hands up to block out his reflection.

"How's my ship? Is she done?"

"Damage is extensive, from what we could see," Gilmour said, not turning away. "How is this ship?"

"She'll stay buoyant enough to get back to the shore...but I don't want to push that."

Gilmour picked up the binoculars next to him and scoped out the horizon, specifically the lit vessel off their bow.

"Any contact from the other ship?"

Clayton frowned. "No, should there be?"

The agent pointed to the idle *Marinochka*. "They're responsible for this...Clayton, radio over to them."

"What?"

"Radio them," Gilmour reiterated, "or hail them. I intend to make sure they're aware we're countermanding this vessel."

"What good would that do? We're in no condition to resist them again if they board."

"You've forgotten," Gilmour said, looking to the captured Soviet crew, "we have this crew as potential hostages. They'll be willing to negotiate, believe me."

Clayton nodded, conceding to him on this point. "Then what do we do after that?"

Gilmour finally turned back to the skipper. "Take their cargo."

"Captain, receiving a hail on the *Amiliji's* channel," the radioman reported.

Krasnowsky rose from his seat and crossed over to the operator. "What now?"

The radio operator clicked a dial on the transmitter and asked, "*Amiliji*, this is the *Marinochka*. Over."

On his earphones, the radioman listened to an unfamiliar voice, one that was distinctly non-Russian, demanding the ship to stand down. The youth's brow furrowed as the first statement from the sister ship finished.

"Sir," he said, removing his earphones, "I think you should hear this." The operator turned the radio's volume up, allowing it to filter to the entire bridge.

"You are ordered to stand down as directed, and allow us to board your vessel. You will surrender all cargo retrieved from the trench shelf and return to your home port afterwards. Until you comply, the crew of this vessel will remain as hostages, only to be remanded to your custody upon completion of our terms."

"Get that man up here," Krasnowsky ordered, referring to Nicolenko. "This is his mission to lose...we'll let him deal with them."

"Bastard...."

Nicolenko stepped to the window with binoculars in hand and gazed through the ink sky. The *Amiliji*, once this operation's dutiful assistant, was now on the warpath, determined to undermine all of Nicolenko's hard won cargo. Thinking back, the lieutenant chided himself for his ignorance...he knew that man, whatever his real identity, should have been eliminated the moment he set eyes upon him. But no, he hadn't follow through, he hadn't done his superior's dirty work.

And at this moment, Nicolenko hated everything about himself.

"So, what are my orders?" Krasnowsky asked, fed up with trying to command his own vessel. If the NKVD were going to commandeer his boat, they'd be the ones to get them out of this mess; Krasnowsky had had enough.

"Keep our distance from the *Amiliji*...at least enough so their inflatables cannot reach us."

"And if they give pursuit? What about your precious cargo?" His voice was devoid of concern for the operation. If anything, he hoped he'd finally have the man by his balls; he was already enjoying watching him squirm under this additional pressure.

"And what?!" Nicolenko snapped, swiveling towards the skipper. "We have what they want. He won't risk harming our vessel in this storm. He will not pursue us," he paused, taking a deep breath to calm his nerves, "it will not be in his interests to."

"Let's pray for your sake, sir. I would not want our commission to be washed back to the ocean floor in haste."

Nicolenko's finger met Krasnowsky's chest. "You are fortunate that I am a son of the people. My colleagues would not offer such a generous amount, nor would they take abuse from the likes of yourself. Count your life as more important than your wallet."

"I would seriously doubt they'll respond," Gilmour said. "Right now, they realize we have them in dire straits...their own dredging mission is jeopardized without this ship to give them advance reports on incoming sea traffic."

Clayton stroked his stubbled jaw as he paced. "What the hell is this all about? Why all the political maneuvering all the way out here?"

"It's all about power, Clayton. Who has it, who can grab more. A deadly war is raging, more terrifying than any in history. Millions are on the way to their deaths...I would venture," Gilmour paused, remembering the chain of events that recreated the world, "this war will reshape humanity as we know it. Everyone, and everything, will in some way be touched by it. Right now, out here, beyond borders and leaders, we are engaged in it. If we don't succeed out here, then we're all dead. It's as simple as that."

Gilmour could feel the trawler crew's fear; they truly had no idea what was to follow in the years hence. Taking a deep breath, he formulated a plan in his mind to get them out of this mess, so that wouldn't be starting a little war of their own. "Can you get us closer to that ship?"

Clayton hesitated, weighing his abilities in light of the crash with his sinking trawler. "You're not thinking...Christ—"

"Just get me close to that boat, and keep your eyes on your prisoners. I'll do the rest."

"If you get yourself killed, don't expect me to do anything but get the hell back to British Columbia."

Gilmour flashed a sardonic smile. "I would expect nothing less."

***

"They're closing, sir," the *Marinochka*'s navigator reported from the window. "Two hundred meters."

Krasnowsky faced Nicolenko, seeing the anger and ire rising in his eyes; the captain didn't have to utter a word to the lieutenant.

"Circle round them," Nicolenko ordered. "Keep our distance as constant as possible."

"That will be extremely difficult in these waters," the navigator said, the frustration in his voice evident. "Going off course and hitting them is a possibility."

Nicolenko hovered over the youth's shoulder, projecting every ounce of fear into the subordinate's spirit. "Then make sure that doesn't happen."

The navigator vacillated, displaying his discomfort to Krasnowsky before finally laying his hands on the vessel's tiller.

Gilmour watched the *Marinochka* leave his binoculars' field of view. "Clayton, they're moving...."

The captain rose and looked out the window, taking the binoculars proffered from Gilmour. "They're not leaving...looks like they're attempting to come about...no," he squinted his eyes, "they're going to encircle us. Why are they doing that?"

In his mind, Gilmour recited a dozen delay tactics an officer might employ, deciding upon one that the trawler would have little recourse but to use in this storm. "They're trying to prevent us from reaching them, but they don't want to leave the trench to us. Circling around would keep the two of us chasing one another until one of us exhausted our patience. He's betting that will be us."

"Doesn't he realize how dangerous that is?"

"He knows that we know. Clayton, they don't have the upper hand here by any means, just like us. They're trying to wait out the storm by any way possible...I just want to make it as difficult as I can for them."

Clayton sighed. "We can't go on chasing our tails forever."

"I don't intend to. Do you think you can calculate their speed reasonably?"

"I...well it's not something I do everyday, you know. But Andersson is pretty proficient at that."

"Good," Gilmour said, nodding. "Track them for as long as you need to. When you have a good feel, set a course for their estimated position, within a few minutes."

A thought dawned over Clayton. "That would put us in front of them, or near them."

"All the better to ram them, don't you think?"

"No, no I don't think so at all!"

"Good, because I don't want them to think that either, just scare them. Maybe, just maybe, it'll give us an edge, tip the balance to us."

"But if we do—"

Gilmour threw his hands up. "You'll make it work, and it will be our way out of here. With their cargo."

"I hope it works," Clayton whispered under his breath, before beginning the calculations with his navigator.

"No change in their course."

Krasnowsky prayed that his navigator's report was correct; he would just as soon give up now and possibly save his skin from Nicolenko's and the NKVD's wrath. At least he knew the Canadians would give him mercy if it all went well.

Nicolenko nodded. "Excellent...keep a wide berth."

"And just how long are we to draw circles in the ocean?" Krasnowsky asked, resting his hands on his hips. "My ship has only enough supplies for another day or so. I should hope your dredging—"

"Do not worry, Krasnowsky. Our stint here shall not pass your deadline. I'm sure the Canadians will be most interested in returning to port after the loss of their vessel."

"Which brings me to another point," the captain said, stepping ahead of the lieutenant. "Is Moscow to reimburse my family for the loss of the *Amiliji*, and my crewmen? Or are they martyrs to the party cause?"

"Your crewmen are not lost yet, Krasnowsky. I fully intend for you to retrieve them, when the time is right. For the time being, per my superior's orders, we will continue to dredge the trench shelf, starting," he checked his wristwatch, "in about four hours, once day breaks and the storm ceases."

Krasnowsky shook his head and scowled, allowing Nicolenko to take notice.

"Is there a problem, Captain?"

Twisting his jaw, Krasnowsky silenced his rebuke. "No...no problem."

"Good. Make certain that is how it remains."

Turning his back on Nicolenko, Krasnowsky looked to each of his crewmen, all of whom reciprocated his rapidly fermenting distaste.

# CHAPTER TWENTY-THREE

"We've got it."

Gilmour stepped around to the cartograph on the small navigator's table. Crosshatches in pencil, some in pen, marked the paper map, all connected by a series of dotted lines and scrawled Cyrillic letters. Clayton and Andersson had done calculations of their own and marked them onto the cartograph. The *Amiliji*'s course was laid down and expanded upon from the Soviet crew, as was the estimated course of the circling *Marinochka*.

Clayton's meaty index finger pounded the map, pointing out a crossmark. "One hundred and sixty-two yards to our starboard bow, bearing eighty-one degrees."

Gilmour nodded.

"At the rate each of our boats are going," Clayton figured, "we should arrive ahead of them by two or three minutes, not giving them nearly enough time to avoid us."

"How much clearance will that give us?"

"Fifteen, maybe twenty yards at the most." The captain rubbed his eyes, then folded his arms. "Do you really think this will work?"

"We have no choice," Gilmour said, rounding the table to get another view of the cartograph. "I can get us out of this with our lives, if you and your crew are willing to follow me."

Clayton considered Gilmour's proposal once more, giving his fatigued brain time to run through it. Picking the sleep from his eyes, he craned his neck to Andersson behind him. "Set the course."

"Aye, aye, sir."

A faint smile crept across Gilmour's lips, so faint Clayton didn't detect it as the agent clapped the captain's arm.

The *Amiliji* groaned under the stress of the aroused ocean waves against its frame. Complying with the crew's will, the trawler deviated from its forward momentum to venture starboard, heading for the calculated coordinates to confront its sister ship, for perhaps the final time.

Salmon clouds rolled into the North Pacific skies, peeking out from behind the typhoon's rear cloud deck, rendering the ocean waters quiescent for the first time in twelve hours. The oppressive gusts that had battered the trio of trawlers now subsided to a mere reminder of the previous night's typhoon.

The *Amiliji* cut through the grey waters, determined to keep her appointment; to the trawler's rear, the *Marinochka* powered ahead, less than an hour from completing a single, counterclockwise circuit of the crash site, waiting for the Canadian-controlled sister vessel to leave the trench to her alone.

Krasnowsky paced back and forth aboard the *Marinochka's* bridge, keeping one eye on his wristwatch and the other on the *Amiliji's* position to their port bow. His sister ship hung around the dredging site throughout the night, refusing to be intimidated by the *Marinochka's* holding pattern. Silently, he was relieved that his other trawler hadn't been lost to the Pacific during the storm, and that despite Nicolenko's aggressive tactics, the Canadians hadn't taken her across the ocean back to North America. Perhaps that thought cast him in a bad light as a faithful party member, but the devil with that...if he could get out of this with his investments intact, and his life, then all the better, Nicolenko be damned. The NKVD and Moscow were nothing but an albatross.

His eyes found his wristwatch again: 0648. Glancing out to the newly sparkling waters, he observed the *Amiliji's* progress, mentally retracing its course over the past hour. Krasnowsky's fingers rubbed his chin, and as he thought longer, the skipper bit his nails to the quick. Another glimpse of his watch gave him pause.

"Hell," he whispered. The *Amiliji* wasn't going away, like Nicolenko had hoped; she was headed for them. And soon—

The clicking of Nicolenko's boots on the deck floor broke the skipper's attention from the window.

"Krasnowsky, I believe four hours have about expired."

The captain did a cursory glance to his wristwatch, for Nicolenko's sake.

Nicolenko noticed the sister trawler forging ahead outside the window, then folded his arms. "Have they been doing this all night?"

"Um…we've been trying to stay to your requested course. The *Amiliji* hasn't been a concern of mine."

"Perhaps she should be." He turned away from the window. "Have your men ready the nets for dredging. We'll begin shortly."

"Readying the nets will take some time. After the typhoon last night, I'd prefer to have them thoroughly checked before we drop them again."

The lieutenant scowled. "We don't have time. The sooner your nets can be dropped, the more time we can devote to the site. I would expect you, of all people, preferring to get back to port as soon as possible."

"And risk losing your catch because I didn't double-check my equipment? This isn't just about my wallet, Nicolenko, it's about my life." Nicolenko contemplated the legitimacy of the captain's reticence, particularly so after Krasnowsky's recitation of the lieutenant's previous warning. With a petulant sigh, he relented. "How long?"

"Twenty minutes."

The lieutenant nodded; that wouldn't put them behind his schedule for long. "Double-check your nets." He pointed a finger at the captain's face. "But no longer, understand?"

"Yes, sir." Judging by Krasnowsky's own timing, twenty minutes would be just about right for the *Amiliji* to intercept the *Marinochka*. By then, it would be too late for Nicolenko to order a change in course, allowing Krasnowsky to perhaps rid the lieutenant of his stranglehold over this ship. The very thought was treasonous, punishable almost certainly by death. Out here, however, the captain was ever more confident that Moscow's long arms couldn't fully extend to him.

Krasnowsky gestured to two of his crewmen, who then followed him to the aft of the vessel. At the furled nets, Krasnowsky paused to see the *Amiliji* decreasing its distance, now less than one hundred yards. He gestured to the sister vessel, pointing out its course to his two crewmen, then unlocked a white box below the net booms, a box whose location was known only to him....

Gilmour felt himself drifting off. Pushing his thumb and finger against the bridge of his nose, he forced himself back into alertness. Checking his wristwatch, he calculated the distance. It was time.

He rose from the corner of the bridge deck floor, where he had been resting his aching frame the last few hours. Walking over to the forward window, Gilmour's stirring had also awakened Clayton, who managed to erect his bulk from the captain's chair and join the agent at the window. Both men spied the closing *Marinochka*.

"Are you sure you want to do it this way?" Clayton asked.

"No question. If we're getting out of this alive, it has to be done."

Clayton nodded, long ago conceding to Gilmour's superior logic. "Keep us steady," the skipper commanded to his crew, "you all know what to do."

With that, the crewmen began preparations for the encounter, scurrying from one cabin to the next, gathering and double-checking the necessary equipment.

Gilmour headed for the corridor and exited the vessel's interior. He stepped out onto the upper deck and watched the two ships' positions. Looking at his wristwatch again, he followed the ticks of the second hand, and at the appropriate time, gestured to the crew behind the bridge window, all of whom had been waiting for his signal.

Gilmour braced himself on the outer railing while the *Amiliji* gained speed and closed in on her sister ship. Estimating their velocity by wristwatch and their rapidly decreasing distance, he readied himself at the bow of the trawler, mentally steeling his training and mind for the coming encounter, hoping that when it was all over, he could finally go home.

Nicolenko yawned, attempting to stifle the fatigue of the past few days. Having had no sleep since the arrival of the Canadian trawler, he battled the creeping ache of restlessness. Wiping his eyes, he studied the *Amiliji*, noting a strangeness about its position; despite the *Marinochka*'s circular, unorthodox course, his instincts heightened to an almost defensive posture.

Grabbing a set of binoculars, he peered out the forward window to the sister ship. Across the sea, a man was balanced against the trawler's railing, holding steadily as white crests of water rapidly fell across the *Amiliji*'s bow. What in the hell was going on? What were the Canadians doing?

Adjusting the focusing power, Nicolenko gained view of the man's face. So, it was him, the one who had seemed much more than he at first appeared. Gilmour, was that it? Yes, Gilmour. Then he had managed to commandeer the *Amiliji*. No real surprise, the Soviet crewmen were weak.

The lieutenant's greater concern was Gilmour's intentions. Losing the *Amiliji* would not ultimately decide the fate of his mission, but this Gilmour was an unknown factor. Having him loose could disrupt everything.

Seeing that man on the bow was not good. Nicolenko scanned the rest of the ship, but saw no one with him. The *Amiliji* appeared to be moving fast...much faster that the *Marinochka*. Putting the binoculars down, Nicolenko felt the rumblings of his own vessel; she was going nowhere near as fast. What was he up to? Surely he would not....

At the rear of the *Marinochka*, Krasnowsky closed and locked the box. Pausing to consider what he was about to commit, he remembered the punishment that would be meted out to him if he did return home, a punishment he couldn't allow his family to share. The skipper and his two crewmen shared a pregnant look, then headed for the interior of the ship. Before following his men back inside, Krasnowsky glimpsed once more at the approaching *Amiliji*, sensing this would be the end of her as well....

Gilmour's grip on the railing tightened. Clenching his jaw, he coiled his muscles, ready to spring to action once the *Amiliji* came within range to the *Marinochka*.

Inside, Clayton eyed his wristwatch. "Steady...steady...."

Andersson's hands were cemented to the tiller. Keeping the *Amiliji* on course was easy; knowing that one could crash into an unsuspecting trawler at thirty knots was not.

The *Marinochka* grew larger in the window, her port flank coming around as the *Amiliji* centered in on the pre-arranged coordinates. Clayton timed their course down to the second, remembering the exact time the larger ship was due to hit its mark. The entire operation was a well-rehearsed ballet without the pretty music; he just prayed that Gilmour wouldn't get them all killed doing his routine.

On deck, Gilmour double-checked his E4.10c at his hip and again ran through a mental list of his mission operatives once he was aboard the *Marinochka*. He knew neutralizing the NKVD agent wouldn't be easy; in fact, he expected heavy resistance once the crew realized he had boarded the vessel. His surprise act, then, would have to succeed to get him through their first line of defense. Glancing one more time back to the bridge crew through the window, he signaled that he was ready. All that was left was distance, and that was rapidly coming to a close.

A gasp blossomed on Nicolenko's face. The pair of binoculars fell from his hand to the deck floor as he leapt from the window and rushed to the navigator at the tiller of the *Marinochka*.

Grabbing the crewman's hands, the lieutenant yelled, "Evasive maneuver! Evasive maneuver!"

Both men looked to the forward window to witness the *Amiliji* appear at the bow of the ship and swipe the stem, plowing into the larger trawler's hull. The bridge crew were knocked to the deck floor after a shuddering wave ripped through the vessel, pitching it to starboard.

Gilmour bristled at the hard connection the *Amiliji* made with the *Marinochka*. Leaping over the railing, his eyes caught the shattered stem of the *Marinochka* before he landed and rolled several meters on its forward deck. Regaining his footing, he pulled his E4.10c and balanced himself with his extended arms.

The agent ran down the length of the trawler's starboard side, searching for the vessel's interior hatch or door. His ears heard scrabbling inside along with several muffled shouts in Russian, but he caught no glimpses of the crew through any of the portholes. Discovering the hatch a moment later, he opened it and jumped inside, finding a sunlit corridor. Seeing no crewmen, he proceeded down the passage pistol first, his back hugging the wall.

Passing a few interior doors, he heard a greater volume of sound emanating from below deck than in front of him. Pausing his advance to listen closer, he picked up what sounded like trickling water. His left hand tried the handle on the nearest door, and when it opened, he peered down to see a ladder which led to a cargo hold several meters deep. The din of splashing seawater was unmistakable now; chances were that the *Amiliji* had sliced open a hole large enough to allow the sea to begin filling up the hold.

"Damn...."

Gilmour was going to have to make quick work. After the *Bradana* sinking, an hour at the most would be his margin before the mass of the "cargo" would force the trawler to the bottom of the trench, losing forever the treasure it held.

Foregoing the common sense of a sane man, he put his hands on the ladder and descended into the black, accompanied only by the trickling seawater.


"Nicolenko!"

Krasnowsky and his crewmen bolted into the bridge to find the lieutenant recovering from his spill on the deck floor. Thrown against the far wall, Nicolenko groaned. Balling his fists, he strained to push himself onto his forearms and chest. His hands patted down his holster, only to find it empty.

The captain produced a revolver from the waist of his pants and held it at arm's length, squarely at the rising Nicolenko.

Nicolenko rubbed his forehead, eyeing Krasnowsky for the first time. "What the hell is this!"

"I've been a patient man, much too patient." Krasnowsky nodded to his two crewmen. "Get him off my bridge."

Nicolenko grimaced as the pair grabbed each of his arms. "Don't be stupid, Krasnowsky. Do you really wish to test the NKVD?"

Krasnowsky walked past the fallen lieutenant. "I'm tired of your talk, and of Moscow's promises. Both mean nothing to me anymore."

Forced to rise by his new captors, Nicolenko seethed under their treatment. Regaining his footing, he took the chance to scan the floor for his lost sidearm, his eye catching a glint just a third-of-a-meter to the right of him. Feigning a limp in his right leg, Nicolenko wrested his right arm and elbowed the inexperienced fisherman in his abdomen, then punched the other man at his left, fully freeing himself.

Krasnowsky heard the commotion behind him. Pulling his revolver, he swiveled on his feet to see his two crewmen tumble to the floor.

Nicolenko dove, sliding head first into the wall, but managed to grab his revolver and cock it, holding it forward to the astonished Krasnowsky.

The men stood at each other, gun barrels frozen in place, waiting for the other to move first.

Toggling a hanging switch, Gilmour illuminated the cargo hold, allowing his eyes to glimpse the haphazard mountains of metal debris deposited on the floor, as if a mining operation had ceased halfway. The profuse stench almost gagged him, but he willed himself forward, forcing his soaked feet towards the glinting material. Wading through the foamy seawater, which rose perceptibly every few seconds, he stepped over to a small mound of the metal, which Gilmour in no time recognized: the same type of debris that had littered the crash sites in Nepal and Yakutia. He gasped at the sheer volume of the material, which, if the ratio was similar to the two previous sites, was capable of yielding possibly dozens or more of the jewels.

"My God...." Gilmour's mind maddened at the thought of the Confederation possessing this many jewels; there would be no future to go home to.

But there was no time to collect nearly any of the jewels; his sample bag was aboard the *Amiliji* now, and the rising level of seawater in the lower depths meant the *Marinochka* was sinking fast. Damn, if there was a way to save the jewels, he'd have to transfer the cargo to the *Amiliji*, a next to impossible task with the trench bottom beckoning this ship down, and that mad NKVD man running around here, somewhere.

Krasnowsky recoiled from the hit to his clavicle. Falling on his back, he dropped the hammer on his own revolver, piercing and obliterating Nicolenko's kneecap. Both men cried in agony and collapsed to the floor, each retreating to opposite sides.

Mustering his strength after taking a moment to wrap his wound, Nicolenko tucked his sidearm into his waist belt and crawled to the corridor, his left leg trailing gamely, smearing crimson behind him. Rising with the assistance of a wooden door jamb, he limped out, knowing all would soon be lost.

Krasnowsky drug his broken frame to the fore of the bridge, his fingernails carving grooves into the wooden floor. Flexing his chest muscles, he forced his rib cage open to push air into his lungs, hoping to last just long enough to crawl to the ship's cargo controls. After an excruciating moment of pulling himself into a nearby chair, he commanded his arms to stretch, extending his fingers to their utmost length. Krasnowsky blocked out the numbing pain wracking his nerves to lay his right hand on the holding bay's instruments.

Allowing his leaking bodily fluids to paint the instruments red, Krasnowsky for once did not care about the condition of his premier vessel, for it was all too late...much too late. No one would stand to inherit her, no one could take his family away from him now.

"Ev...Evgenia...."

Pushing his full weight forward, Krasnowsky toggled the button, setting an end to his troubles and saving his good name. No one would ever have to know about this fool's errand....

# CHAPTER TWENTY-FOUR

With one lead foot stumbling over another, Nicolenko willed himself through the listing bowels of the *Marinochka*, his fist, full of bloodied wool from his left trouserleg, pulling him along, keeping him on the move. Crimson flowed smoothly from his wound, betraying his escape from the bridge with a crisscrossing trail of splotches. Descending a shaft to the lower decks was just short of impossible, but the lieutenant gritted his teeth and blocked out the fire raging in his left limb. His complete focus was on the jewels...nothing else, not even his own health, mattered. They could not fall to the enemy.

The unmistakable roar and trembling of rushing water from below the deck floor filled his ears; had they been hit so hard as to damage the hull? If that was so, and the trawler was taking on seawater, then Nicolenko would have to exhaust every ounce of energy to get to the cargo before it was washed away. Only his death could stand in the way of completing the mission. Perhaps that would be the ultimate reward....

A series of loud knocks along the port and starboard walls of the holding bay startled Gilmour, bringing his attention to the seawater now pouring in fast. Feeling the rising cold around his legs, the agent realized that another factor was in play; the rushing water was coming at much too rapid a pace for the extent of damage he witnessed from the stem, making a deliberate flooding of the lower deck the only culprit. Did the crew see him board? Did they know he had made it to the holding bay?

No matter. His new objective was to get back to the bridge and shut off the flooding water. Even if he couldn't save the ship from eventually sinking, he might be able to buy himself a few minutes. Minding the water level around him, Gilmour retraced his steps, careful not to slip on any of the obscured debris. Placing a hand on the ladder, he felt vibration through the thick, rusted metal. A shaft of brilliant sunlight then poured over him, its warmth piercing the stone-cold bay. Looking up, he saw a silhouetted form descending with difficult urgency.

Gilmour retreated several meters and readied his pistol, tracing the person who was just coming into view. "Halt! I'm armed!"

Nicolenko's boots met the watery floor. Not turning to meet the agent face on, he shrouded himself in the shadow cast by the ladder. "You. Somehow I knew this was all connected to you."

"We seem to be in agreement," Gilmour said, recognizing him as the Soviet "supervisor" aboard the *Amiliji*, the man who alarmed his instincts. He circled round to Nicolenko's right flank. "Men out of our time. Not all that we appear."

"Time?" Nicolenko chuckled, despite the blinding pain. "What do you know about time?"

"No more than you, of course. We're both just grunts, here to do our duties." Gilmour scrutinized the mysterious man. "Who are you? Who do you work for?"

Nicolenko cracked a smile. "You know that I can't answer that. It's all part of our mutual game, don't you see? You do one thing, we do another. You retaliate...it's all how we play."

"I'm afraid I can't let you win. If you abandon this ship, I'll allow you to live, maybe even go back to your own time. But I can't allow you to have the objects."

Nicolenko's hand inched down to his waist belt. "I was about to tell you the same...."

The hair on Gilmour's neck aroused him in time to nearly elude a round from Nicolenko's revolver. Moving to his left, the agent was grazed on his right flank, the slug burning a hole into his overcoat, but missing everything vital.

Nicolenko grasped the ladder, allowing himself to stand steadily with his impotent leg. Gilmour ducked below a pile of debris, shielding himself. Sliding out of the water, he shot off a round, hitting a rung on the ladder.

Nicolenko fired two rounds, then limped into the darkness. The echoes of his awkward steps resonated throughout the holding bay, giving Gilmour a decent idea of his location. The agent hesitated to use his lasersight to pinpoint the false NKVD man, fearing Nicolenko would conversely locate him.

Gilmour crept around the debris pile, careful to mask his

movements under the sound of the incoming water; just getting to the ladder would be difficult enough without his opponent on surveillance.

Gilmour couldn't wait any longer, and the water wasn't getting any lower.

Estimating his distance, Gilmour devised the easiest path around the debris. Launching off his feet, he fired a volley of rounds at Nicolenko's apparent position, then rushed the skeletal ladder. Getting within a meter, Gilmour leapt from the watery deck floor and onto the ladder, clinging hard to the rungs. He then pulled himself up, hearing the air compress after a series of rounds from Nicolenko's revolver zipped under him.

He ascended and stepped into the corridor again, his eyesight bleached by the absolute white of the portholes. Readjusting his sight, he headed for the ship's bow, and an appointment with her captain.

Nicolenko grappled a metal beam and pushed himself to his feet. Around him, the water foamed red with his blood, which was duly churned by the rising ocean level. Threatening to be drowned in the ocean's fury, the lieutenant forded the seawater, his animal-like grunts ringing in his ears and echoing in the darkness, reducing him to the basest of lifeforms.

One hand over the other, he jerked his unwilling body past each rung of the ladder, the grime and rust collected on its surface splattering onto his face and working its way into his mouth. Each second was more torturous than the last, but before long Nicolenko reached the top, pausing only to witness the water raging up the ladder behind him, now just meters away. The last of the metal debris was uprooted from the tallest piles and carried away, taking with them the vestiges of his mission.

It was all going to hell. Nicolenko had no choice but to stop Gilmour, even if the jewels were lost; he couldn't allow the bastard to return...his duty was now personal.

"Sweet Jesus!"

Gilmour stepped over the bloody trail leading to the bridge, then glimpsed the form of Krasnowsky slumped before the holding bay's controls. Gilmour felt for a pulse on the man's neck, then bent down and cradled Krasnowsky's head in his arms, wiping congealed blood from the captain's cheek and mouth.

"Can you speak?" he asked in Russian.

Krasnowsky's throat fought the thickened blood, coughing and vomiting out the fluids just to breathe a meek "Yes."

"Who is he—where is he from?" Gilmour implored, disregarding the man's failing state.

"Nico...Nicolenko...all I knoww—aarhhh...." Krasnowsky burbled out more spit and mucous, which foamed over his chin.

"Relax, I have you...you're not alone." Gilmour cleared away the vomitus, then pressed, "Who sent him?"

"NKVD all I know...please—let me die. I'm just a fisherman...." Krasnowsky's eyes rolled into his head, a final gurgle ejecting from his throat.

Gilmour laid the man to the deck floor and rose to his feet, wiping his hands on his wool overcoat. Turning to the instrument panel in front of him, he discovered the source of the extra water in the holding bay. Reading the Cyrillic characters, and seeing the blood coating the respective switches, he realized the captain had flooded the bay with ocean water, seemingly intending to destroy the evidence of any cargo. Was it an attempt to thwart this Nicolenko, as he called him? Or was it to save his own name, perhaps absolving any relations of his potential criminal activity, since Gilmour was pretty damn certain that the man was not NKVD?

Gilmour crossed over to the radio and tuned the receiver. Picking up the headphones, he said, "Gilmour to *Amiliji*, over."

A crackled voice answered, "*Amiliji*. Osipiak here."

"Get Clayton to send his men over here, and quick! This ship is going down! Repeat, this ship is going down! We're going to lose—"

A pair of gunshots blew the radio board to pieces, showering Gilmour with wood and metal. Ripping off the headphones, Gilmour whipped his head around to see Nicolenko standing there, his smoking revolver gripped in his hands.

"Don't be stupid, Nicolenko," Gilmour hissed, "if that is truly your name. I have the tactical advantage here. Your men have fled this trawler, and your cargo is sinking to the bottom. All you have left is my mercy."

"I have no wish to see you dead just yet, Gilmour," he said, stepping closer. "Tell me what you know, and hand over all that you possess, and I will consider allowing you to swim back to Canada."

Rumbling beneath their feet caused the two to glance down at the deck floor, then back at each other.

"This ship is going down fast!" Gilmour yelled. "I can get you off it, if you allow me!"

Nicolenko shoved his revolver into Gilmour's face. "Your mercy is not worth losing the cargo! Give me the jewels!"

Another rumble below decks buffeted the trawler, allowing Gilmour a distraction. He punched the revolver out of Nicolenko's hand

and struck the lieutenant's jaw with his flattened palm, felling him. Nicolenko quickly recovered to give a swift kick with his uninjured leg to Gilmour's ankle, toppling him with a crack. Despite both men being disabled, they landed repeated punches to each other, scuffling even while they lay flat on their backs.

Multiplying in intensity, the rumbles below deck reverberated at a constant pace, the *Marinochka* buckling under the extreme stress. Seams in the walls and floors opened, with cracks soon growing from the weakest areas of the trawler. Unbeknownst to the two men, the ocean horizon had disappeared from the forward window, replaced by the blue daylight sky.

At once, Gilmour and Nicolenko slid back towards the aft section of the bridge, both landing hard against the metal wall. Gilmour's hand reached out to the floor and grasped a thin, wooden panel that had pushed up. Digging his fingertips into it, he clawed his way up the increasingly angled floor, fighting the combined push of gravity and Nicolenko's own feeble attempts at combat.

"Gilmour! Damn you!"

Looking back, Gilmour saw Nicolenko struggling to free himself from the wall. Gilmour tensed his biceps and pulled himself up using the panel, which was slowly arcing backwards under the agent's mass. Just when the panel began to splinter, sparkles of light cascaded past him. Turning his head to the stem of the ship, Gilmour witnessed the sudden collapse of the bridge window above, bringing a deluge of shattered glass down around him, followed by a heavy metal weight. Bouncing off the floor above him, the weight crashed into Gilmour and sent him falling into the wall below. He opened his eyes long enough to see a creeping blackness overtake him.

# CHAPTER TWENTY-FIVE

An alarm sounded on Waters' holobook, startling her. "Richard, sensors are detecting elevated meV levels..." she paused, "rising to forty-one, centering on the lab!"

"Grab your equipment and alert Anaba," de Lis ordered, picking up his own holobook from the lab desk.

Seconds later in the U5-1 laboratory, de Lis, Dark Horse, Waters, Marlane, Valagua, Roget, Constantine and McKean converged around an array of sensors, emergency equipment and the laboratory's monitors, awaiting the definitive signal.

Marlane and Waters kept their eyes on the bank of holographic monitors, watching a spinning, amorphous black shape grow in scale on the screens.

"Topology is consistent," Marlane said to Waters.

Waters looked to de Lis. "This is it."

De Lis thrust his arms out, yelling, "Stand back, give him room!"

On his command, the group took refuge behind the assembled equipment, waiting for the characteristic hum and sizzle of the Casimir reaction, while Constantine and McKean stood ready with chemical extinguishers, aiming them for the projected area of the return.

At the climax of a cascade of alarms from the laboratory's sensors, a brilliant white sphere ripped open in the center of the room, a vortex of swirling energy that emitted a haunting siren song. The sphere belched, vomiting a beige lump that landed on the tile floor and slumped over. Two instantaneous streams of chemical extinguisher poured over the form, creating a thick blanket of smoke throughout the room.

De Lis pointed to the fallen figure, shouting, "Help him up! Help him up!"

Wearing sanitized gloves, Constantine and McKean grabbed the humanoid form and set it on a nearby chair. The two men then started work on releasing the still-smoking suit's numerous latches. Rotating the metal rings on the shoulder apparatus, they removed the helmet, revealing the perspiring countenance of Special Agent James Gilmour, fresh from the mists of time.

"Thank God, Gilmour," Constantine blurted, "we were beginning to worry."

McKean clapped Gilmour's shoulder. "What the hell kept you?"

Gilmour rose to his feet, slipped off his gauntlets and unlocked the torso piece. "Help get this thing off me...."

After a few moments, the two agents and de Lis stripped Gilmour down to his bodysock. Wiping off his face with a towel, Gilmour inhaled a chestful of air, the first in some time not tinged with diesel exhaust.

Looking at the gathered scientists—colleagues, again, he reminded himself—he felt a pang of remorse, not quite guilt, but disappointment perhaps in a way only he could understand.

"I failed, Doctor...the jewels are still buried there...aboard a Soviet trawler."

De Lis nodded. "We know, Agent Gilmour. The DoD's latest satellite reconnaissance detected the trawler buried under several thousand tonnes of seafloor."

Gilmour perked up at this potentially positive turn. "Than there's still a chance to recover them, despite this?"

De Lis glanced at Constantine and McKean, a sudden, weary cast in his eyes.

Gilmour's jaw tightened. "Something happened when I was gone. What is it?"

"Agents Constantine and McKean returned from their respective jaunts to the Confederation's main manufacturing plants of neutronic particles," he explained. "Estimating forward from the times they each monitored the Confederation, the Russians have enough weapons to level half the Kuril-Kamchatka Trench, if they so pleased."

An ashen pall fell over Gilmour's face.

"It gets worse." De Lis deferred to Dark Horse, who produced a holobook from his jacket. Handing it to Gilmour, the device displayed a holograph dotted with green circles over a map of the North Pacific Ocean basin.

"Those are projected targets for the neutronic devices, Agent Gilmour," Dark Horse said, an index finger tapping one of the green dots. "The plans Constantine and McKean downloaded reveals the Confederation has already scheduled to line the seafloor with them."

A red gash in the middle of the ocean with sprinkles of green was what the trench had been reduced to, a sobering thought to Gilmour. It was no longer land they fought over now, but a series of targets, illusory objects to be divvied up.

"Bastard...."

Dark Horse and de Lis narrowed their eyes. Puzzled, both said at the same time, "What?"

Gilmour rubbed his forehead, a stubborn reminder of his jaunt, and how he had narrowly escaped the sinking *Marinochka*. He whispered, "I should have killed him, now see what I have created by my mercy." He elaborated, raising his voice, "A man, masquerading as an NKVD agent, beat me to the site, by hours, maybe days."

"Beat you to the site?" Constantine asked.

Gilmour put his hands to his hips and walked past the encircling scientists. Not turning his back, he continued, "He knew about the crash site...right where to find it."

"You can't blame that on yourself, Gilmour," Waters said.

"You're only partially correct, Stacia. Allowing him to slip away, yes, I take full responsibility for that. I should have finished him, and not allowed this to happen. But," he faced the group again, "he knows what we are doing...then, and now. He knew I would come. Well, not me by name, but one of us. He knew."

McKean stepped over to Gilmour. "Then there's only one way...."

"The mole," Roget finished, almost in afterthought, as if the group had grown accustomed to, and respected, the everpresent shadow in their midst.

"Do you have a name, an identity, Agent Gilmour?" Dark Horse asked, hoping to stem the mounting conclusions. "Anything to help characterize this imposter?"

Gilmour reflected back to the Russian man who had cleverly imprisoned—then almost killed—him before the agent broke free. "Nicolenko. That's all I know of his identity. A Soviet captain, a man who died in my arms, gave me his name." He shook his head. "I don't know about its authenticity...with him impersonating an officer, it could just as easily be assumed."

Dark Horse nodded. "That may be enough. I'll have Quintanilla check her sources—"

"Actually, Colonel," Gilmour interrupted, "I'd prefer if you didn't, at least not Quintanilla. Are there other avenues?"

Dark Horse swallowed hard; what was with Gilmour's sudden resistance to Quintanilla? He flashed a troubled look to de Lis before saying, "I will...look into other options."

"Thank you, Colonel."

De Lis shelved Gilmour's reticence, for now. "Agent Gilmour, I've instructed Doctor Anaba to perform a post-mission examination on you, the same exams Agents Constantine and McKean received when they returned. After it has been completed, please come by U5-29 for our debriefing. I'm certain your extended jaunt has left you with plenty to share with us."

Gilmour understood de Lis' unsaid motive for hurrying along the examination and debriefing. He was sure de Lis would be more than interested in hearing what he had to say about his opinion of Quintanilla, real or subjective.

Crossing over to the corridor, Gilmour found Anaba waiting at the doorway. He followed her out of the laboratory, certain that de Lis thought he had gone insane; walking under the fluorescent lights once again, Gilmour wished he had.

With each step, Gilmour felt the pain in his body ebbing away, owing all to the swift-action analgesics and stem cells Anaba had injected for his ankle injury. Near top shape again physically, Gilmour was ready to go one more round for the team. Mentally, though, he had to convince himself this third bout would finish the operation, or else lose all hope and concede defeat to the Confederation, who would then stand to inherit complete and utter domination over the world. It was a thought he didn't—and couldn't—relish.

The corridor leading to U5-29 seemed to be unusually active, patrolled by a higher number of MPs than when he had left for his examination hours ago. An alert had not been sounded while he was away; he would have picked up on it.

Regardless, he presented his credentials to the four Marines upon crossing over to the U5-29 doorway, who then obliged him with the standard courtesy of unlocking the entrance and shuttling him inside without so much as a look in the eye; too many other subjects to observe, Gilmour assumed.

"Agent Gilmour."

The invitee turned from the locked door to find de Lis, Dark Horse and another man he realized on the way to the conference table was Solicitor General of the Department of Justice Sebastian Rauchambau. Raising his right hand to shake the Solicitor General's, Gilmour understood that this wasn't to be the standard rehashing of a mission's success/failure ratio. Rauchambau had traveled from Washington, D.C., in the middle of a busy legislative session to Ottawa, no doubt requesting immediate answers to numerous inquiries as to the status of Temporal Retrieve. Gilmour was certain he wouldn't disappoint.

The four took their seats at the table, and after a brief reintroduction, consulted the holobooks before them.

"Agent Gilmour," Rauchambau started off, his Creole dialect flavoring his language, "allow me to congratulate you on your return from the first comprehensive testing of the Casimir jaunt. Being the first to venture into any new technology is breathtaking...I look forward to hearing much more about you as your career blossoms."

"Thank you, sir."

Rauchambau tapped a button on his holobook. "On to our business. My presence here is of great concern to all those assigned to the Ottawa bureau. With our ongoing security compromises on these premises, I felt compelled to meet you face to face, when your schedule dictated, of course. With your absence for some weeks, that had to be delayed until now."

Gilmour nodded. "Of course."

"As a special agent still in the employ of the Intelligence and Investigation Agency, it is imperative that you keep your opinion of the subject to yourself, unless queried by Doctor de Lis, Colonel Dark Horse or myself. Is that clear, Agent Gilmour?"

A hoarse cough erupted from Gilmour's throat...something rank obviously didn't agree with him. "Sir. Yes, sir. May I inquire upon the reasoning of your command?"

"Classified." The Solicitor General's eyes glimpsed over his holobook before he returned them to Gilmour's stern countenance. "Just let it be said that Justice is investigating the matter internally, and we don't need an agent assigned to one of our most classified operations to be free with his reticence to specific personnel."

"Understood, sir." Gilmour wondered just how many ears picked up on his Quintanilla hunch hours ago. Or had Mason, somehow, somewhere, independently voiced both his and Gilmour's prior suspicions of Quintanilla? It sounded unreasonable, unthinkable knowing Greg as well as he had; the man just didn't have loose lips. Taking another tack, perhaps the Department of Justice was close to digging out HADRON, and this was just Rauchambau's routine "don't screw us over mode" kicking into overdrive. If that was the case, then everyone at this conference table had heard it several times already.

"Now, Agent Gilmour, I understand that during the course of your mission to the year," Rauchambau paused to cover a curious grin, "1940—pardon me, I still can't quite believe this sometimes."

"Quite all right, sir, "de Lis said, locking eyes with Gilmour. "We have difficulty accepting the plausibility of it as well."

Gilmour let out a displeased sigh. *Don't apologize for him, de Lis. Let him finish so we can get back on task.*

Rauchambau continued, "You encountered a Soviet NKVD officer known only as Nicolenko. Correct?"

"Correct."

The Solicitor General furrowed his eyebrows. "You suspect he was actually our contemporary? Perhaps a CIS agent, as you state in your report here?"

"Correct. He was fully aware of my activities, once he figured out that my cover was false, and demanded I hand over my Temporal Retrieve technology and the extraterrestrial samples we call jewels. He knew the location of the crash site...in fact he beat me to it, leading me to believe," Gilmour damned the torpedoes, "that our mole—HADRON—was responsible for leaking the information."

Rauchambau half-heartedly nodded. "In the interests of protecting our international standing as a respectable and moral nation, I have instructed the IIA to investigate the suspected identity of this Nicolenko, and to find out if he truly exists as an agent of the Confederation. Unfortunately, I am certain our intelligence experts will come to several firewalls during their international searches."

"I have implicit trust in their capabilities. I am sure every avenue will be exhausted until no byte is left unscanned," Gilmour said, beaming. There was more than one way to fight the bureaucratic malaise, the foremost by giving them his absolute encouragement to expend every ounce of technological capital to track the man down.

In the short amount of time de Lis had come to know Gilmour, he had to credit him for learning to joust with the politicians in their favorite arena: the verbal challenge. Checking another portion of his holobook, de Lis changed the subject and tone of the debriefing. "As for the second topic of our debriefing...Agent Gilmour, your report stated the estimated mass of the retrieved jewels at ninety to one hundred kilos."

"Correct. I would go so far as to say the dredged jewels were double, or most probably triple, the amount we recovered in both the Nepal and Sakha combined. Right now, it's all resting at the bottom of the trench."

Dark Horse shifted in his chair, which now felt constraining, perhaps confining in the wake of the knowledge which had recently been revealed to this select group. "I regret to announce that it won't last. The latest from Washington just an hour ago reports that Vladivostok has begun submarine maneuvers in the Sea of Okhotsk, simulating deep sea retrievals. The DoD estimates a week before the Pacific fleet authorizes an expedition to the Kuril-Kamchatka Trench. It would be only a matter of time before the command is given to launch with live warheads and begin mining the trench."

"Pardon my ignorance on this matter," Rauchambau asked, "but wouldn't the absolute volume of the neutronic yield vaporize these jewels?"

"The latest experiments with our samples indicates that may not be the case." De Lis brought up a schematic on his holobook, allowing it to be broadcasted to all four holobooks. A cross-section of a typical jewel was highlighted in blue, with accompanying text boxes explaining the bizarre properties and metric measurements of the specimens.

"Each jewel," de Lis continued, "is, for all intents and purposes, infinitely dense. Even our most powerful microscopes failed to penetrate them. We have to speculate that these jewels are so tightly packed with matter, almost akin to a neutron star's core, that they would be impossible by conventional or unconventional means to split open."

Gilmour trimmed de Lis' words to a layman's level. "That is, Solicitor General, despite our and the Confederation's best efforts, we couldn't destroy the jewels no matter how much we try."

A vexing frustration crossed Rauchambau's face. "Then what do the Russians hope to succeed in doing out there? Why risk so many lives in starting a new war?"

"I don't believe a new war is what they want," Dark Horse said, countering the positions of many of the government's more hawkish officers, including the lieutenant colonel's own superior. "I believe, and this is shared by many here, that the Confederation hopes to prove its mettle on the world stage. A little nationalist pride, along with rubbing our noses in a prize we couldn't quite control, goes a long way towards becoming an apparent equal with us."

"We think the Confederation will attempt to atomize the surrounding matter, and sift out the jewels from there," de Lis said. "And as Colonel Dark Horse has illustrated, sticking it to us wouldn't hurt, either."

Rauchambau slowly caught on. "Doing it because they can."

De Lis nodded. "Precisely."

The Solicitor General turned to each of them. "Then what can those of us in Justice do to prevent this," he thought back to the curt warning he gave Gilmour, "as an olive branch?"

Gilmour leaned forward. "As a late friend of mine would say, there might just be a way to take a piss in their pool."

# CHAPTER TWENTY-SIX

A symphony of light cascaded across the pyramid-rimmed gallery, creating a menagerie of lucidity and color. The two dozen Temporal Retrieve scientists and special agents, all crammed into a semi-circle, witnessed the simulation of the most powerful weapon mankind had the temerity to create: the neutronic bomb. Watching in rapt fascination, the group beheld the holographic equivalent of a device that was designed to kill them in an instant, but constructed from the very light that struck their retinas every second...and each knew the irony.

Dark Horse stepped forward from the assembly and gestured his right hand towards the holograph flanking him. "Allow me to introduce *Strela*, the Confederation's first practical neutronic warhead."

About two meters in height and sixty centimeters in width, the angled device glittered in the darkness, rotating completely every thirty seconds, suspended in mid-air like some strange trapeze artist. A blue beam soon lanced out from thin air, illuminating the warhead's nosec-one.

Pacing in front of the holograph, Dark Horse continued, "*Strela* isn't the most powerful warhead ever constructed, at least by conventional means. But its unique destructive capability more than makes up for this short-term deficiency."

Dark Horse tapped a button on his holobook, which stripped away an exterior hatch, unveiling a cross-section of the warhead's nosec-one. Another command magnified the interior five times, revealing the intricacies of the device's construction; metal piping ran down a vertical shaft, which then connected to a larger, centralized compartment, complete with two very familiar parallel plates.

"Agents Constantine's and McKean's reconnaissance has allowed us to construct a rough schematic of *Strela*'s mechanics based on the holographs they downloaded. According to our best estimates, the warhead's capability is based upon neutron fusion, utilizing the miniaturization of Casimir vacuum chambers to accomplish this." He raised a finger. "Therein lies the insidiousness of this device."

Gilmour shot a look to Constantine and McKean, then to de Lis and Waters; *Strela*'s Casimir plates were of the same construction as their hazard suits...too much so to be of coincidence. Did the Confederation stumble upon the Casimir's extreme effectiveness, or...surely Dark Horse and de Lis weren't blind to this?

"For those of you unaware of the potential of this weapon, allow me to give you an example. You may remember the volcanic eruption the Global Security Network detected from a previously unknown seismic basin in the Kamchatka Peninsula some thirteen months ago? The Confederation stonewalled the administration's geological investigation into the incident. Thanks to two of our IIA special agents, what you are about to see is the reason why."

Dark Horse punched another sequence of buttons on his holobook, shifting the *Strela* holograph over a half-meter, giving room to another holograph that then took its place. A flat plane evolved into a sculpted mountain landmass, adorned with hundreds of pine trees, accompanied by a rolling grassland from its base beyond. For several seconds it was a serene paradise until a series of flashes above the peak foreshadowed an intense burst of light so bright the photons casted silhouettes upon the gallery's walls. Millions of metric tonnes of rocky crust from the mountain were instantly atomized, reducing the great edifice to a pitiful caldera. Superheated plasma, formerly trapped beneath the mass, quickly escaped into the atmosphere, blistering the Earth's life-maintaining blanket.

Only silence emerged from the gaping mouths of the spectators.

Dark Horse wiped the devastation from the gallery. "Nine-point-one scale aftershocks shook the region for more than two weeks after this...demonstration. The DoD estimates the Confederation detonated six warheads to produce this result."

"Just six?" Gilmour asked, concerned. Reflecting for a moment, he turned to Rauchambau. "Solicitor General, do we have any agents inside the Confederation close to the manufacturing plants for these warheads? Specifically, the Casimir plates?"

"None near any of the manufacturing plants...almost all of our efforts have been concentrated around the quantum smashers."

Gilmour stroked his chin. "Would it be possible to redirect at least one agent to the Confederation's manufacturing base?"

"With some doing, possibly. We'd need to establish new credentials, and provide new accommodations. Arranging all that would be quite a challenge for our regional network in Irkutsk."

"What do you have in mind, Agent Gilmour?" Dark Horse asked.

"Formulating the Solicitor General's olive branch." He looked to Rauchambau. "The IIA will infiltrate and, if possible, overwrite *Strela*'s Casimir transponder codes. You'll recall, Doctor, that your initial attempts at scanning sent the first jewel specimens back in time?"

"Or the next best thing to it, yes." De Lis paused to allow his mind to catch up to Gilmour's. "Intriguing, Agent Gilmour. Eliminating all the jewels in the trench at once, upon detonation."

Rauchambau's eyes narrowed. "Pardon me, Doctor...I'm still two steps behind."

De Lis explained, "Agent Gilmour's plan will theoretically allow us to activate the jewels' inherent properties—time travel—when the Confederation would send the transponder signal to detonate...."

Comprehension crept over the Solicitor General's brow.

"...Rendering the warheads impotent, since the devices should be swept up into a spacetime sinkhole, taking their neutronic yield with them," de Lis finished.

A flood of skepticism washed over Rauchambau's face. "'Should?' Are you certain?"

De Lis crossed his arms, more out of defense than comfort. "It's the only realistic chance we have of preventing war. Now granted, we did this on a much smaller scale—just a single jewel." De Lis swallowed, then intoned, "I implore you, Solicitor General, an investment of a select handful of agents, behind the lines, will be much preferred to a million-plus men and women mobilized to fight your—" he censored himself, careful not to place blame, "a war of attrition, which this world cannot afford. Our century has seen too many sacrifices. Too many children fighting the wars of men, of nation-states, only to come home in body-bags. This is our opportunity to stop it, here and now."

Everyone in the gallery stood mute, taken aback by his polemic; most of de Lis' long-time colleagues knew that the doctor was not given to voicing strong opinions in private, let alone in public. His conviction was impeccable, and voice unwavering. How could they dissent?

"Nobody wants war, Doctor de Lis," Rauchambau said. Remembering all of his reports in the years past that had stated de Lis' strong support for many of Justice's covert initiatives, Rauchambau mulled the team's assertions, even those he considered less than afford-able. He put a finger to his lips before asking, "How do we proceed?"

Shifting to U5-29 once more, de Lis, Dark Horse, Valagua, Waters, Gilmour, Constantine, McKean and Rauchambau took their usual seats. The lieutenant colonel produced a holobook and scrolled down its text, which he referred to before beginning.

"Secretary of Defense McKennitt has made this meeting a top priority; at this moment, he is recommending a motion to the President and the Joint Chiefs, in the event of a national crisis, to secure the North Pacific with military forces. Our job is to make sure that won't be neces-sary."

He tapped a button on his device, highlighting a cartograph of Irkutsk, just a few dozen kilometers from Lake Baikal. "With Doctor de Lis' direction, we are to provide our illegals in Irkutsk with reconfigured data codes. The mission for them won't be easy...we've had a five-to-one failure rate over the past decade in this republic. Security is tight. It'll be up to us to make it as easy as possible for them to retool the *Strelas* under the Confederation's nose."

"How are we to accomplish that?" Waters asked.

"That's where Agents Gilmour, Constantine and McKean come in. Agents...."

Gilmour flicked a button on his holobook. "I'm sure this will look familiar to you all."

The Irkutsk projection disappeared, replaced by a schematic of one of the flat black holographic projectors. Gilmour started, "In tandem with Javier Valagua, who has been putting in some of his own extracurricular hours, we have developed a method to synchronize our experience with that of the agents already in place, utilizing webbed holographic HUDs and modified holographic projectors designed for our hazard suits. By providing them with this live feed, we can instruct them on the spot on how to recode the warheads, while hopefully keep-ing their various covers as maintenance crew at the assorted neutronic facilities."

Valagua looked to de Lis, Waters and Rauchambau. "It's ambi-tious, but we think it's the best way. Giving these agents a live feed without having to bog them down with minutia can only work in our advantage."

"Then we will need to put in some more hours to fine-tune the projectors in time," de Lis declared. The doctor glanced over the sche-matic again and asked, "I gather that you have worked out the problems in miniaturizing the HUD components?"

Valagua gave Waters and de Lis a confident nod. "We've begun the corneal implantation trials, even as we speak."

"You have a deadline of oh-five-hundred Tuesday, and not a moment later," Dark Horse announced. "They're to be dropshipped to the illegals with our weekly briefings, and we cannot postpone. Understood?"

Unanimous voices chorused, "Understood."

"Good. Dismissed."

With that curt ending, the assembled rose from the table and shuffled out, once more determined to beat another of their seemingly endless objectives.

"It has been over six weeks since your last communique! What is the delay!"

"Security here has nearly neutralized my position twice!" the encrypted voice answered, with nary enough time to formulate a response. "I have had to triple-check every move and delay my latest reports. I apologize for my—"

"Enough with excuses! I expected to receive your intelligence on the three missions, but instead silence was my answer! If it wasn't for the extraordinary measures I took to procure this assignment for you, you would have been eliminated long ago! Do you understand?"

"Y-yes. Constantine and McKean were successful in infiltrating the Irkutsk and Magadan facilities...*Strela* will be compromised."

"Compromised? How so?"

"The transponder codes. You must prevent the codes from being changed. They intend on resetting them so that the detonation will acti-vate the specimens deep in the Kuril-Kamchatka Trench. If they succeed, the neutronic particles will not fuse, and you will lose all the warheads." "Impossible! There is no possible way to do this! The neutronic fusion process cannot be halted once detonation is activated."

An angry sigh went into the line. "Please listen to me! It is pos-sible, because the fusion process will not be activated if the codes are changed!"

The old man's bones creaked as he wrapped his hand around the phone. "Then I will alter your mission. I am ordering you to prevent that from occurring. Sabotage the efforts of the Temporal Retrieve agents. Eliminate them before they can jaunt and change the transponder codes. Kill them now, if you so please."

"It...it's not that easy...."

"Why?"

"The Temporal Retrieve agents aren't involved. The IIA illegals working in your facilities will be performing the alterations."

"There are no illegals in Irkutsk! Our purges have eradicated them from the *Strela* centers!"

"They were given false credentials and moved from quantum smashers across the Confederation. They are there, and they will do it."

The old man paused, contemplating what could possibly have gone wrong between the issuing of his commands and the soldiers carrying them out. Perhaps he would order a series of executions; it was the only way to be certain this disgrace would not be repeated. But that still would not solve his ultimate problem.

"Then what is your solution?" the old man asked. "You are the one I am paying—handsomely, I must add—to provide us with neutronic particles and the warhead technology...how do we put an end to this?"

"There...might be an avenue to disrupt the operation. I—"

A double click over the line, followed by loud feedback, halted the conversation.

"What...what is going on?" the old man asked after several seconds of dead air. "What happened?"

"I'm terminating the line! I can't talk!"

"What is going on? What do you think you are doing!" he yelled, but to no avail; the dial tone told him all he needed to know. In anger he slammed the phone onto his desk, smashing the device. Taking a difficult breath, he glared at the suited man across from him. "HADRON," he said, pulling a cigarette from his pack and lighting it, "has been uprooted."

The suited man shoved his hands into his trouser pockets. Walking over to the window, he glimpsed the first descending snowflakes of the season. Cold, it was so wonderfully cold anymore. "His elimination is past due."

The old man nodded. "By all means...end his game now."


"Lionel, this report is half-finished," Waters said, slapping the just-received holobook on her desk. "You promised me Crowe and Ivan would have the QPU calculations three hours ago. Have you any idea how much Richard is going to berate me now?"

Roget rubbed his eyes before retrieving the holobook. "Listen, neither of them have left the lab the past two days...come to think of it, neither have I, except for the occasional commode visit. I just have too many things on my mind."

Waters stood and looked Roget in the eyes. "I understand...but we need to maintain our united front, with all the departments at their peak. The more little discrepancies settle in, the less likely we'll get those illegals out of there." She walked around her desk and clapped his shoulder. "Can you try to get this finished? I'll give Richard some excuse that I was too busy to retrieve it from you."

He nodded and exited her office. Gnashing his teeth, he thrust the holobook into Crowe's hand, ordering him to redo the entire report from scratch, then left U5-1. His heels clacking along the ancient tile floor, Roget quickly bypassed the ubiquitous Marines, who, throughout the months they had been stationed here, admirably disregarded the eccentricities of the theoretical studies department's denizens. Little wonder that Roget did his best to ignore the MPs in turn, so much so they were no more than indoor statuary.

Arriving at his quarters, Roget produced his pass key and ran it through the slot. Giving a cursory glance to the Marine to his right, who nodded in return, Roget walked inside and closed the door behind him, noticing that his usual MP was absent.

Taking two steps into the darkened room, he ordered, "Lights." After another two steps with no response from the domicile computer, he halted and stepped back to the door, his hand finding his pass key and the doorknob. After sliding the card through, he tried the knob, which remained stiff; he was locked inside.

"What the hell...." Roget beat against the door palm first, shouting, "Private, can you unlock the door? Private, unlock the door now!"

Complete silence answered Roget. Beating his fist against the door again, he realized he wasn't going to receive any assistance from the MP. Scurrying across his quarters, his hands scrabbled around a foot table, fumbling for a holobook he left, his only remaining contact with the rest of the U Complex.

A click behind him grabbed his attention. Turning, he discerned a shifting shadow along the depths of his quarters. Roget hopped onto the foot table and kicked a platter towards the far wall, hoping to distract the intruder in his quarters.

"What do you want? I've done nothing!"

Stumbling backwards, Roget landed between the foot table and the near wall. His hands reached down and grabbed a leg of the table, which he lifted off the floor and held in front of him, using the ten-kilogram furniture piece as a makeshift shield.

The stranger's hands gripped the front end of the table, and the two thrust about the room, growling and cursing. Roget finally found leverage and forced the table to the door, which pinned the intruder's right hand, causing him to drop a metallic device on the floor with a clap. The assailant howled while Roget rocked the table over the intruder's wrist, mustering every ounce of strength to incapacitate him. With one great heave, Roget pushed the table onto the man, taking him off his feet; the shadow fell with a loud thump, ceasing his struggle.

Roget peered over the edge of the table, looking for signs of unconsciousness. Satisfied the intruder was incapacitated, he dislodged him, hoisting the table to one side. He stepped away, scouring his quarters for several minutes before digging up his holobook, which he then used to call for help.

It would be the longest night of his life.

"Sit down, Lionel, and tell me again what this is all about."

Flop sweat beaded under Roget's collar, which he tugged at apprehensively. Boring holes into his skull were the combined stares of Rauchambau, Dark Horse, and most disheartened of all, de Lis. The three men loomed over Roget, dissecting his every twitch, stammer and glance, probing him for additional information that his sparse words had not provided them, or perhaps could not.

"I—I cannot for the life of me," he started again, his Quebecois lilt rising to the surface, "understand why an intruder, let alone an MP, would assail me in my own quarters, Richard! I cannot fathom it!"

"Then what was he doing in there!" de Lis spat, his fuse fraying faster than he would care to admit. While Roget's protestation flowed like honey, de Lis' own Quebecois inflection was a staccato castigation. "Given your statement so far, nothing in your quarters had been disturbed. Yet, the private was there nonetheless, waiting for you. Fortunately, you managed to overcome him, but the question remains what his motive was. Can you enlighten us? Is there something else you wish to share?"

De Lis' tone was akin to a parental need to understand a child's incomplete compliance, which wasn't far from the truth; de Lis was the guiding force, the father figure who had assembled his "family" and given all in bringing the theoretical studies laboratory together, expecting nothing but loyalty. Anything less struck him as disrespectful, if not perfidy.

Roget felt the seat tighten around his pelvis, forcing him to endure the figurative flaying. "Richard, I—I don't have any answer good enough—"

De Lis thrust his reddened face into Roget's eyes. "Well by God you'd better start thinking of one!"

From behind, Dark Horse grabbed de Lis' arms and pulled him back, fearing that de Lis would do something to Roget that the doctor would later regret. Walking him a good two meters away, Dark Horse turned his back to the seated man. "De Lis, what the hell do you think you're doing? He's not a suspect yet! And you're sure as hell not an inspector!"

De Lis clenched his jaw, half-listening to the colonel's harangue. *Of all the blasted arrogance...what was wrong here? What was with Lionel? Why, of all the talented men—what was Lionel hiding? And why? Why!*

Roget's hands trembled, despite having clawed them into the seat's wooden arms. "Richard, I think they tried to kill me," he sighed.

De Lis and Dark Horse faced the man again. Crossing over to him, Dark Horse asked, "Who wants to kill you, Doctor?"

Raising his head limply, he blinked several times, gaining the composure and courage to finally say, "The Confederation."

Dark Horse and Rauchambau exchanged heavy, but confused, glances.

"You see..." Roget continued, tears coming to his eyes, "I'm...I'm HADRON...."

# CHAPTER TWENTY-SEVEN

"You *sonovabitch*! You fucking killed my partner! You fucking killed him, didn't you?" Gilmour yelled, ambushing Roget as he, de Lis and Dark Horse exited U5-29.

In the adjacent corridor, Waters and Marlane restrained Gilmour, who still managed to connect a swipe to Roget's cheek, knocking his glasses to the floor. Constantine and McKean ran up behind Waters and Marlane to help contain the rabid Gilmour.

"Stand down, Gilmour!" Constantine said, securing Gilmour's right wrist. "Get a hold of yourself, Agent!"

"I—I'm gonna kill you! Goddammit, lemme go, Constantine! I'm gonna do it for Mason!"

While Constantine pushed Gilmour further from the scrape, Roget crawled on all fours, his hands sweeping the floor for his spectacles. Finding them, he rose gingerly, dabbing his cheek with a handkerchief to sop up the streaming blood. "You...you don't understand, Agent Gilmour...no one understands. No one!"

"Count your blessings they were here, Roget!" Gilmour pointed at him. "I'd kill you, just the way you tried to kill me! Don't forget it!"

"Come on, Gilmour, let him go," McKean said, leading him back against the wall to cool off.

Already four Marines bearing M-119s, led by Dark Horse, had arrived to escort Roget for his protection after the incident two hours earlier, and Gilmour's more recent threat. The lieutenant colonel did not look back as he passed the witnesses, locking Roget's right arm with his, the disgraced scientist's head lowered in shame.

"What will happen to him now?" Waters asked de Lis and

Rauchambau.

"A stern debriefing from the lieutenant colonel," de Lis answered, not at all satisfied with their Pyrrhic victory.

"Doctor," Marlane said, "Crowe and Ivan are competent, but Lionel is the only one who really can run his department. We'll still need him if we're going to succeed in reprogramming the codes."

"I agree, Carol, he's still an invaluable member of our team...that's what hurts the most about this." Rubbing his forehead, de Lis turned to the seething Gilmour. "Special Agent, are you in need of a breather? I can arrange for a temporary leave of absence, if you—"

Gilmour waved his hand. "No, Doctor, we can't afford that, especially now. I need to recollect my thoughts and get back to work on our task, if only double now because of what HADRON—Roget—has done."

The bitterness in Gilmour's words colored everyone's mood to some degree, and just about summed up the real lessons of the past hour: their work was only going to get harder. They would have to strive to overcome the damage inflicted, and hope all their previous work was good enough to pass muster. If not, even rooting out HADRON now wasn't going to save them or the world.

"It's worse than we thought," Waters said, setting a holobook onto de Lis' desk. "He gave them all the pertinent data on our Casimir chamber... judging by *Strela*'s advanced design, he's been at it for at least a year, if not longer."

De Lis pursed his lips while reading the holobook's report. "Then *Strela* is indeed a hybrid of our data and their trials?"

"Yes. Now granted, Lionel did work to improve our existing technology here, even downsizing the Casimirs to fit into the hazard suits. The problem remains, though, that he enabled the Confederation to get a jump on us by providing the Casimir schematics." She crossed her arms and sighed. "Honestly, I think they'd be three years behind us in test detonations if it wasn't for Lionel."

*Damn*, de Lis repeated over in his head. All the while they had been laboring over every minute jaunt calculation and the strategems of the Confederation, Roget had effectively rendered impotent the entire theoretical studies laboratory's efforts to neutralize *Strela*.

Of course, if not more important, the Confederation now possessed portions of the first samples of jewels, thanks to what everyone now assumed was Roget/HADRON who broke into the Lockbox several months ago; this single act seemed to be the starting point for one long domino effect, culminating in the deaths of Mason and Louris and the murders Nicolenko had committed back in the twentieth century, during Gilmour's jaunt.

But still, the question of why rattled in his brain, baffling him. Why did he do it? Money did not seem to be an influential motive to Roget, nor did any power the Confederation could have bestowed upon him. Politics? Roget seemed to be a loyal North American....

Perhaps de Lis could appeal to his junior colleague, maybe give him a reason to repent...after all, Lionel was still a member of this team. If nothing else, de Lis knew that Roget could quite possibly be the man most capable of getting those illegals out of danger before the Russians suspected what they were about to do.

A series of chirps broke his spiraling thoughts. De Lis shoved his hand into his jacket, then removed his phone. "De Lis." He listened for a moment before nodding. "I understand...right, then. Thank you."

De Lis stood and threw his phone back into his jacket. Looking to the intrigued Waters, he ordered, "Gather the team, Stacia—what's left of them. Just got the word from the DoD. We're a go for *Strela*.

"Reports are coming in from all over Irkutsk," Dark Horse said, reading his holobook. "The DoD confirms eight of the ten illegals are in position and ready for the signal link-up."

De Lis nodded. He and Dark Horse entered the gallery, where Valagua, Waters and Marlane manned the holographic weblinking equipment, awaiting the pair's arrival. Next to the group, Gilmour, Constantine and McKean rehashed, for the final time, the reprogramming procedures they were about to relay halfway around the world.

"All right everyone," de Lis said, raising his voice above the chatter. The team members momentarily paused and gave their full attention to him. "We have eight positives from Irkutsk. The DoD has given us full permission to begin when we are in position. Anyone who needs more time, give us an 'aye.'"

The various senior and junior scientists glanced at each other, and in unison looked to the three special agents; no one wanted to waste another second.

De Lis nodded. "Right. Let's go."

Gilmour, Constantine and McKean slapped hands. Constantine and McKean stepped away from Gilmour, who was first on deck, while they entered the gallery's observation anteroom to watch Gilmour's maiden performance. The special agent booted up his holobook and loaded the *Strela* schematics.

Around him, the theoretical studies team put the final touches on the weblinked computers, executing the final diagnostics on Valagua's holographic equipment before the first realtime run would prove or disprove their faith in this once-harebrained scheme, and possibly just save the lives of everyone on Earth.

After completing a myriad of equipment checks, each of the junior scientists came over and clapped Gilmour's shoulders, wishing him luck. Once evacuated, they left Gilmour to Valagua, Waters, Marlane, de Lis and Dark Horse.

"Javier," de Lis commanded, "begin preliminary procedures."

Valagua tapped an array of buttons on the gallery's holo-controls. At once, the gallery's normal fluorescence flicked off, allowing only the two ceiling-mounted track lights to illuminate the equipment.

On Valagua's cue, Marlane tapped a button on one of the weblinked computers, which proceeded to feed the gallery's holographic equipment footage from the very eyes of the illegal operatives. After pausing a moment to verify the signal was indeed correct, Valagua activated the gallery's holographic equipment.

The gallery was soon flooded with raw photons, saturating the room with a resounding brilliance. Shielding their eyes from the light storm, all save Valagua were oblivious to the forms which shimmered into existence. Blobs of pure whiteness were fabricated on a latticework of projected light, almost as if Valagua himself were building the crudely reproduced objects by hand from a set of construction plans.

One by one, the blobs became somewhat recognizable, losing their luminosity as tangibility increased. The staff soon brought their hands down to see a variety of objects emerge from the white soup, the first being a surprisingly good facsimile of concrete walls altogether different than the gallery's trademark pyramids.

The team found themselves in a stark facility, devoid of personality, but full of industrial sterility. Dingy, rusted pipes lay above them, stretching on for several meters ahead into a corridor. Handwritten Cyrillic signs were bolted to several doors along the way, leading into a larger section of the facility, perhaps a laboratory.

"Irkutsk?" Gilmour asked.

De Lis nodded. "It would appear so, although I expected more, for some reason."

Marlane walked ahead of the group a few steps to inspect a holographic handcart left in the corridor. She faced de Lis. "Doctor, this hologram appears rather...well, flat. No movement, nor sound."

Gilmour took note of this inconsistency as well. He felt an unnaturalness, but couldn't place it. Marlane had pinned it, though; nothing made a peep...not a squeaky gear, nor moaning, overworked equipment. It felt dead, perhaps even more so than the holograph Valagua had constructed of Nepal those many months ago.

"Carol, this is a static image just obtained from the web...." a voice out of thin air began to explain, which they all recognized as Valagua's.

The team then scanned the corridor, for the first time noticing that Valagua was nowhere to be found. Somehow he had vanished between the flash and the first appearance of the holographic corridor.

Valagua continued, "...Programmed to orient the gallery's systems. In actuality, what you are seeing is merely a nanosecond, a single frame of time imprisoned in the gallery now."

To the staff's right flank, the corridor wall rippled, stunning them. Light itself curved around an figure which now approached the assembled group. A foot, then a leg, followed by a swinging hand, then a second foot and an arm pushed through. Finally, Valagua was reconstituted, or more correctly, uncovered.

"Pardon my entrance," Valagua said. "I should have warned you that I'd be hidden for a moment over there." He jutted a thumb backwards. "The holographic simulation doesn't quite extend to the gallery's fullest perimeter."

"Nice trick. I'll have to keep it in mind," Gilmour quipped.

De Lis interrupted Valagua's unintended diversion. "Javier, when can we have a full datastream available?"

"At your command, Richard."

De Lis nodded. "Let's allow Agent Gilmour to get to work. Everybody out."

With that command, Dark Horse, Waters, Marlane and de Lis himself stepped away from Gilmour and instinctually headed for the nearest metal door to exit.

Waters was about to set a hand on the door knob when Valagua asked, "Where are you going?"

Stacia looked at the door askance. "Out...?"

"That's the gallery's north wall. Door's over here," Valagua said before breaking away from the group and walking straight into what at first appeared to be a water pipe junction laid next to the wall.

The team exchanged bewildered glances, then decided by following Valagua that the man knew what he was doing.

Gilmour watched the light bubble around the group as they filed out, one after another. The entire exit was one more bizarre moment to add to his ever burgeoning list. *How do I keep getting myself into this?*

\*\*\*

"Take it easy, Alpha...you're doing great."

Gilmour's head spun in all directions; the Alpha illegal's line of sight was bouncing all over the place, leaving the special agent near nausea just by virtue of being privy to Alpha's own point of view. Then again, how often has a man been able to practice keeping his eyeballs steady so that someone else piggybacking on them wouldn't get sick? Gilmour would have to get over it, and fast; there was no time for whining.

"Just get us near the loading bay."

Alpha pushed open a set of double doors, then walked past several fleeing lorries. Red and yellow motion lights flickered and strobed throughout the bay, lending the entire dock an unearthly sulfur pall. Scores of Russian dockworkers, decked out in white radiation suits and yellow hardhats, scurried past Alpha towards another section of the bay. The traffic here was incredible, Gilmour thought, leading him to believe an operation was undeniably imminent; all the better then that the DoD had proceeded as swiftly as they had to relocate the illegals.

"Okay, Alpha, could you do a sweep of the loading bay?"

The holographic loading bay screamed past Gilmour's eyes in a 360-degree panorama, fleetingly registering to his brain.

"Aah-uhh. Take that swing a little less harshly next time, please."

After giving himself a moment's pause, Gilmour consulted his weblinked holobook and decided on the next course. "Head for that metal door straight ahead. Remember, we're just one of the boys here, nothing to see...."

In front of them was an overhead door, large enough to allow a lorry inside. Walking over to a closed door next to the overhead, Alpha spied a sign adorned with an ominous message: "AUTHORIZED PERSONNEL ADMITTED ONLY. UNAUTHORIZED PERSONS WILL BE SUBJECT TO USE OF DEADLY FORCE." The curt warning stuck in Gilmour's thoughts, reminding him of the stakes if he failed; he imagined Alpha's nerves were chilled by now.

Alpha's right glove disappeared from Gilmour's view, then quickly reappeared, producing a pass key. Swiping the card through the door's panel, a green light clicked on overhead, admitting Alpha into what appeared to be a small holding chamber, lined with grey shelves along the concrete block walls.

"Head for those huge, reinforced grey metal shelves to your right."

A few meters away, packed horizontally onto the shelves, were what Gilmour took to be the *Strela* warheads. He looked at them again; they were packed horizontally. Hell, all three agents had drilled the last few days with them standing upright. No one thought to know that the

*Strela*s were being loaded to ship immediately; they must have had only hours to spare.

"Uhh...okay, Alpha, slight problem."

For a second, the scene froze, giving Gilmour the stomach-sinking sensation that perhaps the uplink had developed a glitch.

"All right, bear with me here." Gilmour took a deep breath, then consulted his holobook before he continued. "Haven't worked with the *Strela* horizontally before, only vertically. Should be the same, though," he hoped.

Alpha's white-gloved hands, cut-off from the elbow up, reappeared again just below and ahead of Gilmour's body, waiting for Gilmour's next instructions.

"Next, I you need to pass the interlock on the cone sheath. Here's the encryption code." Tapping a blue button on his holobook, Gilmour transmitted a complex numerical sequence through the weblink.

There was a brief pause before Alpha's gloved hands reached for the bottom-first *Strela* and entered the code onto the nosecone sheath's encryption lock. A green LCD lit-up on the cone sheath, and the gloved hands took off the cone and set it down on the floor. The next stage below the nosecone sheath was the taut red and yellow fluorescent foil Gilmour remembered from their drills.

"All right, this is the security housing for the radiation hood. Swipe the pass key through the microlock," he said, the procedure by rote in his brain. "Underneath that chamber is a blue disk, the QPU. I am going to give you the code to reprogram the disk." Gilmour tapped another button on his holobook, transmitting the second code halfway around the world.

Watching his holobook for confirmation, Gilmour wiped a bead of sweat from his forehead. Time itself seemingly had stopped...seconds seemed to melt into hours. What was taking so long?

A chirp broke his rumination; his eyes looked to the holobook. Confirmation, finally. "Yes! Get that warhead back into shape! We've got a whole set of other ones to do before we can get the hell out of here."

# CHAPTER TWENTY-EIGHT

"Excellent work, Agent Gilmour," Rauchambau lauded. "I have to add that I'm not easily impressed."

Gilmour stepped out of the gallery, two hours and several minutes after entering the room, to find de Lis, Dark Horse, Rauchambau, Waters, Valagua, Marlane, Constantine and McKean waiting for his exit in U5-1.

"Hell, I never thought it'd work. I have to hand it to you, Gilmour," Constantine said.

Dark Horse crossed his arms. "Not to deflate your joy, gentlemen, but we're only a baby step into this operation. Agent Constantine, I believe you are slated for the Beta shift?"

"Yes, Colonel, I am."

"Then we have no time to waste," de Lis concurred. "Javier, get the gallery set-up for Beta."

"Already on it." Valagua raced past the group and headed back into the gallery, followed by Constantine.

Gilmour invited himself along to the gallery's observation anteroom, where he, McKean, Waters and the others reconvened. Peeking through a hole made by the bystanders, Gilmour witnessed the gallery shift from its normal mode to a dark corridor, not too dissimilar from the corridor he was in, but clearly a different location. Constantine did not seem to be distracted by this shift, Gilmour noted; the special agent consulted his holobook, just like he had been trained, and immediately commenced his shift.

Constantine's voice sounded crisply through the anteroom's

speakers as he instructed the Beta illegal through his first leg of the operation. Gilmour again marveled at the humanity of the holographic Russian dockworkers passing by Constantine—every movement was fluid, not stilted as he still expected, perhaps due to the synthetic nature of the holograms the special agents worked with during the drills.

From his new vantage, Gilmour remarked to Waters just how bizarre the floating gloves of Beta looked ahead of Constantine.

"At first, you're right," Stacia answered. "But after the numerous drills you three put yourself through, it's kind of become normal, in a theoretical studies sort of way, just like everything else here since you gents arrived."

Gilmour forgave himself for cracking a smile. "I'll take that to be a compliment."

Back on the monitor, Constantine and Beta's gloves happened upon a well-lit assembly bay. Constantine turned about the bay as he encroached it. "This must be where the *Strela*s are assembled." He double-checked his holobook.

To Gilmour, the bay resembled every old photograph of the twentieth-century-era NASA probe facilities, the ones where, as a kid, he watched the rocket scientists poring over the tall machines, checking every system before a launch. They impressed upon him a sense of the supremacy of technology, of how humanity could make out of all that cold metal and circuitry a better understanding of our place in the greatness of life, of the universe. Now watching Constantine walk over the grey cemented floors of that Confederation facility, he longed for that juvenile wonder, wishing humanity would strive for that achievement again, not the furthering of Armageddon.

Constantine strode past a cadre of white bunny suits, all of whom seemingly took the illegal as normal. Gilmour's partner went left and headed towards a raised platform. The holographic view spun 360 degrees around Constantine—taking Gilmour aback—then returned to the forward position, giving the special agent a feel for the assembly bay. Arriving at the platform's grated metal steps, the hologram of the bay dropped a step down, providing Constantine and the observation viewers the illusion they had ascended the platform. Several more drops like this followed before Constantine and the holographic gloves made it to the two-meter-high top step, which overlooked two dozen buffed and scintillating titanium warheads.

"Okay, Beta," Constantine said over the observation speakers, "take one more view of the surroundings here. I'm not too sure about us sitting atop here."

Constantine was right to have reservations. Seeing the 360-degree swing one more time from Beta's POV, Gilmour was convinced the illegal was as close to a set-up as he could be. Having the high ground was ideal in a battlefield situation, but in the assembly bay, everyone and their brother could see what they were doing up there. Beta had to be great, better than just damn good, like Gilmour's counterpart a while ago.

Once the two began their disassembly of the first *Strela*, Gilmour noticed himself—along with the others in the observation anteroom—giving a recitation of his instructions to Constantine and Beta, so ingrained had the training become over the past few days. All his years of service to the Agency couldn't defeat his natural human tendency to keep his thoughts to himself; it was a sense of duty Gilmour wouldn't allow to be taken away.

Watching Constantine instruct Beta, Gilmour kept time on his wrist chrono, mentally tallying the list of instructions Constantine read aloud, then timing the holographic gloves per each step of the way. The first warhead disassembly was long by about four seconds; seeing a close-up of Constantine's face, Gilmour read the bottled anxiety that perhaps no one, save he and McKean, could detect.

Dark Horse shot a concerned look to Gilmour, but the special agent saw nothing but Constantine. The colonel counted from his own chrono and returned his gaze to the monitor. A rapid twitch in the back of his mind broke through his shielded sense of repose.

The observation anteroom groaned under the mounting pressure; each warhead seemed to drag on longer, and all of Constantine's firm prodding couldn't shave off the few seconds Beta had lost along the way.

Dark Horse stole another glance to his chrono: 00:09:58:92. "Dammit."

Gilmour thought he heard the one phrase none of the Temporal Retrieve team wanted to hear.

De Lis turned to Dark Horse and said again, "So, do we pull him out, Colonel? Abort?"

Fighting every instinct to overreact and advocate a quick mission kill, Gilmour clenched his jaw and pushed his way to Dark Horse. "Pulling him out now is only going to worsen our circumstances, sir! I strongly suggest allowing Constantine to do his job and get that man out of there with the *Strela*s compromised."

Dark Horse rubbed his eyes, showing for the first time in public the rising stress this posting had forced upon him. He glanced at his chrono a third time. "They've been at it for over ten minutes now, barely finishing off two warheads. I'd say it's painfully apparent that the illegal has almost no chance of meeting the deadline."

Surpassing the scheduled deadline automatically killed the mission, no matter what the current status was. No amount of pleading from Gilmour or Constantine could save a mission after that.

"Colonel," Gilmour persisted, "abort this facility once, and kiss it goodbye! The very least we could do is get as many warheads decommissioned before the deadline, maybe increase our chances for a successful end to the mission without pulling up our stakes outright here." Gilmour narrowed his eyes, his pupils meeting the colonel's. Deep down, the special agent felt, Dark Horse knew he had to be right.

All attention was on Dark Horse, who, in spite of de Lis' theoretical studies lab command, was ultimately calling all the shots for the government. Swallowing hard, he nodded his head, which must have creaked terribly inside, paining him.

Gilmour didn't give Dark Horse's say another thought. Turning back to Constantine, his every sinew was consumed with Constantine completing his task and getting Beta out of that blasted neutronic factory.

"I know we've reached the deadline, but dammit, Colonel, we've only got three left!" Constantine shouted to the walls, which echoed his every syllable in the gallery. "We can get it done!"

De Lis shook his head, then glanced to Dark Horse. The lieutenant colonel toggled the intercom switch on the anteroom's computer panel. "Not now, Agent. Not now. Report to U5-29."

A tremendous crack reverberated from the gallery's walls, making Gilmour flinch. Sneaking a look at the monitor, he saw Constantine storm out. Panning his eyes a meter or two, Gilmour caught sight of an abandoned holobook on the gallery's floor, presumably launched by Constantine.

Moments later, Constantine slammed the door behind him. U5-29 and its inhabitants shuddered under his black cloud as he strode past everyone, even Gilmour and McKean.

De Lis and the senior staff seated themselves, holobooks in hand, at the conference table, with lamps lit for the briefing. De Lis stroked his chin, allowing Constantine to stew for a moment in the room's corner. After an acceptable pause he ordered, "Have a seat, Agent Constantine." Constantine pursed his lips and grudgingly pulled out a chair backwards, then seated himself so that the chairback supported his disinterested elbow and chin.

"I feel it necessary to remind ourselves," de Lis began, "that we have definitive orders here from the Defense Department. Breaking those orders, stretching those orders, is not why we were given this mandate. Understood?"

"Understood, Doctor," Gilmour and McKean chimed, followed by a grunt only from Constantine.

"Good. Now, if I'm remembering correctly..." de Lis paused to pick up his holobook. Scrolling down the page, he found the DoD's timetable. "...We have one hour, nineteen minutes before Agent McKean's Gamma shift. Now, gentlemen, this is not a briefing in our usual sense...the need to stress the automatic kill is our top priority. Nothing short of full compliance will be acceptable. We cannot—I repeat, cannot have dissent over this. Too much is at risk here for us to go gallivanting around when a mission goes astray. Is that understood?" The question was directed generally at the agents, but de Lis' eyes shot straight to Constantine.

All three chorused, "Understood."

De Lis slapped his hands down on the table and rose. "Good. I sure as hell hope this is the final time I have to give this speech."

With a round of claps to his back and hooting, McKean exited from the gallery at a new record time and met the senior staff and his partners in U5-1.

"All right, Neil!" Waters cheered, perhaps applauding the loudest of all the theoretical studies group.

Gilmour and Constantine cut through the gathering throng and took turns shaking McKean's hand. "If I'd have known you were going to upstage us, Keanie," Constantine quipped, "I'd never let you out of your quarters this morning!"

"A job well done, Agent McKean," de Lis hailed, a smile cracking his recently dour demeanor. "Truly marvelous."

Dark Horse nodded, satisfied, then silenced the mild celebration with a downward gesture of his hands. "Beautiful work, Agents. At the risk of being a spoilsport, everybody here should allow the agents to get some shuteye before tomorrow's shifts. As much as today's triumphs are good for our spirits, we have to remember it's an ongoing war from now on. Nothing is for granted." Shaking the hands of the three agents once more, Dark Horse looked to the assembled and finished, "Tomorrow, let's kick their asses so hard they'd wished they'd never heard the word *Strela*!"

\*\*\*

A red bulb over the sliding doors signaled the elevator had reached the lower depths of the new facility. Gilmour memorized the surroundings as the Delta illegal took him from cramped quarters above to the bustling underbelly of the Irkutsk military/industrial complex. Judging by the native elements, Irkutsk's denizens could just as easily fill in at any of the Vegas strip spots; the work was equally dirty and certainly unmentionable to the unacquainted.

Proceeding down a dim corridor that would have put the submarine *Hesperus* to shame, Gilmour and Delta found a *Strela* assembly point on the sublevel. Row upon row of warhead fuselages sat on an assembly line, pre-capitation, all waiting for the final installment of explosive mechanisms before being loaded for transport. An automated crane containing two workers hovered over each *Strela*, giving the men topside access while they performed the nosecone connections. After each nosecone was secured, the assembly line's track moved a meter down the line, bringing the delicate warheads to a loading car. From Gilmour's view, each car appeared capable of ferrying about four warheads at once. The key would be to commandeer one of the cars before it hit the loading dock.

"All right, Delta, a little shift in plans here. Hope your skills are up to the task," Gilmour said, scoping out the cars crossing the bay. "Here's where your credentials come into play."

After giving Delta a quick tactical plan, Gilmour had the man do a quick swing pass of the bay. He then walked near the assembly line cautiously, but with deliberate steps, perpetrating his cover, until the pair were past the crane and free to intercept an approaching car.

Gilmour did another scan of the bay with his eyes. "Follow my instructions to the letter. Tell him we're needing a lift to the loading bay...I don't care what you have to say."

The gallery image jumped as Delta picked up his pace and flagged down the nearing car. Once stopped, the car's driver acknowledged a response in Russian that almost passed Gilmour while he lip-read. Delta's hands clasped the car's side and hopped into the tiny vehicle, again making the holograph jump. Several moments passed while the driver facilitated the delivery of the *Strela* warheads into the rear of the car.

Once the car was full, the worker drove off down the corridor, taking Gilmour on a dizzying ride. Looking at the speedometer, they were going only a few KPH, but compared to the slower pace of human leg power, it was lightspeed to the gallery's holographic systems. The trip lasted less than three minutes, the pair soon arriving at some type of

subterreanean transport dock at the end of the corridor, after first passing through a rather porous security checkpoint. A subway train waited
on the tracks while men fed the warheads into a port hatch, putting each
of the weapons into round slots on the car's interior floor.

"Delta," Gilmour commanded, "try to get a closer look at the
*Strelas*."

Delta stepped off the small car and walked around the station
dock, gradually closing in on the subway car. Gilmour did a quick tally of
the warheads between Delta's successive swings.

"I'm counting at least forty *Strelas* in this car alone. Damn, how
many of these things do they have?" Gilmour again watched the dockworkers load the warheads onto the subway car. Counting the empty
slots reserved for the last *Strelas*, this load would be one of the last; there
wouldn't be a better time than now to hit this many warheads.

"Delta, get yourself aboard this subway car. I've another change in
plans."

Delta surveyed the car, then walked to the engine at the head car.
Grappling a handhold, Delta scampered aboard through an unlocked
door and hid in a auxiliary compartment not far from the car's rear.
Before Delta closed the door, Gilmour noted the engine car's exit/
entrance to the cargo car was within sprinting distance.

For now, all the pair could do was wait for the subway car to get
underway to perform the most dangerous part of the mission.

"That's it. Let's go!"

Delta's hand found the lock and cracked the door open, permitting enough light to glimpse the corridor. Satisfied all was well, Delta
stepped out and headed for the car's aft exit, a sliver of a door apparently
designed for children and adults with shoulders less than thirty-five
centimeters to pass through. Removing a lockpick, Delta broke open the
door's lock and wriggled his way past, briefly balancing himself on the
connection arm between the two cars. Flashes of the subway tube's lights
around the speeding cars gave Gilmour glances of the tracks barreling
under them, reminding him just how fast the cars were actually speeding, even if he didn't want to know.

One jump later, Delta had grabbed a hold of the cargo car and
pulled himself onto its slim segment of the connection arm. Quick
work with the lockpick pried open the entrance, and Delta and Gilmour
entered the darkened car. After locking the door, Delta switched on a
helmet lamp. Dozens of shiny *Strela* warheads scattered the light back at
them, casting the car's ceiling and walls with shimmering silver.

What was just a dark cavern seconds ago had suddenly metamorphosized into a forest of machines, each with the capability of obliterating this tube and the ground around it for hundreds of meters; being present with that much power was quite humbling and—dare Gilmour think of it—damned horrifying.

Refusing to dwell upon it, Gilmour and Delta went to work fast, knowing by far this was the mission posing the least threat of interruption by the Confederation, and therefore the greatest fruit.

It was laborious work; the warheads were crammed together in a tight area, forcing Delta to be a contortionist to perform the recoding. Gilmour was able to give Delta new reprogramming shortcuts thanks to the agent's prior experience, but the sheer quantity, and the relatively uneven surface flooring, made for a horrendous experience. Gilmour hoped the train ride was long; he estimated the reprogramming time to run over by thirty to thirty-five percent. In other words, a long night.

By the second hour, Delta had moved to the back section of the car; progress, if it could be called that. Gilmour noticed signs of Delta's nearing exhaustion; repeated mistakes and the continual dropping of equipment started to rankle the agent.

A burst of energy shook the gallery holograph, breaking Delta's attention away from the present warhead. Gilmour was floored by the dizzying perspective. *What the hell—*

Given a brief respite from the haphazard swings, Gilmour saw the car's normal rocking become spasms, building to a series of pulses until slowing to a quiet roll. From all appearances, the car was braking, coming to a halt. Was the car already at its stop, or something else?

Delta instinctively shut off his lamplight, reverting the car to darkness.

"Stay down, don't move!"

After a moment spent absorbing the blackness of the car for signs of movement, Gilmour said again, "Do you hear anything? Men outside, doors sliding?"

Delta extended two fingers in the dim light, answering, "no."

Gilmour was literally stuck in the dark, waiting for signs of confirmation from Delta. Damnable holographic interface's only pitfall was the lack of sound, one of the IIA's most significant allies in field work. Sans eyes, the second best tools were one's ears, visceral equipment harder to fool, making them therefore more reliable in compromising situations.

"Talk to me...what's going down?"

Delta didn't comply, still crouching low behind a pair of

warheads. Periodic swings of Delta's corneal implants gave an incomplete survey for Gilmour to follow the best he could. Seconds of tantalizing torture gave way to minutes, as he waited in mounting frustration at his lack of access to the mission site. Finally, Delta stood—against Gilmour's warnings—and crept over to the car's entrance.

Gilmour dropped his holobook and balled his fists to Delta's holographic gloved hands. "Get away from there, dammit! You wanna get yourself killed?"

Delta continued to ignore Gilmour, instead placing what Gilmour thought was Delta's right ear to the door, cutting off the special agent's view of the entrance, leaving in its place an image of the car's portside wall. For a moment, Delta paused, then bolted away from the door and ran down a narrow corridor between the standing *Strela*s.

"Goddammit, get down! Get down!" Gilmour retrieved his holobook, tapped a green button, then looked to where the gallery's anteroom cameras would be mounted. "Rauchambau, is he armed? Do we have clearance to return fire?"

Over the gallery's speakers, Rauchambau answered, "Negative, they are not armed. All sidearms are restricted inside Confederation neutronic facilities by UN Resolution five-oh-two-one-one-nine."

"Sweet Jesus...goddamned politicians...." Tapping another button, Gilmour patched himself back to Delta. "Give me a heads up, Delta! What's going down?"

A shaft of light split the darkness in two. Gilmour strained to see a silhouette move into the car at the entrance, swing its head once, take a step, then move back outside, extinguishing the light. Delta then rose and crossed to the entrance a second time.

"What the hell do you think you're doing? If they stopped the car, they're coming back! Do you hear me?" Gilmour tore his eyes away from the holograph and yelled at the holobook's web connection. "Is this thing fucking on! Can you hear me?"

Toggling the holobook's audio, Gilmour patched himself through to the anteroom again. "Rauchambau, abort him, goddammit! He's disregarding every command! He's gonna crash it all!"

"You positive, Agent Gilmour?" Rauchambau asked over the loudspeaker.

"Do it now!"

The holographic image continued despite Gilmour's protests, just long enough for Gilmour to see a line of Confederation MPs loading on to the engine car through the cargo car's now open entrance.

"What the hell are you doing!" Gilmour screamed. Desperate, he clawed at the holograph gallery's controls. "Rauchambau! Get him the hell out of there!"

To his left, Confederation soldiers charged through the subway cars directly at him and Delta. Now just centimeters away, Gilmour recoiled in helplessness as Delta attempted to block a baton to the chest. Gilmour groaned after Delta was swiped across the head, throwing the holograph spinning and the special agent to the floor with nausea.

Tilting his head, Delta managed one more transmission through a single eye. Gathering like storm clouds, the blue-suited MPs loomed over the fallen Delta, circling briefly before parting and allowing one last image, one that soon seared itself into Gilmour's brain: a familiar man, in the garb of a Confederation Army officer, reaching down to the special agent before exploding into a shower of static.

A single bellow shattered the gallery's quiescence: "*NICOLENKO!*"

## CHAPTER TWENTY-NINE

"It's all gone to hell!"

Gilmour collapsed onto the floor of his darkened quarters, his hands shrouding his eyes. Alone, time stopped...all was quiet, and his troubles hid in the long shadows, daring not to rouse his ire again. Gilmour's left hand soothed his chapped throat, raw from the past few hours spent damning the fates.

Folding himself into a ball shielded his body and psyche from the universe; it was almost certain not to work, but the act comforted his mind and distracted him long enough to forget for just a moment.

A solitary knock echoed throughout the sullen room, grudgingly bringing Gilmour upright. Filling his lungs full, he breathed out, then rose and stepped over to the door before fumbling for the handle. "Gilmour. Who is it?"

The drowned-out voiced responded, "Richard de Lis. May I enter?"

Gilmour opened the door, flooding his quarters with a blade of fluorescence. "Pardon the darkness. It seemed appropriate."

Setting a foot inside, de Lis didn't hesitate to say "Lights," ordering the domicile computer to bring illumination to the room.

Surprised, Gilmour hid his eyes behind hastily raised hands. "What the—"

"Frankly, Agent Gilmour, I'm tired of your shit."

Gilmour narrowed his eyes and stared straight into de Lis'. *The gall of this—*

De Lis returned the stern stare right back. "And you can wipe that look from your face too. There's a war going down, Agent Gilmour, and niceties such as every man coming home to his wife don't figure much in it. I know you took Delta's capture hard, but the man did it himself. If anything, we know what we're up against."

Gilmour gritted his teeth, not content to have de Lis punching back. If anything, he swore it was Rauchambau he was standing next to. "You sure that was Nicolenko you saw?" de Lis asked.

Gilmour nodded. "I'd recognize that sonuvabitch at a hundred meters."

"Good. Rauchambau wants him eliminated, if he's the threat you say he is."

"We wouldn't be in this quandary if I had succeeded in taking him out in my last jaunt." None of this mess would.

"But we don't have much time." De Lis rubbed his jaw. "Thanks to Delta's bungling, the other illegals have been compromised, as far as we can ascertain. There may be enough warheads still reprogrammed to do the job, but I seriously doubt that's an option anymore. The DoD expects the Confederation to speed up the trench project. That leaves the Navy only a few days to get the North Pacific fleet in place. Honestly, I'm not holding out much hope the military can stop this one." De Lis' face turned a shade of green normally seen on deathbed patients. This was the Big One.

"I apologize, Doctor."

De Lis mustered a stoic look. "Forget it. We need you one last time, James." He proffered his palm, expecting—willing—Gilmour to accept it.

Gilmour's hands had been balled into fists ever since de Lis' reaction. Slowly, Gilmour loosened them, allowing sensation to return, then extended his right palm. Together, the pair shook hands, reaffirming their commitment.

It was time to get this going again.

"If this man is indeed your target, how do you expect to get him?" Marlane asked. Seated across from Rauchambau at U5-29's conference table, she leaned forward. "Without intelligence from the illegals, finding him will be extremely difficult, if not impossible."

"I have a reasonably good idea where in Irkutsk our Nicolenko could be," Valagua said. "Previous missions in that facility have allowed me to corroborate with the latest holographic intel just where that subway train was destined."

For the first time in countless conferences, Quintanilla was in attendance, seating herself between Dark Horse and Rauchambau, apparently showing herself when times were at their roughest. And again, she surprised not only Gilmour but many of the other senior staff by speaking up. "Difficult, but not impossible, Doctor Marlane. There are many avenues not tread with which we have access."

Marlane looked to Waters, who, if possible, would have shrugged with her eyes. To all but perhaps Rauchambau, Quintanilla succeeded in still proving to be the toughest one to read.

"I know of at least one place—one time—where Nicolenko is, was and will always be, where he can never escape, despite his best actions to the contrary."

Constantine and McKean both raised eyebrows and turned to Gilmour, half-disbelieving the words uttered from his lips; what had he mumbled?

De Lis stifled a proud smile, then urged him to elaborate, if only as a formality; de Lis was beginning to draw a good bead on Gilmour. "What's on your mind?"

"Thanks to your mind-bending theoretical studies laboratory, I'm starting to see events in a different light." He made eye contact with his two partners. "Nicolenko is forever bound to spacetime, just like the rest of us. Unless he were to go back into the past and alter events—which I doubt since they turned slightly to his favor—the days he spent in 1940 will always exist."

Constantine scratched his nose, grasping the cusp of Gilmour's thought. "Like a recording?"

Gilmour nodded. "Close, Will. Time isn't as fleeting as we would like it to be, especially nowadays."

"With the proper equipment, we can 'play back' time," Waters added, then cracked a smile. "Excellent, Gilmour. We're rubbing off on you."

McKean leaned back in his seat and sighed. "The monkeysuits." "Has to be. That's the only place and time I can guarantee Nicolenko will be," Gilmour said. "I want to do it right this time, take some back-up, find out where the hell Nicolenko got to and who helped him."

"Sounds like you will need my assistance again, Agent Gilmour," Valagua volunteered.

"You haven't let me down yet. And 1940 hasn't become any easier."

"If I may make a request, Agent Gilmour," de Lis said. "There is one man who can make your mission run smoother...."

Gilmour sat still.

"Lionel Roget," de Lis blurted before the special agents and the senior staff could object.

"Good lord—"

De Lis raised his hands, hoping to drive his point across. "Now I fully understand your objections, Agent Gilmour—"

"The man's a snake, for Chrissakes! You yourself admitted so much!"

"Gilmour's right!" Waters said. "He can't be trusted with overseeing such an important phase of the mission!"

De Lis stood. "Just listen, once, please. Trust me on this. Roget designed the very technology capable of performing our mission. Despite your very reasonable objections—remind yourselves that I by no means condoned his actions—he has insight that perhaps no else here does. It's instinctual to him, and he knows how to get the best out of the equipment. Plus, he will have no oversight authority. Everything final will be made by me, with Crowe and Ivan doing final checks. Is that fair?"

"If he's capable of remorse," Gilmour sneered.

"I interviewed him personally," Quintanilla said. "Remorse is not alien to him. He is capable by far to assist you in your mission once again. I believe its success can be met more by him in the lab than in a jail cell." Dark Horse crossed his arms, perhaps betraying his opinion of security matters. "He will of course be escorted throughout the entire proceedings." The colonel's face was granite hard, reminding the group that he ran the details in the U Complex. "Day and night."

"Then we acquiesce to your judgment, Doctor," Gilmour said, dropping the subject. For better or worse, Gilmour admitted, they needed all the help they could get, even from this snake in the grass.

"This is strictly business. Anything superfluous will most likely earn you a broken jaw, which is what you deserve anyway, if not worse."

Roget removed his spectacles and wiped the lenses free of smudges. "I would expect nothing less from you, Agent Gilmour. Seeing as how I have no wish to waste in a cell, you have my complete word I will do everything to get this mission successfully underway."

Gilmour fought the urge to yell "Shut the hell up!" in order to abide by his and de Lis' agreement. He, Constantine, McKean, the departed Mason and Louris were the better men, not the prestige hungry Roget. Alliances that shifted by the sway of the wind never endeared Gilmour much, let alone the "complete word" of such men.

Gilmour, along with Roget and two MPs, made their way into the theoretical studies lab. Ivan and Crowe greeted their former boss coolly, perhaps as eager to work with him again as Gilmour was.

"I trust everything is still as it was?" Roget asked his assistants. His eyes scanned his abandoned office once they passed near.

"Yes, Doctor," Crowe answered, though without the old laboratory reverence. "We've been updating ourselves on your new initiatives. They look promising."

"New initiatives?" Gilmour looked at Roget, perhaps astounded that the jailed scientist would still be exploring new ideas outside the lab. Roget led the escort inside, then picked up a holobook set there by Ivan. Powering it up, he accessed a file block, then handed the device to Gilmour to read.

After a few seconds of skimming, he looked back to Roget. "Omni-Coordinated Temporal Transportation."

"Until now," Roget explained, "Temporal Retrieve has been limited to two directions in the spacetime continuum, obviously the back and forth movements in time. One of the limitations in such travel is the availability to traverse space. Now, employing the planet's magnetic field lines, we can send you anywhere on Earth."

"Traveling location to location was always something we wanted to work on as a future upgrade to the equipment," Crowe added, "but until recently, never had the resources nor personnel to devote to full-time research."

Gilmour read on. "If I'm reading this right, we would be able to pick and choose our time coordinates, as well as our geographic coordinates, and jaunt there? That would open all sorts of opportunities...."

Roget nodded. "The wider landscape is finally revealing itself to you, Agent Gilmour. No longer are humans dependent on this tiny frame," he said, making a square with his palms, the whites of his eyes growing. "We are creatures of every dimension now. You see, it's bigger, larger, than just one man, one nation, one world. I do this for the enhancement of our species as universal denizens."

For a moment, Gilmour considered smashing the holobook and destroying every bit of data contained within. If a man such as Roget could dream up this Omni-Coordinated Temporal Transportation technology, then fully homicidal men such as Nicolenko could easily obtain it.

"Have you practical models of it yet?" Gilmour asked, more to Crowe and Ivan then Roget, whom he ignored for the moment.

"We have a few more days of actual construction to do," Ivan responded.

Gilmour replayed Roget's crazed eyes in his mind. "Then I'm sure it will be perfected before long." He looked once more to Roget before pointedly saying only to him, "Just keep in mind what happened to the Rosenbergs, Kweiksman and Al-Zawara."

"How'd Roget hold up?" McKean asked later, in the corridor.

Gilmour paused and craned his head back. "Either he's saved the world or damned us to oblivion. Come on."

Constantine furrowed his brow at McKean. The pair jogged by the theoretical studies laboratory and sped up to catch Gilmour, who quickly arrived at U5-17, the previously off-limits offices of Professor Inez Quintanilla.

A tastefully decorated suite—rather than the austere U5-29—greeted them, much to their amazement. Royal blue carpet filled each man's eyes and hugged their shoes as they spread out to explore this inviting new frontier. Portraits of historical figures hung from all four walls, broken up by an occasional landscape or framed flag.

Gilmour walked over to a desk situated towards the rear of the room, perpendicular to opposite, closed wooden doors. The mahogany desk was the home of many framed photographs and a large monitor. Smaller, one-meter-tall cabinets at the foot of the desk housed dozens, perhaps a hundred, book volumes, giving the office an even warmer air than Gilmour had ever thought possible for Quintanilla. Little wonder she never attended a conference meeting in U5-29.

Several moments slipped past them before the door on the left opened, admitting Quintanilla. Her arrival sparked a newfound interest in the professor, replacing Gilmour's near contempt borne from his unchecked ignorance.

"Thank you for waiting, gentlemen," Quintanilla welcomed. She headed straight for the desk that Gilmour was still admiring. An awkward grin from the special agent elicited a curious, arched eyebrow from Quintanilla. She piled several holobooks into one stack, then extended the palm of her hand and said, "Have a seat."

The trio found three chairs in front of the desk and pulled them close while Quintanilla sat down at her desk.

"I have pulled in many favors to give you this briefing...most of my sources were reluctant to provide any help whatsoever. Fortunately, I am quite persuasive."

Quintanilla rotated the monitor around so that it faced all three agents. Toggling a button on a keypad, she activated a stream of webfootage. A holographic scene then played in front of the agents, set in what appeared to be a desolate prairie. Snow fell from the slate sky as a group of men, all dressed in military uniforms, held a vigorous, muted discussion while pointing off-camera. The camera's point-of-view switched several times, closing up on the faces of a few select men, then alternating to a distant, mountainous horizon.

"There!" Gilmour yelled, his eyes widening. "Pause." A blurred face, in mid-turn, froze on the monitor. Gilmour's index finger pointed to the headshot. "Nicolenko."

"Along with five of the highest ranking officers in the Confederation," Quintanilla added. "This footage was filmed over three months ago. My sources are still debating the circumstances of this event, but needless to say, it locks our case for Nicolenko having ties to the highest of the military cadre."

"Do your sources have biographical or psychological information on Nicolenko?" Gilmour asked, perhaps too vigorously.

"Spotty at best." Quintanilla consulted a holobook. "The Confederation has some of the best firewalls our government has ever seen. What little we do know is that his full name is Vasily Zivenovich Nicolenko, first lieutenant, Russian Confederated Army. Awarded the Sword of the White Star, the Cross of St. George, the Russian Medal of Honor twice and the Putin Shield."

Constantine let out a low whistle. "Anything else?"

"Our knowledge of his psych files is even lousier," Quintanilla admitted, ignoring Constantine's facetiousness. "Suffice to say, an officer doesn't attain this level of hierarchy with bipolar tendencies or lapses of judgment."

Unless one could ingratiate himself, Gilmour said to no one but himself. With all respect to Quintanilla, Gilmour had actually dealt with Nicolenko hand-to-hand, face-to-face. If anything, their lieutenant was given to succeed at all costs; schizo, perhaps not, but ego driven, definitely.

Quintanilla continued, "No information on marital status, either. I have located a sketchy birth certificate, but names of birth parents and place of birth have been eliminated, probably during the crash of the old Commonwealth in 2109. Judging by appearances alone, we can discern he is in his mid-to-late-thirties."

"I can attest," Gilmour said. "Nicolenko's a slithery bastard. Surprised you got as much on him as you did."

Quintanilla nodded her head in mute agreement. "I don't have to tell you, gentlemen, this will not be easy. I believe diplomacy has unfortunately run its course in these matters. The Confederation is determined to move ahead with their plan to mine the bottom of the Pacific trench." Her mood grew even darker than before. "In all of my years in the government, I have never experienced the chills I have had these past few months...as a diplomat and scholar, these events have no precedent. I cannot emphasize to you three how terrified I am...."

A pang of guilt, mixed with newfound respect and sorrow, ate at Gilmour's innards. Before all this mess with Roget, Gilmour and Mason had both targeted Quintanilla; their instincts had told them she hid more than she revealed, that there was more to her than anyone would tell them. She was cold, Gilmour agreed. But he was quickly discovering her iciness came from sheer distance, not lack of humanity. All Gilmour could do was pay for his foolhardy accusation by listening to Quintanilla's fear and allowing the guilt to teach him a lesson.

"I know one thing is for certain," Gilmour spoke, breaking the silence, "Nicolenko is an enemy I've learned from well. If anyone was to stop him and the Confederation, it'd just as soon better be us."

Quintanilla looked up from the monitor, where her eyes had been fixed on the static image of Nicolenko, lost in dread.

Gilmour took in a lifetime's full of Nicolenko's visage, recalling every mark on the man, and said again, "I've got a score to even up. I hate to lose."

Quintanilla straightened in her seat. "Needless to say, then, Agent Gilmour, you have the USNA's full consent to take out Nicolenko. Do what you must to locate him, but finish the job."

Gilmour nodded assuredly. "I don't duplicate my mistakes. Neither do my colleagues...we'll finish what we started and go for those warheads."

"Excellent, gentlemen," she complimented, then stood up. "Dismissed."

Gilmour also rose to his feet, followed by Constantine and McKean.

Quintanilla thrust her hand out, which Gilmour shook. "Good luck."

Constantine's and McKean's eyes found Gilmour's. The trio each took a deep breath and headed for the door. With the MP closing it behind them, the agents paused outside in the corridor.

McKean balled his hand into a fist. Constantine did the same, and the pair exchanged glances. Finally, Gilmour formed a fist, looked at it, and held it out before him. "For Chief and Mason," all three recited, then knocked each fist in a single motion. "Let's get it on."

## CHAPTER THIRTY

"I'm going to have to have a few words with my tailor," Constantine said, pulling at his neck's metal collar ring.

Valagua cast an askance eye to the special agent while fitting the abdominal ring on Constantine's hazard suit. "I assure you I haven't performed any modifications."

De Lis stepped around the theoretical studies lab's diagnostic table. "I took some time the last few hours to download several new topographical maps of the 1940-era to your hazard suits' HUDs. The resources Solicitor Rauchambau has come across have been quite substantial."

Gilmour nodded. "Any advantage is a leap beyond what I started with, Doctor."

"I have also recorded a second set of helpware to assist you with Lionel's new equipment, if so necessary."

"Thank you again, Doctor," Gilmour said. "Hopefully we won't get too lost...I'm also packing redundant GPS modules in case of glitches."

Ivan and Crowe wheeled in a cart, on which lay the three pairs of hazard suit gauntlets. The two gave final inspections to the gauntlets, each of which had been visibly modified with enhanced, but slightly larger, holographic display devices. Out of the corner of his eye, Gilmour saw the bigger gauntlets and reasoned the modifications were due to the incorporation of the new systems, Roget's second brainchild.

"I trust all of you read the new specifications and instructions I provided you with?" Roget asked, standing behind his former assistants, making sure all was well.

Constantine winked at McKean. "You bet, Doctor. Haven't had a better night's sleep since I arrived."

Roget pursed his lips. "Then let us pray the Confederation finds you as amusing."

"Did you want us to give them a signed letter from you?" McKean retorted. "Perhaps drop them a hello from your new friends here in the States? I'm sure they'd love to hear from HADRON after so lon—"

"Cool it, gentlemen!" Gilmour ordered, turning back to face them. "We've a job to do. Getting wrapped up in frivolous distractions isn't going to get it done."

Stares grew over the agents, then the slow realization that Gilmour was right.

Roget had a silent thank you written on his forehead, meant for Gilmour, but the special agent disregarded it. He wasn't above reprimanding his men, but giving Roget anything more than common, professional courtesy was too much, too distasteful.

Ivan picked up a gauntlet and presented it to Gilmour, changing the subject in a subtle fashion. "We've written software similar to the holographic interfaces you have become accustomed to. Should work as easy as a cake, Agent Gilmour."

Gilmour nodded and took the first gauntlet from him. Studying the shiny new interface's housing, he slipped the device over his left hand and wrist, wriggling his fingers and palm inside. A second gauntlet went over Gilmour's right hand while his two colleagues finished suiting up, completing their share.

A circle of the theoretical lab's scientists formed around the three agents while final checks were given. Waters and Marlane collaborated on the lab's monitors, reviewing the sensors on each agent's hazard suit. Jaquess and Lux assisted Ivan and Crowe on the last-minute status of the Casimir chambers, actively scanning the casing with EM pulses for cracks or other faults.

"We're a go," Lux confirmed to Crowe.

Crowe nodded to Ivan, and the pair topped off the trio with their respective helmets. Once clicked into place, the pair gave a thumbs up.

De Lis pointed to the Marine standing at U5-1's entrance, who immediately headed for Roget, and brandishing his rifle, escorted him into the corridor. Once Roget had been expelled, Valagua entered the laboratory with the Lockbox and parceled out a trio of jewels to Ivan and Crowe, who then fed them to each Casimir dropchute.

Producing a small voxlink from his jacket pocket, de Lis asked, "Can you hear me?"

"Perfectly," Gilmour responded, de Lis' tinny voice still

reverberating through his helmet speaker. Gilmour craned his head and looked at Constantine and McKean, who concurred.

"Excellent. All systems are at nominal, gentlemen. Your Casimirs are loaded and in wonderful condition," de Lis exclaimed, proudly looking upon his colleagues.

Gilmour's entire hazard suit bobbed up and down in acknowledgement. "Let's fire 'em up." He tapped his holographic interface, powering up the HUD graphics inside of his helmet.

Waters and Marlane supervised the booted-up Heads Up Displays on a bank of monitors, one per agent. "Holographic interfaces functioning normally. All systems go," Marlane announced.

Waters agreed. "Specimens active. Good for start-up."

Gilmour tapped a green sphere on the interface, setting the Casimir vacuum into action. Deep inside his chamber, two plates closed to within micrometers, beginning the whole process over. Feeling the device hum on his back, Gilmour prayed one more time to get through this without being scattered across the four winds.

"Good luck, agents," de Lis said once more into his voxlink. A haggard, weary look crossed his face before saying lastly, "See you on the other side."

Gilmour detected a hint of sorrow (or was it remorse?) in de Lis' speaker-filtered voice, but shelved it and concentrated on the interface's command systems.

The three agents faced each other now, their glinting helmets concealing the visages of the men while they counted down the seconds, their beating hearts not defeated by the climaxing buzz racking their eardrums. Perspiration dripped over and onto the bodysocks underneath the quilted hazard suits as each man primed himself for the ultimate stunt ride.

Green and red HUD numbers—instead of scrolling across the holographic interface—spiraled out of Gilmour's eye view. Glancing down, a sinkhole bored a white hole into his chest, sucking the very photons of the ambient environment into him. Gilmour gasped as, unlike the first time, he could participate as an observer—his eyes glued and head fixed—to this quantum tunnel without distraction from the suit's main systems.

A stalking anxiety soon pounced upon his brain, overcoming his practiced and enforced calm; before he could swoon from the shock of losing sight of his lower extremities, the ever present, insatiable buzz drowned out the universe, flinging him into a black—

—Gravel lot. Lying flat on his chest, Gilmour took in through his helmet the various shapes and dimensions quarried rock had to offer. He pushed himself up, rising in a small cloud of smoke to take in the lapping waters just meters down from this incline. Looking out, several dozen small trawlers, dotted by nocturnal docking lights, were parked along a familiar complex of wooden planks. So, he was back at the Skippsen Marina, glad to know that Roget's new coordinating system actually worked, saving a trip across central and western Canada, unlike his previous jaunt.

"Tell me this isn't a joke," Constantine's voice cracked over Gilmour's voxlink.

Gilmour turned to see Constantine and McKean dusting off their hazard suits, looking like they too had crashed face first. Both men scoured the darkened landscape as they stepped closer to Gilmour, who took again to looking at the docked boats. "This is perfect, gentlemen. Step one."

Once Gilmour had consulted his topographs for directional data, all three men descended the gravel incline and set foot upon the planked path, which ran parallel to the shoreline and the docks.

"This is a marina where I met a captain named Clayton," Gilmour explained, pointing to a distant dock. "His trawler took me to the North Pacific on my first jaunt."

"You think he knows Nicolenko's whereabouts?" McKean asked.

Gilmour nodded. "Or knows who got hold of him."

The agents walked past several docking ports, and after a few minutes—shrouded by the night's darkness—Gilmour led them to the Skippsen Marina's office. For all purposes and intents a shack, the office nonetheless would contain any information on who had filed permits to dock in the marina and who might just have reported sightings of foreign trawlers or steamers. Or if nothing else, what actually became of Clayton, and where he might be found.

Gilmour's gauntlet easily overpowered the rusted lock on the shack's door, and the trio admitted themselves. Three bright helmet lamps illuminated the building, a tight, one-room office, filled to capacity with wooden shelves and many re-bound books. A slender secretary's desk—more of a tabletop, upon closer inspection—sat at one end of the room, accompanied by a stool. Sheets of paper were scattered throughout the room, some on the secretary's desk, most on the floor, lending the room more the look of a child's bedroom than a place of business. Another desk, this time situated with a transmitter on top, sat in the opposite corner of the office.

"All right, fan out and start looking," Gilmour ordered, heading to the secretary's desk.

Constantine sighed at the mess before them. "Hell, we could be here a week."

Beams of light bounced playfully off the walls and floors as the three rummaged through the office's paperwork for the next several hours. Dust and other accumulated detritus from years of neglect were thrown into the air, recreating an underwater diving expedition, with particles of reflected light shining back into their eyes.

"Gilmour, take a look at this," McKean said, holding a logbook open to the light.

Gilmour and Constantine knelt next to McKean as he pointed to a recent entry on the ledger. Above it, and the pages preceding the entry, handwritten Cyrillic dominated. Taking the logbook from McKean, Gilmour flipped through it, skimming the pages.

"*Amiliji,*" he whispered, closing the logbook to read its cover.

"Wasn't that the boat you were brought back on?" Constantine asked.

Gilmour nodded. "Most of this is in the original captain's hand... the rest is Clayton's." Without wasting a second, Gilmour produced his holobook from a side pocket and booted it up. The device hummed while he optically scanned the log book's yellowed pages for the next few minutes, committing the handwriting to quantum memory. "Thank you, Captain," he said again, replacing his holobook. "Anything else, Neil?"

"Nothing I can find for a Captain Clayton."

"Hmm. Looks like this logbook and the manifest file we found on this trawler *Eurus* are going to have to do the job. Will, think you can operate that antique over there?" Gilmour asked, referring to the radio.

"If it doesn't hiss or spit, I'm your man." Constantine walked over to the desk, and raising his fullerene faceplate up, began work on the radio. Within a minute he had the transceiver on, filling the room with a strange and alien din while he rolled the metal dial across the spectrum. Gilmour handed his holobook to Constantine, allowing a brief glance of the *Eurus'* radio frequencies gleaned from the newly discovered logs. "There's your frequency. Let's see if anybody is home this morning."

"Gilmour? What in the hell is going on!" Clayton's static-filtered voice yelled over the transmitter headphones.

Gilmour grimaced at the radio noise and repeated, "I said what are your present course and coordinates, *Eurus*, over."

"Why the hell are you radioing me three-twenty in the morning? And how the hell did you find this transmitter frequency? Didn't I leave you in the hospital?"

"It's a long story, Clayton," the agent answered, fiddling with the radio headphones he held over his right ear. "Are you out in the Pacific again?"

Clayton sighed over the line. "Everything's a long story with you, isn't it?"

"Just give me your coordinates so I can find you. There's information I'm in search of, and you may be the only person able to help me."

"There's a first...Gilmour, I'm not anchored out here on some damned foolish deep sea expedition."

Gilmour studied the logbook again. "That's not important, I can get to you. Just tell me your coordinates."

"Damned...." The insult trailed off as Clayton left for a moment, then returned, another voice sounding in the background. "All right, Gilmour."

Clayton spoke over the headphones while the special agent nodded, hurriedly inputting the numerals into his gauntlet's interface. "Perfect. See you soon, *Eurus*." Gilmour toggled the radio's power switch and returned the headphones to the desk.

"What!" Clayton's voice yelled before being cut off.

Gilmour looked to his two colleagues. "All right, gentlemen, here's our next stop," he said, tapping a button on his interface.

On Constantine's and McKean's respective interfaces, a series of green numerals appeared, along with flashing chronometers.

"Set chronometers for eighteen hours ahead," Gilmour commanded, tightening his helmet. He'd at least give Clayton a chance to bathe before they arrived. "Set?"

"Gotcha," Constantine said, checking his interface one last time.

"All right, boys."

Three whirling vortices ripped open their chests, and before the trio could think twice about venturing forth once more, spacetime had collapsed upon them, compressing and hauling the agents into the voracious, circling maw.

Smoke billowed from beneath the seam of the tiny closet's locked door before a raised gauntlet cracked it open. Three smoldering hazard suits, helmet lamps piercing the haze, walked out into the corridor of the trawler, met by moonlight from the portside windows. After a series of three successive clicks, the artificial illumination had ceased, and the helmets were removed, revealing the perspiring visages of Special Agents Gilmour, Constantine and McKean.

Accessing his interface, Gilmour looked for confirmation that this was indeed the place. So far, two successful jaunts in a row with nary any trouble.

Gilmour peered momentarily at the passive beauty of the crescent moon, then eyed his colleagues and said, "Let's get to Clayton. The less time I have to spend back on a trawler, the better."

Helmets magnetically locked to their abdominal rings, the men moved out, heading to the fore of the *Eurus* without the benefit of a red carpet to guide them. Maneuvering to a central corridor, the men skirted past a half-dozen quarters doors and came near the threshold of the bridge, its metal door held open by a toolbox on the floor. Scanning the bridge at its outset, Gilmour's holobook discerned six heat sources inside, the largest and hottest of which was located at the center; Clayton, seated on his butt.

Charging inside, Gilmour and the other two garnered the swift and startled attention of the crew. Strolling over to the front-facing seat—and the still oblivious Clayton—Gilmour announced, "Clayton! Good to see things don't change much."

"*KEE—RRRRIIIST!*" the skipper growled, jumping from his seat and tossing a set of ribs and barbecue sauce down the front of his shirt. A beer between his legs spilled to the deck floor, foaming like seawater. "Sorry to be a nuisance." Gilmour covered his mouth at the sight and smell of the cuisine, stifling a laugh.

Clayton wiped the red sauce from his forehead and shirt, nearly weeping. "What the hell are you doing here? How the holy hell did you get aboard!"

"I have my ways. Hope that wasn't your only shirt."

"Sod off! Goddamn you, Gilmour!" Clayton flipped excess barbecue from his hands, which splattered the floor. For the first time, he took a good look at the three special agents' attire and the gleaming mechanisms attached to them. "Sweet mother of God! What the hell is that!"

Gilmour stepped closer to the skipper, for once towering over the man now that he wore the hazard suit. "My little secret. Now, where is Nicolenko?"

The skipper's eyes bulged, his gaze skimming over the fantastical gauntlets, boots and bubble helmets at their sides. "Who the hell are you people?" he whispered, more to himself than anyone else.

"Nicolenko?" Gilmour reiterated, his eyes boring into Clayton's.

"Nicolenko...the NKVD man? Probably halfway to Vladivostok by now."

Gilmour grimaced. "Did the Soviets find him? Take him back?"

"Came in a transport ship...they said they were from the government in Moscow after I did some asking around," Clayton said, wiping still more barbecue from his shirt. "Bloody lucky, if you ask me. The sonovabitch was in a coma, just like you."

"You have my thanks by the way, for what you did," Gilmour said.

Clayton grunted. "Ehh, I'd just as soon leave him for dead and give you a fair chance at gettin' home, considering all he'd done to my business. Managed to get a few gold notes off 'em to cut my losses."

Gilmour nodded, halfheartedly hearing Clayton's story. "Good... good. Glad to hear all is well."

"Well?" Clayton gestured to his spill and to the trio of strangely garbed men who had suddenly, inexplicably appeared. "You call this well?"

"What about this transport ship," Gilmour inquired, changing the subject. "A name, destination...a course?"

"Hell, I don't read Cyrillic. If Ghoukajian was here, he could have told me."

Scratching his chin, Gilmour gave askance looks to Constantine and McKean, then looked back to Clayton. "Thanks, Clayton. That's a quite a bit of information." One more quick look back to Constantine and then, "Say, Clayton, when and where exactly was this transport ship when you, uh, were in contact?"

"Must have been...oh," the skipper paused, picking at his fingernails, "eleven days ago, just outside Skippsen's Marina."

Gilmour nodded. "Thank you, Captain, you just did us a major service. We'll trouble you no more. Come on, gentlemen. Let the good captain tend to matters."

Leaving Clayton in a permanent state of confusion and puzzlement, coupled with a gaping jaw, the trio of agents turned tail and headed out the trawler's bridge, giving the crew of the *Eurus* ample opportunity to exchange furrowed eyebrows.

Clayton sat back down. "What in the hell was all that about?"

Hundreds of tinny voices, in dozens of languages and dialects, filtered through McKean's holobook, each talking to one another from such varied distances as the Philippines, China, Japan, Hawaii, Alaska, the continental United States, Canada and the Soviet Union. Especially the USSR. Tapping a button on the device, McKean extracted a certain segment of the radio spectrum, highlighting it in green among a noisy background of red and blue traffic.

"I've isolated their favorite frequencies," McKean reported, his head cocked while he listened to the varied voices, squeaks and pops of the segmented spectrum. "Sure seem to be busy chattering."

"The Pacific's a busy place in wartime," Gilmour said, watching the stars wash out one after another by the impending dawn. The three stood far from the marina's docks, taking refuge in an outcropping of hills. "Catch any call signs?"

"Loads. Right now, I'm working on pinpointing the origins of the radio transmissions. Can probably get a pretty good Doppler shift on them and coordinate each course and destination."

"Good. Will, any progress on lidar?"

On Constantine's holobook, dozens of red circles continued to converge and diverge at the marina's southwestern tip, some two kilometers from the trio's position. "Business as usual on the homefront. Looking out into the deep sea, I've got about four signals headed in the general direction of Asia."

"Keep an eye on them. If one of them meets up with any other ships, give me a yell."

Staking out traffic among the North Pacific was tedious, time consuming, and above all else, mighty boring. Several promising leads intrigued Gilmour's interest, but so far, none could be positively identified as the transport vessel Clayton had contact with until McKean could satisfactorily monitor and cross-index every single transmission, which could take the better part of the day at his present rate. It was tempting to jaunt to every boat out there and cut their downtime in half, but the risk just edged the advantage gained; who knew who was out there, watching every single activity like a spider on its web, feeling out, waiting for the trio of agents to jaunt and unwittingly expose themselves and the Temporal Retrieve project to forces better left in the dark? For all Gilmour knew, Nicolenko had not acted alone, perhaps having colleagues spread from here out to the Asian continent's many coasts and islands. It was not a thought Gilmour relished after coming this far, this close to Nicolenko, that he could almost smell the man, almost...feel his presence in this era. For once, the risk would not be worth it. Another time for the risk perhaps, another era.

The first strains of yellow sunlight lit the barren tree branches above the agents, filtering down to the marina's docks half-a-kilometer away. Winter nesting birds awoke from the night's freeze and began their daily rituals. Soon, Gilmour knew, the marina's denizens would arise as well, putting a new strain on their monitoring duties.

"What do we have here?" McKean said, ending a quiet interlude.

His interest piqued, Gilmour stepped over. "What is it?"

McKean tapped a specific frequency on the holobook with his finger, highlighting it in yellow and eliminating the others for a moment. "Someone's awfully friendly with a frequency I recognized from Valagua's lessons a while back. It's originating from somewhere in the eastern coast or mid-eastern region of the Soviet Union. Whoever it is, they're not losing any time responding. I've recorded five hails between the two and one extended transmission—without a break—lasting ten minutes."

"Hmm...." Gilmour committed a quick glance at McKean's holobook. "They don't appear to be too worried about a trace. Can you get a location fix?"

McKean tapped another series of buttons on the holobook, bringing up a holograph of the eastern seaboard of the Soviet Union. Several red spikes soon grew from the representation of the topographical map, each emitting at a different radio frequency. Further triangulation by McKean revealed the culprit, deep in the mid-region of the Asian continent. "Coordinates 52 degrees north by 104 degrees east. Do you want to listen in?"

Gilmour nodded.

Resetting his holobook, McKean tapped the specific frequency and activated the device, broadcasting it to the trio via a miniaturized speaker. Pops and squeaks were relayed first before a barely discernable voice, speaking in Russian, cut through the primitive radio static and continued with the dialogue. The broadcast lasted less than fifteen seconds before renewed interference extinguished the voice.

"Did you get any of that?" Gilmour asked the pair, still attempting his own translation after the fact.

Constantine shook his head.

"Neither did I," McKean concurred.

Gilmour studied the holograph on McKean's holobook. "Who were they talking to?"

"This one right here." McKean's index finger tapped a red sphere, one ship among many sailing across the Pacific.

"Course data on that one, Will?"

"It's a larger vessel, roughly fitting Clayton's description. According to lidar, her wake is leaving quite a mess behind, scattering oceanic debris everywhere she goes. All indicators are near certain that she was here at some point the past few days," Constantine reported, but added the caveat, "but so could half the ships out there."

Gilmour grunted an acknowledgement. "Still, the nature of the repeated communications and their locations is what sparks me. If you were a transport vessel, what the hell are you doing in typical fishing lanes, talking to someone beyond the coast?" he asked out loud, but to no one in particular. "No, it's too peculiar...stow your gear, gentlemen. It's got to be the one."

Constantine and McKean switched off their holobooks and stowed them in sidepockets. Placing their helmets on and locking them into place, the trio pressurized their hazard suits and then activated the Casimir chambers.

Gilmour clicked his voxlink. "Let's do it!"

Exploding in a crack of thunderous energy, the trio vacated the spacetime continuum, leaving behind a vaporous trail of smoke rising from the frost-covered turf.

# CHAPTER THIRTY-ONE

"Lieutenant Vasily Nicolenko! Where is he?"

Tugging an overhead light bulb chain, Gilmour finally saw the figure he had caged: a bedraggled Russian boy, dressed in oily and perspiration-laden grey togs, fallen upon the floor, gape-mouthed and scared witless; he couldn't have been much older than eleven or twelve, Gilmour estimated, younger yet than the poor sailors on board the *Bradana*.

Gilmour stood over the boy, E4.10c barrel lowered to the child's brown, soiled throat, enough to strike fear into his heart, but without causing him to defecate in his trousers. The boy looked from side to side in the closet, hoping to see a weapon he could employ against the agent. Gilmour had, however, scoured the place before trapping the boy as he passed in the corridor.

"Nicolenko, boy?" the agent asked again, enunciating in his clearest Russian. "Are you deaf, dumb?

The boy shook his head, flinging drops of sweat across the room. "No...."

Gilmour nodded, chiding himself for perhaps being too rough with the child. He was sure not to make the mistake that anybody could conceivably harm or kill you—regardless of age or gender—but this boy seemed sure to run like a rabbit at the instant Gilmour gave him room to wriggle. He holstered his E4.10c, confident the boy would not make a move towards him. "What's your name, son?"

"Pa—Pashenka," the boy coughed out, barely audible.

"That's a handsome name." Extending his hand, the agent helped the boy to his feet. Looking at Pashenka's dingy togs, Gilmour tidied the boy up, straightening his collar and adjusting his shoulders. Reaching into his back pocket, Gilmour's left hand produced a three-by-five-inch, black-and-white emulsion photograph. Holding it up, he handed it to the boy. "Do you know him?"

Pashenka's hands felt the slick photograph, an index finger tracing a line over the image of the man's face. He nodded, then said, "Papa is a doctor on our ship. Papa making him better."

A glimmer of hope galvanized Gilmour, releasing a surge of energy throughout his body. "Where is your papa? I need to talk to this man."

"Papa doesn't like strangers. Papa doesn't like bang-bangs, too."

"Bang-bangs, huh." Gilmour cracked a grin. "All right, Pashenka. No bang-bangs." Turning his head, Gilmour took out his E4.10c and called out, "Will...."

From around the corner of the closet door, Constantine and McKean appeared out of the darkness, dressed in their bodysocks and jackets. Extending his hand, Gilmour proffered his pistol to his colleagues. "Hang on to this for me, will you?"

Constantine raised an intrigued eyebrow.

"I've got a lead. Keep close to the jaunt rendezvous. I'll call with more info in about," he checked his wrist chrono, "twenty minutes."

Constantine and McKean looked at each other and nodded, more out of faith in Gilmour than in what the agent was actually up to.

Gilmour turned back to the boy. "All right, Pashenka."

The pair left behind the other agents and the closet, walking out into the corridor. Pashenka took Gilmour through the cavernous ship, each succeeding deck darker and more foreboding than the last as they descended. The temperature soared the farther Pashenka walked, causing the agent to wipe his brow several times; even the steel walls perspired, meaning the engineering room couldn't have been too far.

Down in the ship's bowels, no one crossed the pair's path, despite their proximity to its essential systems. Stepping down rusty stairs, the boy led Gilmour to a corridor with an arched ceiling, adorned with metal pipes running length-wise. Several doors lined the hall, each no larger than three dozen centimeters in width, not much of an infirmary if indeed Pashenka's father was the ship's doctor. No more than a footstep inside the corridor did Gilmour realize this was the crew's quarters, so low in depth that a rupture or breach in the hull would instantly kill everyone down here.

Pashenka produced a key ring and unlocked an oxidized iron door on his left, which creaked and stalled in mid-push. Giving it a kick with his heel, Pashenka persuaded the door to open. He hurriedly waved

Gilmour inside, then quickly slammed and locked the door behind them.

Despite the dark, Pashenka strode over to a tabletop and lit a match, which flared like the sun to Gilmour's light-starved eyes. The boy held the flame to the bottom of a kerosene lamp, then adjusted the intensity of the light. A mattress was situated in one corner of the room, surrounded by stacks of books and, of all things, what Valagua had once referred to as a phonograph, an ancient music playing device, complete with a bell-shaped horn to one side, to which Gilmour smiled at its quaintness. Three large squares were standing upright beside the machine, probably the recordings.

Pashenka gestured to Gilmour again, almost taking the agent by hand through the tiny living space. An opening in the wall—less than a hallway, but more than a door—was on the room's right, through which Pashenka took the lamp. Gilmour ducked under the low cut in the bulkhead, following Pashenka into the adjacent room, where another mattress, upon which a darkened figure lay on one side, dominated the floor. Pashenka discreetly walked over to the mattress, careful to lower the light output from the lamp.

Placing the lamp on the floor, Pashenka put a hand on the figure's sheet, perhaps to rouse him after a long slumber. Narrowing his eyes, Gilmour tried to make out the form's features; was it Pashenka's father, passed out from too much drink? A quick second look around the room revealed scattered bottles, some tipped onto their sides, all over the deck floor. Small glints of reflected light caught the agent's attention; needles? Turning back to the boy, Pashenka had rolled the bearded man onto his back and was now dabbing perspiration from his forehead with a rag.

"Is this your papa?" Gilmour asked, swallowing a bead of sweat that had dripped over his lips.

A baffled look grew over the boy's face. Setting the rag down, Pashenka pointed to Gilmour's hip.

"What?" The agent's left hand searched his trouserleg, his fingers running up and down over the fabric. Fruitless, Gilmour raised his hands. "I'm sorry...what, again?"

"No." Pashenka reached over to Gilmour's trouserleg and tugged at his hind leg, pulling the agent's trousers closer. Gilmour jumped as the boy fumbled behind his back, finally yanking out something. Pashenka sat back and held out the photograph so close to Gilmour's eyes he momentarily blocked the agent's sight.

Gilmour snatched the photograph, blurting out, "Hey! What the—" Lowering his hand, the agent saw Pashenka pointing excitedly to the man on the mattress. Gilmour shook his head. "No, this man,

Pashenka. Not your...." Another scan by Gilmour shut him up. Rubbing his eyes, Gilmour committed another look at the photograph, then crawled closer to the man on the mattress.

"This isn't your father, is it...." In his mind's eye, Gilmour shaved off the man's beard, cut his hair a few centimeters, than healed the purple bruises on his forehead. He clinched his jaw. "Nicolenko...."

*Kill him now! Do it! End it now!*

Gilmour rose to his feet slowly, never taking his eyes off the comatose Nicolenko on the mattress. "Can you wake him, Pashenka?"

Puzzled, the boy stood also. "He's been sleeping for a long time. Papa says we should let him sleep till he wakes up."

"Then leave the room, Pashenka." Gilmour swallowed. "I'll wake him up myself."

The boy walked closer to the agent, so close now Pashenka could retrieve Nicolenko's photograph again, if he chose. "Are you going to hurt him?"

Gilmour's gaze upon Nicolenko broke, his concentration shaken by the boy's forthrightness. He swiveled his head to meet the boy's cherubic visage.

"Papa says people will try to hurt him...he says he'll be killed."

"H—how does your papa know people are going to hurt him?"

"Papa says he talks to them every day, here on this ship."

Gilmour's hand rubbed his jaw, wiping the dripping perspiration from his skin. It was so bloody hot in here. "Then we must not allow these people to hurt this man, should we?"

A sudden vibration on Gilmour's left leg caught his attention. "Excuse me, Pashenka." Walking across the room, Gilmour stepped under the bulkhead cutaway and paused in the first room. Reaching down, his hand found his holobook. Tapping a button on its side, he whispered, "Gilmour."

"We were starting to wonder about you," Constantine's voice broadcasted softly over the holobook's speaker. "It's been twenty-nine minutes."

"Sorry...I've found someone interesting. Nicolenko's here, still comatose. Do you have my coordinates?"

After a brief pause, Constantine answered, "Affirmative."

"Meet me here ASAP. Bring everything, but be discreet. I'm not alone, and I've got good information that this ship is crawling with NKVD, let alone anyone else. I'll meet you in a corridor outside of some quarters. Gilmour out."

Tapping the same button, Gilmour powered down the holobook and replaced it inside his pocket. Now came the dilemma; if the NKVD were hiding about the ship—and Gilmour had no reason to believe otherwise—was Nicolenko indeed a target of them, or was the target the man or men who came after him, Nicolenko being the bait? The Soviets were devious, curious and dubious, all at once. If they had reason to believe there was more to Nicolenko then the identification he carried and the uniform he wore, then no effort would be spared to discern just who he was, and who employed him.

Killing Nicolenko just to eliminate him from this game they all played may have been warranted—if killing can be warranted, a duty some IIA agents couldn't handle after their first hit—but not on this ship, perhaps now not in front of the boy. Little children weren't immune from the NKVD's tendrils; despite de Lis' belief that Nicolenko was the lone Confederation operative with jaunting capability, who was to know just who and how many watched the Temporal Retrieve team and where they hid? One little event in this era could potentially cause a break in the chain of time, re-linking and weaving a different set of circumstances for the Temporal Retrieve team's contemporary and future eras, essentially erasing everyone, everything the team had ever known or loved.

That left them with the charge of taking Nicolenko back, slipping him out of here, without anyone knowing about it. The problem was, of course, at least two people knew he was here, still leading to the same conclusion about altering time. So, Gilmour thought, do they risk jaunting out of here with Nicolenko, or do they sit tight and wait for this ship to arrive at, most probably, Vladivostok, and discover just who arranged for Nicolenko to get back to their era?

"Charming cruise ship you found us," a voice down the corridor reverberated.

Breaking his vigil, Gilmour greeted Constantine and McKean with a gesture of his hand, signaling them to quiet down. Taking his voice to a whisper, Gilmour jutted his thumb back to the door and said, "The boy is with Nicolenko inside. Did you encounter anyone on the way down?"

McKean looked to Constantine, both shaking their heads. "No one. Not even a rat."

"Good, although if the NKVD could, they'd wire the rats, too."

Constantine raised his eyebrows and nodded in full agreement.

"What the hell's going on, Gilmour?" McKean asked. "Is the NKVD with the Confederation, or what?"

"I don't know...that's what makes all of this all the more

dangerous. We can't trust anyone, anything, to be who or what they appear."

Constantine sighed hard, impatiently. "Then we'll just wrap up the SOB in a blanket and jaunt out of here with him...he can be burnt to a crisp for all I care. Mission accomplished."

"Under normal circumstances, Will, I'd be right beside you. But you've got to remember, that man didn't just blink here by sheer will-power...he's got a Casimir, has to have a hazard suit, and still possesses a jewel or two. And I sure haven't found any of those yet." Gilmour rubbed his temples, still attempting to sort out this mess in his own mind. "Do you really want any of that equipment loose in the twentieth century? Surely you've listened to what Valagua told you these people did during this era? Every two-bit terrorist would pay a wife or two to get a hold of this technology."

"Granted, but when did this—" Constantine caught his breath, then covered his mouth to keep his voice from carrying, "when did this mission change from a simple hit to fifty-two pickup?"

Gilmour looked back to the rusty steel door held ajar at the quarters' entrance. "The moment I saw that boy I realized our actions in this era have consequences far larger than we will ever know, or acknowledge. Don't you think I thought about putting a round between Nicolenko's eyes and dumping him overboard? After what happened to Mason and Chief, I think it'd be perfect. But what about that boy? Think he'll keep quiet? Think he'll stand tough when the NKVD come calling, sticking a baton in his skull and cracking his brains out like an egg?!"

McKean let out a low whistle. "Christ...."

"Dammit, Gilmour," Constantine said, pushing his face into Gilmour's, "I care about the future, too, you know. But I don't want us to have to second guess every step or every leak we take along the way, in the event that perhaps this 'era' is going to be changed by us. De Lis' orders are sound and he has a good reason, I'm certain. But I'll be damned if I'm going to be asked to tiptoe around the time streams because someone got in our way and that someone's great-great-great-great-something ends up saving a species of mold that can cure every venereal disease known to mankind."

Having shielded his eyes during Constantine's harangue, Gilmour now lowered his hand and looked his colleague in the eye. Clearing his throat, he continued, "Point taken, as always, Will. As the special agent in charge, I respectfully disagree, though. These are my orders: We are going to attempt to locate Nicolenko's gear and any jewels in his posses-sion. One of us needs to stay behind here and look after Nicolenko and the boy." Gilmour's eyes darted between the two. "Any takers?"

"I'll do it." Constantine hardened his gaze towards Gilmour, then nodded swiftly. "I'll do it...and if the bastard moves a centimeter, I'll blow his head clean."

McKean raised an uncertain eyebrow at Gilmour while taking a deep inhalation of the ship's stale air.

"Good...excellent." Holding his hand out to Constantine, Gilmour asked for his sidearm back, then said, "We'll keep our life scans constant on our holobooks, but remain silent on vox." He checked his wrist chrono. "I want to limit our recon to no more than thirty minutes, so expect us back by nineteen-fifteen."

Constantine nodded in agreement.

"One more thing, Will," Gilmour said, holstering his pistol in his shoulder strap, "have your bang-bang handy, and keep your eyes on Nicolenko at all times."

"No need to remind me."

Before Gilmour and McKean could turn down the corridor, Constantine proffered his hand to Gilmour. The pair shook vigorously, each forgiving the other's obstinacy. Constantine watched the pair go off into the darkened corridor, then headed back into the quarters to acquaint himself further with the boy Gilmour had dug up. A half-hour shouldn't be too long a stretch for a single man to stay vanguard over Nicolenko, especially while the man lay in a coma. Adapting his eyes to the dark, Constantine studied the room's interior, then ducked underneath the low cutaway he found in the wall to locate a better seat for his wait.

"I wouldn't rule out some sort of shrouding over it," McKean said, walking up a set of stairs.

Gilmour referred to his holobook again as it performed continuous EM scans of the ship. A concentric set of red circles emanated from the pair's current position on the holographic interface, carving out a large swath of the ship. "That'd be a hell of a technological leap to be able to hide that much energy without detection."

"Well, perhaps his hazard suit," McKean noted. Raising a finger, he paused in mid-step. "If he shrouded his hazard suit, it would, at best, hide any EM signatures of the jewels, mostly keeping invisible the same sensors we employed in Nepal and Sakha. But what about gravitational distortion? There's not enough energy in the entire solar system to be able to mask the gravity waves the jewels generate when we use them."

Gilmour narrowed his eyes, tapping his holobook's metal frame while thinking. "Could a short EM burst with our Casimirs do the job? Enough to nudge a response from Nicolenko's jewel, but not send it careening through spacetime?"

McKean nodded his head cautiously. "I think so, but I'm not Doctor de Lis—"

"Nor am I...."

"Well, the damnable part, as far as I can see," McKean added, "is that Nicolenko's jewel is at some distance. If I recall your reports correctly, the first jewels you recovered were actually inside the Casimir chamber when you activated them, or at least you never made mention of any jewels outside of the chamber affected."

"True, but I'm willing to jury-rig with our Casimirs here if we can do it."

"Agreed."

The pair unloaded Gilmour's hazard suit from his rucksack, then detached his Casimir chamber from the torso section of the suit. Spending a few minutes removing the jewel already inside the chamber and securing it in a locked pouch, the agents then synchronized Gilmour's chamber with McKean's holobook, hoping to detect a satisfactory—but not too strong—signal from within the ship. Recovering Nicolenko's jewel was of the utmost importance, if not in the least to regain the pride lost when Roget manufactured the pilfering of several jewels to the Confederation.

Situating the detached Casimir chamber in a shadowed corner of the corridor and careful to brace it against the wall, Gilmour and McKean manipulated the chamber with a set of controls built into the mechanism's flank, bypassing the holographic HUD controls. Tapping a green button, Gilmour activated the vacuum chamber, which hummed loudly after only a few seconds. Both men looked on, as if not quite certain or sure what to do next, while also consulting McKean's holobook.

"What now?" McKean said, his eyes fixed upon the vibrating Casimir.

Gilmour shrugged. "This was your idea."

McKean raised his hands, poising them for the next course of action while his brain tried to create one from scratch. "Let's, uhh...let's initiate the chamber plates. Maybe we can get some kind of reaction going."

Gilmour nodded his head swiftly, then toggled the next button. Inside the chamber, hidden from view except by a tiny hole afforded by the dropchute, the twin plates migrated inward at a methodical rate, squeezed together—or so they had been told by Stacia Waters—by a stew of virtual and anti-virtual particles.

"Anything?" Gilmour asked.

McKean looked up from his holobook and shook his head.

"All right...give it time to join the plates, then we can push the plates apart again."

Once the plates had completed the full squeeze, they made the inexorable drive apart, drifting further as the seconds ticked by on McKean's holobook. Anticipation grew in McKean's eyes as he witnessed, via a holographic representation, the plates nearly extend to their widest point possible.

TTINNNGGG!

The pair broke their stares on the holobook to a metallic stirring behind McKean.

TTINNNGGG!

Rousing his curiosity, Gilmour stepped over to McKean, when a third TTINNNGGG! pinpointed him to something in McKean's equipment.

"What is that?" McKean asked, turning his back to see Gilmour searching through McKean's gear.

Gilmour remained mute, his hands intent on rifling to find the source of—

TTINNNGGG!

"Got it!"

McKean sat up and saw Gilmour with his hands on McKean's hazard suit, specifically the torso, and the pair's other Casimir chamber. Another TTINNNGGG! resonated through the chamber's hollow body as the pair looked on in astonishment.

McKean furrowed his eyebrows. "It's like a damn magnet...."

Gilmour slipped his hand into his pocket and pulled out the rock sample Mason had picked up on the grounds of the LZ in Nepal. Clenching it in his fist, he brought his arm down to McKean's level and opened it. On his exposed flesh, the stone performed a half-turn, acting like a compass needle.

"Scan the ship!" Gilmour exhorted McKean, trying to keep the jewel from flying out of his palm.

McKean furiously tapped several buttons on the holographic keypad, instructing the holobook's sensors to thoroughly check the local gravimetric field for disturbances. In an instant, three signals in the room burned a bright yellow on the holobook.

"I've got three in here," McKean confirmed. "Our jewels and the one in your hand."

Another signal, though fainter, blipped on the holobook, several meters below them. "I've got Constantine's," he added.

The acrid scent of burnt flesh suddenly tore Gilmour's attention away from McKean's report. A piercing pain prompted a bellow from Gilmour, and looking down to his left palm, he saw his curled fingers smoking profusely. Prying his fist open with his right hand, Gilmour let loose of the jewel, only to have it fling from his palm and fly across the room to the humming Casimir chamber on the floor. It struck with such velocity that it ricocheted into some distant corner of the corridor.

"Sweet Jesus...." Calming his trembling hand, Gilmour peeled his fingers back to see a red semi-circle seared into his palm; the jewel had nearly bored a hole through his hand trying to get to the Casimir chamber.

Looking back on his holobook, McKean's eyes visibly widened. "Holy.... Gilmour, we've got a bigger mess than we thought."

Painstakingly kneeling down next to McKean, Gilmour caught a glimpse of the holobook. Before them, a bevy of yellow spheres—some bright, others paler—were separated into two distinct groups among the schematic of the transport ship, both above the two agents.

"Damn." Standing up, Gilmour straightened his back and observed the humming Casimir chamber, along with the newly-created dent in its outer casing. "Well, I failed the first time...let's see if we can get it done now."

# CHAPTER THIRTY-TWO

Constantine's curiosity grew as the two blue spheres on his holobook traversed one side of the ship's schematic to the other, descended one level, then separated. Growing thoughts of the pair's well-being continually crossed him, despite no warnings from their patched-through life scans; elevated heartrate and respiration, to be sure, but that was nothing unusual.

On the mattress, Nicolenko slept peacefully in his coma, almost indistinguishable from the eternal slumber. The boy, however, had been administering to him for some time now, periodically cooling the man's forehead and cheeks with a damp cloth out of a small tin bucket, a luxury Constantine was soon to the point of obsessing over. Considering the damnably hellish temperatures in the bowels of this ship, why should he waste cool water on that man? Rubbing his own forehead with the back of his sleeve, Constantine plotted at least three different ways he could nick the water for himself, but soon thought better of it, lest the boy go squealing and alert whomever patrolled this ship. Constantine became all the more determined to eliminate Nicolenko, if only to rid him of his monopoly on that water.

Close to passing into a coma himself, and determined to stay away from any selfcaused trouble, the agent rose from his squat on the corroded deck floor and passed into the other half of the quarters in an attempt to keep himself conscious. Clicking his torch on, he swung it around the room and performed a rudimentary search, perhaps in the process learning something more about this strange culture.

His hand found several books next to the other mattress and rifled through them, stirring dust into the air and releasing the distinctive odor that only ancient books possessed. Trying to read the old Cyrillic was a challenge, as the language Constantine knew had evolved past the archaic, almost seventeenth-century style all the volumes here seemed to evoke. To his eye, just about all the titles reflected the October Revolution in some manner, praising many of the men history would later come to revile. Men, Constantine realized, who were still alive and breathing in this era he found himself in this very moment. Constantine shuddered to think what these men were capable of in coordination with the Confederation...an unholy alliance perhaps, bridged by two centuries. If it was indeed true, as Gilmour slowly began to believe—and Constantine as well—then Nicolenko had to die.

There was no way around it.

"Just another eleven meters...."

Gilmour and McKean were at a breakneck pace, their respective boots clanging along the steel-floored corridors. On McKean's holobook, a large yellow grouping of spheres was within their grasp, the biggest cache of jewels the pair had yet found, and it was well within distance of its initial detection. Sidling down the slim hallway, the two tried to muffle any noises they produced, but the cavernous tendencies of the ships' veins made it nearly impossible. Echoes of their movement could be heard meters down the corridor, making the mission even more hazardous; any moment now, McKean was certain, an NKVD agent would materialize out of thin air to confront them.

Before them was a large, battered and brine-stained bulkhead with a sealed door set into it. A circular handle was built into the door, designed to crank open a heavy locking mechanism. Referring to McKean's holobook once more, the jewels' signals lay tantalizingly beyond, in what appeared to be a cargo bay. Nodding curtly to McKean, Gilmour set his hands on the handle and cranked hard clockwise. After just a half-turn, the entire corridor shuddered mightily, leading the pair to wonder just what held this hunk of steel together.

As Gilmour set about to give the handle another crank, the corridor shuddered a second time, but didn't pause so easily. Now, the ship felt as though it had been rocked from the outside, its interior twisting and bending to absorb the blow.

McKean looked up at the buckling ceiling pipes. "What the hell is going on?"

"Feels like the ship's been hit by a massive tidal disturbance or another ship." Gilmour quickly retrieved his holobook and booted it up to scan the exterior. The electromagnetic signature of a massive conglomeration of steel sat adjacent to the transport ship. Simultaneously, a dozen new infrared signals quickly spread over the ship's top two decks. "We've got company! Looks like twelve, maybe more, moving fast."

McKean set his hands on the door handle and cranked hard. "Soviets?"

"Hard to tell." Holstering his holobook again, Gilmour's hands joined McKean's in cranking the door open. After two more turns, the lock was sprung with a faint click, and the pair flung the door wide.

McKean fired up his torch and flashed it inside the cargo bay. The light of a thousand crystalline spectra shone back into the eyes of the two, bringing them to a stunned pause. "My god, they're so beautiful...so many of them. It's the mother load."

Gilmour shook his head, reminding himself of their mission. "C'mon," he ordered, clapping McKean's left shoulder.

The pair stepped over the threshold and swiftly made their way to the waiting jewels, which lay sprawled out over a six-meter-cubed section of the deck floor, glittering like some jeweler's prized merchandise. McKean and Gilmour ripped open large sample bags and set them on the floor, hastily scooping the extraterrestrial stones inside.

After several minutes, the bags became so massive that hefting them back to Pashenka's quarters was going to be problematic. At capacity, each bag was nearly thirty kilograms, a heavy burden coupled with the pair's concealed hazard suits and equipment. Perspiring heavily, Gilmour looked over the remaining jewels wearily, fully aware that they would have to abandon the rest until a second attempt could be made, if at all possible. One more bag load would do the job; if only they had brought Constantine or his sample bag with them.

Gilmour couldn't allow that to trouble him now; he and McKean had to get the jewels they did possess back to safety, and fast, if indeed the infrared signatures he detected were reinforcements for the NKVD or the Confederation.

The two agents hoisted the sample bags over their shoulders and headed back to the corridor. Together the pair closed the door once more and cranked the lock back into place, hoping that the crew would pay no heed to the cargo in mid-transit.

Taking off down the dim hallway, Gilmour found his holobook and booted it up, activating the device's vox system with a single command, "Raise Constantine." Automatically, the device webbed the agents' colleague, alerting Constantine's holobook that a hail was forthcoming. After several minutes of silence from his own holobook, Gilmour paused, stopping their progress to double-check his device.

"What's wrong?" McKean asked, giving his shoulder a respite by setting the massive sample bag to the floor.

Gilmour studied the holobook, confident the intermittent green flash signifying a successful transmission was still present. "No confirmation from Constantine."

McKean pursed his lips. "Try breaking web silence."

Gilmour shook his head, his eyes not wandering from the device. "No...I'm not breaking standard operations. Let's get the hell up there. Now."

Grunting, they hefted their equipment and gear onto their shoulders again. The two then fled the vicinity, double-timing it through the corridor.

"How is he doing, boy?"

Pashenka lowered the rag and looked upon Constantine with distrusting eyes, not taking them away from the agent's shadowed countenance.

"Is he near death?" the stranger's voice said, growing closer. Constantine's form shifted, causing Pashenka to retreat a step. "Easy, boy, I don't mean to hurt you." Dropping to his haunches, the agent leaned next to the mattress, near enough now to feel Nicolenko's faint, cool breath in the broiling room. He was within a hand's reach...one quick snap of his wrists, and the world would be rid of Nicolenko and the threat of the Confederation. It was all here, so easily in Constantine's—

A jolt toppled the agent and Pashenka, sending both to the floor in a panic. Next to the mattress, Pashenka's lamp had been snuffed out by the sudden whiff of air through the rudimentary ventilation shaft, rendering the two blind.

Constantine heard a figure scurry into the corner, surmising that the boy had run for shelter, leaving him and Nicolenko alone. The agent's hands sifted haphazardly along the mattress-side, looking vainly for the lamp in an attempt to restore some sense of his environment. Without illumination, he couldn't prepare an adequate defense for himself, nor maintain his vigil.

One more blow throughout the hull and a mightier gust launched Constantine onto Nicolenko. He quickly sprung up after regaining his bearings and distanced himself from the comatose lieutenant in case he stirred. Drawing himself near again after a few seconds away, Constantine took the Russian's pulse; it was in the mid-seventies, and by all appearances, still comatose.

The second jolt was much larger, and Constantine wondered if they hadn't been rammed by a passing vessel. Patting down his right leg he felt the absence of his holobook; somewhere along the line he had lost the device—probably after the first blow—which would make it very difficult for him to scan the ship for details.

"Pa-shen-KA...." he called out in sing-song fashion, his hands roaming the dark. "Where are you, son? Where are you?"

A third jolt reverberated throughout the quarters, although without knocking Constantine over. Swiveling his head, Constantine noted the disturbance this time seemed to be emanating just meters away. Stepping under the cutaway, he went into the quarters' other half and had the impression the noises were getting closer, in fact, just outside....

Grasping his RT-01/9V sidearm from his shoulder holster, Constantine raised it in time to see the door push open with massive force and a darkened figure power his way into the quarters.

Constantine aimed and fired off two rounds, downing the stranger. With the door swung wide, several more figures flooded in and swamped Constantine before the agent could ward them off. Rushing him at full gallop, the strangers overwhelmed him with rifle butts and clubs, beating Constantine to the rusted floor.

Constantine yelped in agony as several ribs, then his collarbone, were crushed by the waves of brutality. The din of repeated cracks filled his mind, soon numbing his devastated body. Bearing the attack for a virtual eternity, Constantine soon lay limp on the floor, drifting between cold consciousness and the more comforting illusions his comatose state brought on.

Sidearms at the ready, Gilmour and McKean crept down the corridor, soon reaching the end where Pashenka's quarters were located. On a nod from McKean—who covered him—Gilmour inspected the closed door, then pushed it open with both hands. It squealed horribly once again, revealing a dark room. With one more parting glance down the corridor, the pair entered and shut the massive steel door behind them.

Setting their respective gear and equipment to the floor, twin torches from the pair lit up concentric white circles on the room's walls. After whirling the illumination around for just a second, both agents gasped and ran to the far wall.

"Jesus Christ!"

Gilmour and McKean jumped to the fallen Constantine's side, quickly checking his vitals. Gilmour nodded to McKean that he had a faint pulse, enough to keep him alive for a few minutes, at best.

Ripping open his own medical kit, McKean produced bandages

and a clean antiseptic cloth, then wiped and sopped up the oozing wounds, while Gilmour, nearby, rummaged through Constantine's gear.

Looking up from his work, McKean asked, "What are you doing?"

"Getting him out of here!" Gilmour pulled up every single piece of Constantine's hazard suit and threw them on the floor. "Give me a hand!"

The pair removed Constantine's overjacket and field boots, put the hood of his bodysock over his head, then painstakingly began dressing the agent in his hazard suit, made all the more tedious by his dead weight. Lifting Constantine's upper half, the two fitted his helmet over his limp head and neck.

"Pashenka!" Gilmour yelled, swiveling his head to the cutaway. "Pashenka, where are you?"

Discreetly, a noise sprung from the other half of the quarters, then a small figure emerged into the room a few seconds later, silhouetted by the lit torches.

"Pashenka, that you?" Gilmour's voice labored.

"Yes...."

"Who did this? Who were they?!"

The boy crept closer to the agents, still afraid, but more comfortable than with Constantine. "Very big men, lots of men. Very loud...I didn't like them. They took papa's man, too."

"Goddammit...." Gilmour uttered under his breath. He stood and placed his hands on the boy's shoulders. "Did they say anything? Anything at all?"

Pashenka shook his head, closing his eyes. "Just the..." a wave of fear came over his face, "man hurting, crying...he cried a lot when they hurt him. It always sounds the same. Papa sounds the same, too."

McKean clicked Constantine's helmet ring, sealing him in completely. "Gilmour...."

Gilmour stepped away from Pashenka and walked over to his gear. "Take him back," he ordered.

An incredulous look crossed McKean's eyes. "What are you going to do?"

"Find Nicolenko." Gilmour removed his jacket and fitted his bodysock hood over his head.

"What about the rest of the jewels?"

"To hell with the jewels!" Gilmour spat. Taking his boots off, he slid his hazard suit's torso and leg sections on. "I want to find out who took off with Nicolenko and did this to Constantine! Jaunt back to Ottawa and tell de Lis what's happened. Don't wait around for me!"

Knowing well enough not to countermand an order, McKean

readied Constantine's Casimir systems, then slipped into his own hazard suit. After both agents had suited up, they lifted Constantine and placed his arms around their shoulders, then walked him and the captured kilos of jewels, with much difficulty, to the door.

Once in the corridor, McKean toggled his suit's voxlink, opening a channel to Gilmour. "Good luck. See you back soon." It was more of a request to his colleague than a farewell.

Gilmour simply nodded. He closed the door and stepped back inside to face the waiting Pashenka.

"Where are you going now?" the boy asked, trauma creased into his countenance.

Gilmour rotated his fullerene faceplate back. "I have to find where the men took Nicolenko. I have to know why they hurt my friend."

Pashenka lowered his head. "How can you just leave?"

Gilmour cleared his throat. Bending down on one knee, he looked into the boy's eyes. "I don't belong here...I can't stay. But I can't take you with me."

"Why not? I have nothing here. My papa cares more for his bottles than me, when he even comes home."

"I am sorry. But if I tried to take you with me, it would hurt you. That's why I wear these clothes to protect me." Dissatisfied, Gilmour rose and found McKean's torch, still lit, on the floor. Picking the slim, eleven-centimeter device up, he handed it Pashenka. "Take this as a gift from me. It's better than your lamp, and will last for a year continuously, even when it's on."

The torch fit plumb in Pashenka's hand as he studied the alien tool.

"Keep it handy, keep it at your side no matter where you go. You'll always be able to find your way home."

Pashenka nodded weakly. "Goodbye. I hope your friend will be all right."

Gilmour's eyes lowered. "I do, too. Take care of yourself, Pashenka." He then turned and made his way to the door.

"What's your name?"

His gauntlet poised to open the door, Gilmour paused. "It's James."

A faint cracking of the lips appeared over Pashenka's face. "I'll never forget you."

"Never." Tilting his faceplate down, Gilmour smiled one last time before leaving. He hoped the boy would find his way, even as Gilmour moved further and further from his own.

# CHAPTER THIRTY-THREE

Gilmour raced to the top deck of the transport ship in time to see a smaller, perhaps military vessel, disembark and set for the open sea. Clanging his gauntlets to the ship's weather-worn railing, he produced his holobook and scanned the ocean currents with lidar, attempting to discern the military vessel's previous course and origination. The problem was, he could spend hours refining and triangulating various currents, time he didn't have. Nicolenko was on that ship; he had to be. His choice was laid out to him thus: Jaunt aboard and kill Nicolenko then and there, or go back to his own era and try to stop the Confederation from finishing the mining of the Kuril-Kamchatka Trench.

Narrowing his eyes, Gilmour witnessed the vessel's lights flicker into the darkness of the horizon. Perhaps he didn't have to choose...he could do both. But it wouldn't be without a hitch. If Nicolenko's rescuers were from Gilmour's time, they'd be more than aware of his presence once he jaunted aboard, and more than likely able to stop him, or at least damage his gear enough to make a single jaunt hazardous enough.

Deliberating into the morning wasn't going to finish his mission; Gilmour had to act now. Activating his HUD, he powered up his Casimir chamber and, once more utilizing his lidar, fixed the coordinates of the retreating military vessel into the Omni-Coordinate system. Once input, Gilmour extended an index finger and tapped a green sphere on the holographic interface. Within seconds, he watched himself being pulled inside the spinning spacetime vortex....

Gilmour landed with a thud on the military vessel's top deck, a cloud of smoke descending over him. Rising up from all four limbs, he estimated that he had materialized almost a meter in the air before connecting with the deck's machine-polished floor; it's a wonder he didn't leave a dent as a souvenir.

His head still locked inside his helmet, Gilmour performed a 180-degree sweep with his eyes, scanning the immediate vicinity for enemy troops. Finding none within sight, Gilmour detached his holobook from the magnetic lock on his torso and scanned for infrared lifescans. A red and yellowish band emanated behind him, stretching from beyond where his back hugged the outer wall of the ship's bridge and topmost sections. Gilmour tapped a blue sphere, isolating the temperatures consistent with human body heat inside the infrared band. Immediately, six white hot spikes appeared on his holobook, each roughly human in shape. Extending the search, several dozens more moved about until all finally melted into the overriding heat of the vessel's engine room, a few decks down.

Slapping the holobook back upon the magnetic ring, Gilmour wasted nothing in advancing to the stern of the ship, prowling the outer wall for any door or access hatch available. Doctor de Lis' specific directives to the Temporal Retrieve team about inconspicuousness and non-alteration of the spacetime continuum was at an end; Gilmour had long ago shelved any qualms he may have once possessed about disobeying de Lis' direct order. The time had come to follow through on the oath Gilmour had cited many years ago to protect his country and its liberties; his duty was to eliminate Nicolenko by any means possible, and disrupt the Confederation's plan. Most important of all, de Lis wasn't here to stop him from doing so.

Eyeing a metal hatch-release bar, Gilmour tried the handle, which didn't budge. Trying it again, he felt the springing action of the interior locking mechanism. Readjusting the power in his gauntlets by several factors, Gilmour clasped the bar and utilized all of his hazard suit's amplified might to turn the stubborn handle, breaking the lock with a pitiful snap.

Gilmour stepped inside the darkened entrance, flicking on his helmet lamp to illuminate the corridor within. Twisting his body, Gilmour turned left and headed down the corridor, away from the ship's bridge. Checking his holobook while he rapidly navigated, several IR sources migrated his way, each seemingly approaching from every conceivable direction, and to Gilmour's dismay, at a rapid pace. Picking up his stride, the agent bore ahead to the back of the vessel, determined to find evidence of Nicolenko's presence, dead or live.

Just as the IR signals were theoretically within Gilmour's visual range, his suit's audio sensors picked up footfalls from behind steel walls and bulkheads, and the subsequent screeching of various doors. Gilmour raced down the narrow hall, which was soon flooded with light from a doorway scarcely meters away. Silhouetted figures burst from the beam of ochre and rushed Gilmour, who raised his left gauntlet and held it at arm's length to meet the charging men. Clotheslining the lead man in the neck, Gilmour's right gauntlet walloped the man's abdomen, felling him. Without missing a step, Gilmour's left gauntlet laid a powerful uppercut to the trailing man, a sickening crack gurgling from the man's crushed throat. Gilmour leapt over the descending body and proceeded down the corridor. With the door left ajar, Gilmour entered a cross-corridor, where a set of stairs took him down a few decks.

Once more in consultation with his holobook, Gilmour scanned IR temperatures, discerning those in accordance with perhaps an injured or mortally wounded body. Damnably, the engine room's excess heat still obscured his IR sensors, making it all the more probable Gilmour would have to extend his search of the vessel to more rooms than he pleased. All around him, his audio inputs discerned the footfalls of men closing on his position. Gilmour furiously propelled himself through the ship's bowels, red and yellow wall lights bouncing around the perimeter of his faceplate.

At last, Gilmour spied a sign painted with the names of several departments posted to a wall. He swiftly read "INFIRMARY" and snapped open the door leading the way. Standing in the corridor, a young man smoking a cigarette yelled a curse in surprise at the mysterious stranger running straight for him. The boy barely managed a defensive stance before Gilmour had shoved him with a light touch of his left gauntlet.

Wasting no time, Gilmour slipped past two more men stationed in the corridor, dispatching them with ease before coming upon an opening in the corridor's starboard bulkhead. Peering inside, the room remained shadowed, his helmet lamp providing the sole illumination. With a foot inside, Gilmour swung his helmet laterally across the room, inspecting the facility visually before committing himself. The lamplight cut a swath through a thick layer of residual engineering steam or high-lying smoke, perhaps emanating from the cigarettes the men had been smoking earlier.

Retrieving his holobook, Gilmour scanned the ambient infrared energy, once more on the trail of body heat. Sweeping the device from one end of the infirmary to the other, the orange band of ambient IR energy was briefly interrupted by a patch of dark blue to Gilmour's right, as if the energy pattern had been erased or draped in that portion of the room. Homing in on it, the erasure shifted ever so slightly, to which Gilmour immediately swiveled to and illuminated.

For a brief second, Gilmour saw a familiar flash of beige and the gleaming of a faceplate, then yelled into his voxlink, "McKean!"

The surreptitious form dashed out of the lamplight and into the darkness again, then broadsided Gilmour's right flank, tackling the agent. Gilmour rolled and crumpled into a ball, the tackle's momentum carrying him a meter-and-a-half until he collided with a wall, stopping his involuntary retreat. In a few seconds that to Gilmour felt like an hour, the agent slowly uncoiled his startled limbs and shocked senses, only to have a sharp kick in the abdomen ignite an explosion of pain throughout his body. Two more rapid strikes from this unknown enemy's boot occurred before Gilmour's instincts took command. Grasping the boot as it went for a fourth attack, Gilmour pulled hard just at the moment the enemy's balance would be the most precarious, taking it to the floor with a massive thud.

Gilmour's right gauntlet supported his tender abdomen while he willed himself up, reclaiming the offensive solidly on both feet. The mysterious attacker proved harder to keep down and quickly regained its stance before the still-dazed Gilmour could counterattack. Both stood facing each other in the infirmary, Gilmour's lamplight inadequately providing any information about his attacker's identity, although Gilmour now recognized the attacker's hazard suit was not from the Temporal Retrieve project.

The dark figure reached behind its back and produced a short, double-bladed axe, then performed a series of figure-eight swings at Gilmour, advancing upon the agent at every upswing. "Did you truly think you would succeed?" a heavily mechanized, male voice filtered through Gilmour's voxlink, still providing an air of stealth.

Another upswing was brought unbearably close to the agent's helmet; Gilmour retreated another step, his right gauntlet clandestinely searching for his magnetically attached E4.10c behind his back. "What business is it of yours?" Gilmour replied, playing the mystery man's game, stalling for an opportunity to find a weakness in his enemy's approach. Gilmour's mind raced through the possible identities and motives of this man, leading him to only one conclusion....

"One should not interfere in the matters of a sovereign nation," the filtered voice threatened. "You should not be here!" He swung the axe again at Gilmour, which the agent barely dodged, giving his attacker a margin of a few millimeters.

When the attacker's axe swing carried his arms upward, Gilmour's hand grasped his E4.10c, which he then swung around and aimed squarely at his opponent's helmet. "I thought the same thing!" Gilmour's index finger pressed the trigger, firing a single round into the clear faceplate.

A cloud of gas exploded over the attacker's faceplate, but the clear material had enough resiliency to remain intact, although a spiderweb crack now obscured the attacker's view by at least ninety-five percent.

Gilmour's left gauntlet wrestled the double-bladed axe away from the attacker. Using its broad, flat end, he swung it against the attacker's faceplate, knocking him to the floor. Now towering over his fallen adversary, Gilmour turned the full brunt of his helmet lamp against the man's shattered faceplate, revealing for the first time the identity of his attacker. Gilmour tipped his pistol's barrel to the man's bobbing eyes. "Nicolenko...."

"Damn you," the Russian gasped, this time without the filtration of a voxlink to disguise his voice. "Even if I have to die, you will not be victorious in our war, my friend. It is larger than any one of us, Gilmour, larger than any man or child born in the next century. It is a war for the very possession of the secrets of the universe itself."

Gilmour's trigger finger twitched. "You sound like your friend HADRON."

Nicolenko's eyebrows furrowed, expressing ignorance.

"Don't be surprised...all you madmen think alike, when it comes down to it. World domination, selling out of colleagues. HADRON is the very reason you're here right now, Nicolenko. Sold his soul for a few dollars from your government. Honor among thieves, and all that, you know."

"Kill me now, Gilmour, that's what you want, isn't it?" Nicolenko hissed. "That's all you have dreamt of since the death of your partner... since your failure in Yakutia. Even after your failure at the trench in stopping me from retrieving all the jewels. Oh, yes, a slight omission on my part to inform you that I have recovered all the jewels, Gilmour. You have lost."

Gilmour detected the hint of a smile creeping over Nicolenko's face. "Even liars believe their own lies, Nicolenko."

"But the truth coming from a liar's mouth would be misconstrued as a lie, no? You and your team have lost, Gilmour. The Confederation now has the capability to use the jewels at our discretion. Kill me now, if that soothes your worried soul. But remember, I exist in any time, in any location. Remember to thank your colleague...HADRON, you say his code name is? Remember to thank him for me, the next time you see him. Kill me an infinite amount of times, and I sprout back again, ready to resume the fight another day, another era. This Pandora's box can never be closed!"

"I beg to differ. Who rescued you from the trench, Nicolenko? Who are you working with?"

Pitiful laughter echoed throughout Nicolenko's helmet. Pausing for a moment, the Confederation vanguard gasped and replied, "You Westerners are dense, aren't you? To think, we all wanted to be just like you once. We were foolish, just like you are now."

Gilmour twirled the axe in his left gauntlet. "Answer the question, Lieutenant! Who are you working with in this century? Who rescued you—"

"Gilmour, the answer is so obviously under your nose, but then again, you have a hard time seeing it. I am working with..."

The agent gritted his teeth. "Yes?"

Nicolenko laughed again. "I saved myself, you ignorant, fucking fool! I told you it was under your nose! That's why I am here right now, to keep you from killing me. I guess it didn't work, eh?"

"You're mad. Your repeated jaunting has rotted your brain."

"I am infinite, Gilmour, you should realize by now. Everywhere, everywhen...as are we all."

Gilmour lowered his E4.10c and the axe. "What...what did you say?"

Nicolenko frowned and gestured with his hands. "Kill me already, dammit!"

"No, you said we are all infinite...." Nearly the same words Gilmour had spoken to Waters, before he, Constantine and McKean had left. Many Gilmours, many Nicolenkos, many Masons? "Then killing you now would do no good, would it?"

"You want to purge your soul, Gilmour? Kill me, then! Murder me!"

Gilmour stepped backwards, retreating several paces from the crazed man on the floor. "Get the hell out of here, Nicolenko. I will not kill you to give you some satisfaction, some small victory over me! Jaunt back to your superiors and tell them your enemies will not be defeated so easily. The most toys will not guarantee your victory." Just how you play with them.

With that, Gilmour turned and walked out of the infirmary, leaving the fallen lieutenant to his own devices, hoping the crazed man would be driven further over the edge by the knowledge he had provided his own enemy a way of thinking perhaps critical to ending this standoff, this Pandora's box, once and for all. It was all about overcoming one's natural instincts, an instinct to automatically kill your enemy, without seeing his point of view, without understanding him. About turning your enemy against himself.

It was Gilmour's only hope in a universe of infinite possibilities, and an infinite enemy.

# CHAPTER THIRTY-FOUR

A brief second elapsed before Gilmour felt his extremities tingle, then the buzzing that always accompanied the jaunt returned, only to be replaced by the sound of his heavy breathing and a grunt as he collapsed in a great heap.

Blinking his eyes, his brain was flooded with an immense white light. One side of his body was then yanked upwards, and a few tense seconds later, jostled into a seated position.

"Agent Gilmour," his ears barely made out through his encased helmet, as if he was underwater, "Agent Gilmour...."

A pair of darkened gloves suddenly made their appearance at his neckline, scratching at the metal ring connecting his helmet to the hazard suit. The gloves then clumsily removed his helmet, and Gilmour caught wind of a noxious stench billowing up from his haz suit.

"Agent Gilmour," the voice repeated again, which Gilmour now recognized belonged to Crowe, even though junior scientist worked behind the agent's back to remove his gauntlets, "hurry out of your hazard suit! They're weren't sure if you'd make it back in time!"

"What the—" the agent started before he had the chest section of his haz suit pulled up over him, buffeting his neck and head. "What the hell's going on, Crowe?"

Crowe proceeded down the haz suit, loosening Gilmour's boots. "He's asking for you, Agent Gilmour! The doctor's been trying to keep him going long enough for—"

At that instant, Gilmour's memory was jogged; Constantine! The agent kicked Crowe out of the way, rose to his feet with his haz suit half on and then ran to the exit, rushing into the corridor past two posted

MPs, who flashed looks of concern to one another.

The cumbersome torso of his haz suit held Gilmour back, even as he punished himself to run faster and harder. Rounding a corner, Gilmour flung himself into a squad of MPs patrolling the corridor, pushing himself past the raised M-119s and glinting body armor to arrive at U5-21, Anaba's infirmary, where Ivan held the door open just in case Gilmour arrived. Ivan waved Gilmour forward, then helped force the agent through the tight width of the infirmary's entrance.

Gilmour sprinted the short distance from the door to a semi-circle of theoretical studies scientists, each having his or her head tilted towards one of the beds. A weak cardio monitor beeped intermittently from behind the curtain of scientists, coupled with the steady pump of a respirator, each of which echoed throughout the austere room, lending it a pall of loneliness.

A few steps away from the group, the approaching Gilmour caught McKean's ashen face. Gilmour shoved his way past Valagua and Marlane, parting them to glimpse the broken frame of William Constantine on the bed, an array of hoses and biomechanical systems perforating his flesh. Bandages and clear antiseptic strips covered most of face, rendering him unrecognizable to the two who had known him the longest.

"Will," Gilmour sang, his arm outstretched to the fallen man's battered face. Beside him, Doctor Anaba's hand tried to still Gilmour's, but the agent wouldn't have it, instead brushing her off and continuing his attempt to rouse Constantine.

The shroud of bandages moved, a small opening gasping, "James...."

"I'm here, Will."

Between the antiseptic strips, Constantine's grey eyelids quivered; the very action of keeping his eyes focused on Gilmour consumed every last iota of the agent's energy. "Did...did you f...finish it? Complete the m...miss...ion? Is...he dead?"

A lump grew in Gilmour's throat; his eyes shifted to de Lis—who nodded almost imperceptibly—then moved back to Constantine, an action the dying agent didn't see. "I—I think so, Will. You did all you could do. Chief would be proud."

A soft, baby smile crossed Constantine's face, a smile full of accomplishment. For the first time, while Gilmour stood there, his hand clutching Constantine's cheek, Gilmour realized Constantine would have killed Nicolenko himself, probably had been prevented from doing so by whomever had beaten the life out of him. Nicolenko had cheated two attempts now to ending his dance with Armageddon, two chances to finish his game.

Seeing Constantine ebb before him, Gilmour felt more determined than ever that a third opportunity be attempted. Nicolenko was responsible—fully or in part—in the deaths of two, and now probably three, of Gilmour's closest colleagues, and friends. If it was in Gilmour's power, if it was in anyone's power, Nicolenko had to be stopped. There was no other option.

Constantine's consciousness flagged; the agent drifted back into a shiftless rest, his body on the verge of losing its battle with his injuries. Gilmour retrieved his hand, allowing Constantine's head to fall back into the pillow upon which it had lain.

Stepping back, Gilmour found Anaba, who was all but powerless to save the fallen agent, as she checked Constantine's fluids and cardiac rhythms next to the bed. She wore a long face, the countenance Gilmour imagined he must be wearing now, and must have had when he found Mason and heard about Chief's end.

The CMO looked up from the various machines and clapped Gilmour's right arm. "He might make it through the night...." Sensing Gilmour's foundering state, Anaba dropped her learned optimism. "If there's any arrangements you wish to have, I'd do it soon."

Gilmour mustered a murmur, more of a grunt than an acknowledgement. The agent knew the routine, he'd done it more times than he could recall, so many times that he had it memorized, something no human should ever have to do.

The semi-circle broke without anyone uttering a word. McKean and Gilmour exited the infirmary together, to which the theoretical scientists gave their acceptance. None of the project doctors would truly share the bond with the IIA agents as the agents did themselves. All silently agreed it was for the better.

De Lis had provisionally given the agents the night off, and would resume operations the next morning. To do otherwise would be foolish and disrespectful, two traits no one had ever attributed to Richard de Lis.

"I'm sorry, Agent Gilmour, Agent McKean...Agent Constantine passed this morning."

In the dark and empty confines of U5-29, de Lis' announcement hit the pair of agents like a brick to the chest, despite its expectation and inevitability. Both men nodded and rose from their seats at the conference table, where they had been poring over various field reports supplied to them by Lieutenant Colonel Dark Horse.

"His body will be flown back to Washington this afternoon,

where he'll receive full honors and a burial."

"Has his family been contacted?" Gilmour asked.

De Lis nodded. "First thing this morning. A full compensation package will be arranged by the government for their loss, just the same as Mason and Louris."

Gilmour held back his scoff; a full comp package was the nice way of saying that the grieving family would have a few million dollars thrown at them to keep their mouths closed about what their son exactly did for the government. Would Constantine have his name trumpeted as a hero in the press? Did Mason and Chief receive recognition that they died trying to save civilization? No, and no. Regardless, Gilmour owed it to the Constantine family that he give them his version of the story, that he tell them how much of a hero he was, and how proud Gilmour was to call him a colleague, and a trusted friend. And how much William Constantine loved his job, his duty, his country. Will could no longer speak, but his colleagues would for him.

"Thank you, Doctor," Gilmour said again. "McKean and I appreciate your efforts."

A muted smile crossed de Lis' face. He didn't want to have to make funeral arrangements for the men he had brought north, for the men he sent out into danger. If he could, de Lis would shut it all down this moment. If he could, he'd go back in time and make sure none of this had ever happened....

"Colonel Dark Horse will be arriving shortly to go over the latest reports from our intelligence bureaus," de Lis continued, putting Constantine's arrangements into the back of his mind for a moment. "At oh-eight-forty-five a full staff conference will be held. Until then, your time is your own, gentlemen."

The two agents acknowledged de Lis' slackened leash, quietly setting out to freshen up for the scheduled meeting with the colonel. It would be a long day.

"Two days ago," Dark Horse started, his hands full with a stack of holobooks, "our Global Security Network picked up four Confederation destroyers escorting eight submerged, *Mavra*-class submarines heading for the Kuril-Kamchatka Trench. Repeated inquiries and warnings from our diplomatic corps to St. Petersburg have gone unanswered. In retaliation to the Premier's refusal to respond, the President has broken off diplomatic ties and authorized the North Pacific and North Atlantic fleets to fire on any Confederation naval vessels suspected of participating in the mining of any internationally held waters."

Gilmour's head lowered to the holobook he held in his hand. The holographic interface traced the chronological course of the Confederation fleet from the docks of Vladivostok to their current mid-Pacific target. In a matter of hours, the trench would be reached by the military flotilla and subjected to the largest mining operation in the history of the world.

"Then outright war is certain," McKean said, more statement than question.

"Unfortunately, our government seems to be heading more and more towards that direction, Agent McKean, unless we can blow the hell out of the Premier's ships before they manage to mine the trench. And I don't find that highly likely. Our nearest vessel can intercept in three days, and the North Pacific fleet will begin massing two days after that, leaving us nearly a week before we can even retaliate. The President is chafing at the idea of lobbing ICBMs over the ocean...somebody in D.C. seems to have talked some sense into him before that option was ever considered."

"Ballistic missiles would have just as easily taken care of the mining as the *Strela*s themselves," Gilmour said, returning his eyes to Dark Horse, "but without the precision."

Dark Horse nodded. "I'd prefer to save us the mess that would create." And the political fallout, he didn't have to add.

"What do you have in mind then, Colonel?" Gilmour asked, fully aware of Dark Horse's intentions before he even moved his lips.

"Suffice to say, Washington can't wait for the Navy to intercept the Confederation flotilla. Once the *Strela* warheads are immersed in the trench soil, they would be virtually impossible to remove, save actually detonating them, one at a time, defeating the purpose in the first place." "Colonel," McKean spoke up, "we did succeed in reprogramming some of the warheads. Can we use those prior operations to our advantage?" "We all know our advantage is slim at best in that department, especially in light of the failures our illegals caused. The only way we can assure complete success is to be there when the warheads are dropped and reprogram them one by one, just like you gentlemen had the illegals do. And for that, Doctor de Lis and his staff have been working on a way to reinforce your hazard suits for that mission."

Gilmour furrowed his brow. "Reinforce? Why would we need them reinforced? De Lis told us when we first started this whole business that the hazard suits could function in virtually any...environ...ment...." He brought his hand to his forehead. "Oh, you've got to be joking."

McKean's eyes darted from Dark Horse to Gilmour and back

again. "What? What are you talking about, Colonel?!"

"He's talking about sending us to the bottom of the trench, Neil!" Gilmour spat out, interrupting the lieutenant colonel before he could answer. "Kilometers under the fucking ocean!"

"You can't be serious! We don't know how the jaunts will be affected by that much atmospheric pressure! No one's done any calculations or simulations showing anything like that!"

Dark Horse's mouth flattened as he held his hands out, palms first, in an attempt to quiet the two. "Gentlemen, listen—"

"Look, Colonel, no one said we'd have to go walk on the ocean bottom with the fishes! That wasn't part of the bargain."

"Agent McKean, I understand your concern, but I've been reassured by Doctor de Lis that his project scientists think it can theoretically be done with existing technology. In fact, he said they've run several simulations in the event a worst case scenario such as this had to occur." Gilmour folded his arms, tipping himself back in his seat. "Colonel, that's not comforting in the least."

Slamming his stack of holobooks on the table, Dark Horse slapped both hands on the tabletop, then leaned forward into the skeptical faces of the agents and said, "If you won't hear it from me, gentlemen, take it from de Lis' mouth. I'm just a simple military man. I'm sure the doctor can synthesize some concoction to make the bitter go down with the sweet."

With that, Dark Horse rose and stormed into the corridor, leaving the pair of agents to stew in their collective gall. Once the door had locked behind the departing lieutenant colonel, McKean shot to his feet and threw down his holobook, which skidded across the table.

"Can you fucking believe that?" McKean spat, his eyes boring holes in the door meters away. "Shit, you'd think they're trying to kill us off one at a time!"

Gilmour remained mute, his arms now crossed over his chest.

"Gilmour, can you believe that!" McKean said again, looking at his seated partner.

Gilmour's face was stone, with no hint he had even heard McKean's outburst.

McKean leaned close to Gilmour's left flank, his head just centimeters from the other agent's ear. "Gilmour?"

"Either way, Neil," he said finally, "we die. We can sit here, booted from our commissions and sulking while the planet goes to hell and we die slowly from radiation poisoning, or we can go into the trench and die when our suits depressurize." Gilmour slowly met McKean's incredulous eyes. "Which do you prefer?"

"What the hell kind of choice is that?"

"Myself, I'd rather go fast...decompression. It'd kill us instantly. I don't want to linger and think about past regrets and other nonsense if we're irradiated like a couple of test monkeys."

Now it was McKean's turn to be speechless.

With a sudden surge of energy, Gilmour sat up in his seat, causing the two to forget for a moment their morbid preferences. "Neil...."

"What?"

"Something I just remembered Nicolenko telling me when I found him in that ship's infirmary...he said he had retrieved every jewel buried in the trench...."

McKean shrugged. "So what? He's a liar, you've said so yourself. We saw a lot of those jewels in that cargo hold, but that couldn't have been all of them in light of the three massive chunks that fell two hundred years ago."

"No, it's not that...." Gilmour stood and paced around the conference table. "If he had found recovered all of them, why is the Confederation intent on mining that trench? The jewels—Nicolenko was intent on telling me—are all recovered, leaving what? *Strela* is designed to obliterate matter, not push it aside like a giant scoop. So, there wouldn't be anything left except the jewels, which would be so dense as to not be destroyed. But if the jewels are all gone, why are they still going? Something...." He paused, putting his index finger to his lips. McKean picked up on Gilmour's thought. "Is rotten. A smokescreen? Could they be mining the trench, hoping that we'll stay a good distance away, that we'll fear the power of their superweapon?"

"It's a start. Still sounds too complex, even for Confederation subterfuge."

"Damn, Gilmour," McKean said after a moment of introspection, "what if they're trying to uncover the trench, not disintegrate the earth, per se. Uncover the origin debris, the object that fell into the sea. But what else could be down there worth mining the place full of *Strela*s?"

"It's the sunken object," Gilmour blurted out, not allowing de Lis the luxury of addressing the assembled senior staff in U5-29. His spine straightened, Gilmour's eyes met the eyes of every one of the seated staff members. "Nicolenko and the Confederation are banking that there are more jewels inside whatever object fell to the trench bottom. And I'm betting they've found remains as well with the jewels Nicolenko dredged up on the *Marinochka*."

"Like the cryptid skull we found in Nepal?" Waters asked, not quite believing bodies could have survived a crash into the ocean.

Gilmour nodded. "I saw firsthand how much material they pulled from the shelf. Chances are there was more than one specimen to be found in all that debris."

"That's a good assumption, Agent Gilmour," Dark Horse said, "but an assumption isn't going to help stop them from removing billions of tonnes of earth."

"No, but it does give us hope of discovering a psychology to their methods, Colonel." Gilmour stared the lieutenant colonel down, then continued, "Especially if McKean and I are going down to the bottom to stop them. We have to be prepared for anything, sir."

Caught off guard, Dark Horse was mute. Realizing the two agents had acknowledged and accepted—in their own way—the colonel's assignment, he responded, "I understand, Agent Gilmour."

"Well," de Lis finally managed to sneak in, "looks like every objective I had planned to discuss has been agreed upon without me having to say a word. So, Agent Gilmour, what do you expect down there, on the ocean bottom?"

Pausing for a second to collect his various theories, Gilmour consulted his holobook. "I'm not a scientist, as you all know, but I do have experience in deductive reasoning and thought, or else the good doctor here wouldn't have recruited me to go to the deepest point on Earth. In light of all we have experienced together, my only conclusion—out of many myself, Agent McKean and my departed colleagues have entertained—is an object capable of interstellar transportation. Or, as they would say back in Washington, a spaceship. And I believe also that the Confederation has surmised this as well and wants their hands on it." Gilmour pursed his lips. "Given this, it would be our duty to prevent them from doing so, or else risk losing the war, and possibly, our freedom and our lives."

"Then allow me," de Lis spoke again, tapping a button on his holobook, "to facilitate you in your duties, gentlemen."

# CHAPTER THIRTY-FIVE

Richard de Lis' index finger toggled the holographic interface of his holobook, highlighting the schematics his senior staff had drawn up of the revised hazard suits. The blue outline of a typical haz suit boot flashed, accompanied by a scrolling text box. "Stacia and I, with some assistance from Ivan and Crowe, have engineered a magnetic locking system on your suits' boot heels, rendering them capable of clasping to any ferric surface you may come across."

Gilmour nodded. "Impressive, but what of the instances when there is no other surface except for trench soil?"

"As you can see," Crowe stated, "we've managed to achieve a gauss ratio of three per square micrometer, suitable enough to bond with the magnetic currents of subsurface magma channels, if need be."

McKean slapped his holobook face down on the table. "That's all well and good, Doctor, but what about the pressure down there? If there're any minute leaks...."

"An excellent question, Agent McKean, one our staff has worked on the most since we first conceived this operation." De Lis toggled another button on his holobook, bringing up a second schematic, which was then transmitted to the agents' holobooks. "Your hazard suits can already withstand the temperature fluctuation, so that isn't an issue. We have, however, to be candid, had more difficulty with maintaining the standard sea level atmospheric pressures inside the suits necessary for the human body's proper functions."

A low whistle was let out from McKean's side of the table, but ignored by de Lis.

De Lis continued, "Several of our follow-up tests in U6's

atmosphere chamber with the modified spare hazard suit have proven fruitful, Agent McKean. We managed to consistently maintain sea level pressure up to levels exceeding three times the norm experienced in the Kuril-Kamchatka Trench. Needless to say, modifications on your haz suits are underway as we speak."

"When can we expect them to be complete?" Gilmour asked.

"I've accelerated the process to fit into Colonel Dark Horse's departure schedule...Stacia is forecasting within the next two hours."

"Excellent." Gilmour stood and tucked his holobook into his pocket. "That answers all my questions. I'm sure the colonel is eager to begin our mission briefing."

"Quite," de Lis said, still wearing a puzzled look on his face. Gilmour's abrupt adjournment had shocked him, if nothing else than because de Lis had been warned by Dark Horse of the two agents' initial objections to the deep sea mission. He watched in amazement as the agents exited U5-29. Turning to his staff, he said half-heartedly, "Dismissed."

A massive, grey-washed valley of ochre soil encompassed the sterile walls of the gallery's holographic chamber, where Gilmour and McKean had assembled to receive their first true introduction to one of the least known regions of the planet, and where they might just end up spending the rest of eternity entombed.

Stepping before them, Dark Horse perforated the photonic construct of the cavernous gash with his torso and upper body, lending the briefing a bizarre preamble. "This is the Kuril-Kamchatka Trench. Thanks to the allowances of our Global Security Network, these are live images reconstructed for us by Doctor Valagua."

The pair studied the deep slopes of the undersea ravine, convinced Dante Alighieri himself had created this subsurface fissure to place his Divine Comedy within. Strange and unearthly caverns pitted the slopes of the valley's walls, perhaps giving refuge to any number of unknown creatures and lifeforms; certainly a habitat contrary to the evolution of the human species as any possible.

Tapping a button on his holobook, Dark Horse set the holographic representation in motion, simulating a voyage through the mid-level layers of the valley at a leisurely twenty KPH. This visible region of the trench was roughly crescent shaped, and the holographic view twisted to the left as they progressed. All four men, Valagua included, where entranced by the nigh extraterrestrial splendor of the trench, much like a child is taken with the first glimpses of life beyond its limited experience.

Further down the trench, the floor sloped ten or more degrees, revealing a field of hundreds of stalagmite-like columns, each ascending several meters into the water.

Gilmour furrowed his brow in curiosity, to which Valagua answered, "Those columns house hundreds of tubeworms, each capable of filtering kiloliters of seawater a second. I'd avoid them if I were you."

The agents nodded slowly in rapt fascination. Their journey continued past the gradual slope, where the columns drifted away and were replaced by hundreds of boulders and smaller detritus, the artifacts of millennia of subterranean eruptions and subsurface collapses. Millions of years ago, lava flows had once dominated this section of the trench, carving out scores of vertical grooves from the walls of the valley which were later recycled as volcanic strata elsewhere on the planet's surface.

The trench's leftward crescent soon ended, beginning a long, narrow, straightforward stint. Now, for truly the first time, the agents were treated to the extreme depths and slopes of the trench valley. Pushing ahead, the severe V-cut of the trench was unmistakable, and the agents were aware of just how forbidding the Kuril-Kamchatka Trench was, second only to the Marianas as the deepest point on Earth.

Both men let out low whistles while the image rolled on, the vast slopes of the trench becoming so deep, even in the enhanced illumination provided by Valagua's holograph, that the floor was nearly pitch black. Seeing this, Dark Horse touched a button on his holobook, brightening the holographic seafloor by a few lumens. Instantly, the seafloor's lowest depths sprung to life with miniature fissures that released plumes of volcanic gases into the ocean water. Yellow and orange patches of material crusted over the tops of these open sores, the spreading sulfuric soot rendering the seafloor a sickening pall. Geothermal energy from the bowels of the Earth itself powered these smoldering chemical factories, the humble beginnings of life on the planet stoking thousands of fires, independently from the sun.

Like clouds of smog over an industrial complex, the plumes blanketed the trench, obscuring the site. Another punch on Dark Horse's holobook cleared the plumes, once again demonstrating the seeing power of the Global Security Network's satellites. Continuing past the colony of fissures, they scoped various ridges that had obviously collapsed within recent centuries, perhaps wiping out more ancient plume-emitting colonies. This region of fallen ridges endured for several moments, giving the agents reason to wonder if it would ever end.

Finally, after a right-hand turn led the trench into another crescent shape, the ridge collapse seemed to come to an end up ahead, whereupon the twenty-KPH flyby slowed to a crawl. Dark Horse then commanded, via holobook, the Global Security Network to zoom in threefold. There, about a third of a kilometer distant, lay a non-descript, fallen ridge shelf, not particularly distinguishable from the landslides they had glided past previously.

Dark Horse paused the holograph and pointed with an index finger, placing it squarely over the rock-strewn and broken ridge shelf. "That's it."

Raising an eyebrow, McKean looked to Gilmour. "Well—not really dramatic, is it? Expected it to be like the Titanic or something."

"It escaped detection all these years because it wasn't," Dark Horse reminded the indifferent agents. "Be thankful...your duty may be easier because so."

Gilmour squinted in an attempt to gain a better grasp of the site. "Where...is it?"

Dark Horse tapped a button on his holobook, which highlighted a segment of the collapsed ridge in red, one of among seven or eight large pieces resting on the floor. The highlighted segment now flashed and was magnified fivefold behind the lieutenant colonel, so that it dominated the holographic chamber.

"Here," he said, his index finger again pointing to the particular ridge segment. "If the Network is correct, the submerged object should be trapped between this ridge segment and the seafloor strata beneath, in approximately four to five massive chunks, the ridge segment itself covering an area approximately two-and-a-half square kilometers."

Gilmour shook his head; it was the same amount of earth the Confederation had obliterated with their first *Strela* test, proving his hunch that the Confederation had planned on removing the submerged object all along.

Another change in the holograph, this time initiated by Valagua, brought up a subsurface spectroscopic scan of the site, coupled with lidar measurements, producing an image comprehensible by a layman. The site's measurements and orientation were held in check, but the visual look of the ridge shelf was stripped away, revealing a rough, unfinished holograph, much like a primitive X-ray scan. An object, or objects, now, were clearly visible, each several dozen to a hundred meters in length, but no positive identification could be made, and none seemed to match any man-made construct. Several smaller pieces had settled around an impactor site, and the larger ones appeared to be half-buried within the seafloor strata. Whatever was down there wasn't budging anytime soon. "That's going to be a helluva retrieval site," Gilmour said, his eyes locked on the holograph. "Do you honestly think we can swim around in there and dig without stirring up the ridge?"

"Just keep the Confederation from planting those *Strela*s, and we'll take it from there," Dark Horse answered. "Your objective is to disable them, while the Navy's is to confront the Confederation with conventional weapons and hope the Russians go home. Until then, we don't need you two to be playing heroes anymore than need be. I'd just as soon blow their warheads up and forget the damned thing ever crashed."

McKean nodded.

The lieutenant colonel walked over to a nearby table and picked up a single holobook. Tapping a button, the device chirped. "Agents, these are your coordinates, just updated and verified by the DoD. Your instructions for this operation are also included. I suggest reading them thoroughly to brief yourselves on the geography of the site and on what the Solicitor General has outlined as your objectives."

Gilmour took the holobook and scrolled through the text, skimming over it before committing it to memory. He already had an objective in mind when he had returned from his latest jaunt, but would humor Dark Horse and Rauchambau by reading the brief anyway.

Dark Horse then glanced at his wrist chrono and clapped his hands once. "All right, we've gotten you as close to the site as possible without getting you wet. Doctor de Lis has scheduled a peek of your new toys. Dismissed."

The Kuril-Kamchatka Trench evaporated, and the gallery reverted to normal illumination, momentarily blinding the two agents. Having now committed the presentation to memory and rubbing their eyes to adjust to the light, Gilmour and McKean exited and headed for U5-11, each man mentally retracing the undersea route several times over, giving their minds advance warning of the arduous journey to come.

A flurry of activity greeted the pair of agents as they entered U5-7. Looking on while Ivan and Crowe worked, Gilmour and McKean expected a brief aside from the normally exuberant and elaborative boys, but apparently they weren't quite ready to cede their secrets to the agents just yet. The two junior scientists orbited the suspended hazard suits, each man wielding a holobook in one hand and a diagnostic tool in the other. In the intervening time period, the haz suits had been shed of their quilted exolayers and now bore leathery, slate grey skins; these were the reinforced, pressure-containing hides, no doubt. Mark III of the suits—or was it IV, Gilmour had lost count—was nearly a complete refit. From the agents' viewpoint, the haz suits looked shiny and pristine, making the transmutations appear effortless, although in all fairness to the theoretical studies staff, the work was most assuredly arduous.

A meter or two away, de Lis and Waters were inspecting some unfamiliar equipment lying on a cart, which the two agents decided was a good place to receive an introduction. As they drew closer, the equipment shone heavily in the bay's industrial illumination, revealing quite well the intricate but robust design of the twin pieces.

"Agents," de Lis beckoned, waving his fingers.

Before the scientists lay two vaguely upside down, U-shaped mechanisms, complete with a convex, half-domed cradle dominating the upper-half of each piece. Gilmour studied the sled-like machinery, which, with a little imagination, could conceivably fit over the Casimir chambers of their hazard suits. "I see you found something else to torture us with," Gilmour said, a half-smile cracking over his face.

De Lis' eyes stayed locked on the machinery. "Quite. Over the course of a few brainstorming sessions, Stacia and I sketched out some diagrams for a self-propelled device capable of functioning in deep ocean currents. These two are the results, one for each hazard suit."

Waters laid her hands on the exterior arms and hefted the sled into the air. She rotated the device around, as if showcasing it for some gimmick-laden webvertisement. "Found a wonderful composite alloy to make them durable and light. Resistant to atmospheric pressures up to seven bars."

Gilmour nodded. "I gather they'll fit over the Casimir chambers?"

"Yes," de Lis said. "Snugly. Snaps into place for easy removal, easy installment. Shouldn't be too cumbersome, or too weighty. All important where you're going."

Gilmour concurred silently.

"So how does this thing work?" McKean asked.

De Lis extended an index finger and set it on a small outtake barrel, not much wider than four centimeters, at the zenith of the upside-down U, which would be directly behind the wielder's helmet. "It's basically a miniature supercavitating engine. The very nature of the hazard suit is aerodynamically sound, enhancing the minimal cavitation we could afford to put into the engine. Carbon dioxide waste from your respiration is employed as the cavitation bubble around your suit, and the engines themselves are standard hydrazine propellant."

Waters handed the agents de Lis' holobook, which provided a holographic simulation of the engine's performance, along with text boxes describing the principles and operations. The pair skimmed through de Lis' technoscience rigmarole and found the design specifications and operational allowances, at least the theoretical ones.

"Sixty-seven minutes," Gilmour blurted, raising his eyebrows. "That's not a lot of fuel to maneuver around down there. We could spend the better part of a day just looking for this wreck. An hour of hydrazine doesn't get us far, Doctor."

"I understand. That's the best we could squeeze into the proto-typical engines, though. Stacia and I talked about adding supplemental canisters, but that could be more trouble than they're worth. Besides, if Dark Horse does his job correctly, you'll get your GPS coordinates as close to the core of the wreck site as possible, so you won't have to expend your hydrazine supply."

"Sounds good." Gilmour's eyes scanned the other shelves, inspect-ing them for any other experimental devices he should be aware of. Returning his gaze, he said, "Anything else, Doctor?"

"Unfortunately, we haven't had time to work on the other improvements I've been mulling over."

Gilmour couldn't withhold a quip. "Maybe you could fit them in on the civilian models, huh?"

"Ugh," de Lis sounded, grimacing. "Let's hope it doesn't come to that."

"Doctor de Lis," Crowe said, turning towards the group.

"Ah, looks like Crowe and Ivan have finished. Agents, let's show off our modifications." De Lis led them to the suspended suits, for which this time Crowe and Ivan were more than willing to allow the agents to study. "As you read in the report, we've reconstructed the hazard suits for deep sea activity. This newly constituted molybdenum mesh alloy will allow maximum movement while also providing for supreme pressure containment."

"If the agents are ready, Doctor," Ivan said, "we can begin suiting them up."

De Lis looked to Gilmour and McKean, who both nodded. They removed their overcoats, revealing the familiar bodysocks underneath. Behind them, Crowe and Ivan pulled up two seats, to which they hung the overcoats over, then de Lis and Waters lowered the haz suits from the two-and-a-half-meter tall suspension frame down to eye level. Gilmour and McKean sat down and began sliding their individual leggings on, which had been proffered to them by the two junior scientists. Adjusting the torso rings, the agents rose as Ivan and Crowe placed the abdomen sections over the agents' heads. The arduous process was made easier over time and practice, to the point where the entire dressing took a frac-tion of the time of the first fitting, many months ago. Four gauntlets, with lidar "cannons" and gravimetric sensors affixed next to the holographic interfaces, were handed to the agents, and after a few seconds of flexing, completed the dress, save for the helmets.

Next, with the two agents bracing themselves, Crowe and Ivan each lifted one of the supercavitating engine sleds and snapped them into place, over and above the hazard suits' Casimir chambers. The junior scientists inspected their work briefly before stating to de Lis their satisfaction.

De Lis then raised his eyebrows, expecting a response from the agents at any second.

"To be honest, Doctor," Gilmour said after jumping in place, "it's not anymore uncomfortable than the original suit. In that regard, I'm sure it'll do the job."

"Excellent. Stacia, inform Colonel Dark Horse that we're ready to begin."

"Already on it."

De Lis gestured towards the threshold of U5-1, then said, "Let's get you gentlemen properly sent off." He led a parade of scientists out of U5-7, which completely emptied, to the theoretical studies lab, where Valagua, Marlane, and several of the other junior scientists waited for Gilmour's and McKean's entrance.

Once the senior staff and the junior scientists had filled U5-1, Ivan and Crowe handed Gilmour and McKean their helmets, and while the agents finished securing them, were witness to the entries of Lieutenant Colonel Dark Horse, Professor Inez Quintanilla, and lastly, Solicitor General Rauchambau, each of whom remained quiet while watching the final pieces of the pre-jaunt process near completion.

Marlane and Waters took to their customary places at a deck of monitors which would soon display the health of the agents and status of their hazard suits. Crowe and Ivan reviewed the final scans of the haz suits, while two MPs guarded the Lockbox a few steps away. After Crowe gave a thumbs up to the pair of agents, Javier Valagua unlocked the Lockbox and retrieved two jewels, which he gave to Crowe and Ivan, who then opened the haz suits' Casimir dropchutes and fed them inside. Gilmour and McKean toggled buttons on their gauntlets' holographic interfaces, booting up the hazard suits' systems. The HUDs responded accordingly in both agents' helmets, in turn powering up all essential systems following voice commands from Gilmour and McKean.

"Holographic interfaces functioning normally," Marlane announced.

"All hazard suit systems at nominal," Waters said. "Bioscans within parameters, although Agent Gilmour has elevated adrenaline levels in his bloodstream."

Hearing the report, Gilmour raised his faceplate and retorted, "Wanna trade?"

Waters grinned and shook her head, then returned to her monitor. "Specimens active. Good for start-up."

The agents tapped green spheres on their interfaces, beginning Casimir chamber activity. Deep inside, the twin plates started their inexorable close, bearing down on the hidden jewels dropped from above.

Again, as before, the Temporal Retrieve project scientists gathered around the two remaining field members, anxious and eager to send them off one final time, on a mission all of them hoped would see them successful and victorious, at the very least for the sake of humankind's survival.

The junior scientists slapped Gilmour and McKean enthusiastically on their backs, pushing them forward into the fray with all their skills, hopes and encouragement. Once the scientists' spontaneous celebration had subsided, Rauchambau and Dark Horse stepped into the semi-circle and stood before the two men.

Dark Horse, never one to use too many words, or get caught up in sentimental reflections, said simply, "We haven't always seen eye to eye, Agent Gilmour and Agent McKean, but I never neglected to respect your dedication to your country. Good luck to you both, gentlemen." He then raised his right hand to his brow, saluting the agents before stepping back and handing the floor to the Solicitor General.

Rauchambau inhaled deeply before starting, "When I granted Doctor de Lis' request, I had no indication that you gentlemen would be truly our only hope in solving this crisis. As the months have come and gone, and the times have gotten more difficult, I now recognize the earnestness to which Doctor de Lis has possessed in his determination to see this project to its successful end, and his near clairvoyance in the seriousness and gravity of the crisis, something I'm not sure our representatives in Washington have always realized. But what I'm most impressed by, Agent Gilmour and Agent McKean, is your single-mindedness in throwing yourselves into situations at which normal men would shrink. You two, and the men who could not make it back, epitomize what our country needs most: dedication, courage, strength, intelligence, and above all, heart, in knowing what must be done, in knowing where your duty lies. I could go on—and most people would say I would..." a smile broke over his face, followed by chortles from his small audience, "but you get my meaning. I'll be quiet now, and let you gentlemen do what you do best. We are all in your debt."

A rousing chorus of applause, coupled with whoops and cheers, echoed throughout U5-1, and if one cared to listen, the entire U Complex.

Gilmour and McKean found each other's eyes among the ebullience and nodded. Closing their faceplates, the agents activated the jaunt processes on their holographic interfaces as the crowd stepped away. Looking around, Gilmour drank in one last moment of this laboratory, creating a mental image of the last time he knew he would ever see this place, these people.

Not allowing his emotions to overtake him, Gilmour focused on the HUD graphics five centimeters from him, blurring out the assembled scientists. He shut off all contact with the world outside, even as he heard "Good luck" filter in from de Lis.

The next few seconds passed like hours...his Casimir chamber hummed rhythmically on his back, vibrating his haz suit, lulling Gilmour into a peaceful, nigh stupor as the holographic interface slowly crept down his faceplate and tapered into a gaping white maw where once his abdomen resided. One heartbeat collided into another until it was one with the spinning jewel, two fiery cores expanding, ripping him apart, consuming all quanta in his body, each millisecond stretching, pulling him further, until finally, he was on the horizon, no longer separate but one, no longer in a present, but in a river of infinity, one with all quanta ever to exist....

## CHAPTER THIRTY-SIX

He fell in an infinite blackness, a ink so dark, so impenetrable, death seemed like it would have been warmer somehow. End over end he tumbled, no sense of up or down, his balance lost to chaos.

In an instant, one word popped into his mind: "Lights!"

A spectrum of color exploded into Gilmour's eyes, his gauntlets rushing to cover up his sensitive photoreceptors. Minutes passed before he could catch a decent breath, and his heart could slow down to properly function. In those intervening moments, though, a hundred different thoughts raced about his mind, each giving him pause. Had he succeeded? Had he just committed himself to death? Was this all folly? Grasping for his left arm through the density of this medium in which he was suspended, he found his holographic interface and tapped it hard. On command, the Heads Up Display came to life centimeters from his eyes, giving him access to every system and the ability to ascertain their functionality.

"Where am I?" he commanded the vocal response computer.

Responding swiftly, the HUD brought up a window to the lower left: "45.79N, 153.05E, -4.838 KMs."

Remembering back to his brief, Roget's creation had taken him to precisely where he had meant to go: nearly five kilometers below the surface of the Pacific Ocean. Gilmour was officially in the Kuril-Kamchatka Trench, lord help him. The realization itself was the most bizarre part; floating in the second deepest waters in the world was as normal down here as it was at sea level.

Swiveling his head around, he lit the ocean water out to a distance of nearly five meters, enough to see what should have been the wreckage site. Particles of floating detritus and opaque, turquoise water were all that greeted him, however.

Toggling a green button on his interface, he activated his voxlink and shouted, "McKean, can you hear me?!" Static ate at his ears in response, raising his defenses. "Increase intensity ten percent, remodulate frequency one hundred megahertz."

On his HUD, a holograph of the vox frequency appeared, the red peaks and valleys of the heightened and distorted signal widening in response to Gilmour's request.

"McKean!" Gilmour repeated, all but pleading with his partner. "McKean!"

Again more static, but a faint "Gil—r...I...m...si...m...ters...pos... tion...." crept through the speakers.

Gilmour squinted, concentrating on the intermittent voice. "McKean, repeat, please!"

"Gil—r...I...m...si...m...ters...pos...tion...."

Raising the interface on his left arm, Gilmour accessed a secondary window, bringing up a sequence of yellow buttons, all labeled under the text "LIDAR GUIDED LOCATER." His right index finger tapped the left-most button, creating a gold circle in the center of his HUD, along with a series of coordinate and distance markers. He then aimed his left arm forward, painting every atom of matter with guided laser pulses from his lidar cannon. Gilmour swept a five-meter radius, overturning nothing but assorted deep sea debris and the occasional eddy coursing through the water.

Having swept the water to his front and flanks, Gilmour slowly rotated his body around, once more combing the water with lidar. Now several minutes into wasting his time, he increased the lidar locating distance and yelled, "McKean! Can you hear me? Can you get a fix on my lidar?"

A distinct "ping" a few seconds later soon caught his attention. Swinging his right arm over to the interface, he ceased the lidar scan and commanded the computer to home in on the source and nature of the clearly artificial noise.

Gilmour's HUD quickly split the signal noise into its components, revealing its source: a second lidar pulse, and from its frequency and distance, emanating from McKean. Initiating his lidar a second time, Gilmour painted the signal with his own pulse and finally gained a visual confirmation of a free-floating figure, six meters to his lower port flank.

Extending his arms forward, Gilmour dove ahead, pushing his legs up behind him. He then swept his arms against his torso ring, commanding the voice response computer to activate the supercavitating engine sled for a short, one-point-six-second burst. At once, a giant plume of carbon dioxide gas shot from the outtake barrel, forming a bubble over Gilmour's haz suit helmet. Within a millisecond, the hydrazine fuel pushed him forward, and an instant later, at a speed of several meters per second, McKean materialized in front of Gilmour before he knew it.

The immediate drag created from the popping carbon dioxide bubble stopped Gilmour in his own trail, causing a cluster of bubbles to push by him in a sudden gust.

McKean reached out his right gauntlet and seized Gilmour's torso ring, keeping the wayward agent from being carried off. Pulling him back, McKean's helmet lamp found Gilmour's faceplate, allowing him to see Gilmour's green-tinged and blurry face. "You always did know how to make an introduction, didn't you?" McKean said over his voxlink. Gilmour nodded his head in response. "Watch it when you activate the sled, Neil. I almost knocked myself out by hitting my faceplate."

"Understood. Say, any idea where this wreckage is at? I did a few lidar sweeps before I contacted you, but couldn't find anything in this damned murk."

"Good question." Gilmour glanced at his own HUD's lidar readings, which was drawing a blank on the site as well. "I assumed Dark Horse had been fairly accurate with his coordinates, but maybe we drifted upwards when we jaunted."

"The only way to be sure is to keep going towards where the floor should be."

"Exactly. Program your sled for a maximum burst of two seconds, and we'll take this a few meters at a time. It might be slower this way, but I don't want to end up as sludge on the bottom of the ocean floor."

"Agreed."

"Ready?" Gilmour asked.

McKean gave him a thumbs up.

The two agents individually commanded their voice response computers for the burst, positioned their hazard suits, and then shot off into the depths with a flurry, leaving nothing but a storm of white, gaseous spheres in their wake.

The first dive ended almost before it began. Checking the individual lidar at the end of their seven meter launch, the agents found nothing but turquoise water and ocean debris. Still no trench floor.

Without waiting for acknowledgement from McKean, Gilmour ordered, "Let's go for another two seconds."

The pair repeated the supercavitating burst, lurching forward with superhuman speed. For a split-second, brackish water buffeted the agents' faceplates, the collective shine of the helmet lamps blinding their eyes and dulling their senses. The absolute hyper-realism of the burst made them slow to the transformation of the turquoise water to a slight ochre tint, then a more opaque sand.

In a flash, the supercavitating carbon dioxide bubble exploded, ending the burst, but not before the agents' momentum sent them flying helmet first towards a vast expanse of seafloor sediment. Unable to stop soon enough, Gilmour's and McKean's limbs flailed as they crashed and tumbled into the trench floor, carving out craters large enough to swallow objects twice their size. Flinging silt and fine pebbles into the already thick ocean water, the pair finally came to rest, but not before their inertia slowed and gravity took over, gradually ensnaring them in a tract of sinking sediment, their heavy hazard suits unwittingly adding to the trap. The sediment quickly began to resettle over them, threatening to not only swallow them whole but bury them as well.

Four hands groped at the devouring sediment voraciously, hurriedly trying to find something to anchor themselves on to avoid sinking into the dozen-meter deep trench floor. Seconds became minutes, before finally the struggling hands descended until only fingertips, then burbling mounds of silt and pebbles, remained. The seafloor soon reclaimed the twin craters, carefully recompositing the vital silt matter abruptly blown into the surrounding water.

A moment later, a single plume of gas ascended from one of the former craters, loosening the sediment floor's grip. Silence, then a second plume escaped, followed by tertiary gas bubbles, strangely lit from below. The darkened trench then exploded in a cascade of light as two gas spheres burst out of the seafloor, launched two meters into the ocean water, and then just as unexpectedly popped, revealing the haz suits of Gilmour and McKean, helmet lamps at full illumination.

Both agents cut through the water, hydrazine nozzles at full, before switching the sled engines off, allowing their ascending inertia to propel them forward. The two haz-suited agents drifted apart until Gilmour regained his wits and extended his arms to grapple McKean, pulling him back.

McKean steadied himself and quipped, "You were saying?"

Gilmour rolled his eyes. "Where are we now?"

"Nine meters from our last position," McKean reported, eyeing his HUD. Raising his upper body, he angled his head around his helmet in an attempt to pick out landmarks with his lamp illumination. He studied the disturbed water for several seconds, scanning beyond the detritus and raised sediment.

Both men now swept the area with their helmet lamps, creating beacons of light that penetrated the ocean water like miniature lighthouses.

"Checking lidar," Gilmour announced, his finger tapping his holographic interface. The lidar targeting circle flashed, painting the environment. Extending the search farther, a shield or wall of material blanketed the target, completely swamping Gilmour's search, as if the lidar itself had been bounced back to its source. Looking up from the target, he widened his eyes in disbelief at the visually indistinct area of water. "What the hell..."

McKean turned to Gilmour. "What?"

Gilmour remained mute before saying, "McKean, double-check my scans. Center on four-five-point-seven-nine north by one-five-three-point-oh-five east, extend to eleven-point-two meters."

McKean nodded his head and performed the search on his own lidar, taking time to center on the precise target. Sure enough, on McKean's HUD, the wall of matter blocked his lidar as well. "Confirmed. There's something reflecting my lidar signal, some type of mirroring. What do you make of it?"

"Haven't an idea. Let's get a closer look the old-fashioned way. Keep the sleds out of it for now."

The agents swam forward, methodically traversing the distance until their individual lidar guidance systems indicated they were within seven meters. Ahead, the twin helmet lamps slowly peeled away the layers of debris and sediment, soon transforming the ocean water from a ubiquitous turquoise to pale sand. Growing closer, waves of dull surface reflection danced in the high-beam lamps, adding to the mystery of the shield, until finally Gilmour and McKean drew to within four meters of the lidar mirror and paused their advance to ascertain just what exactly was in front of them.

"We should be able to discern terrain from here," Gilmour said, his eyes darting from his lidar target to the visual object and back again. "Lidar should pick out soil composition, sedimentary differences."

"I'm not seeing anything with my eyes, either. It's as if I'm missing my hand passing right in front of my face."

Gilmour nodded. Switching his lidar off, he reached around with his left gauntlet and pulled a cylinder from the magnetic ring on his torso. Holding the cylinder in front of his faceplate, Gilmour twisted it twice and aimed it towards an area of the trench beyond their vision, still clouded in darkness. He flicked his thumb up, toggling a button on the side of the cylinder, and then released it. A flash sizzled from its tail end and the cylinder took off through the water at several knots, fast enough to spin away from the agents and disappear into the darkness, leaving only a small, white wake.

Counting down, Gilmour watched in earnest while the wake faded. After a moment, an audible click could be heard through their voxlinks, followed by a larger boom. Out of the darkness erupted a white star, which grew larger until a disk shone like a waterborne supernova, spreading orange illumination and scattering shadows for scores of meters. Within seconds the trenchscape opened to the light of the sun, and before the two agents appeared the sight which brought the face of war to the world once again: a cavernous, collapsed ridge, one of at least a string, towering over them from the right, nearly half-a-kilometer in height, with a diagonal overhang reaching out some three meters above the agents. Underneath that great earthly mass was a wall of sheer metallic material buckled, crushed and cracked after two centuries of wait, running far beyond the flare's reach like some ancient sedimentary strata.

Gilmour and McKean marveled at the immensity of the metallic debris, which, despite the weight of the ridge atop it, still managed to hold up an impressive three meters of height. As the flare slowly lost its intensity over the next few minutes, their helmet lamps threw white circles of illumination against the collapsed ridge overhang and the adjacent crushed metal, highlighting the absolute, otherworldly experience.

McKean swam the interval and extended his fingers, which brushed the twisted corpse, casting an exaggerated shadow along the watery hide. Running his fingers along the wall, he felt the rippled metal reverberate throughout the carapace, his mind failing to fathom the extreme forces required to bring down such a behemoth.

Meanwhile, Gilmour took precise lidar measurements of the collapsed ridge above them and beyond, allowing the flare light to aid his search for potential *Strela* warhead mines; none of his sensors had, so far, detected any electromagnetic pulses or gravimetric ripples thought to be caused by an approaching warhead.

McKean propelled himself along by grasping outcroppings of material, swiftly exploring the hulk much faster than by swimming at its side. Running his eyes in tandem with his gauntlets, he found dozens of pancaked layers, the lines varying in width and duration. Proceeding another ten meters, McKean discovered a mostly preserved section of the metallic hull, saved by a pronounced ridge crevasse. A hole breached the metal layers, and was large enough—just under a meter in diameter—for one of them to crawl through without too much difficulty. Peering inside, cracks along the hull of the metal permitted seams of orange flare light to flow inside for the time being, but not for much longer. If they were going to discover who or what had crashed here, and why, the time to do it was now.

"Hey, Gilmour," McKean said, "I've found us an entrance, a mousehole."

Gilmour located McKean with his lidar and swam forward. "Are you serious?"

McKean craned his neck back and waved his arm, keeping the other one attached to the metal hull. "Come take a look."

Gilmour took a few moments to swim across the expanse, finally meeting the metal wall at McKean's right flank, having pulled himself along the outcroppings as well. While Gilmour approached, McKean busied himself with visually exploring the mousehole, his helmet lamp illuminating the tiny entrance. While the object itself was thoroughly crushed beyond retrieval, the mousehole had been spared, fortunate enough to be located in a pocket where the ridge had not collapsed to the trench floor. An even more fortunate circumstance was that this tunnel allowed access for the two agents, and perhaps a sanctuary if the *Strelas* started blasting all around. Gilmour just hoped the strange, high-density properties of the jewels were shared by this lidar-bending metal. He'd hate to find out the hard way that de Lis was wrong, after all.

"How far does it go?" Gilmour asked, now within arm's reach of the mousehole.

"Let's see." McKean toggled his interface, reactivating his lidar. Placing his left arm inside, McKean measured the tunnel, periodically reading off the distance numerals from his HUD. After a moment, he extracted himself and turned to face his partner. "If lidar is to be believed, at least twenty meters, maybe more. Signal didn't bounce back for quite a while. I'd say we've got ourselves a nice, big wreck here."

Gilmour nodded. "Care to take a dig around?"

"You'd better believe it."

With that, McKean placed his right gauntlet inside and found a good outcropping to wrap his fingers around, then pulled himself inside the mousehole, his left gauntlet pushing his mass forward. Once McKean's boots had cleared the threshold, Gilmour followed, watching his partner move ahead by the waning flare light.

After a few moments of uncertainty, both men disappeared inside the mousehole and headed forward into the unknown, their only assurance being that this would be the most challenging retrieval site of their lives, with the stakes of human freedom riding on their actions, five kilometers below the rest of civilization.

# CHAPTER THIRTY-SEVEN

For the first time in two centuries, life once more echoed throughout the hull of the sleeping giant. Now, after a wait of so many decades, the great, ancient craft had been recovered, and corporeal beings again inhabited its confines. So long, the wait had been interminable....

Pulling themselves along centimeter by centimeter, Gilmour's and McKean's hazard suits clanged against the crushed metal tube, the watery medium in which they floated transmitting the clamor quite well. Periodic pauses to look ahead with the assistance of their helmet lamps seemed to make the mousehole stretch on for kilometers; the agents knew the cumbersome haz suits and the water pressure hindered their advance, bringing their fatigue levels and concentration to lower thresholds, forcing the ever-niggling question, "How much farther?"

After bouncing around the interior and subtly losing his bearings one too many times, McKean halted and signaled to Gilmour to let up. "I—I gotta stop."

Gilmour nodded, allowing his body to come to rest against the tube. Consulting his interface, he said, "We've come fifteen...sixteen meters, the end should be right there. Looking though," he took a deep breath, "I can't see any entrance into this craft. Are you sure you didn't get another lidar echo?"

"Why the hell would I say otherwise? If I thought it was a lidar bounce, I sure woulda said so!"

"I'm not accusing you, Neil!" Gilmour lifted his hand to massage his strained eyes, but the gauntlet ricocheted off his faceplate. "Shit... can't even do that...."

McKean rested his head against the back of his helmet, then turned to Gilmour behind him. "James, is it just me, or...or are we a bit testy?"

Gilmour shook his head. "No, you're right. Stress, or something. Having trouble thinking straight. Mind's clouded."

"Depth?"

"I wouldn't think so. De Lis gave us plenty of nitrogen anti-bubbly to keep that from happening." He gestured his hand around. "Maybe this thing's affectin' our judgment, bending our thoughts."

"How could it do that? It's just a hunk of corroded metal."

"This hunk of metal's from somewhere else. Ghosts...demons...if something died in here, could be some kind of haunted structure."

McKean let out a half-laugh, half-sigh. "Don't start that. We ain't got time for campfire tales."

"Sorry, just a theory. How're you doing?"

McKean glanced around and blinked his eyes several times, readjusting them. "Better. Just needed a breather."

The two picked themselves up and began the crawl again, focusing on getting to the end of the tunnel before it ended them. They traversed several more meters of nondescript tunnel sans complaint, not pausing to think about their monotonous and claustrophobic circumstances.

Making his way past the twenty-meter mark, McKean double-checked his HUD lidar target, his eyes glancing at the sudden shift in return signals. The holographic display, which had exhibited nothing but an indistinct wall of matter all the way there, now revealed a small, central circle of absorbed laser light in the midst of that wall; there was something up there, and it was close.

"Gilmour, I'm getting something on lidar, six meters straight ahead." Angling his helmet so that his lampbeam shown on that spot, McKean swam forward, galvanized by this renewed sense of purpose.

A minute elapsed before the agents were within an arm's distance of the mousehole's end. Twin lampbeams now highlighted it, giving the agents' eyes the first real glimpse of the object, which faintly resembled a hatch, at least in the respect that it was circular, with a crystalline, twenty-centimeter-diameter sphere embedded within the metallic structure. A kaleidoscope of color now danced around the tunnel as they drew nearer, thanks to the queer refraction of the lamp light through the glass sphere. The two agents' highly distorted and mocked forms were also colored in the spherical mirror, adding surreality and a somewhat comical nature to the already incredible adventure of finding this extraterrestrial craft buried below the sea.

McKean laid his gauntlets on the hatch, fingers extended, eagerly searching the metallic structure for a lock, or any other mechanism that could allow them access inside. Gilmour swam up alongside his partner and began his own study of the hatch, his gauntlets focused on the spectrum-bending glass sphere. He tapped it several times, each one sounding as if he had set off a cataclysm of crashing crystal shards. The echoes were hauntingly beautiful, astonishing and peaceful all at once. If it wasn't for the duty they had to perform, he'd be just as content sitting down and playing this makeshift instrument all day.

"I don't see any handle or locking mechanism," McKean said.

"This is the handle," Gilmour determined, then glanced at McKean. "I think."

"You've been playing with it the last few minutes, I should hope you've some certainty of this."

Gilmour furrowed his brow in agreement. "Let me think." He tapped with his index finger once more, letting loose more crystalline emanations into the water. "All right, not touch activated, at least not this sensitively."

"Should we break it?"

"That seems kind of foolish. You couldn't use it again."

"Well..." McKean sighed, pausing to think himself. "Looks kind of difficult to rotate like a doorknob. Can't see pulling it out...well, why not push it in?"

Gilmour shrugged, then put both of his gauntlets over the sphere, eclipsing the shower of brilliant color. He voice-activated the magnetic locks on his haz suit's boot heels, anchoring himself into the metal tube in the event a vacuum on the other side would entice the ocean water to push him through. "Neil, anchor yourself, too."

McKean followed Gilmour's lead, and both men were now prepared for the worst. The only question was, were they prepared for the alien?

Gilmour put all of his mass behind his gauntlets, and pressing mightily, pushed the glass sphere forward until it had all but pierced the metal hatch in which it was embedded. A massive reverberation of the metal structure sent a great creech through their haz suits, rattling their soft tissues. Both men gritted their teeth as Gilmour found himself thrust forward by the action of the hatch, which seemed to be taking him with it. Before him, he could see globules of seawater burble out of the mousehole and travel up his arms and out the circular hole, following in the now-detached hatch's wake.

Taken along, Gilmour passed beyond a series of concentric rings of metal, apparently the craft's inner complex of bulkheads. Clearing a half meter, the hatch pulled away from him and drifted out into a dark beyond, the glass sphere growing fainter as it sped into the distance. Underneath him, he felt the magnetic locks disengage, allowing him freedom to drift sideways into the empty compartment. Globules of water continued to trickle off his haz suit, lending Gilmour the first clue that he was no longer in a watery medium, but an atmosphere. Somehow, it seemed impossible; how could all that pressure be held in check by simple air? He twisted himself around to see McKean trailing behind, water bubbles in his wake, giving himself a view of the whole bizarre process he had just undergone.

Beneath them, the shimmering ocean water roiled softly in the open hatch before subsiding, as if they had just stepped out of a pool and were now flying above it. The curious sensation of floating soon overtook them both, but this was not the water buoyancy they had grown accustomed to, this was microgravity—zero G—for lack of a better metaphor. Gilmour caught McKean's puzzled visage in his lamplight, a face Gilmour was quick to admit he probably wore as well. This was like orbiting in space, but they were nearly five clicks under the ocean...what the hell was going on?

Forgetting for a moment that he was without weight, and drifting aimlessly into a dark abyss, Gilmour raised his left arm and activated his lidar, then swept the interior of the craft for as far as the lidar could go. Glancing up into his faceplate, he readjusted his eyes to the lidar's HUD target, reading the shifting yellow and red patterns the laser guidance was providing. As before in the trench, Gilmour's lidar was inconclusive, leading him to believe that again the craft was absorbing the lidar signal, for whatever reason.

A moment later, McKean matched Gilmour's inertia, sidling up next to him, his ghostly lamplit helmet and face providing Gilmour the only object to focus on. "I'm receiving nothing on lidar. How about you?"

Gilmour shook his head. "Nothing but this absorption pattern, like outside. Not even any spectrum refraction to give me an idea of distance."

"Well," McKean sighed, "judging by the Doppler effect on my lidar scan, I think our inertia is slowing down. There must be an atmosphere in here causing drag."

"I can't imagine after all these centuries this place still being airtight." He paused for a moment, pondering the situation, and how to best utilize the potential boon of microgravity. "The hydrazine nozzles will give us some maneuvering capability, if only for a while." Gilmour craned his neck around, fruitlessly searching their pitch black surroundings for a hint of what this place truly was. "Now if we only knew where we were headed...."

McKean toggled his holographic interface, accessing the engine sled's systems. "I'm setting mine for the lowest possible acceleration... shouldn't take much to give us a boost."

"Agreed." Gilmour did the same on his interface, hoping the infinite blackness wouldn't stretch their allotted fuel beyond the sixty-seven minute limit imposed by de Lis' restrictions.

With two short bursts of hydrazine, Gilmour and McKean were propelled forward into the ink, accelerating to a velocity of approximately two-and-a-quarter meters per second, enough to overpower the vague atmospheric drag and still maintain a comfortable speed at which to take measurements of the craft's interior.

Speeding across the vastness of the craft for incalculable moments, the two agents encountered nothing, scanned nothing, and generally grew bored with the lack of anything in their path, with the exception of the ceaseless, omnipresent black.

"No temperature variations, of small or large degree, no electromagnetic activity, no gravimetric variations beyond nominal," McKean moaned, shaking his head. "As of this minute, I'm not even confident that we're even here!"

"This has to lead somewhere...." Gilmour whispered, refusing to quit searching after coming this far, through this long journey. "There has to be some reason the Confederation wants to mine this trench, wants to possess this craft...."

"I sure as hell hope this isn't some intergalactic joke on us. I'm gonna be pissed if these aliens of yours are watching a holograph of us stumbling around in the dark."

"I'm sure the—" Gilmour's voice broke, his eyes catching a glint of light ahead of them.

McKean turned towards the now-silent Gilmour. "What?"

Gilmour pointed his finger straight ahead. Looking methodically, he yelled, "There! Check your HUD again! I'll get lidar!"

Still puzzled, McKean did as commanded and toggled the controls on his interface, activating the various sensors arrayed on his left forearm. While McKean busied himself with the other scans, Gilmour swept his lidar cannon in the direction of the flash, which still hadn't appeared to his eyes a second time. On his HUD's lidar target appeared another circular pattern, matching exactly the one from the hatch the pair had used to enter. Swinging his helmet lamp again, Gilmour recreated the glint of light, which shone with the same kaleidoscopic colors as the glass sphere.

Gilmour turned to his partner. "I think it's another hatch, Neil."

The pair continued forward, now buoyed by the renewal of the hunt. Closing the gaping distance, the twin helmet lampbeams encircled the glass sphere and the hatch in which it was imbedded, as well as the surrounding metallic bulkhead. Now at a meter's length, the agents held out their arms, allowing their gauntlets to break their velocity and catch them against the metal hatch. The two haz suits clanged violently, snapping the agents back, but both were safely stopped.

Twisting his body around, Gilmour managed to place his boots on the bulkhead and magnetically attach them to the hull around the hatch, giving him leverage once they attempted to open it up. Next to him, McKean had already sealed his boots to the bulkhead, and was now standing upright again, peering into the darkness from whence they had came. Gilmour rose to his height and rotated his head around, glancing at the extent his helmet lamp would allow him to see. Both now stood in the opposite direction they had entered, a thought sure to boggle their minds if they chose to dwell longer then they should.

"Look at that," McKean said, pointing his finger past his partner, to the shadow Gilmour cast on the surface from McKean's helmet lamp.

Gilmour turned to see the sharp outline of illumination on darkness. "What?"

McKean gestured again. "Your shadow is curved."

Gilmour swiveled again and glanced at McKean, who was now bathed in Gilmour's helmet illumination. "So is yours." Gilmour crouched down and ran his gauntlet over the surface of the bulkhead, now under the close scrutiny of his helmet lamp. He then tilted his head up, shining the light, and more importantly, the lidar instrument, outward. On his HUD, a refraction curve was painted yellow, but surrounded by nothingness. He swept the lidar cannon in a complete circle, then came back to where he had started, in front of McKean. "I think we're on a big sphere. I don't pick up anything else around here."

"You mean we're on a floating sphere not attached to anything else?"

"Umm, yeah. I'm not kidding."

"Holy...what the hell can be inside of it? I mean, what could fit inside?"

Gilmour double-checked his HUD, just to rule out hallucination brought about by prolonged superreality. "If the lidar is right, it's calculating a diameter of about one hundred meters, plus or minus."

McKean's mind raced at the thought. He spared himself the impossibility of running through a list, though, and knelt down on his haunches, joining Gilmour next to the hatch and the gleaming glass sphere.

Gilmour's gauntlets brushed the edge of the hatch and found the glass sphere, which, like its twin, bore an exaggerated reflection of his form. "You wanted to know? Then let's find out." Firming his hands, Gilmour applied both to the spectral sphere and pushed with all his mass and magnetically sealed boots behind him.

The glass sphere sank into its mooring with laxness, despite Gilmour's immense exertion and the reinforced strength of his gauntlets. At once, the glass sphere descended into the hatch without warning, viciously slamming Gilmour's gauntlets against the surrounding metal. He cried out as the reverberations rocked his body.

McKean reached out to his partner. "Are you all right?"

"I—I think I am." Gilmour retrieved his gauntlets and folded them close against his chest, then looked down to the circular hatch again. "Why...why isn't it opening?"

McKean blinked several times, staring at the now sphere-less hatch. "What the hell's wrong with you?" He put his own hands on the hull. "Open, dammit...."

As McKean alternately yelled at the hatch and tried to pry it open, Gilmour unfolded his arms and placed them down on the hull structure, running his fingers against the sheer metal. Immediately, his eyes widened. "Neil...it's shaking...."

McKean tipped his head forward over the hatch. "What?"

Instinctively, Gilmour threw up his right arm and pushed McKean's helmet, forcing his partner's body back from the hatch's breech. Like a rising crescendo, the bulkhead beneath the two agents rumbled and roared before a wave of pure white energy bellowed out of the structure, blowing the circular hatch off and flinging it into the darkness. A secondary wave washed a concussive blast over the two agents, launching them away from the open hatch and depositing them oppositely ten meters back. Both Gilmour and McKean then skidded on the cradles of their engine sleds before lurching to a halt, their inertia ceasing unmercifully.

Where once there was darkness as infinite as the depths of the universe, now erupted a fountain of white energy into a river pouring forth past the mousehole's hatch. Shining with an intensity rivaling a supernova, the fountain transformed the Kuril-Kamchatka Trench into an undersea paradise, light spilling, gushing forth, flowing through the seawater with energies unknown save to the power of the largest suns. The massive scar that was the trench now flowed with light, an orgy of swirling and roiling turquoise waves stretching the entire length of the kilometers-wide subduction zone. Life that once inhabited the darkest and deepest edges of the world now were revealed to it for the first time, many blinded, many reveling.

And five kilometers up from this reunion of water and light, many took notice, and many set long-held plans into action.

# CHAPTER THIRTY-EIGHT

"McKean! McKean, can you hear me? Neil!"

Inside his cumbersome haz suit, Gilmour grunted while trying to regain his balance, trapped on his back like a tortoise. Tilting his body to the right, he rolled off the supercavitating sled and back onto his feet, careful not to launch himself into the microgravity. Throwing his mass forward, he was now able to look at the awe-inducing fountain of white light for the first time, witnessing for himself the tremendous power that had blown him away.

"Neil, are you all right? Neil!"

Static crackled over Gilmour's voxlink before he heard McKean's voice. "Yeah, I'm all right. Just about flew off the surface...had to light my hydrazine to keep me from floating away."

"Good to hear," Gilmour answered, blocking out the intense rays of the fountain with his gauntlet so they wouldn't sear his eyes. He followed the fountain upwards, craning his neck to see how far the light river flowed. "Can you believe this? Look at that...it goes all the way out."

McKean took a few steps closer to the former hatchway, now the fountain. "The power and energy in this sphere...what could it be?"

Gilmour shook his head. "A power source? Some kind of reactor?"

On McKean's holographic interface, he accessed his array of instruments with a touch of a button, then scanned the pillar of energy for a few moments. "The sheer scale of the energy is immense, at least several teVs, but the radiation readings are about non-existent, no more than conventional energy sources...actually less. I'd say it's nearly as safe to live in there as anywhere else."

Gilmour put a reticent foot forward, then another; working up the confidence to close the gap, he walked to the edge of the hatchway. At arm's length, the fountain of light did not seem to be repulsive; in fact, he felt no energy beam or wave to ward him off. It was white light... pure photons, glistening against the slate grey of his haz suit. Gilmour's instincts urged him to cover his eyes, but the orbs did not burn with the pain of staring at the sun. Every facet of this fountain flowed with peacefulness, tranquility, with life. It was intoxicating. Kneeling down, he neared the fountain, his faceplate now encompassed with its image.

"Gilmour," McKean spoke, no longer seeing his partner. "Gilmour, what are you doing?"

Extending his right gauntlet, Gilmour pierced the fountain's boundary and plunged the extremity inside. The agent's once-shadowed hand soon burned with brightness; eddies of light licked up his arm and swirled over his haz suit, coating Gilmour with the fountain's purity. Never once did he retreat from the fountain's fantastical beauty...the raw power the fountain displayed was enveloping, heartening, loving. Fear did not have a haven here.

"Gilmour!" McKean implored. "Talk to me!"

Without trepidation, Gilmour rose, and not responding to McKean, extended a boot, then leapt inside the fountain of light, descending into the hatchway, leaving only a crackle of white flame behind.

"Gilmour!" McKean reached out, but his partner had already gone. He shook his head at the impulsive stunt, an act quite unbecoming of the James Gilmour McKean had known throughout his career. For a moment McKean wavered, and realizing that Gilmour most likely wasn't just going to reappear, decided to follow him inside, god help him. Inhaling deeply, McKean's palms perspired while he counted to three, then closed his eyes and leapt as well, hearing his haz suit crackle along the way....

Spacetime peeled away in layers of flame, the universe a vast cycle of fire, ever fueled, ever dying, ever born....

They burned in an invisible fire, a river of flame swirling, rolling, a surf burning through their cores, purified, consecrated by time....

Poured from the depths of the cosmos they sprang, renewed, invigorated, recast, re-bound to the fabric, the cloth, of the universe....

*"Where am I?"*

Infinite whiteness.

No snow had ever fallen so pure...no virgin had ever been so innocent...no sky had ever been so clear...no water had ever been so sleek....

"My god, look at us...."

Gilmour held his gauntlet to his eyes and peered through them to find McKean standing on the other side. Blinking, he turned his gauntlet over to the backside. He saw the machine glove through to his hand, then his veins, ligaments, bones, lipids and McKean staring at him in peaceful disbelief at his own body. Nothing could be so clear to them now, nowhere had ever been so quiet, nothing had ever been so much of everything but yet with no pretense at all. Nothing. And yet, they were everything. This was everything. At once. No past, present, future, yesterday, now, tomorrow. Matter, energy, space, time, was all here, all now. Gilmour tightened his fist...a stiff wind blew through this nothingness...a crack of lightning overhead rendered his fist opaque. Looking out and up, the purity washed away, the whiteness transformed into a chamber... at arm's length, Gilmour became as Gilmour knew himself, no longer able to discern McKean, he moved his gauntlet and saw the other man in rapt attention to the colors flooding back...taking over their senses, the way matter and energy had always lorded over the finite....

"Your journey has been most treacherous. Please, relax."

Gilmour and McKean were startled by the man approaching behind them. He crossed slowly over the smooth metal flooring, his footfalls echoing lightly in the spherical walls of this chamber they mysteriously could not recall entering. Gilmour flashed a glimpse to McKean, who returned his puzzlement with a furrowed brow. The two agents glided carefully over the floor, exploring the sterile chamber from within their helmets. Looking over once more to the man who had greeted him, they were astonished to see him dressed in traditional Sherpa clothing, completely incongruous with the immaculate chamber where they now stood, as if he were an ancestor of Shajda, their guide in Nepal.

The strange Sherpa gestured to them with his dark, reddish hands, flashing them a brief, cordial smile. "Please, come forward," he intoned, without a hint of accent. "I can sense your exhaustion. You have done and seen much."

The two agents nodded and walked over to a set of furniture. The Sherpa proffered a seat to the weary men, who accepted and sat down, although awkwardly in their haz suits. Both agents raised their faceplates and inhaled the sterile atmosphere.

"I am sure you have questions for me. You are very inquisitive. That is how you have survived so long, when others failed. They could not see the possibilities just lying beyond their view."

Gilmour and McKean nodded matter-of-factly. Gilmour asked, "Why us?"

"You?"

"Why us?" Gilmour reiterated. "Why did you come here? Why, when this world has seen so much strife, war, terror, longing...why did you choose us?"

The Sherpa smiled. "They were right to say you were curious. So many questions you have. Your first question is not one any can answer. The universe just does what it does. Your second question is the same as the first. You do have a fondness for repeating yourselves."

"Then allow me to ask this," Gilmour said. "What is this craft? Where are we?"

The Sherpa raised a finger. "A craft, same as any other. I have not seen any more than either of you."

McKean leaned forward. "You mean, you're not...one of them?"

"Ho...no," the Sherpa paused to laugh, "I am not. I am flesh and blood, as human as you two men are. I just watch for them, until they can come back." The Sherpa sighed, then started, "I was there the day this... craft came down to the ground. I led a group of men, of Westerners, ancestors of yours, to a small crash. The Westerners did not react well to seeing the remains of this craft's pilots. Still primitive, even by your standards. As a young man, I was curious, as curious as you two are. I went back to the site, and discovered mysteries beyond that which the human mind had never anticipated, and would never until your time. Here I am." Gilmour and McKean gulped, both attempting to digest what should have been called an outlandish story, except for the fact they knew it had happened.

"And here you two are," the Sherpa continued. "You have utilized their gifts well, as well as can be expected, knowing our species. The jewels you hold inside of your garments are dangerous, but essential. Lessons learned throughout the ages by others you shall learn as well."

"Lessons?" Gilmour asked.

"I can't tell you that. I haven't learned them either. That is for you to do for the rest of our species." The Sherpa gestured again. "Come. They want you to see this."

Gilmour and McKean stood and followed the Sherpa to the center of the spherical chamber. A few meters away, the Sherpa paused on a circular panel inset into the floor.

"You asked where here is?" The Sherpa turned away from the agents and held out his hand. Instantly, the chamber emitted a blinding flash, engulfing them all, becoming a crystalline sphere, in which the trio were now contained. Streamers of light, dwarfing the kaleidoscope of colors the miniaturized glass spheres had displayed earlier, danced and pulsed throughout this sphere, bringing tears of beauty to Gilmour and McKean. Millions of facets radiated and refracted light around, bathing them in pure white illumination. A faint buzz permeated their senses, and the pair looked up to see the fountain of light pouring from the northern pole of the sphere, the same fountain they had leapt into with abandon.

The Sherpa glanced back to the pair. "This is the core of the craft."

"We're inside the fountain...inside the metallic sphere...." Gilmour's voice trailed off; words were inapt in describing his sensory input, which in themselves were inapt to withstand the flood.

"This core," McKean asked, unwilling to take his eyes off the multitude of facets, "what is it?"

"Why you are here, I presume. What the world will die for." The Sherpa walked along the perimeter of the core, then gestured towards the agents. "The jewels you possess, what you have found, all originated here. A facet has been lost, shattered by the accident which brought down this craft."

As the Sherpa explained, a flash of light was generated before the agents, then condensed into a miniature, floating representation of the crystalline core. An horrific explosion was shown fracturing the core and leaving it bearing a tremendous gouge on one flank.

"The jewels you have—the secret wisdom I gained knowledge of so many years ago—are all the result of this," the Sherpa continued. "This sphere that you have been allowed to perceive is a neutron core, the densest matter known to the beings who once inhabited this craft. Its potential is limitless, if employed for purposes of furthering knowledge."

The agents' awestruck eyes remained centered on the segment lost from the core, the pair unable to comprehend material such as this having actually been constructed by nature.

"You are the first to successfully return portions of the fractured facet to its home."

McKean rubbed his temples, trying to grapple with all he had learned about the jewels from the Temporal Retrieve Project. "This core, how—how can we be inside it if its density...?"

The Sherpa smiled at their marveling. "We are everywhere, in every facet, coiled into the numerous higher dimensions no human being could ever see, wrapped inside the core's quanta, infinitely small."

McKean looked over his HUD display, which displayed none of this. "Infinitely...."

Gilmour wiped his eyes, finally breaking away from the image in front of them. "Our jaunt jewels...." He turned to the Sherpa.

"Many have possessed some of the jewels in the past," the Sherpa went on, "but have found them useless, as they cannot refine them... because it is impossible to do so. The accident that split this core was by nature a spacetime rip, and even the most hardy matter cannot withstand the forces of the universe's fabric itself. The core desperately wants to repair itself, but cannot do so without intervention. And that was why I was brought here, to stand vigil for the time when the human species could overcome the hurdles of repairing the core to its natural state."

"Then," Gilmour started, his eyes roaming the confines of this crystalline cage, "it needs the jewels."

"Yes. They are as much a part of the core as our brain cells are a part of us."

"But we need our jewels to jaunt home, after we deactivate the *Strelas*!" McKean yelled, the passion in his voice returning after being rendered dull by the sensory pacification.

Gilmour stared straight at the Sherpa. "McKean's right. We have a duty."

"No." The Sherpa shook his head, scolding them like children. "You have a lesson to learn. Humanity must learn."

McKean raised his fisted gauntlet. "To hell with this lesson! This ship has sat on the bottom of the world for two hundred years! I'm sure it can wait a few more until we take care of the Confederation!"

The Sherpa gritted his teeth. "Children...we are still children."

Gilmour stepped closer to the Sherpa. "Take us back, allow us to do our duty and we'll try to do what's right for this core."

A series of concentric ripples suddenly rang throughout the core, catching the attention of Gilmour and McKean, who dropped their argument with the Sherpa and turned towards the faceted walls. The ripples ringed along the edges of the core, harmonizing as they swept through the crystalline sphere.

"What's that?" McKean shouted, straining his neck inside his helmet.

The Sherpa inhaled deeply, sadly. "Gravimetric distortions in the trench water. The core is highly sensitive to any breaks in the spacetime continuum."

Gilmour and McKean instantly toggled their interfaces and activated their instruments. "I'm not picking up anything," McKean reported.

"Neither am I." Gilmour lowered his left arm and turned to the Sherpa. "Please, tell us what's happening."

The Sherpa extended his hand and placed it on the surface of the rippling core. "Foreign objects are proceeding to the trench bottom. Two have descended three thousand, five hundred and nine meters. Two more are one thousand, five hundred meters behind."

Gilmour and McKean locked eyes. Both shouted, "The warheads!" Immediately, the two agents switched their HUDs to full activation, readying their haz systems for the mission.

"How do we get out of here?" Gilmour asked the crestfallen Sherpa.

The Sherpa finally returned his gaze to the agents. "You don't understand one word I have uttered, have you? There is a lesson that must be taught, and this is the beginning. Their weapons are powerful, yes, but won't begin to harm this craft. You two are the first to come this far. The core will not allow both of you to be distracted from the completion of its lattice."

McKean nearly spat. "People will die!"

"Not if you learn the lesson," the Sherpa countered.

Knowing this impasse could not go on forever, Gilmour searched his mind for a solution, a way out. His heart beating, and adrenaline pumping, his forehead glistened with sweat before blurting out, "What's the lesson?"

"I do not know. I cannot know until it has begun."

"Then let us deactivate the *Strelas*," Gilmour said again, "and make that the lesson!"

The Sherpa shook his head. "No. Both of you will cease to live if you attempt to deactivate the foreign objects, these *Strela*, and the lesson will never be learned."

Gilmour banged his gauntlets together and lunged forward, practically falling on his knees to beg, "Then split us up...one of us to stop them, the other to begin the lesson!" He tilted his head towards McKean. "Neil will stay. I'll go and deactivate the warheads."

McKean narrowed his eyes in dismay. "James?"

"That would be acceptable," the Sherpa quickly acquiesced.

"Dammit, Gilmour, no!" McKean pleaded. "We go as a team!"

Gilmour pointed his finger. "That's an order, Agent McKean."

"To hell with that!" McKean crossed over to the other agent and shoved a gauntlet into Gilmour's chest. "I still hold the best time for deactivating the warheads...if we don't go as a team, you'll get yourself killed on the first one. I'd be back inside in no time."

"Neil, don't countermand—"

"Choose him for the lesson!" McKean shouted to the Sherpa, interrupting Gilmour. "I'll jaunt out there and do what I'm best at!"

"Neil!" Gilmour protested again, but his cry was refused by the Sherpa, who said simply, "The core will allow you to return to the trench."

"Thank you." McKean stepped back from Gilmour and toggled his holographic interface, beginning the jaunt procedures.

"Keanie...." Gilmour looked to his partner, the last tie to the old group at the IIA. "Take care of yourself out there."

Special Agent Neil McKean input his last known coordinates into his haz suit's computer before looking back once more to his friend and colleague. Raising his right hand, he sent Gilmour a quick salute and said, "I've never disappointed you yet, have I?"

With that, Gilmour took a deep breath and watched McKean lower his faceplate, then tap his interface. The agent steadied himself as a swirling vortex pierced his chest and, within the margin of a second, engulfed him in the Casimir jaunt effect, sucking McKean out of Gilmour's timeframe.

Gilmour blinked several times...McKean was really gone. He finally turned to the Sherpa after the short repose and asked, "Now, about this lesson."

# CHAPTER THIRTY-NINE

Water boiled and burned as a form, newly emerged and invigorated, materialized into the turquoise depths. The human figure shielded his eyes from the stellar whiteness permeating the ocean water, then swiveled in the buoyant medium, extending a left arm.

"Activate lidar guidance," Neil McKean commanded his haz suit's computer, which obeyed and instantly brought up the circular target on his HUD. The agent swept the fountain-lit waters of the trench with his lidar cannon, then spoke, "Begin scanning for gravimetric disturbances."

Only a second passed before McKean's ears picked up a single "ping" on his HUD, which was closely followed by another. "Locate source of disturbance." A number block appeared to the right of his lidar target, giving coordinates and rapidly shifting metric distances of the two descending disturbances. "Visual." A second window opened above this number block, showing two flashing red cylinders, slowly rotating after exhausting their fuel.

McKean smiled. "Gotcha, you little bastards." He glanced at the distance marker for the nearest target: 0006.116 Ms, then the second: 0006.852 Ms. An additional window at the HUD's top left displayed the supercavitating engine systems. "Activate supercavitating engine, set for burst of one point five seconds." With the appropriate systems at the ready, McKean set the nozzles to direct him to the first and lowest *Strela*, commanding, "Launch now!"

In a split-second, a small blast of carbon dioxide was released from his sled's outtake barrel, forming a bubble over his helmet. A heartbeat later, he was propelled forward with a powerful burst from the hydrazine nozzles.

McKean rocketed upwards and swiftly met the first foreign object his sensors had easily spotted: a two-meter-long *Strela* warhead descending nose-first just centimeters from his haz suit. His gauntlets reached out and grappled the heavy mechanism; securing himself to it, he re-oriented himself head-first, his helmet lamp highlighting small, hand-stenciled Cyrillic letters warning of the danger of this device. He let out a sardonic chuckle as he crawled to the nosecone. Reaching around his torso belt, he opened up a small tool bag, producing a pass key and a narrow wrench that he applied to the interlock on the nosecone sheath, prying it ajar. He swiped the pass key through the housing's microlock and removed the red and yellow fluorescent foil off the cylindrical radiation housing, revealing the Casimir systems, the neutron fuel, and the adjacent QPU.

Glancing to his HUD's right-hand side, he checked the counter tracking his progress, then promptly put the ticked-off seconds in the back of his mind. He toggled the interface on his left gauntlet, which sounded a pre-programmed EM frequency, emitting a small harmonic squeak aimed at the QPU's blue disk. A chirp a second later signaled a positive response.

McKean checked his descent rate and distance, then replaced the nosecone sheath as he found it. Next, he jumped off the finished warhead and watched it slowly sink into the depths, soon disappearing into the dark sediments below.

Turning his back, McKean caught sight of the second warhead and repeated his docking maneuver. A stubborn lock kept McKean from beating his previous time, but the delay was enough for his HUD's lidar guidance to flash a warning that he was within eight meters of the trench floor. Pulling out all the stops, McKean ripped off the radiation hood's housing foil, banking that once the warhead went off, nobody would be the wiser. He closed the nosecone sheath just in time to see the seafloor reflect his lamplight, and pushing himself free, let the *Strela* drift beneath him. With a quick burst of his hydrazine, McKean killed his descending inertia and witnessed the warhead carve out a small crater just meters from its predecessor.

Now at a safe distance from the seafloor, McKean consulted his holographic interface for the locations of the second pair of *Strela*s the core had detected as gravimetric disturbances. Allowing his HUD to calculate for a moment, the hologram sounded two "pings."

"Location," he commanded his voice response computer.

Two number blocks gave the distances as just two thousand meters from the trench floor, but the coordinates raised an eyebrow.

Double-checking the trench coordinate grid, McKean glanced at the descending *Strela*s and said to himself, "They're mining the other side."

McKean programmed his Omni-Coordinated Temporal Transportation computer for the other side of the fallen ridge, in no way wanting to waste the hydrazine for a long journey. By his educated guess, that would be a distance of about seventeen hundred meters to the right of their initial jaunt. "Two to the left long ways, two to the right long ways," McKean said to himself again, "one to the top short ways, and one to the bottom, if they went with six...."

He promptly tapped the jaunt interface and was engulfed by the Casimir vortex within seconds, plucking him from the fountain-lit side of the trench...and depositing him a second later one hundred meters above the opposite flank of the collapsed ridge, which, corresponding to its former life as a section of the trench wall, was about eighteen hundred meters higher in elevation than the main valley.

Gathering his bearings, McKean could see a glimmering light across the escarpment to his left, which provided a tantalizing glow to this side of the trench. He reminded himself of his duty and dropped his sightseeing, instead focusing his array of instruments towards the approaching warheads.

"Visual."

Two holographic, flashing red cylinders appeared on his HUD, rotating while they expelled their remaining fuel. Looking to his lidar target, the first *Strela* was within ninety meters, close enough to gap the distance with his sled. After a slightly longer burst of hydrazine, McKean ascended towards the nearest warhead, arriving within ninety seconds.

McKean repeated his reprogramming performances of the two *Strela*s, satisfied they would explode at the frequencies to assist the Casimir chain reaction. He allowed the pair to fall into the trench crevasse, burying themselves into the deep fissures created when the ridge broke apart from the main wall almost two centuries ago.

Successful so far, McKean patiently waited for the arrival of the next two, hoping to secure the last pieces to rid the world forever of this threat.

"Three and four have successfully grounded," the Confederation petty officer reported, looking up from his holographic screen, where four green dots blinked.

Behind him, an elderly captain nodded but did not respond, knowing full well the news was not for his ears only. Looking to his left, he said, "It appears your fears have gone unsubstantiated. Our fleet has proven to be more than a match for the Americans, Lieutenant."

Breaking his gaze from a holographic display at his side of the North Pacific Fleet's maneuvers, Lieutenant Vasily Nicolenko rose from his seat. "Captain Kuyneyov, one should never underestimate the resourcefulness of one's opponent. Or has St. Petersburg been keeping you chained behind a desk so long you have forgotten?"

Kuyneyov scowled and turned back to his crewman. "Signal the Deputatsky that we will be loading five and six at the lieutenant's command."

"Aye, aye, sir."

The captain's eyes met Nicolenko's, and the lieutenant lowered his index finger, giving the command for a "go."

Deep inside the submarine Valeska, crewmen dressed in drab coveralls lifted a *Strela* warhead horizontally into a firing tube, then closed and locked a hatch behind it. A second warhead was brought over by a mechanized arm, and placed on a running track, to which the same crewmen hoisted up and placed inside another firing tube.

A sodium klaxon light went on, coating the chamber with a yellow pall. On a command from the bridge, an ensign signaled to a crewman, who punched a firing button on an instrument board, launching the fifth *Strela* into the waters of the Kuril-Kamchatka Trench.

Night on the surface of the Okhotsk Sea was disturbed once more by the whoosh of an undersea launch. Trailing a white wake, the *Strela* vacated the *Valeska*, speeding into the trench at several dozen knots. Half-a-kilometer from its home vessel, the *Strela* pitched sharply downward at a thirty-five-degree angle, expending a small fuel tank within three minutes to get to its target at maximum velocity and inertia.

On the bridge, the petty officer counted down, "Eight hundred meters...eight fifty...nine hundred meters...."

Glancing to Kuyneyov, Nicolenko ordered the release of the final warhead, bringing the pieces to the stage to fight the Americans on equal footing, and for the first time in a century and a quarter, overtake their hated rivals. Nicolenko smiled at the thought...and remembered the words the old man and Doctor Zaryov had said to him. He was old enough not to buy into laurels and sweet words of glory, but the thought of retaking his country's rightful place as legitimate heirs of world domination filled him with pride, even if he had to do the old ways' bidding for now. Once this was all settled, things would be different. The equipment he possessed on this very submarine, locked away behind the securest of doors, would enable that victory.

It was just a matter of time....

***

Lidar pulses bounced off the hull of the fifth *Strela* warhead after McKean positioned himself on the northeast corner of the trench ridge, eagerly awaiting its arrival. Once within range, the agent extended his arms, catching hold of the falling warhead's fuselage and maneuvering himself to open the nosecone sheath.

On this, his fifth go around in forty-seven minutes, his arms and limbs began to tire, dramatically detracting from his reprogramming time. McKean put aside the complaints of his nerves and muscles and pushed forward, allowing instinct, skill and discipline to take over for actual critical thinking. Despite this, McKean lost his patience easily with every shortened breath, making him lose efficiency, and consequently, time, in silly mistakes he wouldn't normally have committed.

After McKean applied the last step in returning the *Strela* to its operating status, his sensor array detected a sixth gravimetric disturbance and sounded a "ping" in his helmet, forcing him to let go of the warhead earlier than he would have cared for, sending the *Strela* pitching forward at a dramatic angle into the seafloor. McKean caught a final glimpse of it in his helmet lamp, witnessing it plow into the sediment, apparently landing just as well, sending a sharp chill down his spine, but afterward, a sigh of relief. Five down....

Checking his interface for the position and distance of the final warhead southwest of the trench, he looked up to see a white trail catch the light from the fountain, a contrail soaring over the sky that was the undersea trench. Before jaunting a last time, he followed the wake a little longer, soaking the warhead with numerous lidar pulses, reducing its trajectory to a fairly straightforward course. Once he had calculated a potential course for maximum yield from the known geography of the trench, he set the coordinates in his interface and jaunted forward...to see the sixth *Strela* zero in on a nine-meter-tall barite tower a short burst of his hydrazine nozzles away.

McKean managed a "Launch now!" command to his voice response computer before the *Strela* exhausted its abnormally long-duration fuel tank and crashed into the tower, showering barite mineral shards and ripping its fuselage about the trench floor. A supercavitating bubble took McKean out of the scene quickly, rescuing him from a meter sheet of clipped shrapnel speeding towards him.

Canceling his short journey, McKean braked strongly, twisting in the water until he lost momentum and crashed into another, smaller barite tower. Grappling the outcropping, he watched the remains of the *Strela* float to the seafloor, spreading out over a field of large boulders and shallow sediment.

Pushing off the tower, McKean drifted towards the debris field and swam over it, eyeing torn metal panels, glints of rivets, bolts and other assorted junk that descended slowly across the floor. Continuing his scan, he lowered his left arm and swept the field with his lidar, hoping to find any remains of the warhead to retrieve. He spent the next few minutes combing the seafloor, fruitlessly coming up with nothing but fuselage and particulates. Dauntless regardless of the shortcomings, McKean understood he had to find the warhead's remains soon, if they were going to recover anything at all before the detonations began.

"Incompetent fools! How could they have miscalculated!"

Nicolenko affixed his helmet and rushed into his quarters, taking last-second stock of his equipment and weapons. Locking the door from the inside, he set the manual controls on his chest interface and accessed his Casimir chamber, beginning the long journey down with an edge of anger, an emotion he had tired of having to throw around with such imbeciles as the government employed to perform such delicate work. Did duty matter to anyone in the military anymore?

Tapping a red button, his Casimir chamber hummed, and the metal plates inside closed their rift, opening a screaming vortex through his abdomen, a sensation Nicolenko himself had never become comfortable with....

The Kuril-Kamchatka Trench burned with the light of the sun, confusing Nicolenko's brain and his own hazard suit's sensors. Holding up a gauntlet to eclipse the immense light, he brought up his HUD and checked his coordinates, hoping to find that he hadn't been taken to the white sandy sea of the Caribbean instead.

His confidence sated, Nicolenko descended in a hurry to the sixth *Strela's* last known position before the stupid drunkard had lost it. Glancing at his lidar, he took note of the shrapnel trail and the apparent cause of the crash; a large, broken tower of some mineral composition prevalent in these waters. Pausing briefly, he grappled the tower and inspected the impactor, which had cracked the tower in half, leaving grey scars three meters or more in length pitched at eighty-five to ninety degrees straight to the seafloor. Panels from the fuselage littered the floor around the impact site, but he could find no evidence of the warhead or the nosecone. Where had it gone? Stupidly, St. Petersburg had stockpiled the scores of other *Strelas* and loaded only these six aboard the *Valeska*. If one of them didn't detonate, the others couldn't possibly shoulder the load and yield enough to uncover the entire craft. He adjusted the lidar cannon on the right side of his helmet, hoping it would uncover the remains of the warhead.

Sifting through the accumulation of data passing on his HUD, Nicolenko glimpsed a curious current that didn't match the rest of the trench water. Following it, his heartbeat quickened; it had to be! Releasing his grip on the tower, Nicolenko fired off a quick blast from his Reaction Control System thrusters on his waist ring, rocketing forward at three meters per second.

Ahead of him, Nicolenko's eyes closed in on the target, still unawares. It was perfect, perfect timing! Extending his arms, Nicolenko approached at just the correct time, grappling the damnable man in the hazard suit from behind. The man tumbled forward, taking them both into the seafloor, scattering debris, pebbles and silt into the surrounding ocean water.

Regaining his strength, McKean rose and saw for the first time his attacker, who himself was recovering from his suicide dive. McKean recognized the man from Gilmour's description: Nicolenko. Now it was McKean's turn to delay the mad Confederate long enough for Gilmour to do whatever the Sherpa required until the *Strela* detonations blew the core halfway back in time.

"Sorry about your little missile, Lieutenant," McKean taunted in Russian over his voxlink. "Seems to have taken a wrong turn somewhere."

Nicolenko dusted his faceplate off and circled round McKean, who did the same, both men sizing up their respective combatant. "Where is Gilmour? Has he sent you in his stead to fight me? Has he grown to become a coward after so many of our meetings?"

"Gilmour? Gilmour is dead," McKean lied, giving Nicolenko something to occupy his mind while McKean surreptitiously searched his lidar scans for the warhead, which he knew he had to be getting closer to.

"Dead? That seems so unlike my nemesis. I recall him appearing just about whenever I counted him out!"

"Maybe," McKean paused, hurriedly looking for anything resembling the forty-five-centimeter diameter, seventy-centimeter-long nosecone, "maybe you have overestimated your opponent. We are, after all, only worthless Westerners. Obviously...inferior to your sensibilities."

Nicolenko walked around another barite tower, circling McKean, hoping his lidar could sift through the metal remains dotting the thin sediment. Everywhere he turned, echoes of metallic debris and phantom mineral signals threw his lidar out of sync, causing him no end of frustration.

"Incapable," McKean continued, "of meeting your logic and military prowess." Moving his eyes to the left of his lidar target, he caught sight of a red triangular object, submerged under a thin layer of sediment, just three-point-seven meters from him. The object was precisely forty-five centimeters in diameter, matching exactly the metal alloy content. And best of all, its radiation housing was still attached, allowing it to detonate.

McKean ignored it for the moment, hoping to lead Nicolenko away from it by doubling back over his own tracks. The lieutenant was a little farther away from the warhead, just on the left side of a massive barite column formation, about half-a-meter higher in elevation, all of which could lend favor to McKean being able to get to it first.

"Bragging is not our way," Nicolenko said finally, after passing another barite tower, "but it is high time North America regard us as little more than a third world country. Only then would a serious dialogue be spoken between our—"

A shower of sediment and metal debris shocked Nicolenko, forcing him to throw up his gauntlets to block his eyes from the force of the blast. Yelling out, he grabbed his double-bladed axe from his torso belt and activated his RCS thrusters, propelling himself forward.

Bursting forth from his supercavitating bubble, McKean landed on the far end of a small flea jump, grappled the submerged nosecone, and launched himself into the water with a short flare of his hydrazine nozzles.

Landing where the warhead was formerly resting, Nicolenko swung his axe blindly into the raised sediment and dust, unaware that McKean had taken off again.

The mass and size of the warhead threw off McKean's jump, however, grounding himself into another formation of barite towers. He landed on his back, still grappling the warhead in his left arm, but cradled inside two closely formed columns. Cloaked for a few seconds behind the sediment storm, he opened the nosecone and found the radiation housing. Cupping the pass key, McKean swiped it twice through the microlock, the silt obstructing his view all the way. Finally, the housing opened and he ripped off the foil covering, revealing the QPU.

Gritting his teeth, he commanded the voice response computer to sound the reprogramming EM frequency. While he waited for the computer to finish the signal, McKean saw a single lightbeam cut through the sediment cloak, then felt the horrendous ferocity of an axe blade chop barely miss his left arm. McKean screamed as he kicked at the invisible assailant, his boots only connecting once. A second chop missed his left gauntlet but found his holographic interface and the instrument arrays next to it, ripping them in half and sending an explosion of sparks into the surrounding water.

McKean's eyes widened as he saw the remnants of his equipment blown away, the only way for him to return to the craft. Without any of his technology, he was stranded in the trench, left to fend off Nicolenko's repeated attempts to exterminate him.

A third strike was deflected by McKean's right gauntlet. He grasped the blade and pushed it away, but their combined struggle over it clipped a segment of a barite column, sending it crashing down over McKean's helmet and chest, cracking his faceplate and pinning him under its weight.

Seconds later, Nicolenko regained control of the axe, allowing the sediment to clear enough for him to see the helpless McKean. Unfortunately, he also saw the warhead trapped with McKean. Putting the axe aside, Nicolenko thought the unthinkable and began to remove the collapsed barite segment to rescue the warhead.

A slow hiss filled McKean's ears, along with a crushing tightness in his sinuses and ear canals; decompression! There was no way back now; if he could help Gilmour fulfill their plan by eradicating this bastard, he'd do it. While Nicolenko struggled with removing the barite segment, McKean dropped the pass key and manipulated his fingers around the *Strela's* Casimir chamber. By touch, he found an emergency arming mechanism he and Constantine had discovered during their experiences with the illegals in Irkutsk and toggled it, sending the warhead into activation mode.

Bearing the increasingly tight pressure, he concentrated long enough to confirm the warhead's activation, seeing a red flash of light below the crushing weight of the barite segment. McKean didn't struggle as Nicolenko managed to use his axe to dislodge the segment; he merely smiled and watched the look cross Nicolenko's face as the lieutenant realized the warhead was now armed, with the fuse set to run out in ten seconds.

Now free from the segment, McKean lashed out with his right gauntlet and found the instrument array on Nicolenko's chest, using all of the remaining power in the gauntlet to rip off Nicolenko's jaunt capabilities, taking his Casimir chamber backpack off in a single stroke. Watching the horror eclipse Nicolenko's face, McKean painfully mouthed "Fuck you!" until the pressure cracked his faceplate entirely, his helmet caving in.

With the red LED flashing down to the end, Nicolenko pounded the RCS thrusters on his waist, rocketing himself up as the *Strela* warhead went to zero. Thrust upward by his RCS thrusters, Nicolenko evaded the initial burst of neutronic radiation, but couldn't escape the force of the detonation below him.

A white sphere soon dilated in a rapidly expanding wave of concussive force, rendering all matter within its grip into energized quanta. The sphere rose steadily, gorging itself on the increasingly abundant matter in its path, creating a brightening wall of flame. The preceding concussion wave obliterated the sediment seafloor and obstructing barite towers, carving out a massive hole tens of meters in diameter before its larger sibling could devour the meal.

Fifteen seconds after detonation, the blast yield reached its zenith, towering over the seafloor, but still dwarfed by the massive, collapsed ridge to the northeast. Lightning arced from the remaining standing structures to the center of the blast sphere, birthing an ungodly storm.

Ten seconds past that, the concussion wave reached its peak, and grown to capacity, rebounded. The supervacuum imploded violently, sending all the matter that survived the initial neutronic blast back to its center of origin in an angry gale.

Tossed upwards to several hundred meters at nearly beyond human survival limits, Nicolenko floundered, only to be pushed back to the seafloor by the onrushing current of ocean water, tossed about like so much flotsam. His helmet lamp still functioning, he watched seawater stream by him while he was slammed down at several kilometers per hour, his only saving grace being his hazard suit. Nicolenko flew about the roiling waves of turmoil, his view quickly encompassed by the charging debris and detritus encircling the undersea twister.

After several moments of sheer terror, Nicolenko's body gradually settled back towards the blast zone, even while the northeastern ridges collapsed and crumbled in the eerily bright fountain of light. Looking down, he saw a tremendous bowl carved into the trench floor, all that remained of millions of tonnes of matter. He descended next to a smoking pustule, landing with a thud onto the molten seafloor. Weakened, he crawled up the tall concavity, reaching the cratertop after an hour's effort of repeated landslides and bursting magma channels. Rising over the top, he climbed out and landed face first into a bed of smoking and charred sediment. Extending a gauntlet forward, he began the long journey to the crash site.

He had taken the Americans' best shot, and survived.

## CHAPTER FORTY

"Six has just detonated!" the petty officer shouted to Kuyneyov from his station. On the holographic screen, a red circle flashed, accompanied by a text box giving the yield, its coordinates and time of detonation.

"What?" Kuyneyov said, rising from his seat. "Where's Nicolenko?"

"Lieutenant Nicolenko has not responded to our hails, Captain," a communications ensign answered, standing at his station with headphones in hand. "Perhaps he left to investigate its destination, sir."

The captain shook his head, remaining mute. Looking over his bridge crew, he pointed his finger to the firing room's liaison, a crewman seated to Kuyneyov's left. "This is all your doing."

"Should I try to hail again, Captain?" the ensign asked.

"Attempt to triangulate his position on the trench floor. Contact *Deputatsky*, and ask to advise."

"Triangulation may take some time, Captain," the ensign warned. "Neutronic radiation will cloud our sensors very well."

"Understood, Ensign. Do it."

"Yes, sir."

Kuyneyov took his seat again, and rubbed his chin. If Nicolenko wasn't going to answer his hails, then he wasn't going to be missed, politics be damned. If St. Petersburg wanted to blow up their trench, by god, they'd get it. And he'd be rid of that political officer. Sacrifices must sometimes be made for the greater good, Kuyneyov reminded himself.

Gilmour and the Sherpa fell to the bottom of the core, its massive facets chiming angrily at the violence bombarding its undersea haven. Steadying himself, Gilmour managed to rise up during the onslaught, bracing his gauntlets against the crystalline wall.

"That one was worse," the Sherpa said, feeling the immense pain the core endured.

Gilmour glanced at his HUD chrono. "It's been about seventy minutes since the initial detonation. This is probably the tertiary bow-shocks hitting the craft...I sure as hell wouldn't want to be around the mousehole right now. I hope McKean got out of the way."

A few seconds later, the shocks passed, allowing the core to settle down.

"I've thought about this lesson some more," Gilmour said, helping the Sherpa to his feet. "What have past civilizations done, when confronted with this dilemma?" he asked, referring to the question of the core.

"There is an inherent balance between those who wish to exploit a neutron core for their own purposes, and those who would wish nothing more than to never see a core again. Judging by your actions, I believe you're in the latter category."

"That's an understatement. I've seen enough people killed in this operation."

The Sherpa nodded. "A core has never been utilized for anything other than exploration, mostly the exploration of the soul through the settlement of the stars. The beings who constructed this craft would never intend to decide in matters such as this balance. But as I have come to know their ways, they would most assuredly want this balance be decided for the greater good."

Gilmour raised his eyebrows. "I can live with that."

"Than it is up to you to decide that the greater good is served. It is your duty, if you do indeed serve the greater good, to put an end to this."

"I understand...but why wasn't I allowed to leave with McKean?"

"Normal human means of settling conflicts will not do," he explained, raising a finger. "The core is the source of this conflict, the core must be the means to its end."

Gilmour threw up his hands. "But how do I do that?"

The Sherpa smiled. "You have already started the path, as have your enemies. Neither of you have realized it yet."

Gilmour looked down, searching his mind and his heart. He remembered the day Doctor de Lis had tracked him and his colleagues down at the IIA; his initial mistrust of de Lis' scientists. Gilmour thought of the many aspects of the Temporal Retrieve Project he was privy to; day-to-day preparations; the hard, long hours he and the others had put in lending their expertise; their investigation of HADRON, Lionel

Roget; how they had been instrumental in retrieving the jewels; stopping Nicolenko from furthering the Confederation's plans as best he could; and the ultimate utilization of the jewels in the operation, this time traveling that had resulted in their greatest victories and saddest despairs.

And now, the whole reason he and McKean were in the trench at all, the reprogramming of the *Strelas*...the *Strelas*....

With surprising self-realization, Gilmour locked eyes with the Sherpa. "You," he pointed to the simple man, "you told us the jewels were a part of this core, just pieces of this sphere. Would the core," he paused, hesitating to find the correct solution, "have the exact properties of the jewels?"

The Sherpa's face remained blank, revealing nothing to the agent. "You know in your heart the answer."

Gilmour pounded his right fist into his left gauntlet, almost allowing a smile to creep onto his face...it was all coming together, all beginning to make sense. "Keanie, let's hope you did it right...."

Tapping his interface, Gilmour accessed his EM transceiver and scanned the QPU frequencies of the *Strela* warheads, hoping McKean had successfully performed the job he promised he would. A chirp sounded from all five remaining warheads, signaling a positive. "He did! I hope he got out of there before it went off...."

The Sherpa said nothing, averting his eyes to the core's many facets.

"I'm going to try and get him on vox, tell him to get the hell back before those things go off." Gilmour activated his voxlink and said, "Neil! Can you read me?" He paused, then spoke again, "McKean, talk to me if you're in range...McKean...."

The agent blinked, then turned his head to the Sherpa. "He's gone, isn't he? Did...did he detonate the warhead?"

"The core," he began, "felt an abrupt change in the foreign object's descent, most likely falling off course. There was no detonation signal given from the origin point."

"Then he detonated it on accident."

The Sherpa swiveled on his feet to face Gilmour. "The core also detected a facet of itself at the origin point...a different facet from the one your colleague utilized."

Gilmour's jaw quickly tightened. "And this facet...where is it now?"

"At the bottom of the crater created by the detonation."

"Nicolenko...our enemy."

"Ah." The Sherpa nodded. "Then you know what you must do."

Gilmour nodded. "Will you help me?"

"No. I am only allowed to unimpede your progress in this lesson. I cannot assist you in any other way."

"Than allow me to transmit a signal. I hoped not to be here when we did this, but...."

The Sherpa placed an open hand on the inner wall of the core, allowing the crystalline facets to impart their intelligence to him. He faced the agent. "It is done. The core will not impede your movement, either. You may leave, if you desire."

"No," Gilmour voiced, shaking his head. "I'll make my stand here, with the core. Somebody from our species has to learn this lesson, don't they?"

The Sherpa, his visage bathed in the core's spectral light, did not answer.

Inhaling deeply, Gilmour activated the EM transceiver once more, praying he wasn't ending life as he knew it.

"No signs of the lieutenant have been found, Captain!" the communications ensign bellowed.

Kuyneyov leaned back in his chair and thought about his next act with the utmost of caution. "Commander...."

"Yes, sir?" a burly, well-groomed man answered from the captain's right.

"Strike my commands from the records. I want nothing recorded!"

"Sir? Yes, sir!" Acting with haste, the first officer whipped over to a station and toggled the command records, hitting erase. A squeak was emitted from the console, then the entire vox system went dead.

Kuyneyov rose from his seat and addressed the firing room liaison, "There will be no mistakes this time, understood."

The young, well-scrubbed boy easily nodded his head, paying extreme attention to his superior officer's order. "Aye, aye, sir!"

"Begin procedures to detonate *Strela*. Signal *Deputatsky* all is in order, all hands accounted for. All equipment is secure."

"Aye, captain." The communications ensign nodded to the crewman at the console, who opened a channel to the lead ship.

Kuyneyov sat in his chair, counting down the minutes until he was the most revered man in all the Confederation.

A slate grey gauntlet brought up a holograph labeled "TRANSMIT." Gilmour's index finger quickly pressed it down, erasing all doubt.

\*\*\*

Vasily Nicolenko fired his RCS thrusters once more, bringing the crash into his sight. It was easily lit from the mysterious fountain of light emanating from the craft's side, coming from what looked like a large corridor. He followed the metallic debris sandwiched into the ridge, none the worse after enduring the explosion almost ninety minutes ago that had devastated the southern portion of the trench.

After traveling down the few meters to the corridor, he would investigate this fountain and find out if it was Gilmour's doing, a deception he had created to distract Nicolenko from detonating the trench. He could not win, Nicolenko knew; he had an entire fleet waiting for his very signal to detonate the rest of the warheads in this trench. Gilmour sending his lackey in an attempt to disrupt the detonations would not succeed, just as Gilmour had not succeeded in his earlier attempts to stop him. Finding the entrance into this corridor, Nicolenko began to unravel Gilmour's plot. The IIA special agent was running out of time....

Kuyneyov swiveled in his chair. Looking to his firing liaison, he ordered, "Initiate detonation!"

The boy tapped the firing sequence on his panel, beginning the countdown.

Buried meters below the trench sediment, five warheads came to life. Red LEDs, adjacent to the EM frequency receiver, started the ten second descent to zero.

Nicolenko blocked the incredible light streaming past him. Slowly, he maneuvered in the tight corridor, his fatigue and the water's buoyancy conspiring to defeat him. His eyes made out an iris of light just a few more meters ahead of him...Gilmour had to be here, had to be plotting his escape. But he would not escape his—

"What! What in—"

Five sequential chirps in Nicolenko's voxlink caught his attention. Pausing, he activated his HUD sensors, checking for the location of these familiar signals. Nicolenko's eyes widened as he saw their origins....

...Zero.

Five pairs of Casimir plates pushed together, producing a gap of just micrometers, enough to begin the virtual particle/antiparticle process. Instantly, quanta filled the chambers of the five remaining *Strelas*, commencing a reaction that pulled the fabric of the universe itself.

Five ripples appeared in spacetime, spreading their influence throughout the trench. Expanding faster than light, the disturbances soon flooded the planet within a nanosecond, sending a cascade of virtual particle collisions streaming across the continuum.

Gilmour and the Sherpa writhed as the neutron core pulled itself apart, reknitting its lattice particle by particle, a cascade of luminescence rivaling the fountain that had brought them inside its very being.

Across the Earth, the crust vibrated with life....

In the Central Asian Conglomerates, Nepalis and Chinese alike gathered to witness a mountain retreat glitter in light. An arc of mountains cradling a particularly secluded valley danced with luminosity, as its mountainside opened spectral light to the heavens above....

Sakha natives danced to the gods...a field reserved for those who had died in a horrible battle was consecrated by the rainbow of colors stretching to the sky from the Ulahan-Sis peaks beyond....

Stacia Waters, Carol Marlane, Javier Valagua, Alik Ivan, Cory Crowe, Hollis Lux, Ryan Jaquess and Richard de Lis marveled as the jewel specimens lit up the trembling Lockbox, casting an eerie, spectral glow across the many subdivisions of the theoretical studies laboratory....

Millions of light rays streamed past Gilmour and the Sherpa, all converging on the empty scar created so many decades ago, above the Earth. One by one, the facets arrived and rearranged themselves within the healing neutron core, positioning themselves as they had been before they were lost. Gilmour watched the rapture curiously, as if witnessing the return of long-forgotten children to a heartbroken mother.

The core's resonance echoed throughout Gilmour's body, filling him with warmth. The kaleidoscope that had been so mighty and impressive before was no match now for this experience, an entire universe ablaze. Within seconds, the streamers waned in number, but the core's brilliant intensity only increased, creating a sense of what could possibly occur next to transcend that.

The scar immediately reknit along to the rest of the lattice, completing the core's healing. Growing brighter still, a wave of white light poured forth from the core, cutting a swath through Gilmour and the Sherpa.

Outpacing the fountain's progress, the light wave broke free from the confines of the craft, illuminating the trench. Trapped inside the mousehole, Nicolenko screamed as the light enveloped him and the supine metal structure.

Five kilometers above, at the very surface of the Okhotsk Sea, the submarine *Valeska*, the destroyer *Deputatsky*, and the other members of the Confederation North Pacific Fleet were eclipsed by the onrushing white light, a warmth that brightened night to morning. The ocean water boiled, tossing the submarine about. Inside, crewmen desperately sealed off vulnerable compartments, while bulkheads cracked and shifted, threatening to take the ship to the bottom as well.

Towering ridge walls on the bottom of the trench shifted under the pressure pouring forth from beneath their masses. Sturdy shelves slid to the floor, coating the sediment with broken and jagged stone. Barite columns disappeared under tumbling walls, causing massive quakes to erupt all along the trench floor's kilometers-long subduction zone.

Under the collapsed ridge shelf that had imprisoned the craft for two hundred years, metallic supports moaned and creaked. Huge structural beams dislodged from their moorings and spiraled towards the neutron core, their matter swiftly swallowed by the hungry core. Metal debris flew into the interior of the ship and were subsumed, as were bulkheads from the ship, all eaten from the inside out, gradually lowering the millions of tonnes of earth above it back to the seafloor.

A massive fault developed along the rim of the trench wall, breaking the ridges into scores of sliding masses. Until moments ago a dominant landscape, the northeast trench wall collapsed, falling inward from the implosion of twenty decades' worth of structural support.

More and more material was launched towards the neutron core, a disk soon growing around its equator, setting the core spinning at a tremendous rate and its sole inhabitants inside flailing.

The ever decreasing sphere departed its last rays of light, then crumpled in on itself, emitting a horrific, sucking moan before its own version of the spacetime vortex extirpated it from the known universe.

# CHAPTER FORTY-ONE

Space split open, howling from an unnatural wound. A pinprick of matter, a mere mote against the ocean of stars, was expunged from the spiral fissure by the awesome powers of the universe itself, battering it with such force as if to forever rid the universe of a terrible irritant.

Deep inside the bowels of the ancient craft, the newly healed neutron core burned with the ferocity of a thousand suns, twin streamers of blinding energy flowing from its magnetically powered poles. Spinning at a rate of five rotations per millisecond, the neutron core seized its inhabitants within its crystalline lattice, who were now beholden to the core of the ancient craft and its whims.

Flung around the core's heart, witness to their past, present and future as if lived out before them, the trio of confined beings braced themselves to the core's multitude of facets, unsure of what was real, of what was illusion.

Gilmour felt his flesh bubble and rake across his body. Paralyzed by the ghostly images ripping past him, he screamed in terror, the spectral lines weaving a streak of many Gilmours, of many Sherpas, of many... Nicolenkos.

Cranking his head to the left, Gilmour's eyes met Nicolenko's, whose body now flooded forth and melded with the special agent's, whose in return melded with the Sherpa's opposite him. The trio were chained to the spinning top that was this neutron core and the carnival game that was the spacetime continuum.

Gritting his teeth, Gilmour pushed his arms away from the crystalline wall, forcing himself forward, immediately introducing a stream of color into the uninhabited central part of the neutron core. Wasting no momentum, Gilmour leapt into the southern pole of the core, capturing Nicolenko's attention. The lieutenant followed Gilmour down, meeting him about two meters away, both men now standing steadily against a hurricane of swirling, spectral energy.

"*GILMOUR!*"

Nicolenko painstakingly reached to his torso ring and produced his double-bladed axe, holding it forward to his nemesis.

Gilmour watched the lieutenant waste his angular momentum, then charged at Nicolenko. Nicolenko swung the axe at Gilmour's helmet, but the agent reached out with his gauntlets and grabbed the axe's handle, forcing it to his right flank, Nicolenko's weak side. The pair wrestled with the weapon until their jockeying allowed both men to lose their grip, which flung the axe into the swirling spectrum. Following the lost weapon with their combined gaze, the axe whirled around the core, gradually losing inertia until it struck the crystalline wall and hung there, fixed upon the latticework with its hilt upright.

Catching Gilmour before he could defend himself, Nicolenko jumped up and kicked Gilmour's faceplate, rocketing the agent into the swirling river of light. The agent's limbs turned and twisted viciously until he lost inertia after three rotations and crashed into the crystalline wall, tumbling end over end, then halting with his helmet cemented to the faceted wall.

Nicolenko growled and leapt at the hapless Gilmour, sensing an easy victory. The lieutenant's boots found the wall just a few paces from Gilmour and held him there while Nicolenko gathered his bearings. Nicolenko rose to his feet, now standing nearly upside down to his fighting stance a few moments ago, and approached the agent's back. Drawing closer, Nicolenko held his gauntlets to his face, and utilizing a voice command, extended two seven-centimeter-long talons, one from each gauntlet back.

Towering above the prostrate Gilmour, Nicolenko recoiled his right hand and swiftly struck, piercing the agent's left shoulder and penetrating the protective outer layers of his haz suit. As Gilmour's helmet reverberated with screams of pain, Nicolenko repeated with his left arm, then extracted both, allowing the wounded agent to writhe on the sphere in front of the lieutenant, who watched in grotesque amusement.

"*DIE LIKE I HAVE IMAGINED FOR SO LONG!*"

Nicolenko grinned like a cat ready to pounce on his battered prey. Crouching down, Nicolenko snatched Gilmour's left arm and exposed his chest and torso, then, using his right gauntlet, lifted Gilmour's helmet and the adjacent locking rings underneath. Nicolenko recoiled once more with his right talon and lunged for the agent's unprotected upper chest.

Centimeters from Gilmour's haz suit, Nicolenko's arm and gauntlet were swiftly, and unexpectedly, knocked away by Gilmour's outstretched right arm, throwing Nicolenko off balance and into the swirling hurricane stream. Quickly gathering himself, Gilmour rose to his haunches and waited for Nicolenko to return again a few seconds later. Readying his gauntlet, Gilmour balled his hand into a fist and smashed it into Nicolenko's faceplate, causing the lieutenant to tumble into the stream for another revolution.

Waiting again, Gilmour gathered his strength, then piled another punch on Nicolenko, cracking his faceplate. Nicolenko came around for a third trip three seconds later, and this time Gilmour leapt out to the orbiting lieutenant, grappling him and forcing both into the circling stream.

Bounding end over end, Gilmour gained control early, leveraging his mass with his left arm, holding onto Nicolenko's torso ring while lobbing punch after punch upon the lieutenant's faceplate, widening a spiderweb crack. With an opaque fracture developing over the entire faceplate, Gilmour extended the talon on his right index finger and repeatedly rammed it into the white fault with all the gauntlet's mechanical power until powdery pieces flew away, revealing Nicolenko's bloodied face once more.

*"DIE YOU BASTARD!"*

With the pulped Nicolenko lapsing into a coma, Gilmour looked up to the north pole of the neutron core. Above the trio, the fountain of light still shone as it had the moment he and McKean opened up the core's metallic shell, a stream of luminescence leading to the unknown. Glancing down to Nicolenko again, and with the lieutenant offering no resistance, Gilmour punched the RCS thruster on Nicolenko's right flank, which burst to life with a white flare. Gilmour released his hold on the man, throwing himself to the mercy of the hurricane's streaming current, while Nicolenko was blown to the top of the core in an ever-tightening current. In the span of two seconds, Lieutenant Vasily Nicolenko was sucked up through the north polar wall, disintegrating into a shower of particles.

Outside the spinning neutron core, a small figure was expunged from the sphere's polar fountain, launched into a sea of stars. A fiery polar streamer carried the form aloft for a nanosecond until the universe took its toll, rendering the tiny speck into a trillion quanta with a spectacular explosion.

A cry split down the middle of Gilmour's brain. Holding on to his consciousness with determination, Gilmour rolled from head to foot as the neutron core's spinning increased, trying to lessen the forces on him while nearly being killed from battery alone. Locking his eyes on the core's walls, he saw the numerous facets bulge wildly, viciously. What was wrong? Was the core in pain? Would it rip itself apart? Would they die here, tearing another hole in spacetime?

"You, you told us the jewels were a part of this core, just pieces of this sphere. Would the core have the exact properties of the jewels?"

"You know in your heart the answer."

Securing his sliced left shoulder closely, Gilmour closed his eyes; he knew what had to be done, what would end this all. He reached for his supercavitating engine sled's release toggle, just behind his left arm. Tapping it hard with his right gauntlet, the sled broke away with a hiss, setting it free into the stream. With blinding pain, he ran both arms up his chest to his shoulders, reaching the Casimir chamber release straps. Pulling these at once, the Casimir chamber on his back came loose in his hands. He flung the chamber over his right shoulder and hugged it close, making sure it wouldn't leap from his arms. Carefully, he led his right index finger, talon still extracted, to the holographic interface. Tapping that, he activated the Casimir chamber, whose display indicated a flashing "0," for no jewel located inside. He proceeded to a second window, accessing the Casimir chamber's EM frequencies. A red button below gave him access to the chamber's memory settings, a list of frequencies Gilmour had programmed into the interface for later use. Scrolling down the list, he found the precise frequency de Lis and Waters employed during their first examination of the jewels, then set a return date. He immediately tapped both, sounding the Casimir's trademark hum and sending the virtual particle stew flying in the chamber he hugged to his chest.

Hurling through the core centrifuge, Gilmour fought to keep his mind from blacking out. A progressively higher pitched chirp filled his ears as the Casimir plates neared the widest gap. Each chirp echoed in his brain, sending spikes of pain up and down his nerves.

*"COME ON DAMMIT!"*

With every last cell of his body shaking itself to the tearing point, Gilmour let out a primal, visceral cry, ripping his lungs and innards apart, a last gasp of the weak, the mortal.

Particles of light shimmered within the facets of the neutron core, an excitement not known for two centuries. Rippling in harmony, the core danced within its lattice, sending shocks of concentric waves ringing throughout the intricately delineated sphere.

At once, Gilmour and the Sherpa spun beyond human capacity, their forms melding in a single ring inside the core's heart. Accelerating faster, the pair no longer existed as human, but were now quanta, beating the circulation of the universe. The ring converged at the core's center, growing tighter until both shone as a newborn star, their quanta collapsing unto a single point....

A single strand descended in the darkness, lit by the luminosity of its own quanta. Dripping onto an ocean of stars, the strand expanded, forming the skeleton of a great and ancient vessel. Hundreds, then thousands, of spindly metal filaments gushed forth from the center of this craft, birthing a massive framework. After a nanosecond, flesh formed over the skeleton, germinating a solid black hull from its bones, coating the hulk with a proper face. A string of circular windows dotted the revitalized organism, revealing a vast central nervous system of decks and corridors, the heart of which was a beating core suspended in its own cavity at the plexus.

Unfolding its invisible wings, the craft soared through this ocean of stars, swiftly cruising past a dusty silver orb, then into the influence of a distant blue planet, its swirls of whitecaps and green lands beckoning the craft and all its inhabitants, native or not, to it.

Reflected in a mural of this azure globe were the visages of Gilmour, the Sherpa and a trio of beings clad in white light, all of whom bathed in this world's beauty. It revolved slowly under them, such peace having been unknown for so long. Waves crested upon verdant shores. Winds blew dust into open continents. Warm air rose to mix with cold clouds. And below, unseen, billions of lifeforms lived, breathed, ate, loved, died, fought, hoped. As they went, invisible to the eye, so did time, passing in increments too small to measure, too stretched to parse. And here, above it all, none of it mattered. Time was not the enemy, time was the medium of these, and more. Time was that wave, that wind, that warm air. Above the blue planet, none of that which Gilmour had fought all his life mattered. It was not essential, it did not have to be the way it was.

How did one explain such things? How did one look upon the world of one's birth, the giver and taker of life and convince them?

Gilmour looked down to his hands, battered, bruised, calloused, coarse, scarred, torn, but here, now. Alive. He had done it. He had saved them. His eyes flitted back to the blue planet and fathomed the billions these hands had pulled from the edge. And he wondered if he was good for anything else.

Gilmour felt the presence of the trio of beings like a child feels the strength and confidence of his parents. With one look, he understood what it was all about, this living, this universe, what he had sacrificed for. Now, they had come to the mural at his request, because he felt the need to have absolution, to know what he had orchestrated to end the stalemate was right. Selfishness was a trait he did not relish in himself, let alone others. He had to know if he was right.

"Your world is remarkable," the tallest being spoke at last, like a wave of sound through water. "You have much with which to be proud."

Gilmour met the being's gaze, not even sure if he could communicate with something so heightened. "It is my home. I have to be thankful of what I am."

"Your friends miss you," another one said. "You have been gone too long, as have they."

Gilmour kicked at the floor, almost shuffling. "Have things been set right? Did I serve good?"

A third being glided towards him. "You still inhale a breath. Your home still provides haven. The one who serves self-interest has been equaled, bettered. It is in your heart to decide, to forgive yourself."

"You have spent many of your days with us, you have learned much," the first one pronounced. "Now it is time to spread that wealth."

Gilmour nodded. "Thank you."

The trio of beings nodded softly—and Gilmour thought—smiled. But then, perhaps he read too much into their warmth. Gathering his haz suit and helmet into his arms, Gilmour detected a hint of lilac, a breeze of cool air that sent him swooning, and the rest, a memory....

His coffee smelled particularly pungent in this early morning, not at all like the sweet scent he had lodged in his head, a remnant of his sleep, maybe. In the jumpjet, Special Agent James Gilmour sat reclined, the latest cineweb stuck in his mind from a day before, scenes of a once long-lost film produced in the early twentieth century, a monochrome production that spoke to him how quaint life was twenty decades ago, before life accelerated to its too quick pace. For once, he remembered life before the IIA and how much simpler it once was. Even the dreaded R-word came to mind in the jumpjet seat.

"Hello...Gilmour, where you been?" the voice in the seat across from him beckoned, his hand waving.

Gilmour shook his head and blinked. "Sorry, Greg. What were you saying?"

Special Agent Gregory Mason smiled and repeated, "I said, I hope this meeting you've set up with us in Ottawa gets us some action. Been in Leeds' starched office too long."

"Don't get your hopes up. I've got a message to relay to an old acquaintance. Just wanted to let him know our progress on a project I've been consulting on."

Mason picked up a holobook and scrolled through its text. "This Doctor de Lis, huh? You know this guy?"

"Yeah. Been communicating with him for about a year. He's been expecting you, and Chief, Will and McKean, as well."

"So how long's this going to last?"

"Long enough to update him."

Mason laughed. "You couldn't web him?"

"No, not this time. After this, I won't be going as a special agent." Gilmour glanced out the window, then sighed. "This is it, Greg."

"Surely, oh...you can't—"

Gilmour nodded. "I've done it all, mate. There are things outside of the IIA I want to do, like begin a life."

"Yeah, heard that one before."

"No, this is it. Have to re-evaluate things, see where they fall." Gilmour leaned forward. "I've done everything, Greg. Things you can't know about, won't ever hear about. Now it's my turn to rest."

"All right, all right. I understand." A smile cracked over Mason's face. "Don't go getting all domestic on me. We still need a guys' weekend retreat, okay?"

"Deal."

"Are you sure you don't remember?" Gilmour asked Doctor Richard de Lis, in the privacy of de Lis' theoretical studies office.

De Lis read the sizable report on the holobook. "Trust me, I would remember something like this, Agent Gilmour."

Gilmour rubbed his palms together as he listened. In U5-1, he watched Mason fraternizing with Doctor Stacia Waters. "It's all true. Every one of my colleagues...Mason, Constantine, McKean, Chief, they're all dead where I come from. Now, I awoke after returning from this experience, and they're alive."

"I'll see what I can do to make sense of this, although I might be hard-pressed to come up with a satisfactory explanation for your experience."

Gilmour turned back to de Lis. "Just make it so my head will quit hurting whenever I think about it."

"I'll be in contact with you. Now, as your doctor, I suggest getting some rest. Go enjoy life...sounds like you've been quite busy."

"You could say that."

"Oh, just one more thing, Agent Gilmour."

"Hmm?"

De Lis laid an index finger on the holobook. "I've never employed a Lionel Roget at the theoretical studies laboratory. Or am I reading this wrong?"

Gilmour felt a sense of justice creep into him. "No. I'd say you're reading it right."

De Lis raised a puzzled eyebrow. "Get you some leave. I'm sure Agent Mason will take quickly to our projects."

"He's a good agent, a good man. It'll be good to have him back around." With that, Gilmour shook de Lis' hand, then departed his office and walked over to Mason and the other senior staff, introducing himself a first time, for the second time. It was all good again.

# The JauntWorld Series Continues...

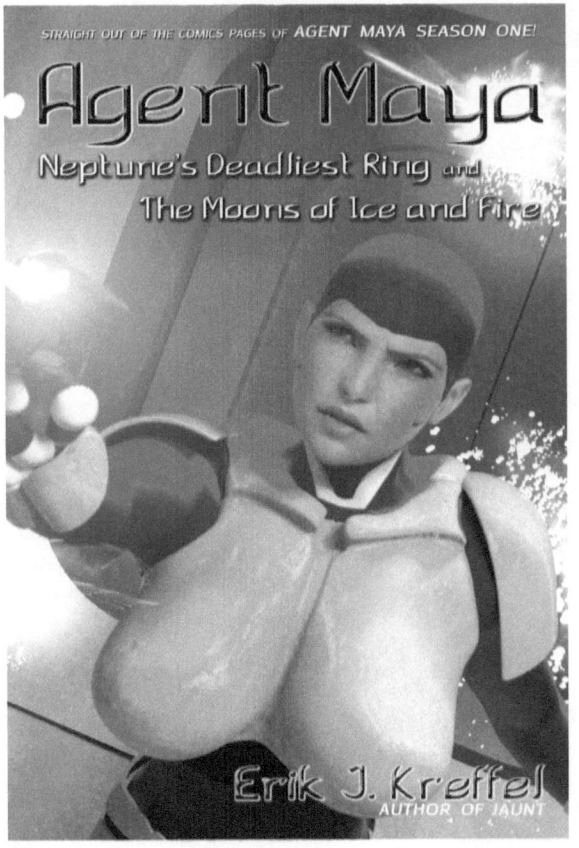

# JAUNT CLASSICS

IS DEDICATED TO THE REPUBLISHING OF CHOICE, OUT-OF-PRINT AND PUBLIC DOMAIN GENRE CLASSICS. THE 2019 SELECTIONS ARE THREE VOLUMES REPRESENTING CLASSIC OCCULT DETECTIVES, PRESENTED HERE UNCUT AND IN THE ORIGINAL TEXTS.

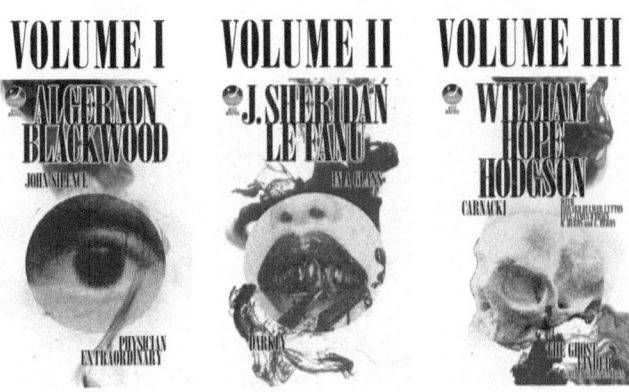

Contemporaries of Sherlock Holmes, the occult detectives were Victorian- and Edwardian-era investigators concerned with all manner of psychic, spectral and paranormal matters, eager to separate reality—no matter how bizarre—from hoaxers and con men.

VOLUME I, renowned psychic investigator Dr. John Silence delves into five cases, ranging from the psychical invasion of a long-dead resident upon a writer of humorous tales to disturbing incidents of lycanthropy, with a twist only Dr. John Silence could conceive.

$8.99    ISBN 9780983331773

VOLUME II, esteemed German physician Dr. Martin Hesselius relates five tales, encompassing the apparition of a beastly creature only its witness can see to the unholy revenant inhabiting the form of a youthful girl, a story that pre-dates *DRACULA* by 25 years.

$8.99    ISBN 9780983331780

VOLUME III, fourteen tales of ghostly encounters with investigators Thomas Carnacki, Mr. Harry Escott and Mr. Flaxman Low, plus an anonymous story of a haunted house in the midst of London.

$8.99    ISBN 9780983331797